ANGELA & JIM & JANICE & JONATHAN & BESSIE & BUD & YAEL & SAM & ROBIN & KEANE

Some of them were respectable, happily married couples who never would dream of engaging in that dread word—ADULTERY.

Others were members of the younger generation, for whom sex was as casual as brushing their teeth.

Both groups had a lot to learn from each other, and a lot to teach, and it all started when Angela went to Boston one Thursday & met Jonathan & went to a hotel with him & set off a sexual chain reaction that changed a lot of intimate lives and a lot of ideas about marriage . . .

THURSDAY, MY LOVE

Robert H. Rimmer's candid and controversial new novel about open-end marriage.

Other SIGNET Books by Robert H. Rimmer

Thursday, My Love

by
ROBERT H. RIMMER

A SIGNET BOOK from
NEW AMERICAN LIBRARY
TIMES MIRROR

Library of Congress Catalog Card Number: 70-183524

ACKNOWLEDGMENTS

With the kind permission of the Boyce family and Duncan Littlefair, who performed the wedding, portions of Father Lereve's marriage of Robin and Keane are based on the wedding of Joyce Christine Frye and David Allan Boyce in the Fountain Street Church, Grand Rapids, Michigan, September 12, 1970. Additions to the ceremony are from a translation of the Tao Teh Ching by Lao Tzu, translated by John C. H. Wu and preserved in a written document by Ardeshir Mehta of Jerusalem and India. The first lines of the chorus of *Catulli Carmina* are printed courtesy of Associated Music Publishers, copyright owners.

The poem "To My Daughter" by Emil Deutsch is reprinted courtesy of Emil Deutsch and *The Friends Journal*.

General permission to quote from Abraham Maslow's writing was given to me in a letter from Abe Maslow prior to his death.

The author and publisher also express their gratitude to the following authors and publishers for permission to quote from their books:

Sex: The Radical View of a Catholic Theologian by Michael Valente. Copyright © The Bruce Publishing Company, 1970. The Bruce Publishing Company, New York, New York.

Toward a Quaker View of Sex, Alastair Heron, editor. Friends Service Committee, Friends House, Euston Road, London, N.W. 1.

Infidelity: The Way We Live Today, by Brian Richard Boylan. © 1971 by Brian Richard Boylan. Published by Prentice-Hall, Inc., Englewood Cliffs, New Jersey. Reprinted by permission of Prentice-Hall and the author's representative, Gunther Stuhlmann.

"Pollution of the Mind." An editorial by Jeremiah Flynn appearing in *Printing Magazine*, published by Walden-Mott Corp., 466 Kinderkamack Road, Oradell, New Jersey.

Subjectivity and Life by Alan Watts, published by the Society for Comparative Philosophy, Inc., S. S. Vallejo, P.O. Box 857, Sausalito, California.

Feast of Fools by Harvey Cox. Copyright © 1969 by Harvey Cox. Published by Harvard University Press, Cambridge, Massachusetts.

(The following page constitutes an extension of this copyright page.)

This is a reprint of a hardcover edition published by The New American Library, Inc. The hardcover edition was published simultaneously in Canada by George J. McLeod Ltd., Toronto

SIGNET, SIGNET CLASSICS, SIGNETTE, MENTOR AND PLUME BOOKS are published by The New American Library, Inc., 1301 Avenue of the Americas, New York, New York 10019

FIRST PRINTING, DECEMBER, 1972

PRINTED IN THE UNITED STATES OF AMERICA

"Thursday, the fifth day of the week, following Wednes-day."

—*Webster International*

"Thank God, it's Thursday!"
—Slogan for the Four-Day Week

"Thursday's child has far to go."

—Mother Goose

"Thursday, we kiss."

—Mother Goose

And, Maundy Thursday, the Feast of Passover, when Jesus, following ancient custom, washed the feet of his disciples and gave them a New Commandment: "Love one another."

As for Solomon Grundy who took ill on Thursday, Edna Millay who said, "I do not love you, Thursday," and Mother Goose who also said, "Friday, we cry . . ." we'll excuse her and assume the others were misanthropes.

For all the Angelas and Adams . . .

If they are your fathers and mothers, love them . . .

Someday, they may be you . . .

If they are you, you are a beginning . . .

☆ 1 ☆

Angela drove her Ford station wagon down the curved driveway in front of the Thomas home. It was Thursday. At last, after the long summer, she could go to Boston again. John Barleta, their gardener, was on the front lawn giving instructions to two of his employees, tired-looking, placid men in their late sixties whom John hired to do the lawn mowing, trimming, and flower planting he contracted every year from the more affluent residents of Valley Stream Estates. It was rumored that Barleta made more money than the people he worked for, but the community was the kind where a man lost status if he ran his own power lawn mower.

When they had first moved into their new home Angela would have been happy to mow the lawn herself and tend the flower beds. "I'm really a *paisan*," she told Jim. "It makes me feel passionate to dig in the earth and taste my own sweat." Actually, Angela had even more erotic ideas. Their new back yard was nearly an acre of forest. The neighbors on either side were at least two hundred feet away. That first spring she had fantasized herself dressed only in a cotton dress, planting a garden. Maybe Jim was helping. Maybe he was just watching her, proud of his sexy wife. Then suddenly, heedless of the perspiration flowing from her body, overjoyed with their land and their earth and their kids in the house, he would tumble her on the ground, pull her dress over her head, and yell his enthusiasm at their bodies slithering naked together in a joyous orgasm.

But Jim had ignored her hints and even her chiding that he enjoyed upper-middle-class game-playing. "We can

11

afford Barleta . . . for God's sake, Angela, I don't work my ass off to spend my leisure trimming lawns. I don't like gardening. I want to play golf. Even if it does look pretty silly for a lawyer's wife to be using a pitchfork or pushing a wheelbarrow, you can putter around the yard if you want to." That was eight years ago. Barleta even planted their tomato plants now. Angela still didn't play golf, but she was usually waiting at the club when Jim returned from an all-day foursome.

Angela waved at Barleta. "I'm on my way to Boston," she told him. "Jim will mail you a check tonight." Momentarily, she wondered why she hadn't just smiled at John and continued on her way. Her closest friend, Bettie Kanace, wasn't so friendly with Barleta or any of the tradesmen in Acton. But Angela couldn't help herself. She liked people . . . especially down-to-earth people like Barleta. Grinning back at her, his several double chins creased in happiness, his huge belly held together by a four-inch belt, John was the perfect portrait of a gardener who probably planted Astro-turf around his own home. Angela knew that several photographs she had taken of John were among her best. But neither Jim nor John knew that Angela Thomas' "snapshots," as everybody called them, were any more than a hobby. That she was really quite professional, whether her family realized it or not.

Driving through the side streets that would bring her to the Mass Turnpike, she remembered last night and couldn't help chuckling. Jim had dropped the subject of Angela's Thursdays on the griddle again. They were sitting on the veranda of the Valley Stream Country Club with the Kanaces and the Vinings, sipping a second before-dinner cocktail. In the distance the crickets were chirping. The early evening sky was cool and remote. She wanted to tell them all to sit still a moment and listen and feel. But if she had, they would have laughed. They all knew that Angela was a romantic. "Nothing wrong in that," Ed Kanace said. He approved of Angela. But she knew it was only to convince her of his in-bed potential. "If it weren't for daydreamers like Angela, who would buy sports cars?"

"Thursday is Angela's day off." Bettie and Martha knew it well enough, but Jim, Ed, and Harry were on the subject of Women's Liberation, mouthing all the male platitudes, and wondering what suburban women did all day. Jim couldn't help it; occasionally he evoked the slight question mark that Angela's Thursdays left in his mind.

"Every Thursday for the past six years, Angela has gone to Boston for the day." He grinned indulgently in her direction when she told him it was scarcely every Thursday. "What in hell do you do all day Thursday, Angela, beside dispose of our surplus income? I'll bet you have a lover."

Angela knew that when Jim kidded her about having a lover it was his way of saying, Look at my wife. She's beautiful. She could have a lover. But she's mine. As for spending Jim's hard-earned money, both of them had long since outgrown their acquisitive days. While Jim might not have phrased it the same way, it was her contention that they had become sophisticated enough to appreciate time more than material things. Long ago she had lost interest in frenetic home decorating. They lived in a comfortable accumulation of furniture and styles, mementos of the passing phases of their lives. Worn furniture and rugs had been replaced, but Angela had never pressured like Bettie Kanace "to toss all this crap out . . . stuff that dates back to our wedding day, and start all over again."

About once in three months Angela did go on a shopping spree, buying clothes for herself and the kids, and shirts with French cuffs for Jim (the only clothing he trusted her to buy for him), but she shopped with precision. She knew her own style . . . breezy, casual, little makeup. Extremes in fashion made her feel silly, as if she were a kid again trying to find a new image by putting on her mother's clothes.

As for extracurricular romance, she had occasionally given it a passing thought. Not particularized. Just daydreams. But the truth was there were no men in her environment who were basically much different from Jim. Whether Jim had any fantasies, she couldn't tell. Like most middle-class Americans, Angela and Jim were careful never to reveal to each other any strange sexual drives. A few years ago Jim had seemed a little interested in Bettie. But his entrée to seduction seemed to be largely based on suggestive conversation. He aimed his innuendoes at Bettie when they were all together. Bettie told Angela Jim really wanted to "take a flyer," but he didn't dare ask. At forty-five, Angela guessed Jim wasn't "adventuring." He enjoyed the serenity of his routine. Another female somewhere on the fringes of his life could prove disruptive and demanding.

The truth was the Thomases had both aged well. Jim's

youthful Sicilian coloring—"I look like a Mafia gangster," he had told Angela when they were just married—had lightened considerably. His black hair had grayed with charming random streaks of white. The iron-gray bristle moustache he had grown several years ago contributed to his country gentleman look. Angela was aware, too, that while she might not appear so youthful and nubile as her daughters, Ruth and Robin, nevertheless men whom the Thomases had known for years seemed suddenly to rediscover her, and were amazed that she was forty-three. Not that she was beautiful. She guessed some men simply responded to her bright cheerfulness. So many of her friends approaching menopause had turned inward. While they might try to maintain their physical appearance, they often exuded a dreary conformity coupled with a belief that they knew all the answers. Angela couldn't help herself . . . she bubbled instinctively. "I have an affirmative brain," she told Jim. "People in love with their own navels bore me."

But with Ruthie nearly twenty-two, beginning her last year at Radcliffe; Robin, twenty, at Julliard (spending more of her time studying ballet), and Richy starting Dartmouth this fall, Angela had accepted at least one fact of life: the days when love was shining and trembly, and sex was an endless male and female adventure, were mostly rememberance of things past.

☆ 2 ☆

At the toll booth Angela picked up her entrance card onto the turnpike. The clock on her dashboard read a quarter of nine. She hadn't wasted any time. Even before Jim had left for the office, she was piling the few breakfast dishes into the washer. She kissed him good-bye, and gave herself a final mirror check. She watched him drive his Buick onto the street. And then she was on her way. Over her shoulder was her tote bag. Her camera was loaded with thirty-six exposures, and a couple of additional rolls in case anything interesting turned up.

Actually Thursdays had become a way of life in the Thomas family. In a vague way, Jim was aware that at the beginning she had spent Thursdays taking pictures of ancient Boston buildings that still survived the modernization of the city. Later, the people of Boston, the flotsam and jetsam that float on the current of life in any big city began to intrigue her. Jim warned her against getting too friendly with unwashed bums and dropouts. But Angela never worried, she was certain she would wriggle out of any tight situations. She continued to accumulate her photographs. Jim seemed happy to assume that in a larger sense Thursday for Angela was just, plain and simply, a day of escape from the suburban merry-go-round. After all, he had golf. Anyway, Thursday was usually Jim's day in court. Thursday, Jim worked especially hard to make a living. Angela knew that Thursday night Jim was "pooped." She managed to be home by five-thirty or six . . . well ahead of him. She even had time to whip up dinner before he arrived.

When Angela had first ventured into Boston on Thursdays the children were much younger. Although it was no longer true, her original excuse for the weekly excursion to Boston was to visit with her mother, who lived in the North End. Jim could only approve. It saved him the necessity of more formal weekend visits to the old lady and Angela's sisters. Their husbands (unlike Jim Thomasello) hadn't anglicized their surnames, and didn't think too highly of "ambulance chasers" anyway. Angela guessed that her sisters, Kathy and Alma, resented her a little. Jim came from New York. That in itself was suspicious. The first day Angela brought Jim home (the boy she had met at Boston University), she knew she was introducing a stranger into a tight little family group. Being Italian wasn't sufficient to bridge the gap. Jim really had made no effort to try. From the beginning it was a growing intellectual separation. She and Jim were the only ones in either of their families who were going to college. Angela knew that Alma had told Maria, their mother: "Ange, with her sixty-thousand-dollar home in Acton . . . what does she care if you have to run a fruit and vegetable market for a living?" But Maria was well aware that her older daughters and their husbands, who had taken over the family bakery on Salem Street, made a very good living indeed. They had stayed in their original homes in the North End not because of lack of money, but simply because anywhere else would have forced them to live among strangers—Irish and Protestants who were definitely not a part of their world. As for her mother, Angela knew Maria wanted to work.

The old lady enjoyed the tough world of men in the market, and she had been admired by all of them. After she died at eighty-one, hit by an automobile of all things, Angela still presumably visited her sisters but the timing had dwindled to every seventh or eighth Thursday. Maria was buried four years ago. Ruthie had been in high school then, and her job on Thursdays was to corral Robin and Richy at two-thirty, after junior high classes were over, and see they more or less stayed around the house until mother came home.

Only half concentrating on the familiar drive toward Boston, conscious that she was holding the car at seventy, necessitating an occasional glance in her rear-vision mirror to see if the fuzz were after her, Angela mused that history was repeating itself. She had no more closeness with Ruth than Maria had had with her. She would have bet that in her younger days, her mother, calmly obtaining weekly absolution from her priest, had known more than one man postmaritally. With a twinkle in her eye, the old lady often told her daughters stories from Boccaccio (her favorite author) in minute detail, especially delighting in cuckolded husbands.

"Men," she would snort. "They think they own you. Let them think, and do what *you* must."

Angela hadn't dared to use the hint as an invitation to question the old lady. Now, she wished she had. Females in her mother's generation could accept an extramarital relationship as dangerous (Italian husbands killed their wives for less) but an inevitable phase of marital life. Angela smiled at her thoughts. Even in Italy things were changing. Now, if they dared, females could get a divorce. But as for her own life, if there were any lovers peripheral to the Thomas household, they were premarital.

Robin was secretive. Angela hoped that she wasn't concentrating on any one boy. If Robin fell in love and got married that would be the end of her dream of being a dancer. Richy had shown no interest in girls, as yet . . . but Ruthie had tossed Angela a flaming torch. Then she withdrew across a moat and behind her own castle walls, leaving no real bridge on which Angela could launch a discussion.

Two weeks ago Ruthie had confided in her—not the details . . . just the unadulterated fact. This fall, Ruthie

16

had moved into an apartment in Cambridge with a young man. She was obviously in love, but the boy (Bud something or other, Ruthie hadn't yet brought him home) was going to graduate school at Harvard. Bud had no money. Obviously he couldn't support a wife. So why should he have one? It was an interesting question. If a male couldn't support a woman, it no longer meant he couldn't make love to one.

"We're sharing expenses," Ruthie told her. "Maybe Bud will marry me someday. Maybe he won't. It's the way it has to be." Angela couldn't really share Ruthie's laughter. Was it forced?

"Of course, I know Daddy! If he knew about Bud, my share of the expenses wouldn't be there to share," Ruth had continued quite calmly. "It really shouldn't worry you, Mommy. Bud and I want to live together. I think we're in love. At least, I love him. If it isn't going to last, it's better to find it out now. If you tell Daddy, and he gives me Army ultimatums, he won't accomplish anything. I can get a job afternoons in Harvard Square, typing for a law firm, and pay for the apartment and school myself."

Ruthie had once told Jim, when he informed her of the hours that she must keep when she was in high school, that maybe, since he had already become a major in the reserves, the Army would retire him as a general. Actually, it wasn't a fair criticism. In his handling of the children Jim may have been a little patriarchal but he wasn't militant. They all could wangle anything out of him they had ever wanted.

What could she say to Ruthie? That living in Acton, Massachusetts, in a sixty-thousand-dollar home, having security and three children was the acme of an ecstatic life? That she, Ruthie, shouldn't surrender herself to a man until she was sure she would achieve a similar status? That would be irrational. She had slept with Jim twice before they were married. He was in his last year of law school, then. There had been no guarantees that he would be financially successful. She hadn't given a thought about middle-class success then. But she and Jim *had been engaged*, and the wedding date had been set. Didn't girls get engaged anymore? If many females were like Ruthie and "wouldn't be caught dead wearing a rock like yours, Mother" ... the diamond manufacturers must be going out of business.

☆ 3 ☆

Angela was sure of one thing. She wasn't exactly unhappy with what the sociologists termed her upper-middle-class way of life. By contrast with the way most people lived, she at least had the freedom of money. Jim had never tried to be a millionaire, but, of course, his earnings (at least four times the national average) made her Thursdays possible. She refused to speculate whether her way of life made Thursday necessary. Rich or poor, one thing she was sure of: a man or woman needs a personal purpose, a nexus on which their lives can revolve. She guessed that if she hadn't rediscovered her interest in photography and combined it with her Thursdays, the Thomas marriage might have been shipwrecked on the shoals of her boredom. It bothered her, but she really had no answers for her children, except possibly that a bird in the hand was worth two in the bush. Jim was a good man. A concerned father. Given a second chance, like Ivan Osokin, she'd probably live the same life all over again. And really, *she was happy,* in a calm sort of way.

There was no need to rush home to dinner on Thursdays. The nest was empty. If she got tied up (silly idea, what could possibly tie her up except deciding too late in the afternoon to go to a movie?) or making dinner just for Jim and herself was too much of a nuisance, they could always eat out. The Red Coach Grilles, the dining rooms of the Holiday Inns, and a few of the more expensive eating places around the suburbs had become meeting places for the middle-aged. Roadside clubs, where the bartenders quickly recognized them, became their friends, and introduced them to others who were likewise fending off their loneliness by eating out, enjoying vacuous conversation with temporary acquaintances. Stopovers on the final road to a senior-citizen center, she told Jim, but he didn't think that was funny. Besides, they only ate occasionally at those places. Saturday and Wednesday they were with their friends at the Valley Stream Country Club.

Thursday was really her day. A day to drift on the

current . . . a day to be lonely but not alone . . . a day to be herself, whoever her real self was. Angela admitted that she didn't know the answer to that. All that she was certain of was that after twenty-three years of marriage, there was at least twenty-five percent of herself (the percentage seemed to be growing in recent years) that somehow she couldn't share with Jim. Except for one or two weeks after they were first married, had she ever surrendered herself completely? Why was it that most people learned to withdraw a fraction of themselves? . . . Why were most people, even after they were long married, afraid to reveal the trembly, insecure people they really were? . . . Perhaps it was just because they were married. Could anyone ever dare to be utterly defenseless with the person one lived with every day and night? Certainly whoever or whatever her real self might be, she had never revealed it to Bettie Kanace. In fact, a few years ago, when Bettie suggested that, now, she too was free of the kids and could join Angela on her "Boston Adventure," Angela had hemmed and hawed out of it. Bettie finally took the cue and told her confidentially, "You don't have to answer, Angela . . . but I'll bet Jim is right and doesn't know it. You *are* having an affair."

On secure grounds, Angela could only laugh. "Some affair. Who would want a forty-three-year-old matron between nine and four-thirty on Thursdays?"

"My husband thinks he would." Bettie stared at her quizzically. "You turn him on. The trouble is that Ed could never devote a whole day to you. His attention span with females exhausts itself in about forty-five minutes."

Though she had had several propositions from their male friends in the past few years (including Ed, who was so determined to sack with her that he had offered Bettie to Jim in exchange), she had remained faithful. Jim and Chuck Zendella (who had broken her hymen in the back seat of an automobile when she was seventeen) were the only males who had ever touched her body. All that she could now remember about Chuck was his frantic haste, and his sad gasp and clutching of her as he spilled his seed on her stomach. It was amusing. She couldn't recall his face, or how he managed to wiggle her out of her panties, but she could remember his penis. It had looked so swollen and helpless. Afterwards, she had wanted to hold it. Then it was so subdued and unresponsive. She wondered why neither Chuck then (nor Jim later) enjoyed being

19

touched afterwards. Once the seed was discharged, the essential man together with his penis seemed to withdraw, to retract together. . . . Even a female's tender mouth, which finally could hold the male without choking to death, was an anathema. Angela wondered if Jim was aware that she was sure she was capable of going from orgasm to orgasm and making snuggly love all night. Of course, it was just a feeling. She had never had the opportunity to prove it.

Over the years, she had more than once thought about sex with another man. Did the ephemeral lover, and the love that stayed poised forever on the plateau of wonder, really exist? How could you not consider the possibilities when every movie, most of television, and seventy-five percent of the book-club selections reminded you that man's dreams and reality rarely coincided . . . that in real life after a while the bells didn't ring so loudly anymore, rockets didn't go off? Screwing was as casual as hot buttered popcorn, and just about as sensuous. Would sexual intercourse with a stranger be an antidote? She dismissed the idea as impossible. Not that she would be repulsed at the thought of a different male entering her body, kissing her breasts. It wasn't that. Long ago she had liberated herself from any ideas about sex being nasty. Her problem was that she would need complete involvement with a man (obviously not possible with one husband already) or she would want no involvement whatsoever.

If she could have said, in response to Ed Kanace's cajolings, "Okay, Ed, let's screw. I want a fierce joyous orgasm. I want to feel your body plunging into mine. I want your semen to burst in my vagina. But afterward I don't want to pretend I like you or you like me. I won't dislike you. I won't think about anything except getting dressed, giving you a peck good-bye, and that will be that."

In her fantasy, if Ed protested about her male attitude, she would have just chuckled and replied, "Ed, let's not mix sex and personality. If I ever decided to discover whether you are a different kind of screwing machine from my husband, that would be a separate thing. The rest of you I know about. I really couldn't bear listening to you talk about selling Buicks or playing golf. Your gisum flowing out of my vagina is nowhere near as repulsive as your thoughts would be boring my brain."

Of course, females from Acton, Massachusetts (or Middletown, Ohio, for that matter), may have fantasies like that but they only thought them in popular novels. Angela knew how to hold her tongue. It was simpler to smile and look wistful, and leave a male with his illusions.

☆ 4 ☆

At the Newton toll booth she paid her tax. Thursday. The long summer over once again . . . the girls were back in college. Richy had reluctantly been escorted to Dartmouth. She grinned as she recalled his embarrassment. Why couldn't sons let their mothers hug them . . . and hug their mothers back? Not sick . . . Mother's Day style. But warmly as female friends. But Richy had other problems. He couldn't wait to begin the transformation of his nouveau appearance. . . . His long hair was not quite long enough. His new baggage and trunks were too obvious. While he didn't say it, his nervousness proclaimed his need to be rid of his quite square parents, comparing notes with other parents about to be separated from their male progeny for the first time.

Thursday. The first Thursday in Boston since last June. It wasn't that she couldn't have continued her Thursday routine through July and August, but with the kids home, with Jim, on some of the hot summer days, extending his Wednesday afternoon golf into long weekends, this past summer it had seemed kind of ridiculous.

There were still Thursdays in the fall, in the winter, and in the spring. Thursday. The neither here nor there part of the week. Thursday, September 28th. For some people, a beginning was in January. Late September with the colleges opening, the city was a new child suddenly aware of itself. September was prelude for Angela.

The day was bright and crisp. A light northwest wind had blown the smog out to sea. The earth already smelled of October. Though she tried to put her lovemaking with Jim last night out of her mind, the moments kept drifting back. Unless she made the overtures, they made love less frequently now. Still, if they had averaged three times a week in the past twenty-three years, last night would have

21

been the three thousandth five hundredth or so time. Yuck. It was a wonder they hadn't worn each other out. In the act of love, Jim was still delightfully male as he sobbed the ecstasy of his release and his appreciation of her. For maybe a half hour they even seemed to break through to each other in a joyous kind of intimacy and laughter at their own silliness. Why couldn't this be a way of life?

Then it was over. Jim took his usual quick leak because maybe the flushing helped avoid prostate . . . and she lay on the bed, uncaring that his semen oozed out of her vagina . . . wondering, bemused, if at this late date she could still get pregnant. (She knew she could. Doctor Green told her not to take chances.) Lying there, she wanted something more than the television, now turned on and booming . . . she wanted something more than his friendly final kiss . . . "It was nice, Ange." Wanting, wanting something inexplicable to herself even. It would have been useless to tell Jim. In fact, it would have upset him. My God, what did she want? Her climax had been violent enough. She kept thinking about Ruthie and Bud, who thus far, though he probably slept every night with her daughter, had scrupulously stayed clear of the Thomas home and Acton, Massachusetts. Not that she was jealous of Ruthie . . . no, rather the truth was (she grinned as the thought burbled into her mind), the truth was she was nostalgic for the kind of lovemaking she and Jim had had for the first few years of their marriage. What had happened? Why couldn't a male and female hold on to that joyous involvement and need for each other? How did they get to fear the defenselessness that would make such intimacy possible through their entire lives? Now, after twenty-three years, Jim managed to beat the Kinsey statistics. He could stretch their lovemaking to a half-hour . . . but after their climaxes they quickly retreated into their separate shells. What she had really wanted to say last night (and didn't dare) was, "Jim . . . pretend you just met me . . . pretend you don't know me." But, alas, he did—at least seventy-five percent of the time.

✩ 5 ✩

Angela only vaguely remembered the feeling of time passing—time being lost forever—that had culminated in her first Thursday. It was six years ago ... her thirty-seventh birthday, October 16th. For some reason birthdays had become a kind of accounting time for her. While the balance sheet balanced, some of the assets were depreciated. Her lovely home that had occupied her and Jim for years, planning and saving for it, was finished. After two years it had become routine. Once Jim left in the morning it became a silent prison punctuated by a morning delivery from the mailman. No surprises, except an occasional book-club selection she thought she had rejected. Then the interminable phone calls from female friends, either planning the day at hand, or the weeks and months ahead. Should they play bridge? Would she take charge of the entertainment committee this year for Acton's Women's Club? Really, she should accept the presidency. Everyone wanted her. The club needed her. Or, the latest ... the *MUST* drug program. Doctor Keynes was so dynamic. He told everyone he would never have gotten *MUST* off the ground without Angela. *MUST* would rehabilitate the kids. This marijuana kick was nothing to joke about. God knows where it would lead. Had Jim told her? The Reece kids and three others and their families were going before Judge Hastings. They'd all be busted (her friends knew all the current vernacular). Of course, it wasn't that pot was so bad ... but everyone knew marijuana led to worse things. Angela hadn't forgotten the Harvest Dinner at the Valley Stream Club, had she? A week from Saturday. Was she or Bettie in charge of table decorations? It's your birthday Angela? Oh, dear Angela. Happy Birthday! Time is passing. We're getting older. What did Jim get you?

Maybe that wasn't the exact conversation on her thirty-seventh birthday, but it was close enough. Angela remembered she had slammed down the phone on Martha Vining, held back a tear of frustration, and dialed Jim's office. "It's my birthday!" she said, detesting her plaintive

23

voice. Jim knew it. Two hours before he had kissed her his usual morning good-bye, patted her rump thirty-seven times, and gleamed his assurance that tonight was diaphragm night. "I just wanted you to know," she told him, "in case you telephoned. I'm going to Boston."

Jim had been beamish. "Great, Ange, you need a change. Have fun. I bought you a little surprise for your birthday, but go whole hog. Get yourself a new fall outfit!"

Angela turned off the expressway down the ramp into the garage under the Prudential Plaza. She could no longer remember what she had done that first day. But it was declaration of one-day independence a week. Give or take a few weeks that was six years ago. The second Thursday she had driven to Boston the die was cast. At the beginning it was impossible to explain her motivations. She had unearthed her old Yashica thirty-five-millimeter camera from the junk in the front hall closet. She remembered telling Jim she was thinking of going back to work. It was a good decision for one's thirty-seventh year. She needed something constructive to do. Maybe she would set up a studio right here in the house.

She hadn't anticipated his violently negative reaction. Why in hell did she want to get involved photographing babies and new brides and grooms? He was right, of course. On weekends when he was free she would be up to her ass in wedding receptions. Besides, Jim had launched into a discussion of why couldn't she take up golf and play with him. He never pretended that he was any pro . . . it was just a clean, invigorating way to relax. The Vinings and the Kanaces played together . . . foursomes. They had fun together. She was letting herself become too damned introspective. Why did she keep withdrawing from social commitments? Okay, maybe she didn't like golf, but if she really wanted to help, cutting a little swath in the town as president of the Women's Club could be useful. He was beginning to think that he might step off the fringe of politics and run for office. Nothing big. Selectman, maybe. An antisocial wife would be a noose around his neck.

She denied that she was antisocial. She couldn't verbalize it, but the superficial contact that most people seemed to relish—endless conversation that existed largely to assure the speaker and listener they were both alive—left her uneasy and dissatisfied. She wanted an involvement with individuals and small groups of females that seemed

24

impossible to achieve. It was an interesting fact of her life that if she suggested to Jim or the Kanaces or Vinings that it might be fun to spend an evening listening to music (a symphony or an opera) or attending an avant-garde drama at one of the theaters in Boston, they would enthusiastically agree. "Ange is right, we need some intellectual interests. There's too much crap-talk and boring television" ... but after a half-hour or so, if she put a concerto or symphony on the turntable, their minds wandered, and pretty soon Ed or Jim or Martha or Bettie couldn't stand it any longer. One or the other would speak in a hushed whisper "Gee, Mozart was quite a guy wasn't he? ... Did you know Dan Seward was in the hospital? Phyllis isn't saying much ... but the rumor is it may be cancer. Live it up, I say. Did you say that Mozart wrote this concerto, Ange?"

As for the theater, Jim told her he was a simple guy, why suffer? She knew her friends were bored and simply trying to please her, and she guessed she must be a dreamer. In her world and in her time, very few husbands and wives, let alone groups of friends, were interested in learning together, or even dared to be silent together.

It wasn't that she couldn't play the suburban social game. She could and did, and there were moments when she enjoyed herself, but she was plagued with the growing awareness that in the past few years she empathized more with the people she photographed on the streets of Boston than she did with their friends. Angela smiled at her thoughts. Despite her conviction that her best photographs passed beyond simple portraiture into the essence of the person, the truth was that her contacts with her "street people" were superficial. The people in her favorite photographs, in one way or another, all seemed about to say, "I'm alone. I don't want to be alone, but there is no bridge, is there ... is there?"

☆ 6 ☆

At least Jim hadn't locked the door of his doll's house. If she couldn't contribute to the family's economic welfare, she could pursue the unanswerable questions with her camera. Without telling Jim (it had really seemed kind of childish at the beginning), Angela spent most of her Thursdays "streetwalking." It was her secret world. Certain that his wife was a one-man woman, Jim would have been delighted had he known. "My wife's a streetwalker" . . . then, after a big guffaw, he would roll his eyes happily at the innuendo. "She moseys up and down the streets of Boston soliciting bums . . . and begs them to take their pictures."

As the escalator brought her to the level of the Plaza, Angela couldn't help herself—she smiled at the people hurrying past her. The gay notes of melody she couldn't identify danced below the surface of her mind. She was in love with being alive. Walking past the art stores, book stores, restaurants, and boutiques on Boylston Street, she occasionally caught a mirror reflection of herself in the store windows. With her camera tote bag swinging against her hip, her long legs stretching in a purposeful stride, her calves rebelling against the confines of her skirt, and her ungirdled buttocks in a joyful cadence of their own, Angela was sure that the people smiling at her pictured her as a matronly den mother about to join her scout troop, or an apple-cheeked tourist from Sandusky, Ohio, or Boise, Idaho, newly arrived in Boston, trying to find her historic roots on the Freedom Trail while her husband peddled his wares at some convention or other. It would have been better, of course, if she had a brood of kids milling around her as they embarked on a whirlwind tour from the Old South Church to the Paul Revere House, to Bunker Hill, and finishing at the Charleston Navy Yard to see the *Constitution*.

Actually, people stared at Angela and smiled because they really couldn't believe their eyes. Someone passing them seemed in a deeper harmony with life. Momentarily she tripped into the brains of the plodders and worriers, and the dark shadows of their own making assumed a new perspective. Life just couldn't be so bad when there were sunshine and Angelas in the world.

Of course, this was a Thursday Angela. Today she was *allegro*. "Mirth, admit me of thy crew, to live with her, and live with thee, in unreproved pleasures free, to hear the lark begin his flight . . ." Once she had known the whole poem, and Jim told her he had asked her to marry him because she recited it to him over a bottle of chianti in an Italian restaurant on Hanover Street.

But it was no longer so easy to force her environment to conform. To bubble, to be buoyant proved you were still childish, and hence suspect, in an adult world. Just this morning she told Jim, "I suppose sometimes I sound as if I were a Christian Scientist or I had swallowed Candide whole, but I have made a startling discovery. The sun that is shining today is the same sun, in the same sky, as when I was a rag-tag kid in the North End. Yesterday is only different from today because the man-world seems different. We tend to lose our perspective. We confuse the man-happenings on television, in the newspapers, on radio . . . the wars, the hatred, the suffering . . . with reality. All man-life is ephemeral; we coat it with dullness or a gloss as our mood dictates. The universe pursues its destiny, uncaring. Why am I melancholy one day, moody or sad, and a few days later in the identical man-world I'm happy, laughing, joyous? Isn't it because I am reacting to the kaleidoscope of the man-world? . . . Now the patterns are good ones, now they are bad. Most of us have simply forgotten that we are creatures of much more stable, unchanging patterns. The light from the stars in the sky may come from worlds that no longer exist, or worlds that are disappearing toward the edge of the universe, but it is the same light and the same patterns that Jesus or Socrates saw, and probably will be the same light that men will be staring at another two thousand man-years from now." Angela noted that Jim, his eyes perusing the headlines of the Boston *Globe*, hadn't been listening too closely. "Jim, do you understand what I'm saying?"

She guessed Jim might have reversed the question on her, but he didn't. Years of marriage make one politic . . . "Of course, I do, honey." As he left the breakfast table, Jim pecked her lips in an absentminded way. "You're telling me that you are a joyous creature of the world. I agree. After twenty-three years, I'm still happy I picked you."

Slowing her pace as she came to the Public Gardens, Angela watched a police paddy wagon cruise off the road onto the sidewalks toward a middle-aged man who had just dropped his pants and underwear. Poised drunkenly against a huge chestnut tree, he was urinating. The last reluctant dribbles trickled over his black, greasy trousers. With a glazed look he stared in the direction of Angela and the police car (she had already found her camera and clicked off three pictures), and then he slid gracefully to

27

the ground. His uncircumcised penis, hanging lifelessly between his legs, seemed unnaturally long, and his protruding belly in contrast to his sunburned face was much too white.

Angela was still taking pictures when one of the policemen accosted her. "You a reporter, lady?"

She shook her head. Why did the police always make her so damned nervous? Beneath the uniform and the helmet he was just a burly young Irishman leering at her. She had been brainwashed by the image. But he did look mean—as if he were about to snatch the camera out of her hand.

"Who are you? What's your name? We didn't hurt that lush."

You didn't have to toss him into the wagon like a sack of potatoes. Angela didn't verbalize her thought. She just grimaced and started to walk away. He grabbed her arm. "Wait a minute, sister. I have a feeling we should take you down to the station, too."

"Take your hands off me." She was jittery, but she managed to suggest cold anger. "If you arrest me, you'll find yourself in more trouble than you've ever been in your young life."

The bluff worked. He dropped her arm and walked toward the paddy wagon. "It takes all kinds," she heard him tell his buddies. "She probably never saw a prick that size before."

Angela shrugged. There was only one thing to do. Don't mix the man-world with reality. It still was the same lovely day.

☆ 7 ☆

Black, white, yellow mothers with their kids; students and drifters stretched indolently on the grass holding onto summer . . . young lovers, some dreamy in their discovery of each other, and others so passionately embraced that only the faint recollection of the police stopped them from stripping and copulating before they burst. And why not? Angela grinned. If it could be accepted as a way of life, why shouldn't willing genitals experience fresh air and sunshine? The Gardens and the Common were a moving panorama. In European cities—on the Via Veneto, the Galleria, the Dam, the Champs Élysées—or in Tel Aviv on Dizengoff Street and in hundreds of other places in the world, older cultures knew there was no more charming, free entertainment than people watching each other. Would Americans ever learn how to build cities with streets and sidewalks that mirrored men rather than machines? At least Boston had its Common . . . a lovely word that most people had forgotten really meant people sharing people. Here even the pigeons shared the swan boats meandering in their fixed tracks, and New Leftists and Right Birchers proclaimed their separate paths to nirvana, while on the sidewalks young actors mimed their desperation with the older generation and the followers of Hare Krishna danced and sang their way to eternity.

It was a summer stage, a living theater that too soon would give way to cool northern air and the wintry blizzards that would sweep the actors into hibernation. For Angela the bustling audience was the actors, and the question trailing into infinity was, Who watches the watcher?

At the intersection of Winter Street and Tremont she paused to watch the desultory spectators on their lunch hour staring at boys wearing saffron dhotis and girls pristine and virginal in their purple saris. Kids, really (Robin, Richy, and Ruthie were all older), the boys with shaved heads, the girls with plaited hair singing their never-ending chant to God: "Hare Krishna, Hare Krishna, Krishna, Krishna, Krishna, Hare, Hare, Hare Rama, Hare Rama, Rama, Rama, Hare, Hare." And while they sang, they danced, a lilting little jig to celebrate their abandonment of temporal things.

About fifty feet away from the circle the crowd had formed around them, on a slightly higher elevation, Angela panned the gathering through her telescopic lens, snapping an occasional picture to add to her collection of the dancers. Was their ecstasy assumed or real? The faces of the shifting lunchtime audience reflected curiosity, disgust, and simple bewilderment, as if they were personally trying to answer the dancers' basic question. "Is it simply the aim of life to eat, sleep, have some shelter, some sex pleasure, and die?" One of the dancers had directed the question at Angela a few weeks ago and then answered it. "No, this is not the aim of life. Your aim of life should be to realize

29

yourself . . . that you are part and parcel of the Supreme Absolute Personality of Godhead, Sri Krishna." The girl had danced away with the dollar Angela gave her, surprised that a stranger had her own answer and voiced it. "I think the aim of life is to celebrate life." The watchers and the watched epitomized two worlds—those who would never dare drop their grip on whatever tiny reality they had lived by, and the followers of Krishna who knew their truth. The only reality was never to die by never being born again.

The psychedelic kaleidoscope suddenly reshuffled itself and Angela was staring through her telescopic lens at a man in conversation with one of the female dancers. Perfect. A tall, craggy Bostonian. The patrician type with a prominent Roman nose inherited from the Caesars who had penetrated Britain. A cross between Prince Philip, whom she admired, and the Cabots, Lowells, Sargents, and Saltonstalls. Crinkling eyes and a warm smile softened his face as he listened to the words and supplications of one of the female dancers. What was she telling him? Angela snapped off five pictures in rapid succession.

As she took the last picture she was suddenly conscious that he was staring across the space of sidewalk and milling people that separated them. He was watching her with a merry, puzzled expression on his face. She saw him give the dancer some money for the japa-mala prayer beads she had put in his hands. He grinned directly at Angela, put the beads in his pocket, touched the girl's shoulder in a gesture of friendliness, and then turned into the crowd. With a strange sense of loss, Angela watched him disappear among the people flowing down Winter Street. Momentarily he had embraced her with his eyes. Across the intervening space—had she imagined it? was he saying?—I have something to tell you. It was silly, of course, but Angela wanted to listen. She laughed softly and told herself to grow up. It was a schoolgirl emotion. Still, she couldn't shake the feeling. The idea of "some enchanted evening" might be sheer romanticism . . . but a moment of unspoken, deep-felt communication could exist between strangers, couldn't it?

She wasn't hypnotically following a Pied Piper when she too, walked down Winter Street toward Filene's. One mundane thing she had to do today. Close out an account at the Provident Institute for Savings. It was the last link Jim and she had with their first year together. To save

30

money they had moved in with her mother and father. The few dollars a week she deposited in their account, earned from her job at Bachrach's Studios, were something toward the day when Jim would finish Boston University Law School, set up his practice, and get his foot on the first rung of the middle-class financial ladder. The eighteen hundred dollars she had saved then, left untouched, had grown to four thousand. Now, Jim wanted to buy a block of business property in Acton. The price, two hundred and fifty thousand dollars, seemed dizzy and dangerous to Angela. They would commit their total savings and still have a mortgage of one hundred and seventy-five thousand dollars. But Jim insisted the time was now. Between forty and his late fifties were a man's money-making years. He had ten years to do it. *The Block,* as Jim characterized it, had assumed an avuncular reality. Eventually, it would support them in a Florida retirement. Angela wondered, when the day arrived, what she would do in one of those artificial island developments for the upper-middle-income aged. Jim would play golf and fish, of course. He could wax enthusiastic about the joys of such a carefree existence. Did he think she was only kidding when she told him it was too bad they didn't have senior-citizen centers for elderly whores? Maybe she was joking, but even in her sixties she was sure she'd enjoy that kind of work more than playing bridge with suburban matrons while she waited for Daddy to come home from his retirement games. But, alas, older men put their teeth in cups and daydreamed about young girls who wore mini-skirts a finger-length from their crotches. And most young men enjoyed their mechanical, high-pressure, Playboy dream worlds more than the actual flesh of a female, young or old. As for women of forty-three, they were already in limbo. They were either old maids whose vaginal juices would no longer lubricate a male, or if they were married and still aware that they had pussys, they had been thoroughly conditioned that the mining rights, used or not, were staked out long ago.

She was so preoccupied with her meandering thoughts that she walked into the bank almost unaware that someone was holding the door open for her. He smiled benignly at her . . . her Boston Caesar enjoying her, a blushing gasping schoolgirl. What did they call the new female phenomenon? Groupies? Teen-agers who chased after the youngsters who sang rock music. She had read a book about them recently. It belonged to Ruthie. One of the groupies gave full instructions on how to prepare plaster of paris, so a loving female could make reproductions of her favorite musician's erect penis and testicles. She wondered what Ruthie had thought when she read it. Worse . . . since this stranger seemed to have a weird kind of telepathy with her, what would he think if he were receiving the thoughts flashing through her brain?

"I'm not really following you." She knew she was blushing. He was at least six inches taller than she was. Looking up at him made her feel ineffectual.

"I just wondered if you were going to ask me to pose for another picture." Somewhere in his background was a Harvard education. Did the undergraduates practice the accent? A trademark equivalent to a Masonic handshake? His eyes were recording her physical person with a cool intimacy.

"Oh, dear. I hope you didn't mind." Angela knew that she had completely lost her poise. Why couldn't she just say, "I'm a professional photographer"? Good lord, it wasn't a lie. Once she had been. "Really," she stammered, "taking pictures is a hobby of mine."

"Delightful. Do you come to Boston often? You can count on me. I'll offer myself. An enthusiastic hobby, looking for a hobbyist . . . especially one who looks as if she is about to burst into tears from embarrassment."

Angela couldn't help laughing. "I'm not really embarrassed." She was aware of people passing between them as he continued to hold the door. "I was just a little fearful you might react like one of those voodoo natives I've read about. They refuse to have their pictures taken. They fear

32

the photographer might imprison their soul. Whoever owned their pictures might possess them in reality."

Again she was overwhelmed with a need he evoked in her. It was mad. Even if she had known him for years, she really wouldn't have dared put her face against his and murmur, "I like you."

"The Krishna followers would say that this is only a temporary body." He chuckled. "Since you only have a picture of the shell that encases the essence of what is both of us, you are welcome to it." He picked a business card out of his pocket. "Have a nice visit in Boston. If the pictures come out, send me a print or two."

I'm letting him go again. Angela stared dumbly at his back as he wove through the crowd on his way to Washington Street. Why? Why did she have this compulsion for intimacy with this stranger?

Please sir, I think I could talk to you. Would you listen? Do you have time? Could I snuggle in your lap while you tell me a story? That was it. At forty-three, somewhere inside her an Angela in pigtails refused to grow up.

Walking into the bank she remembered his business card still clutched in her hand. She read it and nearly collapsed in laughter. It just couldn't be! J. Q. Adams, President Adams National Corporation, Financial Printers, Boston, Massachusetts. Impossible . . . not John Quincy Adams!

Even as she filled out the forms to withdraw her savings, she was really thinking of his last words. "If the pictures come out . . . send me a print or two." She tucked the check for four thousand three hundred and sixty-seven dollars and twenty-six cents into her pocketbook . . . "If the pictures come out" . . . J. Q. Adams obviously didn't know that Angela Campolieto Thomas might be old, tattered, and worn, even a dud in some ways, but with a camera she never missed. Didn't her initials spell ACT? Damn. When the time for action had occurred she had become a stuttering idiot. She must be getting senile. Why should a man . . . not a young one, either (he probably was a year or two older than she) make her feel so giddy? No, not giddy. Young. Alive. She had seen in his eyes a different image of herself. Not mother, not wife, but female, with all the full potential of being female. That felt good.

Outside the bank, vacillating as to what she would do now, she tried to put J. Q. Adams out of her mind. While it wasn't a matter of urgency, she had promised herself to look at some new earrings. Getting her earlobes pierced, urged on by Robin and Ruthie, and decried by Jim as kind of insane at her age, really had been kind of silly. She had removed the gold plugs a week ago. If she didn't put them back, or put something in the holes, pretty soon they would grow together, and Jim would have proved his point. She wasn't the seductive earring type anyway.

Damn it. Jim was wrong. Dangly earrings changed her image . . . for herself at least. Wearing them made her feel maturely sexy. At a costume jewelry counter in Filene's she dawdled through trays of twisted metal and stone. She knew the young female salesgirl was rapidly losing patience with her. Staring at her with a vacant look, she implied a subtle pressure that made it impossible for Angela to make a decision. Then, as she was vacillating between two choices . . . unbelievably, in the mirror on the counter, *she saw him again*. Talking to a salesgirl at one of the perfume booths, he was standing profile to her. Thank God, he was still unaware of her. This time he'd be certain that she was following him. She dropped the earrings she was about to buy on the counter. Not daring to look in his direction, she walked quickly toward the door.

☆ 9 ☆

Amused with the salesgirl's conviction that some men were erotically aroused by the musky quality of Belogia, J. Q. Adams was sniffing the perfume when Angela flashed across his vision. Was that damned woman following him? Was she signaling in some subtle way that she was available? Maybe her picture-taking was a great deal more than just coincidence. If she were a pick-up, she was no ordinary one. The expensive type. He had read about call girls still operating in their forties. Still, that kind of female . . . in business . . . would have dyed her hair. The careless flecks of white in her black Italian hair, even the clean brushed look, was not the work of a hairdresser. Momentarily, he felt sinister. Just this morning, Janice had insisted that the thirty, ten-foot-tall marihuana plants he had carefully cultivated all summer in his back yard garden should have been harvested weeks ago. It was insane for a responsible citizen to have grown them. They hadn't even dared to tell their best friends, or have anyone in their back yard all summer. Maybe this female was a Federal agent. No, that was ridiculous. If he were a suspect, all the police had to do was raid his home. He chuckled. The evidence, like Jack's beanstalk, was reaching to the sky.

While J. Q. Adams might have termed himself somewhat introspective, he was still able to translate thought into action. Before Angela had reached the exit he had closed in on her. "Really," he smiled into her startled face, "I hope you won't think I'm presumptuous, but perhaps you can help me. Once a year, for her birthday, I buy my wife a bottle of perfume. For the past few years I've followed the path of least resistance. Chanel Number Five. Perhaps you have a better idea."

Once again they were standing in a doorway with people passing between them. Unreasonably, Angela wanted both to talk and to run. "I'm sorry," she said. "Nobody likes my choice of perfume except myself."

"I do," he said, grinning at her surprise. "I caught the scent of early spring flowers when you were standing near me at the bank. I wasn't wrong. Either the aroma is you, or it's your perfume. Anyway, it makes me nostalgic."

Angela couldn't repress her laughter. "To tell you the truth, you frightened me. I thought you were going to complain that I was following you. I was going to scream. When the cops came I would have told them the truth. You are following me."

"You don't look like a woman who screams." As he said the words two matronly shoppers, interested in their verbal exchange, got stalled between them. He squeezed around them and took her arm. "Do we have to let the world come between us? If you haven't had lunch, perhaps you'll have it with me." J. Q. knew he was taking a calculated risk. This woman seemed to be unaware that she had a style and attractiveness rare in women her age. Of course, she might prove a colossal bore. But did it matter? A lunch set its own termination.

Angela wanted to ask him why. Why would a stranger want to buy another stranger lunch? A man might want to pick up a young woman, but her? . . . What could he possibly gain? Even as she nodded acquiescence, the thought prickled through her mind that in her entire twenty-three years of marriage she had never had lunch, dinner (or breakfast, giggly thought) with any male, alone, except Jim. She knew that Jim had occasionally dined (small-town lawyers can keep few secrets) with a female client, but knowing Jim she believed him when he said it was for business not for pleasure.

Thinking, My God, Angela, you are provincial . . . she let herself be guided by this confident stranger. "It's a little walk," he told her. "We could take a cab, but this is more companionable. We'll dine at the restaurant on the top of the State Street Bank building. A nice view of the harbor. You can get some interesting pictures. May I ask your name?"

She was about to say Mrs. James Thomas, but caught herself in time. "Angela. Angela Thomas. I feel kind of silly, as if I may be putting you out."

"Not at all. I'm delighted. Are you visiting Boston?"

"I visit Boston every Thursday." She laughed at his surprise. "My home is in Acton."

He allowed himself to be engulfed by the merriment in her eyes. "Good Lord, I thought you were a tourist. We're not at opposite ends of the compass . . . only right angles. My home is in Cohasset."

As they stepped into the elevator that would take them to the top of the building, Angela couldn't resist the question, "What about your wife's birthday present?"

He grinned. "I have a day or two left. Maybe instead of Chanel Number Five I'll buy her the fragrance you are wearing."

Sitting opposite him at a window table she silently watched the traffic on the Central artery, thirty floors below them. A God's eye view that gave the beholder a feeling of immanence. "The perfume is *Pois de Senteur*. Sweet pea," she said.

She chose a martini, he a Cutty Sark on the rocks. "Make the martini with Beefeater's," he told the waiter and smiled at her. "On second thought, I don't think sweet pea is Jan's style."

"You said the odor made you nostalgic."

"I did, didn't I? For me memory often gets linked with smell. A certain odor and something buried in my past will be recreated in the present with a surprising vividness. Marcel Proust wrote most of *Remembrance of Things Past* on that premise." He toyed with a spoon and stared at her. "To be honest with you, I had a moment of total

36

recall when I was with you in front of the bank. For a second I was a youngster on vacation in New Hampshire with my parents. They had left me for the day with a farm girl. I was five. She was about sixteen and enjoyed being a pseudo-mother. We picked flowers for the hotel tables. We were friends. She was dark-complexioned like you, probably Armenian. I've been in love with her ever since." He smiled at Angela, his hypnotized captive. "Conditioning. Positive reinforcement. It can occur unknown to us. Perhaps it explains the impossibility of *not* asking you to lunch."

"Is Jan your wife's name?" Angela clung to a log in the whirling rapids.

"Janice."

"Your initials are J. Q. Do they really stand for John Quincy?"

"Jonathan Quincy. Someone prevented my mother from going whole hog."

"Does your wife call you Jonathan?"

"No. Jon." He smiled at her. "My employees call me J. Q. One of my boys is named Sam, a name I would have preferred since I have more in common with John Adams' brother. If I took a tortuous course I suppose I might claim a relationship, but in truth I feel stronger blood ties to the man without the 's'."

Angela was trying to listen but at the same time she was wondering if she dared to ask him whether his wife would approve of this luncheon. Not a very sophisticated thought. His last words slowly penetrated her own thoughts. "You mean, Adam? Funny, I was adding some vowels to J. Q. and I had arrived at Jake. But I like Adam better." She shrugged. What ever made her say that? He had an artless way of leading her into deep waters.

"Would you be Eve?" His eyes twinkled. "Heavens, no! . . . Angel is better. Does your husband call you Angel?"

Angela sipped the last of her martini. She tried not to appear too bubbly. "Jim calls me Ange, or when he's provoked, Angela. I'm no angel."

The way J. Q. (Adam) was staring at her seemed to deny that. A married man shouldn't send such erotic signals toward a married woman. Angela tried valiantly to squelch her effervescence. Why was it that this stranger could suddenly make her feel so defenseless? It must be the martini. It was gone somehow, and the waiter had returned with a second. She had ordered a shrimp salad and he had seconded her selection. Was that only ten minutes ago? They were talking like old friends.

☆ 10 ☆

"I'm interested in the followers of Krishna," he was telling her. "Despite a New England inheritance and a pretty solid conditioning in the Puritan ethic, I'm aware that happiness lies somewhere between doing and being. Maybe some of us can learn to live our lives as a bridge. We need cross-culturists, hybrids. We need people who devote their lives to depolarization, finding the common threads between the hundreds of subcultures, separating man from man, that are burgeoning in the world."

Angela was intrigued. "Maybe you and I are trying to arrive at the same goals. I guess I never philosophized it, but I'm trying to create what I call living pictures. Pictures of people and things that exist on two or three different levels." She shrugged. "It's just a hobby, of course. It keeps me from expecting too much from people." Angela wanted to tell him that in this super-transient, throwaway world, most people—even husbands and wives—had little involvement in each other's interests. But even though it was true that Jim knew law and golf, and she knew homemaking and photography, to suggest that she lived some of her life in her own world was only stating the obvious. For better or worse, most people lived that way.

Perhaps he was just being polite, but Adam kept probing her with question after question. Forced to verbalize what she had been doing for the past several years, Angela was surprised to discover herself. "I guess Ruthie, my older girl, is the only one interested. When she's home she helps me in the darkroom. She can't believe that her mother is the same person who took the pictures." Angela smiled. "Funny, I reach her with photographs, but when I try to be a mother, Ruthie vanishes."

"Maybe the Angela who takes the pictures is the real person. Maybe Angela, the mother, is just an acculturation of old beliefs and proprieties." Adam was enjoying himself. This woman sitting opposite him was daring to tell him. This is me . . .

"I guess I'm kind of crazy, Adam. I know normal females don't make friends with panhandlers like Jim Yates, who works the Government Center during the day and sleeps in a rat-infested cellar at night, or with the skinny bearded man I call Henry Miller. He rides a bicycle around the city delivering messages. I asked him if he worked for the Cosmodemonic Telegraph Company. And do you know something? . . . He actually had read *Tropic of Capricorn*. In fact he taught high school for ten years, then his wife died. They had no children. God knows where he lives now. He writes poetry which someday he promises to read to me. Or Fanjan, that's his name, really. He weighs over three hundred pounds. He wanders all over the city, soliciting. When he isn't begging he sits on a wooden butter barrel he carries with him and thinks. I can't get him to tell me what about. And there's old Black Hattie who waddles along in worn shoes and ankle socks. I haven't seen her since last June. Poor thing, she used to count on me for lunch on Thursdays. And there's Ansel Gates, parading up and down in front of the Old South Church with a sign asking why people don't love one another. The expression on his face makes you feel he's about to burst into tears. Ansel marched in Selma when he was younger. Now he gets by on his social security. Or there's Bill Teffler. You must have seen him. He hobbles through the city at a furious pace on two aluminum legs. He lost them in an auto crash. He was driving and his wife died. Every block or so he stops and grimaces with the pain of walking on metal. He told me that God took his legs to remind him that the television commercials he was writing were an abomination. "Oh . . ." Angela blushed, "I've got running off at the mouthitis. I'm sorry. There's hundreds of others. The city and its people. Did you ever see the Cruikshank drawings illustrating Dickens? I have a feeling that the basic styles of human beings haven't changed much—their clothes, yes . . . but not the fundamental bewilderment with life and what it's all about. Please, forgive me. You uncorked me. After nearly an hour, all I know about you is that you are president of something called Adams National, you have a son named Sam and a wife named Janice, and you must be quite sorry you ever challenged yourself with me."

He touched the ends of her fingers which were resting on the table. "On the contrary, Angel." His eyebrows were raised in wonderment at himself as well as her. "See . . . you sentimentalize me. I know . . . an angel, you're not! As for me, let's say that I'm the exception that proves the rule. I have a theory that when a man gets to the top of a company he should stop being a specialist. What's more, it is a good place to look around and consider the illusion. Maybe, a life of horizontal movement would have been more fulfilling than a vertical one." He grinned at her bewilderment. "Adams National, among a great many other things, prints the annual reports for quite a large number of top companies in the United States. If you'd like to buy stock in the company, it is listed on the American Exchange. It's probably a safe but unspectacular investment. Despite the fact that its chief factotum is something of an oddball in the business world, its earnings are reasonable and its future growth quite bright."

While he was talking, Adam kept lifting the tips of her fingers, one after the other. She could have withdrawn her hand, but the elusive touch seemed to establish some kind of needful communication. "Sounds as if you enjoy reconnaissance," she said. "Taking me to lunch is obviously a horizontal movement. Is it a way of life for you?"

He shook his head, but her innuendo delighted him. "I guess fundamentally I'm like most people. I have a few daring ideas, a few theories which have never materialized in fact. The basic organism rebels at change. The familiar rut provides security. Most of us want novelty, but nothing that really endangers our life-style. I was thinking these thoughts this morning. In effect, you have become the second confrontation I have had with myself today. I nearly flubbed both of them."

Amused, Angela listened while he told the waiter they would have no dessert . . . just coffee. He seemed to anticipate her thoughts. "You didn't keep so lithe, making a fetish of eating. Strange, as I was saying . . . initially I dismissed you out of hand. I could have spoken to you when you took my picture. I vacillated at the door of the bank. Even in Filene's, when I threw caution to the winds and leaped, I was thinking: J. Q., at forty-six years of age don't you know enough people? Why are you cornering yourself with a strange female . . . in what can only be a surface contact?" He seemed pensive. Angela wanted to squeeze his hand, but she didn't. "Fortunately, I rejected

40

the thought as inappropriate to an executive who preaches the merits of curiosity.

"If I were you," Angela said, knowing it would provoke him, "I would have satisfied my curiosity with a younger, unmarried woman. Do you love your wife?" It was a mad question to ask a stranger. But the whole luncheon had the unpredictability of an encounter group. More fascinating, Angela suspected, because there were no voyeurs. Just two strangers who could say anything to each other because they were reasonably secure they would never meet again.

"I like Janice." He grinned. "From my viewpoint I would never hurt her. Of course, my viewpoint might not be hers. Do you love your husband?"

Angela smiled. She had asked for it. "Seventy-five percent of the time."

"That leaves room for a lover."

"I don't have one."

"Do you want one?" His look said, say yes.

There was nothing to do except to cool him gently. "I'm too old. I've been too faithful. I wouldn't know what to do with a stranger." She laughed. "This is quite crazy. Why would you or any man pick a forty-three-year-old mother, with three children, for an affair?"

He shrugged. "Because it would be comfortable. Furthermore, I have a theory which I've never had an opportunity to test: the initial contact between a male and female who are strangers should be naked, in bed together, *before* they get acquainted or really know each other. Then they could discover each other mentally and physically as a combined laughing act of slow duration."

Angela felt shaky. She couldn't remember ever responding so completely to any male. He was so seriously insane. "Adam," she said softly. "You picked the right name for yourself. You are either quite mad or as simple as Adam. Any Eve could hand you the apple."

"You'll have to admit one thing. Adam and Eve slept together naked for quite a few years before Cain or Abel. Adam had fortitude." Even as he persisted, he wondered at the folly of it. Jan never refused him in bed. But it was impossible not to capitalize on Angela's obvious interest in being pursued. No. That wasn't true. This female's reaction was more like Sleeping Beauty. He alone had awakened her, and naturally she was his. No. Damn it all! Closer to the truth was this strange magnetic pull.

Whoever she really might be, she was his flower-girl of long ago! once again putting sweet peas in his hair, hugging him and telling him that he was beautiful.

"Don't abandon the idea," he said, knowing it was quite hopeless. "Consider it. Tonight. Tomorrow. When you are securely ensconced in Acton. You might look upon it as a historic experiment. A new phase in human relationships. Two middle-aged lovers sneaking into a hotel room."

"Please," she begged. "You make me feel very peculiar. Almost guilty. Like I've already said yes. You said I was a second confrontation. Tell me about the first."

☆ 11 ☆

They both knew the dining room was thinning out, but for the moment the table was their world. She listened while he told her about Sam and Keane. Keane, his younger boy, twenty-two, was in New York playing with the Philharmonic . . . violin. He was equally competent on the piano. Conducting smaller orchestras and composing modern operas and music which as yet intrigued no performers. Keane was a musical revolutionist in a world whose ears still ached with rock and country-western. Sam, his older boy, had come to work in Adams National based on the condition that he be placed in charge of research and development. Adam smiled. "Sam is twenty-six. He spent most of his time in college and graduate school making films. Adams National isn't General Motors. We have no R & D. I should have said 'had.' Now, we have! Sam is testing me. He wants to diversify the company into videotape recording. We would manufacture video cassettes, the software, based on exciting original material produced by and for people who are fed up with commercial and even educational television. Sam visualizes it as a new kind of underground which could function as a critical medium independent of government and business. A departure from commercial television, which at present makes few value judgments."

"Sounds fascinating," Angela said. "Maybe I could switch from still photography to video. Then your company could hire me." It was a silly thing to say. She had no intention of working for anyone. Fortunately he ignored it. "I don't see how you are being tested. Everything you read says videotape will change the world."

"That's the point. Our board of directors agreed to set up a division, Adams Video, but the direction we'd take would be in the area of video cassettes in a magazine format. A weekly moving picture magazine. We agreed that the day of the *Life* type magazine is past. *Look* has already succumbed. In the not too distant future people will subscribe to monthly or weekly tapes, living magazines, which they will play through their television. . . . The tapes will carry national advertising, just like a magazine . . . and that's the rub. Adams National is a public corporation. If we develop a video magazine, it will be center-of-the-road. You see, Sam's calling my bluff. He's already produced a videotape questioning the validity of the approaches of organizations like the Freedom Studies Center, in Boston, Virginia, which by its own words is in business "to expose the communist and revolutionary challenges to American Freedom." Sam wants to be more honest . . . to tell another version of reality. In his words, 'the truth.' "

"What is the truth?" Angela was following him with an interest and fascination she had forgotten existed in her.

"That communism and the threat of it is simply a current whipping boy. The Nazis used the Jews. Did you ever read Erich Fromm's *On Narcissism*? Sam wants to do a videotape on the difference between benign narcissism and virulent narcissism, which affects most of our twentieth-century leaders. The tape Sam and a few of his friends have already made is dynamite, suggesting that the United States is involved in a kind of undirected fascism which requires communism as a whipping boy." Adam laughed at the intensity of Angela's concentration. "Really, I'm not trying to convert you."

"You are, but not to what you think." Listening to him Angela was happily astonished that strangers could so quickly pass beyond the usual amenities. In her environment intimacy was hard to come by. Even close friends played mental poker with each other to avoid revealing the essentially lonely people they were behind their brave facades. She asked him, why, since he was president of Adams National, he couldn't, for a while at least, pursue both the moderate approach of the company officials and at the same time give Sam rein in his direction. His eyes sparkled agreement. Sam might object to half a loaf but it was better than nothing. Angela was about to tell him about Ruthie. In a sense, Ruth's refusal to conform to the accepted patterns of courtship and marriage paralleled his own concern over Sam. But, even as she had the thought, her eye caught the huge clock atop the Custom House Tower. It was quarter to four. A three-hour luncheon, and the hours had vanished in minutes.

"I really have to go, Adam." Her voice was a whisper, a denial. She didn't want to leave. Her expression was proof enough that the entire night ahead would be insufficient. "My car is in the Prudential garage. By the time I cab back there it will be four-thirty, and I'll be plunk in the middle of the evening commuters. Oh, dear, I wish I knew how to thank you for such a lovely afternoon."

"Your glistening eyes are thanks enough." Adam led her to the elevator. "The time did go fast, didn't it? Will I see you next Thursday?"

They were standing on the sidewalk in front of the building. The first empty taxi would ring the curtain on the last act, not of a drama . . . a vignette, a happening, shading off into nothing. They both sensed it, and Angela gave it voice. "It would be either pointless or too tempting." He held her hand, and looked at her like a lost child, missing his flower-girl.

"I like you, J. Q. Adams," she said softly. "Thanks."

The taxi driver he had waved toward the curb was honking impatiently. She kissed Adam's cheek fleetingly and got in the back seat.

"Send me the pictures, at least," he said.

It was silly. A married woman with three children and tears in her eyes for a passing stranger. She didn't look back. Maybe the thought she hadn't evoked summed it up. They lived in a world of rebellion, but when you got to be forty your brain froze. It was too late to challenge the unknown. It was easier to settle for the familiar and secure. If she had accepted his mad proposal, if she met him next Thursday or the Thursday after, if their liking grew to love, if . . . and what if the ifs should turn to hows, and whys, and lonely whens? No. No. Lord, *no!*

☆ 12 ☆

The morning after she had married Jonathan Adams, in the chapel at Wellesley College, Janice had awakened him with a good-morning kiss. Lying on top of him, as he sleepily opened his eyes and found his way back inside her, she had told him solemnly, "I know our life can't be all honeymoon, Jonathan, but promise me something ... no matter what ... even if we are peeved at each other you will always kiss me good-night, and I'll always kiss you good-morning."

Over the years, except when Jon had been away on business, though often the two kisses were a ritual—a kind of reassurance performed without too much thought or a come-hell-or-high-water feeling that "we're in this together," at other times the forced continuity of the kisses, given when one or the other was angry, or sulky, or dispassionate, had the effect of enemies forced to shake hands. Like children cajoled out of their occasional sullen withdrawals, the kisses tumbled them into unexpected laughter at their failures to live up to each other's expectations.

This morning, Janice not only kissed Jon lightly awake but she signaled to him with a playful caress of his penis. He grinned at her, receiving the message. "It's seven o'clock. There isn't time. You should either stop entertaining every evening, or knock on my door at six."

"And have you a grouchy bear? No thanks. Anyway, why should I always initiate proceedings?" She swung out of bed. Jonathan watched the nightgown flip over head. At forty-four Janice was in good physical shape. Her breasts were small and had stayed firm. Her behind was taut and her stomach only had a slight curve. There was a reason. Janice worked at it. She swam, played tennis a little, played golf a lot, and watched her calories with a fortitude and determination that Jonathan attributed to her Puritan lineage. Janice Bradford could trace her heritage back to the original Pilgrim colony. Once she told him that it was written in the stars that she should marry Jonathan Quincy Adams. Maybe. But whoever had been doing the stellar writing hadn't followed her scenario. Ten years ago, when he had been president of the Boston Chamber of Commerce and could have easily used the position as a springboard into politics—first as a State Senator, with his sights on Lieutenant-Governor and ultimately Governor—he had been operating within the expected groove. While Janice had never quite evoked it, he suspected that once she had fantasized herself in the role of First Lady of Massachusetts. Governor Adams' wife. Jon and Jan Adams, that wonderful couple on Beacon Hill who might not only have set the social style and flair for Boston Society, but ultimately might have become the party's great white hope for Washington. The party, of course, would have to be Republican. And that was the rub. Politically, Jonathan Quincy Adams described himself as a Platonist. The problem was that the day that "philosophers would be kings," and society really planned for the greatest good for the greatest number, seemed to be disappearing into the anarchic seas of mass democracy. Jonathan wasn't even sure he could explain this pedantic thought to Janice, and if he did, whether she would understand it. All of which made it obvious that he was born too early for a life of politics. But he was convinced that destiny, if not personal time, was on his side.

At her Spartan breakfast offering of an orange (no juice), dry toast, a little jam, and black coffee, Janice reminded him that it was Thursday. "See you at the club about sixish. Don't forget we promised the Lovells we'd have dinner with them. It'll be an early evening."

He understood her meaning. Tonight . . . *if he made the overtures* . . . they would make love. Jonathan smiled. Janice was a planner. She enjoyed the anticipation as much as the consummation. He had never been able to convince her that sex and marriage could function better off the cuff . . . spontaneously. Alas, most Americans were too busy emulating their machines. Their data-processing equipment ground to a halt and all the lights flashed frantically when the preplanned software received strange input. *"Che serà, serà"* might have been a popular song hit, but it was an anathema to most marriage programs.

As for dinner with the Lovells, that was predictable. He knew that Janice and Barbara Lovell would play golf in the morning, go to the hairdresser in the afternoon in the hope that he and Jack would appreciate their femininity that evening, when they would all spend several hours

46

together prying and probing into the shells of lobsters in search for dinner. For the most part he enjoyed the Lovells. They were in relatively the same income bracket. Their children (the Lovells had three) were all past their teens. As President of the Graniteville National Bank, Jack had been helpful in financing the construction of the hundred-thousand-square-foot Boston plant of Adams National. Of course, as he had pointed out to Janice, Jack kept in trim by playing golf but his mind was potbellied. Usually, without too much forethought, Jonathan would introduce some subject into an evening with the Lovells that would thoroughly incense Jack, who firmly believed that Jon played the role of devil's advocate not because he believed his theories but rather to test the mettle of his opponent. Tonight, because unaccountably he had been thinking about it for several weeks, Jonathan thought he might sound Jack out on the subject of suburban zoning laws as an insidious form of social control beyond the reach of any sound city planning. That should be a nice red flag to wave in front of a Republican bull.

He was dimly aware that Janice had mentioned something about taking the afternoon off. It brought him back to the last swallow of his second cup of coffee. He suddenly realized that while he had been thinking about Jack, and dinner with the Lovells, on one surface of his mind, on another he had been thinking about Janice, naked, and Angela Thomas, naked (obviously suppositional since he hadn't seen Angela naked) and wondering *if* he had made love to Janice, could he have also made love to Angela . . . in the same day? Well, why not? A really mad idea, because the truth was he had no idea whether he would ever see that damned Italian woman again. He grinned feebly at Janice. "Sorry, I guess I was already in my office thinking business." He kissed her head. "Do you think I look like Adam?"

Janice scowled at him. "I asked if you could come home early and play golf with us." She wasn't going to give him any reaffirmation until he answered her. He didn't enjoy lying, but there was no choice. If Angela telephoned, he wanted to be in his office. "Really, Jan, I've got a heavy workload this week. Oakes has called in the regional salesmen and I should lend him support. Jack Lovell should understand . . . I'm not in banking. The printing business is vastly competitive. I don't need the challenge of extracurricular competition, I have enough of that all day."

Jan patted his cheek and gave him a quick kiss. "Adams . . . not Adam. Your inheritance gives you away." She didn't notice the quick look of surprise on his face when she said, "On the other hand, I suppose there are a lot of Eves who would find you tempting."

☆ 13 ☆

Slouched behind the wheel of his Porsche, which he excused himself owning because it was already five years old (and he not only got good mileage, but if necessary could tinker with it himself), Adam wove in and out of the traffic on the Expressway toward Boston. He smiled at his reflection in the rear-view mirror. Jon, Jonathan, J. Q., Mr. Adams, Adam. He burst into happy laughter. Of course, he was all five people and possibly some others as yet unnamed. The real problem, as he had more than once tried to explain to Jan and the Lovells, is that most people have been conditioned by society to believe that growing up, maturity, becomes the unreasonable process of integrating into one consistent self the many selves you had enjoyed as a child. And then, before you had lived through your teens, daydreaming, fairy tales, fantasies . . . even releasing the deep-down laughter and tears that made you you . . . became verboten.

Today he was Adam. It wasn't exactly a new self. He couldn't give Angela Thomas full credit for that. But it was a mutation he rarely attempted in Cohasset. In fact, the last time he had let go, other than his joyous venture of growing marihuana among the flowers in the back of the house, facing the ocean (a deed which had given him new esteem in the eyes of Sam and Keane, if not Janice), had been last July Fourth. A particularly warm day. The Cramptons had invited him and Janice and the Lovells to spend the day on their fifty-foot houseboat. Janice was charmed with the Cramptons' boat, so much more comfortable than their own thirty-foot Cal 30 sailing sloop, on which Jon had finally reluctantly installed an auxiliary engine, though he preferred not to use it.

Though Janice had occasional moods when she would sail alone with him, now that Keane had gone to New York, and Sam came to Cohasset only occasionally with his new wife (Jewish, of all things), still, for Jan, sailing with Jonathan alone seemed like an antisocial act. Really, she asked him, weren't they getting a bit aged to continue the rugged life of old salts? All their friends had long ago graduated to power boats. Giving up and becoming Jonathan was probably inevitable. Adam shrugged at his melancholy thoughts. In four years he would be fifty. The motorboat age extended its hoary hand of welcome.

The marina crowd followed one or two patterns. The more daring boat owners, who devoted their full spare time in the winter to studying navigation and planning summer cruises to Martha's Vineyard, Nantucket, and Long Island, and in summer took weeks off from their work exploring the coast of Maine or Massachusetts, insisting they enjoyed the minor hardships and inconveniences of boat living (roughing it at marinas that catered to their every need, from electricity to modern hotel living), or the less adventurous, like the Cramptons, who spent most of their summer tied up at a marina and used their boats as floating summer cottages—rendezvous that might revive or romanticize tired marriages, or at the least provide a summer environmental change and give the illusion of informality that couldn't be achieved in the winter dwellings of upper-middle-class New Englanders.

Adam turned the Porsche off the Southeast Expressway toward Columbia Point. Though the day was warm, tiny currents of cool air advertised that it was October. Last July he and Jan hadn't really known the Cramptons that well. Bud Crampton was in the construction business and owned several apartment houses. Even before they had cast off the dock, Adam knew that unless he drugged himself with a few drinks, the idle afternoon, anchored somewhere off Cohasset, would bore hell out of him. Janice had a much greater ease and tolerance in parrying vapid conversation. Jack Lovell moaning with Bud about world conditions and the perils of inflation scarcely provided a good fire to throw fuel on, but after several hours, Adam, desperate, couldn't resist trying.

But Bessie Crampton, who had told them to bring their bathing suits, purposely "broke up" their boring discussion about money. She suggested they all should change in one of the cabins and then go swimming off the boat in clear,

49

unpolluted water. Of course, there might be a shark or two around, and the water out here was a little chilly, but that added challenge. Knowing it would cause some consternation, Adams offered a more intriguing challenge. It would be joyous and more friendly if they all swam naked. He tried to convince Bessie, since she was the hostess, that she should lead the way. Chuckling and probably silently agreeing with the idea, Jack Lovell announced that Jon was at it again. But despite Janice trying to frown him into silence, Adam had persisted.

"You go first, Jon." Bessie grinned at him, obviously intrigued by the idea, but afraid of Bud's reaction. "Any of the rest of you who want to be bare-assed, it's okay with me. But I'm too old and flabby."

"You look in pretty good shape to me." Adam ignored Janice's frown piercing him to silence. "Has anyone ever seen you naked, Bessie, except Bud?"

Bud, a *chevalier sans raproche,* protected his wife. "What's all this bit about being naked?" he demanded.

Adam had tried to explain. It wasn't really a question of whether being naked was good or bad. It was the possibility of experiencing a friend, or an acquaintance, in another dimension. He tried to explain that to Bessie. Neither Janice nor Barbara, for example, were total physical creatures, even to each other. Perhaps a totality of human exposure, on occasion, could act as a substitute for alcohol. How could you be remote from another naked human being?

"I'd be damned remote and embarrassed." Bessie looked at him provocatively. "But I'm not inhibited, Jonathan Adams!" She slid down the zipper in the front of her flowered bathing suit. "Come on, Mr. Adams. One, two, three. We strip together."

"For God's sakes, Bessie. Act your age!" Bud Crampton exploded.

Bessie shrugged at her husband. "Haven't you heard of Women's Liberation? I believe in it. I even signed a petition to do away with men's and ladies' rooms. Think of the money you could save in building construction." Although Bessie obviously enjoyed aggravating her husband, she refastened her zipper.

Adam gave the muddy waters another stir. "What I'm really asking, Bessie, is not to see you naked, but to convey to you that it might be a joyous form of escapism to snuggle in your tits."

50

Although Janice only raised her eyebrows . . . as if to say, that's Jon . . . and Barbara shrugged, Bessie blushed charmingly. "What's the matter with Janice's tits?" she demanded.

"Poor Jon." Janice patted his shoulder. "With my cupcakes I've deprived him of a certain voluptuousness. He was raised on *Playboy* girls, and lately seems to be developing a Don Juan syndrome."

Adam persisted. "Please understand, I'm speaking figuratively as well as literally. Think of how much time we all spend dancing around the periphery of other people's lives. With encounter groups and sensitivity training, some people are trying to break through, but you will note that this is always a group effort. I have a theory that the only real encounter, at least for this period in man's history, is dyadic. One male to one female, or vice versa. The problem, even in that relationship, is that our basic narcissism gets in the way. We are, each and every one of us, scared to death to let go of our little ego identities. So we either conceal the real person we are, or we wrap an ogre around ourselves and end up making unreasonable demands on someone else. In any event, most of our lives we don't dare to be defenseless. Bessie doesn't have to answer, but probably if we weren't all living in such a tightly structured, monogamous situation, she would be delighted to have some appreciative stranger snuggle on her breasts."

As he turned his car into the parking lot next to Adams National, into the space reserved for J. Q. Adams, Adam was grinning. Without particularly intending to, he had launched them into a discussion of wife-swapping. Jack Lovell admitted that for years he had had a yen for Janice, but suburban affairs were too complicated. Barbara immediately gave Jack her okay to sleep with Janice, but only if she got Jon in exchange. Bud Crampton was convinced that secrecy and not open knowledge was the only practical way to have an extracurricular love life. Bessie said it would be fun but Bud was too jealous. If she had a "fun affair" and Bud found out, he'd divorce her . . . and really, how could anyone become involved with . . . committed to two people? Surprisingly, Janice disagreed with her. "At my age, it's too late, of course. We live in a society where even the children believe that only youngsters can make physical love . . . that sex past forty is a maudlin idea." She had grinned at Jon. "I love Jon

51

and our two boys, so why couldn't I love another man? If one additional male needed some love, I'm sure I could offer it to him. The advantage of being past forty and already loved by one man is that I wouldn't overwhelm a second one."

At the very least, for a moment on that hot Saturday, six people had started to wonder. Maybe that was the first step. To dare to be a wonderer.

☆ 14 ☆

The double-glass front doors of Adams National Corporation opened on a reception office furnished with the usual aluminum, vinyl-covered furniture. An indication that a wry spirit was at work somewhere on the premises was *Ramparts, The Village Voice,* and several New Left newspapers dropped on the reception room tables among the copies of *Fortune* and *Business Week* and the usual printing trade magazines available for visiting salesmen, who might be waiting to see an Adams National executive.

Harry Carswell, Vice-President and Comptroller, had complained to J. Q. "Your son Sam hopes to set some visiting Republican afire. It seems to me more like biting the hand that feeds him. Really, J. Q., that far-out stuff doesn't contribute to our company's image." Harry might have said the same thing about Sam himself, but as yet he hadn't gathered courage.

With a clipped black beard and rather shaggy hair, Sam looked as if he belonged in the office of an advertising agency or a television network. Sam had forestalled his father's comments by simply pointing to the murals that J. Q. had commissioned for the reception area. One section depicted the Pilgrims landing on Plymouth Rock. "One of them looks just like you, J. Q." Laughing, Sam had pointed to one of the foreground figures, and there was a startling facial resemblance. But to Sam's delight, all of the men in the landing boat and on the shore were heavily bearded and wore their hair Prince Valiant style. "What's more, J. Q., by their standards I would be considered ultra-conservative. At least I'm staying in my middle-class environment and fighting. These guys were the first drop-outs."

Even before the front door swung closed behind him, the transmogrification was usually complete: Jon . . . Adam . . . became J. Q. The Adam slouch, slowly straightening as his feet touched the front steps, gave way to the crispness of a general inspecting his battalions. Strangely, this morning the change wasn't so instantaneous. Adam lingered on. The alphawaves in his brain refused to give way to the beta. He nodded at the girl behind the reception desk. A new girl . . . Italian . . . marvelous breasts. Maybe Janice was right—lately he seemed to have a breast fetish.

"Good morning, Mr. Adams."

Angela Thomas was Italian, too. But Miss Canetti's eyes were just brown eyes. Angela had amber saucers that beckoned you to come behind the looking glass. " 'Twas brillig, and the slithy toves did gyre and gimble in the wabe."

"Good morning, Miss Canetti."

Obviously an afterthought. What was Angela's maiden name? Today he would ask her. If she telephoned . . . why did he persist in thinking she would telephone? She had made it quite obvious that she wouldn't. How well do I want to know this stranger, he wondered. If she telephones, what then? Wouldn't she actually be saying, "I've thought about it, Adam, and I'm willing to go to bed with you"? Hadn't he encouraged her? Asked for that kind of response? If he had (he knew that he had), then why? Why? Damn it! It was simple enough. He met a woman who appealed to him, who had attracted him in some indefinable way. Would it be such an earthshaking event if they made love? For Angela, at least, he guessed it would.

He took off his suit jacket, removed his initialed gold cufflinks (a birthday present from Janice), and folded his French cuffs to just below the elbow. J. Q. always worked in his shirtsleeves. He had no private secretary. Vice-Presidents and various upper-echelon officials of Adams National were permitted their "girl Fridays," and at certain levels J. Q. agreed they were necessary, but for himself they blocked communications. He believed that presidents of middle-sized companies should be easily accessible. Eager subordinates often provided so much insulation that the chief officer didn't know what was going on. He smiled at his thoughts. He should have told Angela that she could telephone him without being forced to identify herself, either to a switchboard operator or a secretary. Callers often were surprised to be passed directly through to him, and be greeted by his brusque. "J. Q. Adams speaking . . ."

J. Q. permitted callers to pump themselves dry before he would respond at any length. It was unnerving, and he knew it. Salesmen who congratulated themselves that they had reached the president of the company often wondered, as they spouted their stories, if the phone had become disconnected.

He noted the time on the ship's clock that hung on one of the mahogany-paneled walls of his office. Nine-twenty-five. If Angela left Acton at nine, she probably wouldn't be able to telephone before ten. If she hadn't called by noon, she obviously had decided against it. Waiting for a telephone call that might not come changed his morning schedule. He opened the connecting door into Sam's office and noted that Sam hadn't yet arrived . . . or if he had, Sam was already in the videotape department.

In June, after the board of directors had given their okay, a five-thousand-square-foot space in the storage area had been cleared out. Within a few months Sam not only had exceeded the first year's budget, but was demanding a doubling of the area for the ultimate production of videotapes. The whole business could be a wild gamble. J.Q. didn't deny that videotapes could ultimately change the whole environment of television, but he was still dubious of Sam's approach. Too idealistic. It was discouraging to admit it, but that New York publisher who was presumably developing an extended library of video home pornography would clean up. While the crusaders might eventually close down the public viewing of blatantly sexual movies, it would be a long time before anyone would challenge the Supreme Court decision that, in the privacy of his own home, a person had the right to look at or read anything he chose. Videotape sex movies—delivered by the post office and viewed on home television sets—were inevitable. Instead of contributing to the improvement of television fare, videotapes might accelerate the decline.

J. Q. suspected that Sam had his own ideas in this area. A few days before, Sam had left a copy of a new edition of the *Kama Sutra* on his desk with the notation that he should examine the·photographs by William Graham.

Adam was impressed. There was no denying that the act of love could be photographed beautifully. In about fifty soft-focus photographs, Graham had captured every aspect of copulation and oral-genital lovemaking, creating a visual hymn to the innate loveliness and mystery of man and woman defenselessly engrossed with each other. He wondered what Angela would think of these photographs. Did Angela have this kind of photographic talent for expressing the human condition? If she did, Sam would be interested. No. That was impossible. Sam must never know about Angela.

J. Q. fidgeted at his desk. He couldn't leave his office and be paged for Angela's call. Ordinarily, at this time of morning he would have toured the plant, inspecting the activity in various departments. Stopping in the composing, press, binding, shipping departments, he would review the workload with Peter Dasman, his Vice-President in Charge of Production. His tour today would have to wait until afternoon ... or perhaps he wouldn't make the rounds at all today. Would anyone miss him? He knew the answer was no. His child, Adams National, created from scratch by him a little more than twenty years ago, no longer needed him. Except in emergencies, the ship ran very well with the first mate and crew. The captain could take up knitting.

The estimates on the Johnson Corporation annual reports were on his desk for a routine final okay. A four-color job, forty-eight pages and cover, with an eighty thousand press run. It was a bore, really. Every year Adams National submitted bids competitively. They wined and dined the Johnson buyers, and Oakes fretted that they would be high bidder this year ... but every year they got the contract. Many of their customers didn't bother with competitive quotes. It was a hell of a lot simpler to do business with companies who trusted you. His designers had gone all out. The cover of the report this year was both embossed and gold-leafed. Conspicuous consumption, really, to give the stockholder an image of prestige and wealth. Just so long as they got their dividends, most stockholders never waded through the pages of self-congratulation that made up most annual reports. The estimate totaled $42,500. J. Q. scribbled a memo: "Last year we waited three months for final payment. Build an additional two percent into the final price to cover the delayed payment." Chuckling, he attached it to the estimate and tossed the report into his out basket. Someone had to cover Sam Adams' research and development.

Staring at his clock again he suddenly realized that only ten minutes had gone by since he had last looked. Ten-fifteen. Angela, enraptured with his words, sitting opposite him at lunch, kept summoning back Adam. It was quite insane, really. No one would be more certain of it than Janice. She might be able to understand the involuntary attraction of a middle-aged man for a younger woman, but Angela Thomas was forty-three, only a year younger than Janice. Perhaps it wasn't wholly Angela. Maybe he had been reading too much of the sensitivity stuff that Sam left around the house when he visited them, or perhaps pictures like Graham's in the illustrated *Kama Sutra* were throwing him off balance. Or maybe he was just getting old ... the compartments of his life didn't open and close so easily anymore. He carried bits and pieces of his Adam self into the J. Q. environment where they didn't belong. Of course, the idea of Angela ... what was the idea, anyway? Discovery, of course. The joy of daring to be involved with another human being. Immature? No one could be more certain of it than Janice. Wasn't it really an admission that Adams National, Janice, Cohasset, the tiny record of his life needed to be occasion-ally taken off the same turntable. There were other lives being lived, other records being played. Temporarily, An-gela was the unknown ... hence piquant and adventurous. Why couldn't he face it simply? A woman had taken his picture. He'd been aware of her and she of him. No matter what her thoughts had been, her eyes had flashed the message. I need to know you. If you give a need security, it could become love. At forty-six, why shouldn't he discover if he still dared to love another woman? I love you, Janice. I love you, Angela. Today for a change ... zing ... this minute, he had come to life! He was unafraid to evoke his motives consciously. Quite simply, after many years of marriage, he wanted to know what it might be like to penetrate another woman mentally as well as physically.

☆ 15 ☆

At ten-forty-five he gave up. The deadline had passed. If Angela was coming to Boston this Thursday, she had convinced herself not to explore the byways that J.Q. Adams had offered her. He was thinking it was probably just as well, when Sam strode into his office and wished him a hearty good morning. It flashed across his mind that if his telephone rang right now, and it was Angela, how in hell would he talk to her with Sam listening? He felt unreasonably antagonistic. Sam plopped into one of his leather chairs. He was puffing on a corncob pipe. J.Q.'s expression asked the question without saying the words.

"No, Father." Sam grinned. "I am not smoking grass. I would no more come to Adams National stoned than I would come here half-crocked on juice." He blew a cloud of smoke into the air. "It's aromatic tobacco. All the girls love it. All the advertisements tell them a pipe-smoking male is virile. On the other hand, when I occasionally smoke pot, I do it in the evening, or on weekends. Since you've now grown your own supply, you and Jan should give it a whirl. It could give your sex life a new dimension."

J.Q. pointed at the *Kama Sutra*. "This edition, with the Graham photographs, is sufficient to do that without marihuana."

Sam laughed. "See, I told you there is more to fucking than stag movies. Your generation still wants to see the penis plunging into the vagina." Sam dropped a couple of paperback volumes on his desk. J.Q. noted the title, *Sex in Marriage* by Wendall Koble. He flipped the pages.

A very beautiful Scandinavian girl, staring cooly at the beholder, and an equally handsome blond male were demonstrating, with detailed genital display, every conceivable act of lovemaking. Paralleling the perfection of their bodies, their faces were unemotional masks. It was incredible that such intimacy could be photographed with such a lack of joy. J.Q. was aware that Sam was pointing up the difference between these photographs and the sensuous, warm eroticism of the Graham photographs.

Sam grinned at him. "This marriage manual may be a step in the right direction, but it's too clinical. Obviously it will soon be available on videotapes and film for home viewing, but even in motion, and with grunts and groans, it will be boring. On the other hand, I believe ultimately people will be using video cassettes as a kind of mirror. As the video camera becomes readily available for home use, every male and female will be able to assuage their basic voyeurism, quite simply, by taking their own home video movies of themselves making love. Notice I didn't say 'fucking.' I believe that Adams Video should develop a series of cassettes that in a sense will be instruction cassettes to teach, not only video camera placement so that a couple, or two couples could photograph themselves, but we could go way beyond the clinical aspects and teach them how to produce entirely new sequential relationships via the camera, and in a thousand ways discover their surface selves as well as each other in a new kind of depth."

J.Q. knew his astonishment was showing. "If I look bewildered, please realize it's not wholly for myself. I grasp what you're saying. I'm just dubious that I have the nerve to try and sell some of your wild ideas to our rather staid board of directors."

"Don't worry, Jake. A picture is worth ten thousand words. When the tapes are ready, we'll project them at the next board meeting. That'll do it!" Sam waved the pipe smoke away from his head.

Sam obviously wasn't in any hurry to leave. With half his mind on the telephone, wondering how he would talk with Angela with Sam listening, J.Q. flipped the pages of the Johnson estimates. He hoped that Sam would take the hint. He was busy. Now was not the time for extended discussion. But Sam evidently felt conversational. "I wonder what Jan would think of these photographs."

"Your mother wouldn't like them." J.Q. grimaced. "What about Yael?" He could guess the answer. Sam's wife, like most of the females of her generation, were unafraid of their own sexuality.

"Oh, Yael is way beyond this. We've made videotapes of ourselves making love. We'll show them to you and Jan one of these days when Yael is satisfied with the editing."

"Show them to me! I don't feel like trying to convince your mother that her daughter-in-law isn't completely immoral."

"Yael's amoral." Sam smiled. "Most women are. It comes from a lack of the kind of possessiveness that has trapped the male. Maybe amorality is the female's perfect retaliation in a male-dominated world." Sam was silent for a moment, and then evidently decided to verbalize his thoughts. "There's something I always wanted to ask you, J.Q. Have you ever been to bed with another woman besides Mother?"

J.Q. scowled at him, but deep inside Adam was grinning. "That's a hell of a question for a son to ask his father. I've known my share of females."

"Premaritally or postmaritally?"

"For God's sake," J.Q. exploded. "Let me tell you something. Despite all the talk about female freedom and the sexual revolution, the large majority of human beings have been unable to devise a successful social method of sexual freedom within monogamy."

"I'm aware of that." Sprawled in the leather chair, Sam looked as if he were ready for an extended bull session. "That's why Yael and I didn't make a big deal out of getting married. We have agreed that we're in the exploratory phase, no children until we determine if we have the stamina and a mode of operation for the long haul." Sam stared at him. "Would you go to bed with Miss Canetti if you could get away with it?"

"She's just a child."

"Come on. Have you looked at her lately?"

Despite himself, J.Q. laughed. "The act of intercourse with a stranger doesn't scare me. What has kept me on the straight and narrow is the fear of afterwards. Even for you, Miss Canetti might prove difficult. She doesn't seem to have your range of intellectual interests. What would you talk about afterwards?"

"Marriage." Sam eased out of his chair, greeting Billy Whiskers, the eighty-year-old Adams National interdepartmental messenger, who hobbled into the office. Smiling apologetically at them, he dropped a few pieces of mail into J.Q.'s basket. As he shuffled out of the office, he listened for juicy bits and pieces of Sam's conversation that he could spread around the plant. "Miss Canetti told me she enjoys screwing, but she's honest." Sam smiled at Billy Whiskers' retreating back. "She can't afford to indulge herself. She wants a fighting chance. No married men. What about Barbara Lovell?"

"What about her?"

"For adventure. Not for me. For you! I don't have even a muted Oedipus complex."

J.Q. shrugged. "Let's knock off this conversation. I'm busy." He picked up the large envelope that Billy had dropped in his basket. There was no postage on it. It was addressed in a flowing hand. *Jonathan Q. President, Adams National Corporation, Personal.* In the upper corner, startled, he read the return address. *Thomas, Valley Stream Road, Acton, Massachusetts.* "Sam," he said abruptly. "I've got work to do. Your mother wants to know why you and Yael can't come out to dinner once a month. Give her a ring and tell her why. Now!"

Sam saluted. "Okay, chief. See you later."

Even as he flipped open the envelope, J.P. guessed the contents.

Four eight-by-ten photographs in Ektachrome of himself and one of the female Hare Krishna dancers. Even in quick examination the prints had an ingenuous sparkle. An Angela Thomas trademark. It was obvious they had been hand-delivered. Was Angela waiting right now? He sauntered through the outer offices, deliberately holding his pace to a walk, hoping his bubbly feeling was not apparent. It was eleven-forty. But even before he opened the glass doors into the reception area he could see that the lounge and the chairs were empty. He probed Miss Canetti, trying to appear cool and casual. Had a woman come here within the past hour and left an envelope for him?

"I asked her if she would wait, Mr. Adams. I told her you were in your office." Miss Canetti smiled innocently at him. She obviously had drawn her own conclusions. Angela was obviously something more than a female saleswoman. "She seemed a little nervous, Mr. Adams. She said she just wanted to leave an envelope for you. Billy picked it up a few minutes ago. She said she couldn't wait. That was about an hour ago. I'm sorry that it wasn't delivered to you sooner. Mr. Oakes told me that the only time I should leave this desk is during breaks or emergencies."

Back in his office J.Q. dialed Saul Meers, his sales Vice-President. "I'm tied up, Saul. You'll have to carry on the luncheon meeting without me. You can fill me in tomorrow."

Outside the plant he deliberated whether to take his car. Taxis were hard to find in this part of Boston, but if he drove downtown, he'd spend more time trying to find an empty parking lot than it would take to get there. Luck was with him. He saw an empty taxi heading away from the city, toward the Army base. For a couple of dollars' bribe the driver turned the cab around. "You can drop me at the corner of Winter and Tremont Streets."

Adam knew that he had reverted to a schoolboy . . . so enamored with his first date that he couldn't think sanely. The probability that he would find Angela in the Boston crowds was extremely small. Still, Thursday was Angela's day. She would have no reason to go home until late afternoon. Why did he have this mad compulsion to see her again? He grinned. "See" was a euphemism! He wasn't being honest with himself. Unaccountably, he wanted to hold Angela in his arms .. not just to make love to her but to discover if she would respond to his certain feeling that they would know how to float . . . to bask together in the lovely aura of a temporary new entity that would be neither of them separately. What quality did she have that gave him a sudden awareness of himself as a male, vis-à-vis a female? With her he felt a unique merger of personalities. Something that had occurred only once or twice in his life. With it was the overwhelming need to be both himself and the other person.

"To be" expressed it consummately. With Angela he wondered if it might not be possible to be wholly himself. Was the need to be defenseless simply an illusion, a striving for nonexistence in life? It was more likely that Angela's "reality" was in his brain. Was she simply an illusion that began long ago when a flower-girl had hugged him to her breast and whispered: "Jonathan, you're beautiful."

The taxi driver patiently repeated his message. "We're here, Mister . . . corner of Tremont and Winter." Adam shook himself out of his reverie, paid the man, and crossed Tremont Street to the Common. Like Japanese dolls who were wound up religiously by their owner every morning, the Hare Krishna dancers were still jigging and singing their never-ending promise of a world without end. One of the girls recognized him. She smiled in his direction. But among all those faces, Angela's face was missing. She wasn't there. He was suddenly aware of his insanity. An old fool. Why would she come back here? He smiled ruefully. He was either a romantic, or growing senile, to believe that she would understand.

61

☆ 16 ☆

Aware that the organist in the Park Street Church was playing "Somewhere Over the Rainbow" on the amplified church carillon, Adam wandered up Tremont Street toward the Government Center. The music temporarily blended the crowds of lunchtime people into a harmonious whole.

Was the sense of expectancy in the air simply of his own making? If he were Angela, what would he have done? Two things were obvious. She had developed the pictures and thought about him sufficiently to have attempted to deliver them. She could have telephoned, but that wouldn't have been her style. He sensed she would feel that words, without the physical presence of the speaker, were a frightening form of communication. She would have been afraid of the possibly cool, second-thought reaction of the male. The surface J.Q., who might have indulged himself in a madcap luncheon with a stranger, but later would regret the time he had wasted on a housewife running from her suburban boredom. And now she was on the telephone trying to proposition him. Yes, Angela would think that way. But if she were like him, she still might need to know why this stranger exerted such a compulsion on her. Was it more than a basic human need to plumb the unknown?

She must have taken a taxi to South Boston and found his office. Then, when she arrived and opened the glass doors, and was confronted with the cool efficiency of Adams National . . . impersonal, without love . . . she had fled. Adam smiled. By God, if he were female that's what he would have done. Where was she now? She could be in a restaurant eating lunch. The odds of finding her were stacked against him. And so, here he was, an ancient Ulysses, a man bereft, searching for his soul in the form of a middle-aged lady. Really, it was a good thing the drives that motivated the actions of most human beings were never fully exposed to one another. Or was it? Maybe if all the young and old people passing him now, as he leaned irresolutely against the iron rail fence of the Old

Granary Buying Ground, were aware that he was simply a man in love with the smile on a woman's face, they might have shaken his hand, or put their arms around his shoulder, and they might have been overjoyed to know that they weren't alone. There really was another loving human being in this world.

He was about to hail a taxi and head back to lunch in the Adams National cafeteria when the quiet charm of the ancient elms and the people ruminating on human transience as they stared at the nearly indecipherable slate markers, commemorating the remains of the founders of Boston, reminded him that it had been fifteen years since he and Janice had brought Sam and Keane to see the tombstones of Paul Revere, John Hancock, and, of course, the doughty Samuel Adams.

Walking through the gate, he floated on memories of nearly forty years before when his own father had first taken him to see the stone that marked the grave of the old revolutionist. "They don't write too much about Sam or give him proper credit, son. All the historians remember is John and his son J.Q., who became presidents. But without Sam, the English might still be running things." Even a hundred and fifty years later such a thought was abhorrent to an Adams.

And as his father's words reverberated in his mind, *he saw her*. Sitting far back in the cemetery on the edge of an ancient tomb, her legs dangling, she was following him through the lens of her camera, quietly snapping pictures of him as he walked toward her. He didn't run. He told himself that his heart wasn't nearly jumping out of his chest, but his purposeful gait, and the bubbling laughter that flooded his mind and surged through him like a cascading waterfall would have revealed, to even a casual passerby, Adam was a man come alive.

She greeted him through a blur of tears, and he realized that she too had restrained herself from running to hug him as he threaded his way past the worn gravestones.

"I really did it," she whispered, the tears now uncontrollable in her eyes. "For a moment, I didn't think you'd get the message." She was a radiant schoolgirl, with an orange ribbon through her hair, who had just won honors at graduation exercises. How could this woman, practically a stranger, reach so deeply into the man he was?

"What message?" he asked. Resisting the temptation to take her in his arms, he reveled in the clean simple femininity of her pale green knit suit and her wind-askew hair.

She took his hand and pulled him along the walk, pointing at a large gravestone near the iron rail. They were standing close to the city sidewalk. Even before he stood in front of the stone, he remembered the words etched on the marker. *Samuel Adams, Born September 16, 1722, Died October 2, 1803.*

"I told his spirit to send you a thought wave." Her eyes and eyebrows danced in quizzical delight. "He really did it, and it reached you!"

Adam squeezed her hand. "Please . . . from now on don't count on Sam. He was a political revolutionist. I'm sure he wouldn't approve of the sexual revolution. Sam wasn't very interested in affairs of the heart. For him, we would be shockingly dilatory, and unessential to his Puritan scheme of things."

"Oh, I trust him better than that. After all he did have two wives."

Adam laughed. "Not at the same time."

"If something telepathic didn't bring my message to you, why did you come here today?"

"It's a good question. To tell you the truth, I haven't been in Old Granary since the boys were seven or eight." Unaccountably, a picture of Janice flashed across his mind. Nearly twenty years ago . . . her hair, natural blonde, page-boy style on her shoulders. She smiled at him. His wife . . . a young mother with two yelling enthusiastic boys tugging at her hands and skirt.

Angela seemed tuned to his momentary reverie. Happily silent, she watched him, a tiny grin flicking around her mouth as she unconsciously ran the tips of her fingers over his wrist and the back of his hand. "So, really, why did you come here today?"

It was a puzzling thought. "I was looking for you. Not here, especially . . . in fact I had given up. I was wondering why you came to my office, and then didn't ask for me."

Angela sank to the ground near the Adams grave. She pulled Adam down with her, and then searched in her tote bag. "I was so sure you'd find me that I brought two chicken sandwiches and two cans of root beer . . . they're probably warm. Oh God . . . you know the truth . . . even as I bought them I chided myself for such wishful thinking."

64

Adam chuckled. "The Sons of Liberty. Revere, Hancock, and Adams would love you for one thing. No one else has ever dared to make this a picnic ground."

"It's all right. I know Jimmy Venuto, the policeman who patrols this area. A few minutes ago, I told him, if he saw me sitting here with a man, not to worry. His name would be Adams, a pillar of Boston." She bubbled. "At the very least, Adam, you do look like a character out of William Dean Howells, or J. P. Marquand . . ." She was silent for a moment. "When I got to your printing plant and saw how formidable it looked . . . I was afraid to ask for you. The truth is I never took the initiative with a man. Even now, I know I'm being too obvious."

Her skirt had slid back on her knees, and he could see the soft slope of her under calves and the curve of her buttocks in her pantyhose. She watched him as he ate his sandwich, her eyes filmy with delight. Seeing him through the soft-focus lens of her happy tears, enjoying the chiseled lines of his face, she told herself she didn't care. She was old enough to dare to be herself.

"You were afraid that I might have second thoughts." He wondered what she would do if he gave in to his desire and touched her face and kissed her lips. "You were thinking I might be wondering how I ever got involved with you."

"More than that." Angela really wanted to ask him why he had bothered to look for her, but that would be forcing the impossible into the open. "I was really scared to death. You must be very important to be president of such a big place. Why should you be interested in an insignificant housewife? Besides, Jim has often told me, a man's place of business is inviolate. Don't you have to work?" She liked his crinkly self-questioning look.

"I'm beginning to think that a day off, once a week, would make J.Q. a less dull boy," he said. "Thursdays, Adams National could do without me. I could carry your camera, and you could teach me photography. My son, Sam, would approve of that." He really wanted to say, let's not play games. You could have mailed the photographs to me, or not sent them at all.

So, in a sense, she had taken the initiative and, though she might be a long time in admitting it, she was tacitly offering more than simple friendship. How did he want to respond? There was no doubt in his mind. For the short term. Right now, he would be delighted to take Angela

Thomas to bed . . . and worry about the consequences later. Was he reacting like a typical male to what seemed like an available female? No. In the past years there had been other females. Some of them would have been delighted to have a brief affair. But he had never felt this driving need. It was more than sex. Angela invited an intimacy that made him forget himself. Of course, it was quite insane. She was married. He was married. They were on a carousel that played "forsaking all others" . . . but they weren't listening.

Angela guessed his thoughts. "A man and woman can't just be friends, can they?" Her eyes were pleading. She knew that she was trying to say something else. Like Adam, I know my being here is obvious, but don't make me aware of it. Don't rush me. Maybe if you'll have patience, I'll dare.

He pulled her to her feet. "We can't stay here. People are watching us through the pickets, wondering when I'm going to put my arms around you and kiss you."

Angela knew that they looked like lovers. She hoped no one she knew would see them. Husbands and wives weren't so aware of each other. They walked through the entrance hand in hand. He pointed across the street. "That's the Parker House."

"Where they have the Parker House rolls?" She giggled, and then looked embarrassed as she was suddenly aware of the innuendo.

He thought it was funny. "See, I told you a woman of the same generation is more enjoyable. Most young females never heard 'Roll me over, in the clover . . .' " He stopped in the doorway of the hotel. "We could take a room for the afternoon."

She didn't answer, and they slowly walked past the motel toward King's Chapel. "How could we?" she finally asked, feeling a little safer that the hotel was behind them. "We have no luggage." There, she thought. Now, you know the truth. I'm willing to go to bed with you. If it weren't the truth, why hadn't she squelched the idea immediately?

He was amused. "We'll just walk right up to the clerk at the desk. I'll say, 'Good afternoon. My wife and I want a room.' "

She stared at him, wide-eyed.

"I couldn't. He'd know the truth. I'd blush. I'd stam-

66

mer. It would be quite apparent what we wanted a room for."

"To rest . . . to clean up, silly. Because we didn't want to drive to Cohasset. We are staying in town to a dinner, and a show."

Angela was incredulous. "You mean you would actually register as Mr. and Mrs. J. Q. Adams from Cohasset?"

"Why not?"

She clutched his arm, urging him even further from the hotel. "You know what Hamlet said about you? 'The devil hath power to assume a pleasing shape.' Adam, I couldn't. It's not just that it's too soon, or it's immoral, or that I really don't know you. All those reasons are true enough plus a million others. But quite practically . . . what if someone recognized you or me? *Then* what would we do?"

Adam laughed. "I'd stand my guns. 'Well, if it isn't Joe Doakes. Meet my wife, Angela Adams.' "

"Your wife's name is Janice."

"Joe wouldn't remember. He's stupid."

Angela couldn't help smiling. "Maybe we'd run into Harry Doakes. He would be smarter than his brother." She took his hand. "I want to show you something."

They were standing in front of the cemetery next to the ancient Boston church, King's Chapel. "Good God, Angela . . . not another burying ground."

She led him inside the gate. The sunlight filtered through a canopy of leaves already frost-tinted red and yellow. She pointed to a weathered stone, and waited while he deciphered the worn letters. "Elizabeth Paine? A relative of yours?"

She stared into his eyes, wondering why she couldn't look at him without feeling so overcome, so damned helpless. "Sisters under the skin, perhaps. Do you remember Nathaniel Hawthorne's *The Scarlet Letter*? Legend has it that there was more truth than poetry in the story. Some people say Elizabeth was the real-life Hester Prynne."

He couldn't help himself. He brushed her lips with his and kissed away a tear in the corner of her eye. "Angela . . . Angela . . . you are a delight. Let's stop worrying about sex. There's other things we need to discover about each other. Do you dare to be carefree? If it has nothing to do with murder, or robbery, and the only sex will be the inevitable current between us, will you do whatever I ask?"

She grinned dubiously. "I guess so."

"Okay, come with me. I'm going to buy you some new clothes."

<h1>☆ 17 ☆</h1>

As she matched his brisk pace, his only answer to her bewildered questioning was, "Trust me."

He propelled her into a store almost before she had grasped the name emblazoned over the door and on the windows. *Slacker Jacks and Jills.* Before she could protest he cornered a salesgirl. Dimly she realized that he was testing her ... but for what? The store displayed every imaginable type of male and female slacks, mostly in vibrant colors, for youngsters who would delight in wearing the hip-hugging styles. They were the oldest people in the store. In fact, they were ancient enough to be the parents of most of the customers, who grinned happily at "Daddy Warbucks" and his girlfriend.

"My wife wants a pair of slacks," he told the girl, who was entranced by his easy command of the store. "I think orange will go nicely with her brown eyes. As for me, I will contrast with her by wearing green slacks. We'll both need pullover jerseys. Can you fit us?"

Angela was about to say, No, Adam, I can't! These styles are for youngsters. I wouldn't be caught dead in orange slacks. But somehow she held her tongue. Maybe it was the enthusiasm of the young salespeople who had gathered around them, delighted that someone past thirty dared to cross the generation gap. Of course, they could fit them. Slacker Jacks came in all sizes. The "sex-prize in every package was you. Wear our cool pants and all your friends will get hot pants." While she was hiding her confusion at the array they spread before her, Adam chose a pair of burnt orange slacks. "My wife will take these." He surveyed Angela's body, a huge grin on his face. "About size twelve. She'll put them on now. We'll both need shopping bags to carry the clothes we are wearing." Pleased with Angela's astonishment, he pushed her toward the dressing rooms. "Hurry up. We only have a few hours."

The store didn't have sneakers. Adam was grinning at her when she emerged from the dressing room wearing the orange slacks and a green jersey. "Where we're going, you can't wear street shoes," he said, "but don't worry, I'm sure we can solve the problem." He was charmed by her obvious self-consciousness. "My God, you look pretty sexy."

Angela was certain that everyone in the store was staring at her. Someone's mother trying to recapture her youth. She was trying to tell him . . . it was impossible, she just wouldn't go out in the streets wearing this mad costume. But it was too late. She suddenly realized he, too, was transformed. A slick roustabout from Piccadilly Circus . . . right out of Soho. She burst into laughter. "Adam . . . you look like a racetrack tout . . . all you need is a floppy English cap."

"Aye, a prettier bird, I ain't never seen. All the blokes will go off their rockers when they site you, me lass." His accent was Boston Cockney.

There was nothing to do but follow him into the street. Clutching the bag containing her suit and pantyhose in one hand, and her tote bag in the other, she still managed to cling to his arm. She tried to ignore the good-humored people who stopped to stare at them.

"Enjoy yourself," he told them loudly. "We're wandering minstrels." He sang a snatch of the song to a bewildered old lady. "A wandering minstrel I, a thing of shreds and patches, of ballads, songs and snatches, and dreamy lullaby!"

"What if someone recognizes us?" she wailed. She had a vision of her sisters, who could easily have ventured into this part of town, accosting her in astonished horror. Maybe it would have been better to have gone to the Parker House with him. At least, in a hotel room there would have been no voyeurs.

He finally waved a taxi to a standstill by standing in front of it in the narrow street. "Community Boat House," he told the bewildered driver, and then inside he pulled her into his arms. Laughing at her consternation, he kept kissing her lips and nose and eyes. "You were great, Angela. Charming. I didn't think you had it in you. I still can't believe it."

"Can't believe what?"

"That, if I were your husband Jim, you'd be sitting here in a taxi with me, wearing tight orange pants, that show your delightful rump in stunning detail and altogether make you look quite voluptuous."

The answer was that quite honestly she wouldn't be, but it was a two-way street. "And if I were Janice, would you have dared to spring such a zany idea on me, and expect me to be joyously enthusiastic?"

Adam shrugged. "The history of my life is an unending series of rejections of J.Q. Adams' unrestrained nuttiness. Jan doesn't like surprises. It would be impossible for her to go sailing on the Charles spontaneously. She would think it unreasonable that I hadn't told her several days before, so she could plan for it. Jan has lost the charm of 'off the cuff' behavior."

Angela was relieved to finally discover where they were going. She wasn't at all sure that she was really more amenable to sailing on the Charles River than Janice would have been, but she wasn't going to admit it. "Most women get involved with their image," she told him. "It's the only security we have. Now, take me, I'm a middle-aged woman . . . set in her ways." She grinned at his dismayed look. "Really, Adam, these pants are harder to get used to than the thoughts of adultery. It isn't only my behind that is sculptured by them; I really don't know whether to walk backwards or to crouch frontwards with my hands in front of me, à la September Morn."

"Walk forward. You have joyous buttocks. In those pants each cheek is its own boss!"

☆ 18 ☆

As they drove along Storrow Drive, he explained that the Community Sailing Club was run by the Metropolitan District Commission. "They have fifty or sixty sailboats, mostly one-class designs called Mercurys. Membership is very reasonable. It's not a yacht club as such—the boats belong to the club. Mornings they hold sailing classes for Boston youngsters. Afternoons . . . particularly Thursdays . . . are for lovers."

He chuckled at her confusion and obvious embarrassment as she emerged from the taxicab. At the entrance to the boathouse he suddenly remembered that Angela would have to sign a guest release. "They're very Bostonian snickety about it. Don't panic. The card just says, 'I can swim at least seventy-five yards and am a capable swimmer and will abide by the rules of the boathouse.' "

"Whose name do I use?" Angela demanded.

"Your own." He was holding her hand ignoring the reluctant look in her eyes. "Angela, stop worrying, we're only going to sail together. When we finally sleep together, you can be Angela Adams."

"Adam . . ." She looked at him pleadingly. "Do we have to go sailing?"

"Can't you swim seventy-five yards?"

Angela grinned at him. "Of course I can, but I'm not sure you can sail a boat."

The attendant who greeted Adam dispelled that fear. "Haven't seen you since you won the Inter-Club race in August, Mr. Adams. Guess they're keeping you pretty busy." Trying to ignore the attendant's interested appraisal of her slacks, Angela signed the release that he handed her. She noted the signs conspicuously posted on the club walls. "No one permitted in the boats without sneakers."

The attendant picked up her card and stared curiously at the camera tote bag slung over her shoulder. "I hope you have sneakers, Mrs. Thomas." Angela tried to ignore his questioning look, which seemed to imply that she was contravening more than the house rules about sneakers.

Adam assured him that he had an extra pair in his locker. Following Adam out to the dock, Angela accentuated the sway of her hips, thinking that since she was dressed like J. Q. Adams' little sexpot, she might as well act the part. The dockmaster who assigned Adam a boat watched her, intrigued. As he was picking up the tiller, rudder, and sails for the boat, Adam returned the dockmaster's conspiratorial grin. "I think he likes you," he whispered, as he led Angela to the locker. "The last time Janice was here, she left a pair of old sneakers. She has big feet . . ." He handed her a pair and stared quickly at Angela's feet. They seemed to be about the same size.

"You mean that I have to wear your wife's sneakers?"

"Why not?" He chuckled. "You know, Angela, the way you are staring at me with that wide-eyed look, it's very difficult not to hug you. Don't you want to find out what it's like to be in Janice's shoes?"

71

A few minutes later they were tacking toward the middle of the Charles River. He finally eased the tiller and dropped off from close haul until they were idling on a reach. The sail bagged the air making an easy sack on the port side of the boat. Slumping against the stern he invited her to sit beside him. Laughing, she levered herself down, using his ankle for a handhold. Staring at Janice's sneakers on her feet, she tried to relate her feeling of carefreeness and sheer joy with a lady from Acton called Angela Thomas. Momentarily that Angela was another person: a rather mundane housewife and mother who came to Boston on Thursdays and would have rejected out of hand the thought that she would ever have a lover. No, that was wrong. Adam wasn't her lover . . . yet. But there was no doubt she was tempting fate. For a moment she saw herself through Jim's eyes. Was this the reality? Was this really Angela Thomas, married some twenty-three years, romantically play-acting like a young college student? Wasn't the real truth that J. Q. Adams was just as mixed-up as she was? With his arm around her, his hand lightly touching her breast, wasn't he acting out fantasies as much as she was? She wanted to ask him something she could never dare ask Jim. Did growing old mean that you couldn't be just plain silly and hilarious? Did everything in life have to have meaning and purpose? Why couldn't she have told Jim, a few nights ago, that it didn't really matter if she missed an occasional orgasm? He didn't have to stand on his head or make her pleasure a life-and-death mission . . . Why couldn't he understand? Sometimes her joy in the act of love was as simple as pleasing him. Angela shrugged and she felt Adam's leg, intertwined with hers, respond with a quick pressure. She couldn't even explain to Adam why she was grinning to herself. How could you tell a potential lover that you were thinking about the act of love with your husband? Oh dear Lord, why couldn't love be as simple as laughter? Laughter of humans momentarily being gods.

Adam turned the boat into the wind. "We'll let the wind come across the bow," he told her. "The sail will just flip flop over our heads as we drift." He took her in his arms, and kissed her, and then he smiled into her solemn face. "I like you, Angela," he said softly. "You're a lovely human being."

"No, I'm not . . ." There were tears in her eyes. "Damn it. I don't know why I'm making such an issue out of us. I

72

guess I'm just shocked at the way I seem to me . . . a love-starved suburban wife . . . right out of a novel by John Updike. It's dishonest. I'm not love-starved, or looking for sex sensation . . . the truth is that I love my husband."

Adam kissed her cheek. He swung the tiller to catch the wind. With the boat close-hauled again, she sat next to him on the railing and leaned far out. The spray dashed across her face. The little sailboat seemed happy too, bouncing gaily over the light chop.

Their backs were nearly parallel to the water. He twinkled his own happiness, turning his face to hers and shouting into the wind. "Maybe our confusion is the simple discovery that it's possible to love at least one other person in this mad world."

Angela wanted to kiss him "Even if it were possible . . . your wife or my husband wouldn't believe it. Nor would any of our friends. I think the best thing is to face reality. We've had a tiny adventure. We could easily be involved in an affair. If we did, soon the temporary 'us' would have no place to go. I'm afraid I'd be the unhappy one."

"Why not me?"

"Because men shed overeager women pretty quickly." She looked at him quizzically. "I'm afraid you could easily make me into that kind of female."

They sailed silently for a while. Adam wanted to ask her bluntly, why wouldn't it be possible to make love a few times . . . experience each other for better or worse, and then walk away. But even as he had the thought, he knew she was right. Even before having sex with this woman, he knew that sex alone would be insufficient. He would want deeper involvement. He tacked the boat back and forth across the Charles, pushing it to its limit. As the warm October wind increased in intensity, and they heeled onto the starboard, less than an inch away from taking on water, Angela sensed that he was pushing the boat to its limits, challenging the elements.

He handed her the jib rope. "Brace your feet against the center board box. Hang onto the jib lead. Now stretch. Hang out as far as you can!" He whooped his enthusiasm at her as she complied. With her body poised threequarters over the water, she laughed into his laughter. She would ache tonight from the unaccustomed exercise, and she'd have to have an excuse why her face was wind-burned, but right now nothing else mattered. She

73

was incandescent, lighted by the bright questioning look of love on his face. "Oh, God, Adam . . ." she whispered the words, "please . . . please, I mustn't like you so much!"

He was quite enchantingly mad, singing: "Blow ye winds of Boston .. blow ye winds, hi ho. Clear away the running gear and blow . . . blow . . . blow. . . . Come on, sing with me, Angela!" And she learned the words and sang with him. " 'Tis advertised in Boston, New York and Buffalo, five hundred brave Americans awhaling for to go . . . So blow ye winds of morning . . ." He bubbled his exhilaration back at her. "I love you Angela. Is it so bad for a man to love in a world so devoid of love?"

Back at the dock she wanted to say, "I love you, too, Adam." But she didn't. It was four o'clock. Thursday was over. "I can't go home in this outfit" she told him. But there was really no place to change in the tiny yacht club. Besides, the attendant was too inquisitive. Angela snapped Adam's picture on the dock, and he took one of her. She wondered what she would tell Jim if he ever saw them. Her picture she would have to destroy. But Adam's could join her collection. Why not? A proper Bostonian in his sailing togs on his afternoon off.

"We can change our clothes in your car," he told her.

She was dubious. It seemed the wiser course to separate here. If he drove with her to the garage he would only have to retrace his route back to his factory. But he wouldn't consider it. Another half an hour with her was worth the inconvenience. In a taxi, she held his hand and they rode together silently. Bemused. Lost in thoughts of the swiftness of time, and the hopelessness of containing a moment of happiness. The taxi driver left them at the entrance to the garage beneath the Prudential Plaza. She told him that her automobile was buried somewhere in the winding catacombs. She could never remember where one section began or the other left off. But he found the car quickly. Parked near one of the ramps, it was in much too exposed a position for them to undress, and then dress again. He asked her for the key. In a moment he reparked the car next to one of the far walls where the neon lights seemed dimmer, and the cars near them looked as if they had been abandoned forever. She sat in the back seat of the station wagon and spread her pantyhose and three-piece suit over the back of the front seat.

"Do you have to watch me?" she demanded, as she unfastened her slacks and wiggled out of them. Smiling, he

74

nodded yes, and then before she could pull on her pantyhose, grinning at her nakedness, he moved in beside her on the seat. She couldn't summon up the will power to say no. She kissed him frantically, aware that he had unsnapped her bra. She arched to his fingers, incredibly light and delicate as they searched her flesh.

Impossible! She tried to chuckle, and it came out a sob. Who ever heard of a forty-three-year-old woman sitting practically stark naked with her lover in an underground garage? "This is a life insurance building," she whispered. "Jim told me once that some insurance companies won't insure a man's life if they know he has a mistress." She gasped, both at his lips and tongue tasting her breasts, as well as at the truth. He was hungrily ready to make her his mistress. Sliding down on the seat, afraid that a chance passerby could see them, she inadvertently exposed her body more fully to his kisses. What could she do but relax and enjoy the warm delight of his caresses? Then, with his face warm against her belly, he startled her back to reality by blowing a rat-a-tat-tat on her stomach just above her delta.

"My God." He smiled at her. "Benjamin Franklin said a woman grows old from the top down . . . but he never saw Angela." He hugged her. "Naked, with your eyes wide open, and that jersey just covering your shoulders, you look like a bewildered adolescent."

Angela grinned at his obvious joy. She didn't tell him, but compared with her own memories of her youthful self, her breasts looked a little saggy. Happily, they didn't feel one bit less erotic. She was aware of the bulge in his pants and touched him lightly for a second. "Really, Adam, we've got to stop. In a minute you'll have your pants off. I may look young and schoolgirlish to you, but I'm not so liberated that I want to make love in the back seat of an automobile." She pushed him gently to the door, insisting that he let her get dressed.

"I want to know you," he said quietly, as he took off his slacks. "In the ancient Biblical world, *knowing* a woman was a euphemism for having sexual intercourse with her. It's really an aspect of the word we should teach the younger generation. A kind of gestalt word that means so much more than the banal words for intercourse." He chuckled. "Can I know you one day? Ah, isn't that much better than the brutal word? Or even than saying, let's make love, let's go to bed? . . . Used properly, it could be the key to sexual love . . . *knowing one another* . . . a dialogue of minds and bodies, communing together over their essential mystery." As he chattered Adam had stripped to his shorts and quickly dressed in his shirt and business suit. He watched her comb her hair.

She kissed him. "Adam, it can't happen. I'd be too guilty. Sweet love, I'm not trying to give you the impression that my genitals are so sacrosanct that I couldn't just have sex with you and pray that Jim never found out . . . and maybe even let it go at that. I'm quite ordinary, really." She sighed. "I guess what I'm trying to tell you is that I would only be able to know you sexually, if you understood that I didn't love Jim any less. You see, I just haven't any reason for being unfaithful. I love Jim. He loves me." She looked at him helplessly. "Damn, I'm not convincing you am I?"

Adam shrugged. "In a way . . . but I would hope we might both be capable of 'in addition to' rather than 'instead of.' Meet me upstairs, in the lobby of the hotel, next Thursday . . . between nine-thirty and ten. Please don't say no, now. If you have to say no, say it to me on the telephone next Wednesday morning."

He waved to her as she drove out of the garage to the Mass Turnpike. On the seat beside her were the shopping bags with his green slacks, and her orange ones, and their jerseys. In her camera were pictures of him at Old Granary and the yacht club. Memories. Trails she must destroy, or they could lead to her destruction.

☆ 19 ☆

A hundred times before Thursday Angela told herself she wouldn't meet Adam at the Sheraton Hotel . . . maybe this Thursday she wouldn't even go to Boston. That would be the safest thing. Wednesday, the simplest solution would be pick up the telephone and call Adam directly. "I can't meet you Thursday." She would say the words softly, trying to conceal the huskiness in her voice, thankful he couldn't see the tears that would be in her eyes. "No, Adam . . . not tomorrow nor the Thursday after." And there would be silence on the phone and then maybe

Adam would respond, his voice deep with the warmth of his understanding. "Well, maybe someday . . . someday, I'll be walking through the Common, and once again a wide-eyed Angela will take my picture. And once again we will have luncheon, and we'll be happy that even though we liked each other we resisted."

No, Adam wouldn't be that effusive. More likely he would mask his feelings. J.Q. would answer her. "All right, Angela. Perhaps it's for the best. Take care of yourself." And then the hum of the dial tone as the connection was severed forever and she sobbed her bewilderment and unhappiness . . . and the plain silliness of denying herself a few hours of joy, of discovery with a man she really liked. What kind of world was it that legislated against love? . . . that inculcated and made a virtue of self-denial?

And if she did meet Adam, did their mutual discovery have to be based simply on sex? Obviously, if they spent the whole day in a hotel room, they would have intercourse. Joyous or not. They might be so tuned to their own guilt that their lovemaking could be self-destructive. They couldn't escape. The environment they would have created ultimately would make it necessary they undress and copulate.

Angela fantasized the Thursday encounter, from the shivery moment she would meet Adam in the lobby of the hotel, to their constrained disrobing, to the penetration, and the ultimate orgasm, and then she tried to convince herself that the whole madcap venture was quite unrealistic. Insane, really. After all, Adam was a man. Why should he be any different in bed than Jim? He actually could be worse . . . intent on his own pleasure and devil take the hindmost. If she arrived in the hotel by nine-thirty, before ten-thirty or eleven the sexual encounter would probably be over. Then, Adam, with his passion dampened, would suddenly realize the woman he was in bed with was, in truth, a rather prosaic, middle-aged matron . . . a long way from the sexpot he had created in his imagination. He would have to be polite, of course, but the four or five hours remaining before they could say good-bye to each other (with sighs of relief) would be deadly.

Angela pre-lived what she would or wouldn't do about Thursday so many times, vacillating between yes and no, that Wednesday morning came before she realized it.

Then, there was a club luncheon and a session of bridge after the luncheon. She had been unable to wiggle out of it (Angela, you can't let us down, we need you to fill out a table). Afterwards there was scarcely time to get to a private cocktail party at Ed Kanace's showroom, arranged so that Ed could unveil the new Buicks (completely redesigned this year) for a few close friends and hopefully take their orders; coupled with a quick surreptitious tete-à-tete in which Ed asked if Angela had heard the news. "Bettie and I are washed up. Bettie is divorcing me." . . . Wednesday was gone, and tomorrow was Thursday.

There was only one thing she could do . . . telephone Adam early Thursday morning at his office, or perhaps the simplest thing was simply not to show up at all. He might be disappointed, but he would finally realize their brief affair had nowhere to go. She and Jim finally escaped from the Kanaces—a frightening evening during which Bettie confirmed to a mixed group that she and Ed were going their own ways, and cheers to those who faced facts: when love was gone, it was gone; and Jim, evidently happy and relieved that his marriage was standing firm (good old Ange was a rock . . . a rock of Gibraltar), suddenly became romantic.

For some reason Jim rarely ever made love to her in the middle of the week, but tonight he only shrugged when she told him that she might be getting her period . . . *that cinched it*. Jim couldn't help but be aware that her response was more fiercely passionate than it had been recently. Could he guess that she was making up for her guilty feelings when she moaned her love for him? Finally unable to restrain her passion, she raked his back and his buttocks with her fingernails. Was she dishonest? . . . playacting? Maybe. But momentarily she had been excited, too!

And later, when Jim was watching the eleven o'clock news, and she was vacillating again, utterly convinced that she couldn't be with Adam after making love with Jim, and then feeling giggly as the thought occurred to her . . . why not? She had never pretended to Adam that she was a virgin schoolgirl, or more realistically, an unhappy housewife. Quite simply, Adam would never know. No more would she know, if he had made love to his wife . . . what was her name, Janice? She fell asleep wondering why a female who had a good husband, a good provider and lover . . . a female who had just reached a reasonably violent climax could think about making love to another man. She was bad. But damn it, she felt quite good and loving.

She didn't feel so well in the morning. The fates seemed to be conspiring against her. It was raining and the radio weatherman didn't help with his dire warnings of a storm off the coast and heavy rain and winds in the coastal areas. At breakfast, Jim questioned her. He realized it was Thursday, but surely she wasn't going to Boston today? What could she do all day? It was no day for picture-taking.

"I don't take pictures every Thursday," she explained patiently, trying not to appear on the defensive. "As a matter of fact, there's an open rehearsal of the Boston Symphony Orchestra this afternoon, and there's an exhibit of Wyeth paintings at the Museum."

Jim kissed her good-bye. "Okay, sugar, but drive carefully. I wouldn't know how to live without you."

His words were still circling in her brain when she took the elevator out of the Prudential underground garage to the hotel. As if she were being drawn by an irresistible post-hypnotic suggestion, Angela walked into the lobby. It was only nine-twenty. Somehow, she had averaged better than sixty miles an hour, covering the distance from home in a little less than thirty minutes. Of course, she was trembling . . . almost praying that Adam wouldn't be here . . . hopefully, wouldn't come at all.

A quick tour through the lobby revealed that he hadn't arrived. He had said between nine-thirty and ten. Should she wait the whole half-hour? Better, could she stand the tension of waiting? She wandered over the broadloom carpet in a trance, staring dubiously at an empty lounge chair where she could have sat and fidgeted. But she couldn't sit. She examined the tiny newsstand just off the lobby, thinking she might buy a package of cigarettes. But she hadn't smoked in years and years. It would be silly to start again now. She stared at the paperback books, not really reading the titles, and then the cover of one sank slowly into her conscious mind. *Adultery for Adults*. Both repulsed and entranced, she picked it off the rack and skimmed the pages. One paragraph caught her eye. "Ho-tels are for married people. Tired old married people who keep regular hours. Besides, they think it's funny if you check in and stay only for two hours."

Horrible. She fumbled for a dollar and gave it to the

counterman quickly so he couldn't see the title of the book. She didn't wait for her change. Then, as she walked back toward the entrance, she saw him coming through the revolving door. Wearing a light raincoat, no hat, carrying a black umbrella, he looked handsomely cool and unperturbed. A bright bubbly smile transformed his face as he saw her. His hand, grasping her arm, seemed to have a certainty and strength that flowed through him into her body, as if somehow he sensed her nervousness and was silently saying, Don't worry, I love you.

He guided her onto the escalator that led to the Plaza level. She smiled at him through her tears and handed him the book. "I bought you a present." He looked at the title, chuckled, and casually dropped the book into his pocket. "Thank you, but I reject the appellation. For you and me, adultery is a word that doesn't apply."

She couldn't help respond to his easy good humor. "Adam . . . you're a dreamer. You refuse to admit to reality."

"Reality is in the eyes of the beholder." He led her into a coffee shop. "Let's relax a minute, and have a second breakfast while we deliberate strategy."

They were silent while a waitress took their order. Coffee and toast. She really didn't want either. Angela finally dared to evoke her thoughts. "I was thinking . . . maybe it would be better if we walked around the city . . . but, of course, that's impossible. It's such a dismal day." She looked at him brightly. "Maybe we should go to the Museum of Fine Arts." She actually had a momentary vision of herself and Adam discussing paintings and sculpture, spending a frustrated but platonic afternoon.

"Or we could go to the movies and hold hands." Adam's expression was both mocking and filled with love for her. "The fact is, Angela, I made a reservation. All we have to do is to go down to the desk and register."

"Register?" Angela was appalled. "Who am I supposed to be?"

"We covered that ground last week. Mrs. Adams. Who else?" Adam's grin was captivating. A mad schoolboy prankster.

"We have no luggage."

Adam took her hand. "Angela, I'm not implying that you aren't breathtakingly lovely, but really, no one would suspect us as lovers. They'd look at me and think . . . he's

80

a fortunate middle-aged man whose wife has retained her youthful charm and beauty."

Angela couldn't help laughing. "Two old fools, you mean. You're probably right . . . but humor me, Adam. If we must take a hotel room, you register alone. Tell them that your wife will be in later. I couldn't face the bellboy." She stared at him earnestly. "Really, if I manage to go through with it at all, it's got to be sneaky."

Ten minutes later, the key to the room in his hand, Adam led her to the elevators. She breathed a sigh of relief when she discovered they were alone in the elevator. "We're near the top," he told her. "A good view of Commonwealth Avenue and the Charles River." Angela was silent. She was in the fire now. It was ridiculous to complain of the burning.

☆ 20 ☆

A maid in the hall greeted them politely. "My wife and I are checking in. We won't need maid service," he told the woman. Angela didn't dare look at her face. To make doubly sure, Adam hung a "Do Not Disturb" sign on the outer doorknob. The room was impersonal. Two huge double beds, a couple of lounge chairs, a desk-vanity, the usual television, and modern art reproductions on the wall. Had other illicit lovers ever occupied it? Angela didn't voice her thought.

Adam admired the beds and maneuvered her toward one of them. "I told the clerk my wife liked big-sized twin beds."

"Wasn't he surprised?"

"About what?"

"That you'd rent a room for the day to go to bed with your wife." She sat down beside him, still wearing her suede jacket. "This is really silly, isn't it?"

Without taking his raincoat off he stretched out on the bed and grinned at her. "No. It isn't silly or bad. It's nice. I'm joyous that you came. I didn't think you would." He touched her hand. "Good Lord, you're trembling." He pulled her down beside him and hugged her. "Honey, we're safe. For the next few hours we are lost to the

81

world. No one knows where we are. We've escaped." He kissed her enthusiastically. "Are you really jittery?"

She grinned at him uncertainly. "No. Not now. But I'm going to be scared to death to leave."

"No problem. The elevator goes directly to the garage. You can go down alone and I'll meet you there."

Amazingly, though she had known him less than seven or eight hours, she felt a warm empathy with this man. Indecisively, she watched him hang his raincoat and suit jacket in the room closet. She took off her jacket, and he hung it beside them. "Look out the window." He put his arm around her as they stared at the city below them. "Even through the fog and rain you can see the Charles. A week ago we were sailing. Now, we have a prelude to winter. Come on, take off your dress, and snuggle with me. It's a good day for a man and woman to share each other's warmth."

She slipped out of her dress and draped it across a chair. She wondered why she didn't feel embarrassed to be with him, half-undressed. The truth was he gave her a warm feeling of security. She curved into his arms and he unsnapped her bra . . . pushed it back on her shoulders and kissed her nipples ever so lightly. Through her stocking panties she could feel his hard excitement against her belly, but he made no effort to get undressed or take off her pantyhose. She shivered but insisted she wasn't cold. The room was warm and it was nice to lie here on top the sheets . . . to hold the moment somehow . . . as intimate as penetration, really.

I've been thinking about us," he whispered into her hair. His hand, underneath her panties, caressed her buttocks lightly. "I could say that I'm attracted to you because of your contagious enthusiasm for living, or because of your lovely face, or your body . . . or simply because I have an intuition that we look at life and loving the same way . . ." He was silent for a second.

"But," she said, filling in the word for him.

He grinned. "Not but, exactly. Something else. That book, *Adultery for Adults* . . . Janice read parts of it to me when it ran in *Redbook* or *Cosmopolitan*, I can't remember which. It's very sophisticated. Gives you the feeling you haven't lived unless you are having an extra-marital affair . . . *and* getting away with it." He held her hand and brushed his lips over her fingertips. "I think you and I could discover a depth relationship beyond anything that book ever contemplated. But let me warn you. A lot of people think I'm too intense. My puritan ethic doesn't let me relax." He laughed. "I'll give you an example. While I'm fully aware of the productive processes of the printing industry, it's not the competition that intrigues me, nor the moneymaking process, but rather the interpersonal actions and reactions of human beings, and the never-ending tendency for human organizations, and the very structures that humans need for their material and emotional survival to disintegrate or simply be self-destroyed by some internal, suicidal masochism. Yeats said it, I think: "Without a center things fall apart . . ." As he spoke, Angela was aware that his fingers inside her pantyhose, first feathery on her stomach and pubic hair, were now lightly cupping her vulva. It was an insidious form of pleasure and she was hypnotized.

"What you are saying is that you and I are a temporary organization." She burrowed against him, shivering a little.

Adam hugged her. "My God, I'm raving, aren't I . . . and you are freezing. Let's get undressed, and get under the covers."

Angela agreed. "First, I have to go to the bathroom. I always have to urinate after I drink so much coffee. It's a diuretic."

Adam undressed swiftly and followed her into the bathroom.

"I can't go when you're watching me," she said. She had hung her pantyhose on the shower door. She tried not to see his well-formed body and erect penis. "Oh, Adam, I'm embarrassed. Please stop looking at me. I'm no young thing."

Laughing, Adam pointed to himself. "Obviously, he's happy about you."

There was no choice. She had to urinate, and she did while he kneeled in front of her, kissing her breasts. She grinned at him. "This is plain silly. I'm sure you don't follow your wife in the bathroom . . . I'd murder Jim if he tried to do what you're doing."

"Is it because we're lovers?"

She nodded. "Of course, and I'll bet you . . . after the second or third time we're together, when I go to the bathroom, you won't follow me."

"Don't count on it. I'm very unpredictable. A few

weeks ago I jumped into the tub with Janice. She screamed, of course."

Laughing, Angela dried herself. She stood up and hugged him, and kissed him with a long kiss. "I'm glad you like your wife, Adam." His penis, hard against her belly, excited her. "If we don't get to bed soon, you're going to burst."

She wanted to watch him urinate, but he pushed her toward the door. "It isn't that ordinarily I would mind you watching," he said, twinkling at her. "But until you leave, my friend won't recover his secondary function."

"Primary, you mean. If you don't urinate you won't live long enough for the secondary joy. Adam, I really have to take a shower . . . I'm kind of smelly."

He managed to finish. From behind her, he encircled her waist. Kissing her neck, he gently pushed her back to the bed. "We can take a shower later. I want to discover if I was attracted to your perfume, originally . . . or seduced by the natural odors of your body." With the covers over them, he let himself be lost for a moment in her wide-eyed expression. "Angela, do you always say 'urinate'?"

She giggled. "Of course not. . . . To myself, I say I need to take a leak . . . or like Jim, I even think, 'take a piss.' To tell you the truth, I never say urinate. To other women, I'd say I have to go to the bathroom or to the john."

"Okay, then that's a good place to begin. From now on, we use the words and say the thoughts we would ordinarily repress. Defenselessly. No games. No cover. No fear. Anything that comes into our heads we dare say it to each other." He made a cave out of the bedclothes and deep under the hump he kissed her knees, her calves, her vulva. Stopping for a moment he tasted her labia and clitoris, while she protested and tried to keep her legs closed. "Oh, Adam . . . please. I do need a shower."

"No you don't." He grinned at her. "I like the taste of Angela." He kissed her pubic hair, belly button, and then stretched beside her and teased her erect nipples with his tongue. "So, my lovely . . . while the chance of you getting pregnant at this late date in your life is less than it was, I don't think we want to complicate things." He looked at her with raised eyebrows. "Who's taking care of birth control . . . you or me?"

She kissed his face passionately. "Adam . . . Adam . . .

84

why do you make me feel so delightfully shivery? Sometimes I'm on the pill. Sometimes I use a diaphragm." She smiled. "To tell you the truth, right now we don't have to worry about anything, except I may start menstruating." She hugged him. "My God, I've been afraid all morning that today was the day. Maybe I'm late and it's tomorrow."

"What would you have done, if you had your period?"

"I'd have told you we couldn't make love."

"I'd have answered. We can't let time, tide, or moon months stop us. Our hours together are too few."

She was silent. Present joy could be lost wondering about future joy. "Do you really think we'll last . . . that we'll be together a year from now . . . even next Thursday?"

"Every minute with you, I'm becoming more convinced of it."

"It isn't going to be easy. We're extramarital, aren't we, Adam? Oh, God . . . I hope . . ."

"What do you hope?"

She shook her head, concealing her original thought and telling him another. "I hope that only a few minutes have gone by . . . She chuckled. "That you have the stamina to make love all day." Her hand brushed his penis and she pulled away. He opened her palm and she understood and held him gently, and he lost himself in the wonder of her flesh and the warmth of her skin and her heart beating.

"I think you're love-starved," he said softly.

She shook her head, thinking it was little less than twelve hours since she had made love with Jim. "No . . . I'm Adam-starved!" She kissed him wildly, amazed at herself that she could let go so completely. She nibbled his chest, bit the softer flesh on his stomach, held his penis erect and lapped it, laughing at him and telling him it was a sweet lollipop. "My God," she gasped, as she flung herself back on the pillow. "I'm bad! You're right . . . for forty-three years I must have been repressed. I was very sexy when I was a little girl . . . but I never did anything about it. Oh, Adam," she sobbed. "You taste nice, too. But this *is* madness I'm afraid. Honey . . . honey, I'm afraid."

She merged her face into his neck and cried. Her tears slid down his chest, and he held her close to him, and the rain slashed against the window, and her sobs diminished, and she slowly spread her legs over his leg, and she helped him find his way into her, and she inched on top of him so that her face and lips were next to his neck, and he held her buttocks with the palm of his hand and his fingers were gentle on her flesh but they imprisoned her body against him, and with his other hand he caressed her until she felt a serenity so pervasive . . . a letting go of her body . . . so that she both existed and ceased to exist, and she heard his whisper in her ear. "This is the way . . . this is Tao . . . together . . ."

☆ 21 ☆

Four weeks later Angela realized she was measuring the new joy of her life by Thursdays. A memory book of Thursday hours that she could open when they weren't together . . . plus the anticipation of the unlived Thursdays yet to come. She refused to think of how many, or how few Thursdays might be left to them. In ten years there could only be a maximum of five hundred and twenty . . . in twenty years (ridiculous, she would be sixty-three and Adam sixty-six) there would be one thousand forty. In reality, of course, in the five or ten years that they might have together, there would be many less than five hundred or a thousand Thursdays. But those were fearful thoughts. She wanted to believe Adam when he told her, "We're irrevocably committed. I'll make love to you when you're a wheezy old lady of eighty-three." In a world of transience, it was nice to deny the inevitable.

One thing she knew. Her sense of uneasiness was rapidly disappearing. Adam was a part of her life. Maybe less than one-seventh, but the shorter time cast a warm shadow over the remainder. The biggest problem was to keep Adam and Thursdays in a private compartment of her mind. Could she make this tiny "extra life" enhance her relationship with Jim? It wasn't her idea alone. Adam and she had discussed it in depth. My God, what hadn't they talked about in the thirty or so hours since they had really known each other?

She still remembered that first day vividly. An hour or two later, encapsulated in their first blending of flesh, she realized that amazingly Adam was still linked to her. She had opened her eyes and smiled dreamily into his smile.

"You're still almost inside me. You do have amazing qualities."

Adam laughed. "Not without your help. Whenever I seemed to be shrinking something inside you gets the signal, and a slow undulation of your vagina keeps me alive in a most ecstatic way."

"Adam, I'm not love-starved." It was madness, but she had to be honest with him. "My husband makes love with me several times a week. I like Jim. He's been good to me . . . we have nice children. We have a good life." As she spoke her hand strayed idly over his penis, and she held it, unthinkingly, her fingertips a wispy rake.

Adam smiled. "You may not be aware of it, but you're holding another man's penis while you tell him about your husband. What would Jim think?"

Her eyes were glistening round mirrors of wonder. "He'd think I must be depraved." She sighed. "But what can I do? When a man feathers a female's labia and clitoris so delightfully, pretty soon she's beyond morality or immorality. She has to demand that the sword be put in the scabbard!"

Angela remembered screaming her ecstasy into his mouth, trying to muffle her wild, joyous release, lest the whole hotel be aroused. She remembered their laughing thrusts and counter-thrusts and the screaming summit that tumbled them off the bed together in a wild gale of hilarity, leaving them panting and breathless and delighted with their helplessness as they awaited the temporary calming of their throbbing blood.

Lying on the floor, too pooped to crawl back into the bed, Adam had been philosophical. "Angela, I'm dangerous. In you, through you, and with you, I want to see if we can consciously do what escapes most people. See if we can integrate our strong sexual attraction into a unitary whole." She snuggled against him and listened while he rambled. "In a sense, you and I are symptomatic of the times. The younger generation have grown up in a world where every value, every ethic, every moral approach to life has lost its mythic appeal. Our generation has devalued and debunked and even removed the poetry from much of the ineffable aspects of life. Many of us in our superiority call ourselves liberals. We're no longer hung on past taboos or the superstitions of the church. We only partially believe in God, and then most certainly not a personal God. Even the flag-wavers, crying to restore pa-

87

triotism, don't really believe anymore in a nationalism that says 'my country right or wrong.' Many of us are beginning to realize that the economics of capitalism which still gives lip service to a personal laissez-faire has lost its reality in a world of increasing populations. In one breath we sing songs like 'I gotta be me,' and 'I'll do it my way,' and at the same time we look for a great white governmental father who will make us believe that we really care about one another." Adam had suddenly stopped talking and was kissing her again. Angela had kissed him back, fascinated that he could switch from philosophy to passion with such ease. "See, I told you I was slightly mad. It's intermission at Jordan Hall Forum while the main speaker makes love to his hungry wife." He scooped her back onto the bed.

"I'm not your wife," she reminded him.

But he only patted her cheek. "I have a curious mind." He snuggled against her breast. "I may not be entirely accurate, but if you look up 'wife' in the dictionary, old Webster will tell you to see 'vibrate.' If you really dig around in a delightful book, like Partridge's *Origins,* you'll discover that wife is derived from an old Norse word, *'veifa,'* meaning vibrating . . . and is also related to the medieval French, *'gaif,'* meaning 'an abandoned or unclaimed animal.' " He was grinning at her wide-eyed absorption in his words. "Also possibly derived from the Old English, *'wafian,'* meaning 'wave.' Hence, you are my loving wave, with some, if not all of your vibrations unclaimed."

She grinned at him. "I surrender. But I still don't know what you were trying to say before your genitals took command of your brain again."

He thought that was funny. "That's it . . ." he told her, delighted. "That's the key. A new mystique for men and women based on a realization that we have come one step further than the animals. A new kind of value system based on the amazement of love. Man could enhance his sexuality by a new integration. What better religion is there than the wonder of your breasts? . . . Being aware both of their surface beauty, and the limpid loveliness of the mammary itself capable of producing milk, or as now, flowing with contained blood that is both Angel-a and not Angel-a?"

At first, Adam's wide-ranging interests stunned her mind, and then as the weeks went by, she knew she was slowly awakening to life as Adam saw it ... a world full of vast unexplored potential that vibrated in ratio to one's wonder and curiosity and commitment, and she found she was able to match and even exceed his enthusiasm for learning and knowing. Her problem was concealing from Jim that the Pandora's box was opened. Angela had discovered that a body may grow older, but a brain only does when the owner fails to feed it. But, she really didn't want to conceal the woman she was slowly becoming. Rather, she had to be careful to reveal herself in small doses, so that she could entice Jim into this exciting new fun-world of the appreciating mind.

It wasn't easy. Occasionally she would be so obsessed with an Adam approach to life that she wanted to hug Jim, and in some mad way have him be happy that she was in love with him and Adam, too. Ah, if only Jim could understand her need for Adam and not be angry. Angry was mild! He would be raging! If she could only tell Jim that it was really no problem at all. She actually did love two men. She loved Jim because he was warm and comfortable and affectionate (at least when he wasn't preoccupied with law or golf), and she loved Adam because he was intemperate and intense and driving, a megalomaniac, convinced there were answers to everything ... even their unstable extramarital relationship.

☆ 22 ☆

The real difficulty was that there was no one she could share Adam with. Not even Bettie Kanace, who poured all the bitter details of her life with Ed into her unwilling ears, and then asked her point-blank what she would have done.

Bettie had begged her to come to the Kanace house for lunch. Ed had moved into the Holiday Inn. When Angela finally arrived about one-thirty, Bettie admitted that she had waited until noon and then in little more than an hour had consumed three Scotches. Angela rummaged in the refrigerator and made tomato and lettuce sandwiches for both of them. She brought them out on the patio with a very light Scotch for herself. Bettie was on her fourth.

"Don't think I haven't known about Ed and that Karen Ainsley." Bettie's voice was a little slurred. "You remember her. She was active in all the Acton social events. Everyone expected she'd be president of the Women's Club. Then her husband, Bill, was killed in an automobile accident. After that no one ever saw her. She dropped out of everything ... too busy putting out to every rutting male in sight."

"It must be kind of difficult," Angela said. "You have a husband, you get used to sex; you need it as part of your life. There's no provision in monogamous society for a female who loses her man. Yet someone like Karen must have feelings and emotional needs."

"She can masturbate!" Bettie was feeling very aggrieved. "I thought you'd heard about Ed and her. You can bet your husband did. Once he even covered for Ed when Ed was supposed to be playing golf, and wasn't. I don't know what it is about you, Angela. You never seem aware of what a cruddy world it is. You go around like one of those damned Christian Scientists. 'God's in his heaven, all's well with the world—crap. Tell one of them, like Carol Gaines, that you have a cold or pneumonia or are even dying and they give you that big sweetness and light deal. 'It really isn't pneumonia at all,' she'll tell you, 'it's just error that has hold of you!' "

Angela watched the maples and elm leaves floating to the ground, and rippling restlessly across the Kanaces' back lawn. She was only half-listening to Bettie's ravings. She smiled mindlessly when Bettie insisted that if Ed were having an affair with Angela, that would be understandable (and what's more she, Bettie, wouldn't have really minded). But Angela, lost in her own wonder, wasn't listening. Here was a private, fence-encircled world. Quiet, peaceful. Few people who lived in urban areas could afford such sylvan privacy. Yet, only in the best of the Kanaces' married years, when the kids were growing up, was this tiny world-within-a-world ever used. Coming through Bettie's living room, Angela had noticed a book titled *Living With More Zest in the Nest* . . . a guide to what to do with one's life after the children were gone and the nuclear family had deteriorated and became simply a bored husband and wife rattling together in their home, waiting for death or Godot or for the grandchildren to visit them. The grandchildren who drove them crazy and cluttered the place and made too much noise when they finally did arrive.

And she remembered Adam (was it last week . . . no, the week before) showing her some secondhand editions of J. H. Fabre's *The Life of The Spider* and Maurice Maeterlinck's *Life of the Bee*, and his *Life of the Ant*. "They're only a dollar each," he told her excitedly, and when she admitted to him she hadn't read them, he bought them for her. "You can't buy them in paperback," he said. "And that proves something or other. The man-world is so concerned with navel-gazing that the world of insects, pursuing their destiny, without reference to human beings . . . is boring to them. Yet, how can we understand ourselves when we ignore an unknown world in motion, the cosmos . . . in our own back yard . . . beneath our feet. I think we rush to the moon and the stars simply for the feeling of power it gives us to get there . . . not to really know about them except in a superficial way."

How could she explain Adam's magic world of curiosity to Bettie? How could she tell Bettie that, viewed with perspective, the total mystery of life made human problems, especially when they were self-induced, assume a relative significance; that it could even make it possible to laugh a little at one's concerned self?

"I've been doing a lot of reading and thinking lately," Angela said finally. A bubbly vision of herself flickered through her mind. Luxuriously naked, half her body stretched over Adam's naked body, his penis deep within her, his glasses on (looking a little like a professor), he was reading to her from a book called *The Prometheus Project*, a chapter on aging, and the kind of world that might be possible if human life were extended. What if man could live as long as five hundred years? She knew she couldn't communicate the idea to Bettie, the changed world it would be. Would monogamous marriage exist at all? Could one man and one woman stay together, forsaking all others, if they spent a hundred years together instead of a possible fifty?

When her thoughts did crystallize, she knew her words were partially Adam's words, happily copulating with the words in her mind and producing a wealth of offspring. "I don't think I would mind if Jim discovered another woman. Maybe our angle of vision is wrong. Most of us don't make any effort to understand love. Remember that novel *Love Story*, by Erich Segal. The wife died of leukemia, I

91

think." Angela shook her head. "But what if she had lived, Bettie? Would anybody have bought the book? Because then the only thing to cry about would be that their lives were boring duplicates of practically every other middle-class married life. I don't remember the characters' names but they certainly weren't the brightest people, even vis-à-vis each other. Had the wife lived, by the time they were in their thirties, their very different backgrounds and interests would have ripped them apart. Or, think about it another way. Let the book stand just the way Segal wrote it. Now add the next chapters that Segal didn't write. The man wouldn't mourn his dead wife forever. A few months, a year goes by, and he's going to find another woman, and before you can say Jack Robinson, he'll get married, have children, forget his first wife entirely. If Segal had written the next chapters, the book would have flopped. American women are very unrealistic about love."

"That's because most men are bastards." "Bettie sniffled. "Frankly, Angela, maybe I'm a little crocked, but I don't know what the hell you're trying to tell me."

Angela shrugged. "I was just wondering what would happen if you telephoned Jim and told him you'd changed your mind . . . you wanted to stop divorce proceedings. Then you could call Ed and tell him to come back home. You decided you love him, no matter what he has done . . . and if he has a little fun occasionally with Karen Ainsley . . . okay, you wouldn't mind sharing the wealth. In fact, since Karen must be lonesome, why not bring her around some evening and Ed could buy a bucket of Kentucky Fried Chicken and the three of you could all have a few drinks and all get squashed together."

Bettie stared at her, astounded. "Angela Thomas. You must be out of your mind. Ed is screwing the ass off that woman, and I'm supposed to love her?"

Angela laughed. "Why not? Thirty years from now we'll all be dead, or if any of us has any sex interest left they should write us up in the medical journals. Jim told me last night that Ed still loves you. He doesn't want a divorce. Think about it. Ed put his penis in another female's vagina and he discharged a dropper full of semen. Karen and he had a moment of physical ecstasy. But it's still Ed's penis, not Karen's, and after he washes it and if you're nice to him, he'll put it in you, and he'll tell you he loves you, too."

Bettie was shocked. "Angela, I don't know what's come

over you in the last month or so. You've either been reading some pretty wild books or keeping bad company. I don't think you believe a word you're saying. Wait until it happens to you. Then, you won't be so damned liberal."

Angela was conscious that weaving in and out of her thoughts as she talked with Bettie, she was really thinking, Janice. What was Janice really like? How would Janice respond if she discovered Adam was involved with another woman? If Adam didn't exist and Jim were having an affair, how would she have reacted? With fright and a feeling of insecurity, probably. Incongruously enough, Angela knew that her continuous fear that she and Adam might be recognized and Jim would discover what she was really doing on Thursday created her own environment of insecurity. In one breath, she could lose both Jim and Adam.

But Adam blithely ignored the possibilities. He embraced their love as a unit that somehow seemed to have both a present and a long future. In his words, their extramarital life "must have input . . . objective experiences beyond lovemaking that would give stability and strength to their private world." Madness, obviously, and unrealistic—how could you make a once a week love affair into a full life—but intriguing!

The second Thursday she had been captured by Adam's enthusiasm that they could begin by making a tour of Boston bookstores. "Not that we couldn't devote our six or seven hours today wholly to lovemaking." Adam had a pixie expression on his face. "After all, a man would be quite insane not to take care of a hungry love-person like you." Angela had responded to his teasing with a naïve solemn look of agreement. "But," Adam continued, "we must never stop searching for the larger objective. Ultimately, we should be able to merge our sexuality into every objective outside contact that we share. Thus, no matter what we may be doing together, or where we may be, we'll really be making love. The only fundamental difference will be that at a particular moment it might be inconvenient to take off our clothes."

They were in the Howard Johnson Motor Lodge. Laughing, she accused Adam of being a time-study man. They made love (or, as Adam insisted, "knew each other") between nine-thirty and eleven, ate lunch at Au Beauchamps, a tiny French restaurant on Beacon Hill, and then went on a tour of bookstores . . . Book Clearing

House, Paperback Booksmith, Lauriats, Old Corner, Brattle and Starr, and even the Federal Book Store in the Government Center. In each store Adam was greeted by someone—managers, clerks, cashiers—and ignoring her embarrassment and fear that they might be recognized, he calmly introduced her as Mrs. Adams. They staggered back to the motel with a load of books (which Angela insisted she couldn't take home all at once ... Jim knew she read a lot, but mostly she borrowed books from the Acton Public Library), and finally back in their Thursday room, laughing hysterically at their hectic pace they flopped panting on the bed. There wasn't time for a shower, but there was time to undress again and to breathe each other's special body odor, which she had to agree with Adam, occasionally at least, could create a most powerful aphrodisiac.

☆ 23 ☆

Thursday before Thanksgiving they were suddenly aware that they wouldn't be able to see each other for two weeks. (The last Thursday in November was for families not lovers, as unfortunately were most holidays.) Adam was pensive. "You've become a way of my life, Angela . . . today, let's have room service, a few drinks with lunch, and create a temporary Thursday womb in this uncertain world." Undressing, he remembered a poem. "Ah, Love! could you and I with Him conspire, to grasp this Sorry Scheme of Things entire, would we not shatter it to bits—and then remold it nearer to the Heart's Desire!" He grinned at her surprise. "In my callow youth, I used to learn poetry for the hell of it. I once knew most of the *Rubaiyat*."

"Did you recite poetry for Janice when you were at Harvard?" Angela knew the question sounded tacky. She wasn't jealous of Janice, past or present. How could she be? Jealousy demanded a one-to-one possessiveness. "I hope you understand. I think you know more about Jim than I know about Janice." She snuggled against his chest. "Oh, I'm not saying what I really mean. I guess what I want to say is I want your love, but not at Janice's expense."

Adam grinned at her. "Each person should love the people they love because they are unique. I love Janice because she's Janice. I love you because you could never be Janice. I suspect that you love Jim because he's not Adam."

Angela laughed. "One thing is certain, Jim and my relationship is on a different plane entirely. I'm much cooler and calmer with Jim . . . pragmatic, I suppose, because, after a long time together, a man and a woman do become pragmatic. It will happen to us." She looked at him sadly. "One Thursday soon, Angela will be put aside while Adams National or Janice takes precedence. It's the way the world is."

Adam lay on his back and stared at the ceiling. Angela twisted his pubic hair in little curls and kissed his nipple through a forest of hair. She explored his penis so tentatively that Adam was only slightly aware that it was growing bigger.

"One of the joys of living is synthesis—the relationship between seemingly unrelated, irrelevant ideas and things." He whispered into her shoulder, while his tongue tasted the warm hollows made by her clavicle bone. "That kind of approach to life takes a touch of madness. You're right. With me, at least, Janice is pragmatic. But I have a feeling when she plays golf with Jack Lovell she's quite existential, and that proves my point. Anyway, last night I was skimming the personal columns in *Boston After Dark* ..." Leaning on his elbow, Adam brushed his lips over Angela's nipples, enjoying their firmness and her large areolas, pinkish brown. "Janice wasn't interested. Perhaps she thought I should have outgrown my interest in man's basic loneliness and begin to pay attention to the reality of the obituary columns." For a moment he stared at Angela, entranced by her open-eyed attention to his words. It made it hard to concentrate on what he was saying. "Actually, I clipped the ad to show it to you. It's in my jacket pocket."

"Tell me, instead." Angela slid down so that her head was resting on his stomach. From this vantage point she didn't touch his penis with her fingers, but occasionally tasted it with her tongue. "I don't know whether it's your semen or me, but you taste like potato soup. Tell me about your clipping."

Enjoying the pure eroticism, Adam lightly rubbed her back. "The advertisement read approximately like this: 'Dynamic but frustrated, forty-one-year-old man wants daytime relationship with frustrated married or single woman. Discretion assured. Write Box Something-or-other.' "

Angela laughed. "Sounds like us. Sure you didn't write it yourself?"

Adam shook his head. "We're not in the same category. The thing that struck me is that there were numerous other advertisements in the same vein. Married people attempting separate adventures, couples looking for other couples. It begins early, with the youngsters using matching services or going to dating clubs where they can telephone the table of the opposite sex to get acquainted with each other. The act of finding a friend depends on the same mechanical manipulation as our total living environment. Anyway, I was wondering whether people seeking one another were really aware of the nature of their loneliness or how to resolve it together once they found each other."

Angela pouted her lips loosely around the tip of his penis. Adam had blossomed with a new erection.

"You little witch, I'm not sure I want to ejaculate again. But there isn't any doubt about one thing—I'll feel more comfortable inside you."

"No hurry," Angela murmured. "We've got hours. Concentrate on the thought you were pursuing."

Adam pulled her to him, kissed her breasts and lips, and reversed positions. "Maybe," he said, chuckling as he put his face against her belly, "this will give me a new perspective."

"I doubt it." Why did she feel so female . . . and bubbly alive? She curved her body so that her mouth was on an intersection with his penis. She held it firmly with her hand. "Don't worry, I'm really quite passive. If I put this silly fellow in my mouth now I'd choke to death. So I'll just gently kiss him. I'm waiting."

"For what?"

"For why Janice wasn't interested."

Adam kissed her delta and lay with his cheek on the inside of her calf. She couldn't see his face but she suspected he was grinning. His effervescence enveloped him . . . and her, too. "My God!" She heard his voice muffled as he kissed her upside-down. "You're something.

You look very lovely down here. I love you." He was silent a moment contemplating the amazement of the female. "If you let them, ideas can jump across wide synapses." His voice seemed far away, and it wasn't easy to concentrate because occasionally he stopped talking and lightly tasted her. "A few days ago I read an article in *Life* that told how President Nixon was enlisting Frank Borman, the astronaut, as a special Presidential representative to try and secure the release of prisoners of war held in North Vietnam. The writer spelled out his conviction that Nixon was enthralled with the astronauts. Presumably he identified with them because he had no sons, and even more because they epitomized the pioneer spirit. According to the writer, the President broods over a nation which has turned in on itself, has become spiritualless, ceased to explore, or be challenged by the physical environment." Adam kissed her vulva and tasted Angela with a quick nuzzling motion. Then he swung around, and took her in his arms. "A few weeks ago two men scaled the sheer cliff side of a mountain in the Yellowstone National Park . . . El Presidente. After an arduous week they got to the top and they were greeted by reporters and well-wishers who had come up to meet them on the side where there's an easy access road. Their answer as to why they did it was the old empty challenge: 'because it was there.' Adam laughed. "Astronauts, mountain climbers, professional football, baseball, and basketball players are part of the system that most of the people in this country empathize with. They are not rebels like us."

"We're worse . . ." Angela twinkled at him. "Jim occasionally accuses me of being one of the 'radical liberals.' Jim would rather see a John Wayne or Gregory Peck or Charlton Heston movie on television than go to see what he says is mostly 'freaky, way-out stuff.' If they ever made a sympathetic movie about people like us and Jim saw it, he would be convinced the society was going to hell."

Angela's voice deepened a little, and he sensed that she was imitating Jim in a warm, good-natured way. "Ange, we've got to get back to the old virtues. The day when a man believed in the work ethic, and had pride in his work and believed in honor, and the importance of a good name." She was silent a moment and he realized that there were tears in her eyes. "In Jim's book, what we are doing is about as bad as any bad guys could get."

Adam kissed the tears on her cheeks, and held her hand.

"Honey, I'm not so impervious as I may sound. Occasionally, I feel guilty. Janice and Jim could take up the collection together for us, and sing Hymn No. 138 to remind us of our sins. The trouble is I don't really believe they are sins, and that has something to do with the point I failed to get across to Jan."

"What was it?" As if she decided that she was beyond reclamation anyway she responded fervently to Adam's kiss, and burrowed into the curve of his shoulder . . . listening absent-mindedly, she played with his soft penis, enjoying its transformation to boyishness, as if it had forgotten, forever, its hard-driving urgency (less than a few minutes ago) to discover a vagina.

"I don't know if it makes sense to you, but I felt sad that our President was so one-dimensional, as are most of our political leaders. They can't see that the frustrated man, searching in the personal columns for the frustrated housewife, is really a pioneer. Instead of wondering how it feels to experience no gravity, or what the moon's surface is like, or to cling to a side of a mountain (all, incidentally, emotions that could psychologically be connected with a death wish), the really exciting adventure is to discover the layers of thinking, feeling, emoting in another human brain. Too many of our leaders are trying to recapture a nineteenth-century world, or a time even before that. The adventure of the twenty-first century is man. Imagine if I could relate to you so perfectly that the alpha-waves your brain is releasing in profusion could merge with my alpha-waves, and we could be even more aware of each other than we are."

Angela smiled dreamily. "How do you know my waves aren't theta-waves?"

Adam slipped his arm under her and blended his mouth with hers. Her calf glided over his and then as her buttocks swayed over his hand, she undulated against him in an erotic tidal rhythm. Their bodies touched lightly in gliding caresses, oh so lightly . . . seeking not fulfillment, but timelessness.

☆ 24 ☆

Though she had insisted that she never would, the Wednesday before Thanksgiving, Angela telephoned him at his office. Adam could hear the repressed sob in her voice. "Adam, I had to call you. I have such a sinking, hopeless feeling." She told him she could only talk a minute. She was in a pay station in the shopping center. Had she told him that Jim's mother and father were coming for Thanksgiving? That they had sold their home in New York, and were moving into a senior-citizen center? God, she couldn't remember what she had told him about her "real" life. In their beautiful fairy-tale Thursday existence there hadn't been time to be their dull, unglamorous selves.

"What could I do?" Angela sounded depressed. "Jim left it up to me. I feel badly about Lena and Gramp having nowhere to go. Jim's only sister is in California, and she lives in an apartment. I suppose I should have insisted that they come here to live ... but Jim wasn't enthusiastic. Oh, Adam, the least I could do was to invite them to stay until after Christmas, and now I'm trapped. There'll be no more Thursdays for us until after New Year's."

Adam heard the catch in her voice. The operator told her that her time was up. "Angela, give me the number in that phone booth. I'll call you back."

In a minute he heard her pick up the phone. "Adam ... Lena's in the car waiting. I can't take too long."

"Six weeks isn't going to separate us. I'll call you every day if you want."

"Adam, you can't. How could I talk with you sanely? Our telephone has four extensions. Someone might be standing underfoot, or I'd never know who might be listening on another phone. Robin won't be home for Thanksgiving. She going to a girlfriend's house in Westchester. Richy is staying at Dartmouth to do some studying. But Ruth will be home. She's bringing Bud. Jim's not happy about that. Then in two weeks they all will be home for the Christmas holidays." He heard her sigh. "It's all been a dream, hasn't it, Adam? You and I have no reality . . . no basis for existence. Adam . . . maybe I should just say good-bye."

"Angela!" It was J.Q.—not Adam—commanding her. "Wherever we're going, we're not saying good-bye over the telephone. You can find a way. Telephone me. A week from tomorrow morning. You got to a pay station once. You can do it again."

"Oh, Adam . . . what's the use?" She was crying now, and her voice sounded husky. "We're only kidding ourselves."

J.Q. stared at his phone. Should he agree with her? He intuited that she was offering him a way out. Masochistically? No, heroically. Angela had the ability to project herself into a role of quiet self-denial. *But he didn't.* They owed it to themselves to discover whether their need was the occasional delight of stolen fruits or whether their joy in each other ran deeper. He tried to explain it to her, and she listened, and she agreed when he reminded her that she had promised to give him a collection of her photographs.

"I want them now. You can mail them to me next week," he told her.

"I'll have to make new prints," she said. "Most of the good ones are framed and in the playroom."

"Is that a way of saying you don't want to?"

"No, I will. I'll work in the darkroom Monday."

"Do you have a cassette tape recorder?"

"Yes," she sniffled.

"Well, either telephone me next Thursday or send me a tape."

"To your office?"

"Why not? Angela . . . do you want to make love?"

"Oh, God! . . . Yes! Yes! I want to *know* you. Adam, please, I can't talk any longer."

"Angel-a, I love you. Give your Lena a hug. Tell her you were talking with your lover."

When she hung up, he tried to conjure the magic of her face, and he was altogether too successful. Troilus' soliliquy jumped into his mind, and he said the words aloud. "If no love is, O God, what fele I so? And if love is, what thing and which is he? If love is good, from whennes cometh my woo? If it be wikke, a wonder thynketh me. When every torment and adversite that cometh hym may

100

to me savory thinke, For ay thurst I, the more that ich it drynke.' "

"Reciting poetry, now, J.Q.?" For a moment Adam was startled, wondering how long Harry Carswell had been waiting unnoticed in his office. Obviously, he had been in another world not to have heard the door open. But J.Q. quickly replaced Adam. "I felt Chaucerian this morning . . . lusty!" He smiled mockingly at Carswell, noting that, as usual, Carswell was immaculately dressed: custom-made suit, polished shoes, perfectly knotted tie, white shirt. A heavy-built man, Carswell exuded a security and inner self-confidence that contrasted sharply with J.Q.'s casual attire. Particularly so when, like today, he had dressed Adam-style with a flamboyant striped shirt, wide floppy tie, and hush puppies. A few years older than J.Q., Carswell gave the impression that he was a man on the move. One day a story about his business acumen would appear in *Fortune* or *Dun's Review*. J.Q. knew that since Sam had come to work, a generational friction had developed between him and Carswell that neither of them made any attempt to ameliorate. He wondered if Carswell was coolly deciding that Adams National might be as good a springboard as any. In the past few months he had occasionally hinted that the company was vulnerable to a stockholder coup. A takeover, and when the smoke cleared away Carswell could be president and the Adamses, father and son, could be sent out to pasture.

"How do the November sales look?" J.Q. noticed that Carswell had a magazine in his hand. It was apparent there was something in it he wanted him to see.

"Sales are holding . . . it's not sales, it's profits." Carswell shook his head. "I estimate they'll be down twenty percent. When the story comes out that we may have to cut dividends, the stock will take a tumble."

J.Q. shrugged. None of this was news. It had been hashed over at the last directors' meeting. "We'll survive. We'll turn around with the economy."

"Did you see this editorial in the November issue of *Printing Magazine*? It's called *Pollution of the Mind*." Carswell opened the magazine. "Listen to this, I think it will interest you." Carswell read the words with slow and maddening emphasis: " 'Let's define pornography. It's whatever debases that singular sexual capability of man and woman to reproduce one of their own kind. It's whatever tears away at the family structure of a nation so

101

as to hold up to ridicule a common sexual right shared by husband and wife. It's whatever someone outside a family would use in an attempt to subvert the sexual values taught to a child by his parents. It's the portrayal of sex in such a manner as to make it an end purpose of life rather than a means toward strengthening the individual, contributing to the nation, and benefiting mankind.' " Carswell paused, obviously for dramatic effect, and then, since J.Q. was silent, continued reading. " 'We doubt that anyone will argue the point that when family life is disrupted, the result is a chain reaction of discord and discontent. Do the words sound familiar? Destroy the concept of family unity and you hit the foundation stone of the nation and civilization as we know it. That's what the printer should think about the next time he is approached by a literary pimp.' "

Momentarily as Carswell was reading, J.Q. wondered if perhaps Carswell or someone at Adams National was aware of his Thursdays with Angela. But what if they were? . . . Really, what business was it of Carswell's? If the ship was sailing a relatively smooth course, did the crew have the right to question the captain? J.Q. decided the simplest approach was not to react at all. Ultimately Carswell would reveal his hand.

Carswell dropped the magazine on his desk. "I'd think about this, J.Q. Remember Adams National isn't your private preserve. You have a responsibility to the stockholders. Some of them might not take too kindly to the fact that we have pumped over a hundred and fifty thousand dollars into this video diversion with no return in sight."

Suddenly, the direction Carswell was taking was apparent. "I think you're beating a dead horse, Harry," J.Q. said calmly. "The directors are all in agreement. We couldn't expect a return in the video area, if at all, for at least two years. It was a calculated gamble. I'm not pushing Sam's ideas . . ." J.Q. knew he was, but he wasn't about to concede that to Carswell. "For my money, since the Federal Communications Commission has taken the position that cable television was not only a common-purpose carrier, but a broad-band link that could be used in two-way communication, and could be expected to generate its own local programs, I've been convinced that Adams National could move into the gap. We're a peanut-size company, but if we stay abreast of things, we don't always have to be. The world is changing. Network television will take a back seat when you can dial into a central location and get any kind of program that you want." J.Q. stood up behind his desk, a signal that the discussion was over. "What we should really be doing is proposing a new stock offering of about twenty million dollars, so we could move in *now* and lay our own cable. It we did, we could dominate the Massachusetts market. Right at the moment we are just on the fringes of a major technological breakthrough. Believe me, Harry, five years from now network television will be on its way out. People are becoming so polarized, we'll have thousands of fractionalized markets. The technological age doesn't need or want mass markets. Like it or not, the breakthrough in cable television and home video cassettes will ultimately create an educational and political revolution in this country."

Carswell listened patiently, determined, obviously, to put J.Q. back on the track. J.Q. guessed Carswell was offering a kind of straw in the wind warning. Obviously one day he hoped to be able to say, I told you so. "J. Q., I'm not questioning cable television . . . or the potential in the future. I just want to remind you that Sam is spending money like a drunken sailor on what some stockholders may consider dubious video material. From the little I've seen, Sam is too left-oriented, both politically and sexually. This used to be a conservative New England company. Keep one thing in mind: I told you quite a few years ago when you started the expansion of Adams National that you either retained actual control, or one day you might jeopardize your position."

J.Q. shrugged. "At the time there was no choice; we needed every dime we could raise. My family still retains thirty-nine percent of the stock."

Carswell met his cold look with an equally frigid stare. "I don't have to remind you, Charlie McMasters has at least twelve percent of the stock. Look, J. Q., I'm just trying to keep things cool. Dividends will tell the story. A dissident group of stockholders could be mobilized. Things could get pretty hot around here."

"And you'd go along with McMasters?"

Carswell suddenly grinned. "J.Q., I like screwing as much as any man . . . but all this blatant sex disgusts me. What's more, I'll wager most of the Adams National stockholders would agree with me. Our customers are a pretty square lot. Financial printing and sex aren't good bedfellows. Talk with Sam yourself. Find out a little bit more about what he's doing."

When Carswell left, J.Q. read the editorial in full. The conclusion irritated him. According to the editor of the magazine, Jeremiah Flynn, sex was not an end-purpose of life, but rather "a means toward strengthening the individual; contributing to the nation and benefiting mankind." It sounded so logical. The role sex should play in life was unquestioned by most religious and secular morality. Most of the leaders of society would agree with Carswell . . . certainly all the business leaders. Sex was something a man and woman did together to have children and get genital relief. A biological imperative. Afterwards, when their minds were clear, men (not women despite the efforts at Women's Liberation) could get down to the serious business of "working" (or fighting wars) until finally the mystique of work became an end in itself. Without his "work" man lost his purpose ("Without my walking stick, I'd go insane . . . I'm not a man without my cane"). Instead of being joyful, interhuman play; instead of being a respite from the never-ending conundrum of life; a marvelous glimpse in ultimate mysteries that might actually be; sex and the coupling of man and woman had become a devalued, trivial escape mechanism.

Was it possible, as humans approached the twenty-first century after Christ, that human brains could gain a new transcedence over their animal inheritance? A new breakthrough that would reveal the truth. Copulation was the essence, the prime purpose of life! Could human beings discover that thinking brains were capable of making the act of love an act of complete intimacy, surrender, and wonder. A prime peak-experience and insight that was continuously renewable. This man and this woman . . . Angela and Adam, Angela and Jim, Jonathan and Janice, Janice and . . . ?"

Adam burst into happy laughter at his thoughts. Of course . . . Janice and Jack . . . arithmetic progressions of man and woman locked together in an ongoing process that beyond all else was the pinnacle purpose of life. The gross national product, at least so far as it represented the accumulation of junk, was simply gilding the lily.

Carswell, wake up! Adam is in charge!

☆ 25 ☆

Rather than telephoning Sam on the interplant phone, he decided it would be simpler to interrogate both Sam and Yael on the way home. While Sam could have hired Yael to work with him at Adams National, after they were married, Yael had decided to keep the job she had when Sam first met her, as assistant producer at V.T.R. Educational Films, a fledgling company in video recordings for schools and colleges. Without being in each other's hair, they were working in the same vineyard. The cross fertilization and input into their marriage created what they called a "livelong marriage." When J.Q. had questioned the word "livelong" as meaning tedious, Yael assured him with a grin that there was an older meaning that meant durable.

J.Q. realized that in the past month he had paid little attention to Sam or new developments in the video research department. It wasn't wholly his preoccupation with Angela, but rather the day-to-day involvement with over-all strategy for Adams National. Adam might stand aside and wonder at the folly of it, but someone at the upper levels of any organization spent a good portion of his time planning for the future one or two years hence. While J.Q. didn't like to think of the ramifications of this approach, as a necessary philosophy of business survival, it was an undeniable fact that a business organization either grew or it declined. There were no midpoints, no static times or plateaus that could be maintained. The economics of capitalism from the government down to the entrepreneur was predicated on an ever-increasing production of economic wealth. If you denied the value of much of the wealth that was created, if you felt in your bones that this way was insanity, it didn't matter. Both the ends and the means and the name of the game was profit. It made no difference, really, at what level you played the game; you couldn't escape, except to die or dare to drop out. For most it was easier to die.

But these were grim thoughts. Despite the Carswell episode, J.Q. was in a buoyant mood. To both his and

Janice's happy surprise, Yael and Sam had decided to spend the Thanksgiving weekend in Cohasset. The frosting on the cake came with Keane's telephone call from New York last Sunday. Keane was coming home for the holidays, and perhaps he would be back in the Boston area permanently. He was considering a job with the Boston Symphony Orchestra. It would give him time to compose, and he was interested in organizing a performing group on his own. Despite J.Q.'s dire warnings that Boston audiences would support a six-million-dollar basketball stadium, but would let a small theater company like the Charles Playhouse bleed to death for a few hundred thousand dollars, Keane was optimistic. Boston seemed to have a brighter future for small-scale live performances than New York City.

Keane told them he was bringing a girl home. "She's studying ballet at Juilliard. We'll be home Wednesday afternoon about four. And for God's sake, when we arrive don't give us any of that old-fashioned mother and father stuff. In fact, don't say anything. She's sleeping with me in my room." No. He wasn't married . . . His girl wasn't even sure she wanted to get married. She was a dancer. Dancers didn't keep house, or want to get married at twenty. For God's sakes, he was only twenty-two!

Janice was happy that she didn't have a daughter. It was difficult enough to decide about post-marital morality, let alone have an unmarried daughter who was floundering for answers, but she saved this observation for Jon. Keane was coming home! Her family would be reunited again.

Though they had promised to eat dinner with the Lovells (whose children were spending Thanksgiving with their various in-laws), there was a simple solution which Janice immediately put into effect: invite Jack and Barbara to spend the weekend with them. Janice told Jon that it would be a chance to experience their home as the kind of happy commune Jon had occasionally envisioned for her.

J.Q. guessed that Janice's enthusiastic preparations for an old-time New England celebration were partially motivated by their occasional differences over whether they should sell their house in Cohasset and give in to the inevitable. One began married life in an apartment and moved to the suburbs for the children. The reverse steps were an apartment again, and then a room in the womb of a home for senior citizens. The Adamses were finally back where they started with no young children, and fewer illusions. It was interesting that neither he nor Janice remained for long on the one side of the argument. The pros and the cons of giving up their home carried too many conflicting emotions, and deep roots that were hard to sever. Right from the beginning (three years after they were married, with just two boys and a dog) the house had been too large. The main section, with a rambling fieldstone exterior, had been built nearly two hundred years before by a former patriarch of Boston and the South Shore. The first remodeling by a later owner had added two newer sections, one for three additional bedrooms and one for an artist's studio with a huge north skylight. The studio had ultimately intrigued Janice into taking up art and painting as a hobby to make the house "somewhat practical." The living room, flanking one end of the house, sixty by forty feet, was definitely not practical. With a fieldstone walk-in fireplace on the long wall, and a small stage on the far end, which had been added on by a former owner who liked orchestral music (and years before had invited the entire Boston Symphony Orchestra and the conductor Koussevitzky to practice there), the room could have been turned into a mini-theater. Janice had decorated it by arranging the furniture in several intimate clusters with the main gathering area centered around the fireplace. But after the boys had gone to college they rarely used the living room. Other than the possibility of screwing naked in front of a roaring fireplace (an idea which, after they tried it once, Janice rejected as being kind of silly and not anywhere near so comfortable as a bed), it was not a room for dyadic intimacy. Besides there were ten other rooms, and Jon usually "holed up" in his library after dinner.

Perhaps to a great extent the character of the house created the people who lived in it. Because she had her own studio, Jan had adopted the image of an artist and had finally become a competent painter, specializing in New England sea-coast scenes. Sam and Keane, who for years kept the house filled with their friends, operated on the assumption that the living room was their own private club and intimate theater. Long before they went to college, intrigued by the real stage with real footlights and a curtain, they became entrepreneur entertainers, producing plays and running home movies for an audience of enthusiastic kids, whose parents were often incensed by "the rich Adams kids" who charged admission, and once ran a "stag movie" for a mixed audience of fascinated high school kids.

When Sam got married, and Keane pursued his music career to New York, Jon had suggested, with enough seriousness to startle Janice, that they could adopt a black family from Roxbury . . . not just orphans but a complete family, or if Jan didn't like that idea they could start all over again and have another family, or they could turn the house into a commune. Quickly rejecting these mad schemes, especially the thought of getting pregnant again (abhorrent idea), Janice countered with her own proposals. Why not offer the living room to a small theatrical group? Or why couldn't they start a colony for a group of selected writers and artists . . . the Adams Colony? Or if Jon rejected those ideas, why not invite the Lovells, who were in the same predicament, to sell their big house in Graniteville and move in with them? And, since it seemed the "in-thing" to do, if Jon wanted occasionally to sleep with Barbara (who would be delighted), Janice would give him permission.

J.Q. chuckled as he remembered the seriousness with which Janice had offered him Barbara. Was she suggesting a trade so she could go to bed with Jack? Maybe she and Jack were actually having an affair. If she was, he could understand that, but Barbara's lush figure, in striking contrast to lean Janice, was an insufficient inducement.

"How do you know Barbara would like the idea?" he demanded.

Janice assured him that he must be very dense not to see the obvious. Barbara adored him.

"What would I say to Jack? 'How about it, old man? Tonight you take my wife, and I'll take yours'?" It wasn't being quite fair. He guessed that Janice, after seeing one of those sophisticated movies devoted to wife-swapping, would have enjoyed a discussion of the possibilities, but while he could imagine himself in bed making love to Barbara, it was afterwards that bothered him. What would they talk about? Barbara was a flit-brain. He probably wouldn't have to talk at all. Just listen to oceans of nonsense. If Barbara had been Angela, what then? But then Jack would have to be Jim. There really was only one good solution. If Jim met Barbara and they liked each other, and the good Lord could attend to a three-couple reshuffling, it would be fascinating to play the new game . . . at least Adam thought so.

But whatever their reality might be . . . probably as simple as staying entrenched in their Cohasset home . . . for Janice, the Thanksgiving weekend was a showcase performance to prove that given the proper ingredients, the big house could offer its own "Adams-reasons" for being.

Driving him to Boston this morning, so that she could do some last-minute shopping (Sam and Yael would drive him out tonight), Janice was bubbling, new-bride alive. "I know it's silly," she said, "but for the first time in a long time I'm looking forward to something. It's amazing how simple the ingredients of happiness are." Janice's enthusiasm flickered over her face in tiny smiles, impossible to restrain. "I've got a dozen things to buy in the North End. Fresh fruits, vegetables . . . Yael asked me if I would get a few gallons of hard cider. Sam told her that he wanted to drink like an old-time Adams . . . I hope that means he will leave the marihuana alone. Jon, you ask him to for me. No grass. He wouldn't have it, if you hadn't been so insane to grow it. I heard it's hard to get and very expensive." She nudged him playfully. "Really, I'm not a spoilsport. But that damned stuff makes everybody so remote, wrapped up in their own little worlds. And anyway, I can't smoke it. It hurts my throat. And the Lovells will be shocked. I've never told a soul. It scares me to even let close friends like the Lovells know we have it. . . . Oh, and I forgot to tell you, Sam talked with Keane. He's elated that the boat is still in the water. If the weather is as balmy as it has been, they want to sail to Plymouth early tomorrow morning. We can have dinner late, around four o'clock. Maybe we can all sail over with them. Sam said he'd drive the station wagon to Plymouth tonight. The boys could tie the boat up at the dock and sail it back Friday."

Janice shrugged. "I'm not too enthusiastic about the Plymouth Adventure, as Sam calls it, particularly by boat. The weather is too unpredictable. What's more I hear a group of full-blooded Indians are going to demonstrate at the Rock and at the Mayflower to protest the treatment of American Indians. I'm not so stupid. That's why Sam and Yael want to be there."

109

☆ 26 ☆

Walking through the plant, wishing his workers a Happy Thanksgiving, shaking hands with them and inquiring about their families, J.Q. wondered how much Sam's rebellion was a reflection of his own attitudes. What would his employees think if they knew the real Jonathan Quincy Adams wasn't the hard-shelled Puritan he seemed to be? Few of them knew anything about what was going on in the video department. Occasionally someone would ask him how Sam was doing. "Hear we're moving out of printing into TV." But mostly at the level of hourly workers, the employees did their jobs and had little interest in the future, except somehow to earn more money and work less.

It occurred to J.Q., as he was talking with the women in the bindery, that many of them were younger, or at least no older than Angela or Janice. Was it the access to more money, or more leisure, that made it possible for some women to maintain the appearance of sexuality into their sixties? Most of these females were married, most had to work. More than half of the middle-class families in the United States would drop into a poverty income level unless the wife worked. Was it work or continual worry about money that made many of these women in their forties appear sexless? He would guess that much of their in-bed offerings were an accommodation for the male, a sense of marital duty rather than a paean to life. Most females past forty seemed to have turned off sex and taken up eating. The lithe young women of today, feminine and provocative in their youth—twenty years from now, would they emulate their mothers? If that happened, then neither the sexual revolution nor Women's Liberation would have accomplished much. He couldn't help grinning at his thoughts. What man really needed was a new kind of genital affinity with life. One day the medical profession might even discover that sparkling, unrestrained, natural sexuality was not only the key to youthfulness but to longevity. Atrophy from disuse affected the entire psyche.

As J.Q. examined jobs in various stages of completion, and his surface consciousness checked the efficiency and productivity of the Adams National operation, a parallel line of thinking merged in his mind. Perhaps in a small way he could contribute to the beginnings of a new kind of world. A happier sexual world could only flourish in a better work environment. This year Thanksgiving weekend encompassed the Friday after. It was part of a proposal that J.Q. was exploring with Adams National employees and the union to shift the work week to a ten-hour day that would begin Monday at seven in the morning, and end Thursday at five in the afternoon. The four-day, forty-hour week not only offered three-day weekends, but five or six times a year, with the addition of the regular Monday holidays, a worker would have four vacation days in a row. As a further logical development, instead of two- and three-week vacations, crowded into summer months, it would be possible for some workers to take their normal vacation in three or four increments of two weeks each by spreading their present vacations. Thus a worker who had earned an annual four-week vacation, instead of taking it at one time could work twelve weeks and have two weeks off, without sacrificing his regular three-day weekends.

Because the printing of financial data for corporations in the form of new prospectuses and annual reports was often on an extremely rapid service basis, J.Q., by giving support to a four-day week, was in conflict with several of his executives. Carswell had suggested that it was another of J.Q.'s subtle ways of bucking the tide. It was the kind of business innovation that became rebellion, and opened a company wide to competition until the rest of the business and industrial world joined the insanity. Adams National, in Carswell's views, could only be a follower not an innovator.

As for his own feelings, J.Q. silently agreed that Carswell's belief in work as the salvation of man had some merit (particularly in a society where the more leisure a person had, the more it was squandered on spectator amusements), but lately when Carswell or Bill Oakes assumed the role of *bête noire*, he had to restrain Adam from taking command and suggesting "the Angela-solution" . . . a once a week adventure in defenseless self-discovery with a member of the opposite sex. A joy not only for those in his age and income grouping, many

111

of whom might be in a position to commit Thursdays as well as Fridays to the enjoyment of a second love, but an opportunity for a new kind of interpersonal growth for the average working man and woman who would be able, at the very least, to devote Fridays to an additional life-style. Since, in any case, this would involve a maximum of two-sevenths of any particular person's life, it could solve, in an active way, the problem of what to do with one's increased leisure, and it certainly would be much more enjoyable than spending empty hours gazing at television.

Following his flight of fancy wherever it might lead, Adam wondered why, ultimately, a socially approved second kind of marriage commitment couldn't develop, permitting every husband and wife, after some years of marriage, to enter into a second marriage relationship. Tentatively, until he could think of a better term for it, Adam called it *duogamy*. Carried to its logical conclusions, husbands, wives, and lovers would all be married to each other. It was a chuckling thought, but sadly, at the moment, Angela was the only one he could ever tell it to.

He was still surprised at how quickly Angela and Thursdays had dovetailed into the fabric of his life. Leaving aside that he was taking an extra day a week off (excusable as an executive prerogative, if he needed an excuse; or as partial recompense for the years he had devoted seventy hours a week to establishing the company), the big question was still unanswered. Was his behavior immoral? The moral approach was easy to rationalize. He didn't love Janice less. In fact, knowing Angela had actually made it possible to rethink his relationship with Janice. Perhaps, even more, it had involved him in a reconsideration of commitment and what commitment could mean in expanding the quality of interpersonal relationships, from marriage to work orientation. No. He had no moral guilt, and he suspected that Angela, despite her fears, was morally untroubled. Perhaps some new kind of two-way polygamous structure was a basic human need. Not spouse-swapping—rather, a partially structured spouse exchange made viable by deeper commitment than casual adultery. Why not a morality based on St. Augustine's statement? *"Love God and do as you like"* . . . and for God, substitute Man . . . one and the same.

The real problem, of course, was ethical. Angela had summed it up. "My relationship with you seems so good and normal that occasionally I react to Jim as I would to a father, or mother. I want to tell him and have his approval."

☆ 27 ☆

Sam drifted into J.Q.'s office at four-thirty to wait for Yael, who would pick them up in the station wagon. Without giving J.Q. the opportunity to tackle him, Sam immediately took the offensive. Had Jake finished the book, *The Greening of America*? J.Q. nodded. Charles Reich's study, based on the changing consciousness of Americans since the founding of the country, and dealing with the mindlessness of the corporate state, had become required upper-echelon-executive reading. For many businessmen, Reich's "love affair" with the younger generation (he was forty-two) was both a kind of betrayal and a way of knowing the enemy!

At the moment, J.Q. felt like playing the role of devil's advocate for the Establishment. A sop for his irritation with Sam for not being more circumspect with Harry Carswell. He knew that Sam delighted in baiting Carswell. He didn't seem to understand that purring tigers could bite your arm off. "I enjoyed the book." He leaned back in his chair, momentarily wondering why fathers couldn't hug their bearded sons, if they felt like it. "But Reich is typical of many liberals, who fail to recognize the kind of world they are predicating would require a dictatorship." J.Q. knew that he sounded ponderous, but he couldn't help playing the role of elder statesman. "Reich gives you the feeling that the revolution by what he terms Consciousness III is inevitable; then, a few chapters later, he gives the impression that to really make it come about, the blue-collar worker must first be converted to the new awareness. According to him, all you have to do is say the right words and the 'hardhats' will jump on the bandwagon."

J.Q. knew Sam enjoyed the fun of father and son mind-boggling each other. "To tell the truth, Sam, Reich's background is probably similar to yours . . . upper middle class. Neither of you really have any idea of what makes lower-income people tick. Reich pits what he calls Consciousness I, the American Horatio Alger dream, the laissez-faire society created by the Carnegies, Vanderbilts, Fisks and Goulds and their like, and Consciousness II, the belief in an impersonal, all-powerful, fascist-style industrial state, against the coming millenium of Consciousness III, supposedly your generation's deeper understanding and awareness of the great new age of nonmaterialism and human self-actualization."

J.Q. shrugged, trying to erase a picture of Angela, naked in his arms. She was shaking her head wistfully, wondering why he was being so obtuse today. "Don't think I'm not for Reich's kind of world, Sam. But ultimately, you can't have any world without structure. Near the end of the book Reich says that even a millionaire would be better off if he chose liberation instead of the plastic world of material wealth. 'If he exchanged wealth, status, and power for love, creativity, and liberation he would be far happier and he would make a good bargain.'"

J.Q. chuckled, and since Sam seemed to be listening somewhat placidly, he uncovered his bigger artillery. "There's two problems here. The millionaire might be able to give up what he has because from experience he really comprehends the shallow rewards of materialism. But the low-income man will be hardest to convince. Status and power and money to buy all of those nice material conveniences and gadgets is everything he has ever worked for. It's the American Dream . . . and nobody, particularly blacks or long-haired intellectuals, is going to make him give us his dreams. The second fundamental ecological fact is even more important, and Reich and most Utopians overlook it. For example, I don't think you would deny the importance of sewage systems. Yet, I have a feeling that you and Reich would consider an engineer, obsessed with sewage-disposal problems to the exclusion of "recapturing his humanity," a very dull fellow. If this engineer went a step further in his pursuit of solutions and invented what is now a crying need, a new kind of home sewage that reprocesses urine and packages and deodorizes shit right in the home or apartment building instead of wasting gallons of clean water to flush the excrement into our rivers and oceans, and if he was motivated to invent this process by a desire for materialistic gain, wouldn't you categorize him as one of Reich's throwbacks to Consciousness I?"

114

J.Q. grinned, pleased with his own perspicacity. "Now here's the point: if you cite the historical destruction of our natural resources as one example of the need for a revolution, you overlook the fundamental point. What kind of value structure is the new society, or the New Left, or Consciousness III going to offer Joe Smith to get that home sewage cabinet invented? Carswell would say profits, that personal monetary gain and personal materialism are the only motivating incentives that work. Maybe you have some other answer. But unless your new society develops a structure that intrigues people and rewards them for their effort, we'll all be up to our ass in our own shit".

Sam whistled. He clapped his hands in mock appreciation. Before he could answer, the intercom buzzed and announced that Yael had the station wagon backed up to the shipping door to load Sam's video equipment. Sam hugged J.Q. "By God, Jake, you've missed the point. That magnificent shit box won't be invented by just one Joe Smith. One little guy doesn't invent anything anymore. It will take hundreds of minds working together, all of them knowing that crapper is more important than supersonic transports or trips to the moon or ABM's ... And that's what we're going to do at Adams National! Tell them why!"

☆ 28 ☆

Yael greeted them from the shipping platform, where she was helping one of the Adams National employees load the station wagon with portable video cameras, playback equipment, and two monitors, which Sam was borrowing for the weekend from the Adams National video studio.

J.Q. waited until Sam was on the expressway, headed toward Cohasset, before he introduced the subject of Carswell. Sitting between them, Yael watched J.Q.'s reflection in the windshield, an amused smile on her face.

"You were supposed to keep me posted on what's going on in the video area." J.Q. was feeling a little irked, but he wasn't sure whether it was because of Sam or Carswell.

115

"What in hell kind of sex tapes have you produced, anyway? Carswell is ready to call in the fuzz. If you must go in for sex, why do you have to wave a red flag in front of a bull?"

Sam chuckled. "Harry's a pussy-footing ass. He's shocked as hell, not just at the tape I showed him but everything else that is going on in the studio . . . beginning with the six video cameras we've bought, plus all the other video source material. He's scribbling it down in his big account books in red ink, waiting for me to drown in it." Sam was driving at a pace that reflected his anger. It didn't make J.Q. feel any more at ease. "Yael and I made a video film on our own . . . at our own expense. Oh, we used the studio, and the electricity, and some of the fellows helped us, but there was no payroll expense for Adams National. I did it that way to keep you out of trouble. The corporation still owns the tapes, if it wants them. It's a half-hour tape. We call it *Oceanic Love*. I showed Harry the first few feet of the tape. Yael posed for us naked. The original source cameras explore her body simultaneously from three different locations with a unique visual intimacy that even I, for example, able to know Yael from only one perspective, have never experienced. Using a number of video techniques, keying, wiping, debeaming, inserting images into each other, you, I, we—the viewer—merge into Yael's breasts and vulva, and slowly float into her vagina. Whirling into her womb in amniotic fluid, we finally unite with her brain in search of a cosmic consciousness."

Sam was smiling now. As he spoke he slowed the car down. "While this is happening I appear in the form of Siva, with three eyes and a lovely erection. Siva is the Hindu god of destruction who is concomitantly creator, since continuous change implies creation as well as destruction. Slowly, I dissolve into the ultimate female principle, which in Hindu cosmogony is feminine . . . Sakti." Sam was silent for a moment. "Essentially the film is beyond word description. It's a mystic experience based on ancient Tantric beliefs in maithuna, or sexual intercourse, as a religious experience."

Yael squeezed J.Q.'s arm. "We've got the tapes with us. And we've got a special surprise for you and Jan. Keane did the music for *Oceanic Love*. We sent him the tapes. He has a friend at WNEW who ran it for him while he composed the score. Sam just did the synchronization last night, so we can all see it together. The trouble with Harry Carswell is he probably never saw a vulva in his whole life."

Sam was bubbling with laughter. "It's worse than that, Yael. I'll bet he screws with the lights off, and his wife only opens her legs one inch and tells him to hurry and get it over with."

"He certainly didn't think it was very funny when I told him the vulva was the other lovely face of the female, and like a human female face, no two vulvas were alike ... or no two penises, for that matter."

J.Q. groaned. He guessed that Sam had given Carswell what Sam and Yael called the "honest sex" treatment, calmly saying all the words that Carswell had been trained from childhood were obscene. But he had no idea it had gone this far.

"Don't worry, Jake." In the dim light from the dashboard he could see the warm smile on Yael's face. "You'll love this tape ... so will Janice."

The first day Sam had brought Yael to Cohasset flashed into J.Q.'s mind. For a swift second as he grinned back at her, it was three years ago and Sam was introducing them. An erect young girl from Israel, a Sabra. Yael's bearing was still military, a carryover from her service with the Army. Much in love, Sam had told them he was going to marry Yael, even if he had to become an Israeli citizen. Yael had been in the United States as an exchange student for a year, but she still wasn't at all sure she could grasp the American way of life. She was uneasy, too, about a sense of duty to her own country. When she finally agreed to marry Sam and become a United States citizen, she told him it was because he was like his father ... essentially Jewish. Laughing, she suggested that his father's real surname must have been Adamsky. It wasn't Jon's appearance. No one could mistake J.Q. Adams for anything but a damned Yankee. Rather it was his intensity, and driving belief in learning. "Every time you get wound up in discussions with me or Sam," she told him, "you remind me of Jake Epstein, my favorite professor at Jerusalem University. He taught Philosophy. I was really in love with him, but he wouldn't sleep with me. He said he was too old."

So for Yael, J.Q. became Jake. J.Q. smiled at his memories. Angela, too, had nearly named him Jake. The boys, who had never felt easy with "Dad" or "Pop," had quickly adopted this new manifestation of their father. Essentially, wasn't Sam trying to evoke the same idea when he said that for the first time he had seen Yael in a new dimension? Human beings needed multiple images, multiple names—for themselves. Different names became new avenues for self-discovery. Both the "namer" and the "named" could see each other from different viewpoints.

J.Q. suddenly realized that he had lost the thread of the conversation between Sam and Yael. Yael was questioning Sam on video techniques in a language and at a technical level that was impossible for him to follow. He sensed that technique and philosophy were merging to create an entirely new art form. "If you're going to have a glimmer of understanding of some of the things Adams National is underwriting, you'd better read Gene Youngblood's *Expanding Cinema*," Sam said. "Really, Jake, it's more than film or videotape, it's intermedia; a blending of all the art forms into one complete kinaesthetic experience. There's hundreds of men and women all over the world merging sculpture, music, dance, painting, and the life-flow itself, by using a combination of film, videotapes, and the computer in a search to rediscover human consciousness. The joy for Yael and me is that while a great beginning has been made, and there are already hundreds of tapes and films that have gone way beyond anything any of us ever experienced in this life, we still are only on the threshold. Ultimately, a Michelangelo of intermedia techniques will appear. An artist who has the breadth of vision to create in visual motion a new conceptualization of the world."

When she spoke, Yael was as excited as Sam. "You have to understand, Jake, that from the beginning, movie and television forms of storytelling have simply been extensions of stage drama. The basic techniques are exactly the same. The author of the play or the movie, or the novel, is following time-worn structures that produce a *known conditioned response*. The audience is expected to respond with tears or laughter or fear, and up to now it has. The viewer is as programmed as Pavlov's dog. Some of the films we have made are simply a kinaesthetic experience completely removed from storytelling. We believe we can bring about, via film and videotape, an entirely new kind of subjective understanding of each other as human beings. We can create a moving, in-depth experience that goes deeper into human consciousness than any art ever produced in the world."

118

Sam, inching the car along the expressway, enlarged on Yael's thoughts. "Right now, Jake, it would be possible to experience us from the God-viewpoint. A wormlike five o'clock exodus. . . . Thousands of people being slowly exuded from the womb of their mother city. Scurrying humans trying to find a temporary birth in the suburbs. Men and women not really waking up in the morning to go to work, but returning to the city to die, and then at four or five to be born all over again." Sam chuckled. "Through video techniques, the most important of which is probably instantaneous superimposition, or sequential montage, an artist could translate my analogy into a nonverbal, moving imagery that might give us a new glimpse of ourselves."

When Sam paused with his ideas, Yael jumped into the breach. J.Q. liked to listen to them catalyze each other. Because of their common interests, input became throughput. Yael and Sam were a perfect team. "All you have to do, Jake," Yael was saying, "is to go see some of the current crop of movies. You'll soon realize the old-style movie story is running out of gas. There's been a quarter century of television exposure to movie plots. Kids, in the United States at least, can no longer be conned. The television generation not only can predict the plot, but can cue the actor's lines, giant-steps ahead of the author, or the poor actor, who in many cases becomes an empty puppet. He can no longer believe the worn, trumped-up misery he's supposed to bring to life. There are no new stories. But something sinister has been happening. Because of instantaneous exposure to the whole world, man seems to be in the process of acting out the old stories in real life. There isn't a day goes by that 'news' doesn't have the style and content of old movie plots. A senator drives off a bridge and kills a woman who is not his wife and with whom he was probably having an affair; the Jordanians capture our jet planes and hold hundreds of passengers hostage and as a by-product kick off a civil war, in which thousands are killed; our Army, under the order of the President, flies helicopters into enemy territory to rescue prisoners of war in an episode that only needed Gregory Peck in the chopper to make it indistinguishable from a Hollywood plot; in Detroit a man kills his daughter and two other kids in such a perfect reenactment of Joe Curran in the movie *Joe* that the judge insists both the prosecuting and defense attorney see the picture before

119

the trial." Yael shook her head. "Temporarily, moving pictures are surviving on a pent-up voyeur-demand to see how people look when they are fucking ... which is really a hidden need to see how they themselves look fucking."

"The problem is that we live in the age of instant overexposure," Sam said. "We have begun to equate the phenomena with people themselves. Every kind of human interrelationship is quickly reduced to trivia. The R movies don't show you the actor's genitals, but seeing their behinds or tits quickly gets as boring as seeing penises plunging into vaginas in the X movies. What Yael and I have tried to do in *Oceanic Love* is to visually blend a male and female at a new level, at the height of their consciousness. Once that blending has taken place, the next step is to merge two consciousnesses into the cosmic consciousness. This is a religion as old as man. It is actually codified in some of the Tantric mantras. A love yoga ... in the original meaning of yoga—'to join.'"

"Incidentally," Yael said, "not to change the subject, but Sam showed me those pictures of you with the Hare Krishna dancers."

J.Q. wondered if Yael could see the shocked expression on his face. He'd forgotten all about those pictures. They were in a brown kraft envelope at the bottom of the "things to do" basket on his desk. Why in hell had Sam been looking through that stuff? What's more, he had a damned nerve to bring them home to Yael. Somehow, he managed to listen to Yael without reacting verbally.

"Whoever took those pictures of you would understand everything Sam and I are trying to tell you. Maybe not in the technical jargon, but intuitively. The processing of those negatives into the final prints was a work of subjective art." Yael smiled at him. "Jake is in those pictures ... the Jonathan Q. Adams that most people are unaware of. ... A beautiful job of subjective photography."

Before J.Q. could recover from his surprise, happy that in the muted light from the dashboard neither Yael nor Sam could see the obvious question in his mind, Sam said, "We could use someone like that in the studio. I hope you don't mind that I borrowed the pictures. I was looking for the invoice on the last TV camera. Carswell said it was on your desk for okay. I want to hold up payment until Fairchild comes through with a few missing items. Anyway, when I found those pictures last Thursday, I meant to ask you about them. I brought them home to show

Yael. The're in my briefcase. Who is Thomas in Acton? . . . Male or female?"

"Female." J.Q. decided to pass it off lightly. . . . How much did Sam know really about Angela? Had he seen them together? "She's a woman who enjoys photography as a hobby. A housewife. She was quite embarrassed when she realized that I had seen her take my picture."

"Maybe I should give her a ring," Sam mused. Irritated, J.Q. wondered how he could divert Sam into other areas. "What's her first name?"

"Alice, Abigail . . ." J.Q. muttered. "I really didn't pay too much attention to her. I can assure you she's not the type for the kind of stuff you're doing." Working on the theory that the best defense was a good offense, J.Q. attacked. "Besides, you've got a payroll of over seventy-five thousand a year, now. Since we okayed this video diversion, Adams National is in for over three hundred thousand. No more people . . . no more overhead until you change the money flow."

"Jesus," Sam exploded. "Don't get misled by *Oceanic Love*. Someday it will bring back the entire A.N. investment. But in case it doesn't, you know damned well we are building a library of video cassettes of management and sales techniques that Oakes has already sold to a dozen top companies. The celebrity cassettes of composers, artists, and writers will be in every library in the country. If Adams National is going to get in an uproar, I'll get a group together and we'll buy out the entire investment with a profit for the company."

J.Q. was still trying to soothe Sam as he turned into the driveway. At least he had diverted him temporarily from the subject of Angela. Angela working for Adams National! Ye Gods! That *was* insanity. Crazily enough, there wasn't any doubt in his mind that if Sam could offer her a job, Angela would be intrigued by the idea. But then what would happen to Thursdays?

Sam drove the station wagon in front of the three-car garage. Keane's Volkswagen and the Lovell's Cadillac were parked in front of them.

A little upset by the sudden economic-business dueling between Sam and his father, Yael tried to clear the air. She asked J.Q. if he knew how the Mormons spent Thanksgiving. J.Q. admitted that he didn't.

"Well, the day before Thanksgiving, around midnight, in the old days, the Mormons would organize a big hunt-

121

ing expedition. Then all the men marched up into the Utah hills and shot a tiger, and they carried it home. Proudly, singing all the way. Then Thanksgiving Day, all the men walked around with their chests stuck out, and were happy and thankful. Because on Thanksgiving, at least, they had all the pussy they could eat!"

Chuckling, J.Q. suddenly became Adam. A picture of Angela, upside down, flashed across his mind. Sam was right, one vulva was as different from another's as a female's face. It was nice to have a friendship with more than one.

Taking some of the equipment out of the wagon, Sam was still acting a little gruff. He was obviously unhappy over Jake's fear that he was blowing the corporation's money. He told Yael that old chestnut was a past-forty joke. It turned him off. Why did she want to deride something she obviously enjoyed?

Yael laughed. "What do you want me to do? Cry? Besides, I've never had to beg you ... so how do *you* know I enjoy it?"

She tickled Sam as he was struggling toward the front door with a load of equipment. "At heart, Sam ... you're just like Jake ... a Puritan."

Sam exploded with laughter. "Like hell I am, Yael Adams. It's the word 'eating' that gets me ... it's cannabilistic. I'm a gourmet. I enjoy pussy like vintage wine."

☆ 29 ☆

Thursday, Thanksgiving morning, dressed in heavy woolen sweaters, woolen socks, ski pants, and corduroy pants, the motley crew of the Adams' Cal 30 boarded the auxiliary sailing sloop at the Cohasset Marina and were duly checked off by Jonathan Adams, skipper and, according to Sam, reincarnation of Captain Bligh, who assigned their locations with nautical precision.

Wearing red and green Portuguese fishing caps (donated by Janice Adams, who had purchased a dozen of them a year ago, when she and Jon were in Lisbon), they were singing a Portuguese *Fado* taught to them by Keane, who claimed it was sexy but untranslatable. Feeling exotic and debonair as the flappy peaks and tassels of their caps bounced against their cheeks, Keane and Sam hoisted the sails. The wind was blowing about twenty knots, the temperature was around fifty degrees. But as they sailed away from land, it would get colder. Jack Lovell, a golfer not by profession, but in his own words by "preferred-hobby," watched the activity and confusion of ropes with some bewilderment. Below in the cabin, as Sam and Keane announced they were about ready to cast off, Yael and Robin were organizing Thermos bottles of hot coffee and clam chowder, and a picnic basket filled with sandwiches that the latter-day Pilgrims would eat en route to Plymouth.

Standing on the dock, Janice and Barbara waved goodbye. Last night, over the objections of the others, they had decided that some members of their informal, four-day commune, should retain a modicum of sanity and not go sailing in the North Atlantic three weeks before winter. As the mother hens of the tribe, they would tend to the turkey baking in the oven. Later, around noon, they would drive over to Plymouth to meet the voyagers. Grinning, Jon told Janice that if they weren't docked at the public landing by two o'clock to immediately call the Coast Guard. The Plymouth Adventurers would be lost at sea.

At the helm, still exuberant from Barbara's and Janice's enthusiastic bon voyage kisses for all of them, and Janice's slightly sarcastic "Don't start another war with the Indians," Jon steered the *Wah-kon-tah*, translated the great-spirit-that-inhabits-everything (a name chosen by Keane and Sam for the boat some years ago), out of the harbor on a broad reach. The offshore, southwesterly, blowing puffily, meant that they would have good sailing until they stood off Plymouth. Then they must haul the sails and go in under power, or waste hours in endless short tacks.

With the helm still in his hands, waiting for Sam and Keane to trim the sails, Jon silently admitted to himself that sailing the sloop to Plymouth in November involved a blithe madness. Even though the boat was responding to his touch like a happy lover, heavier air would turn her into a bucking hellcat. The forecast was for continued mild, unseasonable weather, with increasing offshore winds. It was probable that even before they sighted Plymouth, the crew would get a workout. Of course, if the wind got up to thirty knots, Sam and Keane wouldn't be able to sail the boat back to Cohasset this weekend. "After the boys have deserted you, don't count on me," Janice had warned him. "You can leave the boat in Plymouth till hell freezes over. I'm not sailing it back with you this time of year alone. And don't forget, Friday afternoon we're playing golf at Coonamesset with the Lovells. We're not sailing." What was more, she reminded him (for at least the tenth time), the *Wah-kon-tah* should have been hauled out of the water three weeks ago. In New England, after November first all regular marine insurance expired except for boats that had been snugged on their cradle with dry land under them. Even Christopher Jones, Captain of the *Mayflower*, three hundred and fifty years ago, with a boatload of sick Pilgrims, wondered how he dared to be in the North Atlantic in November, when he should have been sailing in milder weather off the coast of Jamestown, Virginia.

Jon chuckled. He was reminded of the discussion he had had with Angela about astronauts and mountain climbers. Was sailing to Plymouth this time of year attempting the same kind of empty challenge? No. This was a participative adventure . . . not to challenge the elements (there really wasn't too much danger), but to recognize by intimate contact with the ocean, sky, and wind man's essential puniness. It could have been an even better adventure if Janice and Barbara had sailed with them, or if by some joyful broadening of human relationships, Angela, Jim, and their kids could have been aboard.

But Robin was here! On board the *Wah-kon-tah*. She swayed toward him, balancing easily along the slightly slanted deck. She grinned at Jon and sat beside him, impressed by the wheel which he put in her hands. "Oh, Jake, I'm having so much fun." She watched Keane coiling ropes, and the expression on her face, overflowing with love for his son, was Angela's expression. My God, was he going off his rocker? *No! Robin was here. This was no dream! . . .*

Angela, your daughter Robin is here! Impossible! After fifteen hours I still can't believe the reality of it. Robin Thomas, in the middle of a "naked parade," led by Sam and Yael with Keane bringing up the rear, ringing a huge dinner bell, charged into our cold morning bedroom just a few hours ago. Shivering. Hilarious with their own daring and bravado, they all jumped naked on top of a bewildered Janice and me. Yelling for us to get up, it was time to go sailing, they stripped off our blankets, delighted and giggling their approval that Janice and I were naked, too. A thrashing pig-pile of people, yelling and screaming joyously in a king-sized bed.

Robin, blushing at her nudity and ours, but choking with laughter (Angela . . . *your daughter*), gasped: "Oh, Lord . . . Jake . . . your sons are completely, joyously mad. I love them both. I wish my mother could see me now . . . I'm in bed naked, with my boyfriend and his father and mother! Oh God . . . no, I don't, Mother would die on the spot. Or if she didn't and she told my father, he would have a heart attack. Or he'd challenge Jake to pistols at ten feet at sunrise tomorrow for corrupting his daughter's morals."

I tried to protest. I was guiltless. I hadn't invited Robin into my bed. She was here of her own accord, but no one was listening. Keane was regaling us with a vivid description of the Lovell's consternation.

"They're probably still wandering around in a state of shock!" Keane yelled happily. "If we'd been invaders from Mars, they couldn't have been more surprised. When we pounced on them, Jack Lovell jumped out of bed to save himself. He was wearing purple pajamas. Barbara, in a wooly red nightgown, was crouching to hide her tits, which for some reason were dangling out."

"Maybe we surprised them making love," Yael giggled.

"With nightclothes on?" Sam snorted. "Impossible!"

"Oh, my God," Janice wailed. "How did I ever get mixed up with such a family? It's all your fault, Jonathan Adams. After last night and all that business about Barbara's behind, and then all of you smoking grass, and now this. They must be convinced that the Adamses are completely immoral." Janice tried to wriggle out of the bed. But Sam on one side, and Keane on the other, held her in place. She burst into laughter. "The Lovells have three very moral children, and several grandchildren. They would never jump into bed naked with their naked mother. Let me go, you naked nuts!"

"Why shouldn't sons and daughters jump into bed naked with their mothers and fathers?" Sam demanded.

Keane grinned across Yael and Jake to Robin, who was clinging to the outer edge of the bed beside me. "After all"—Keane's eyes were saying I-love-you-Robin— "Yael and Robin could be your kids, too, and you could

125

have wiped their asses too . . . I remember Jan wiping mine. I remember it well."

"Oh come on," Janice said. But she couldn't help laughing at Keane's serious expression, as if he were recalling the details of his infancy. "No one can remember that far back."

"I can, Janice." Yael leaned against the pillows, her breasts dangling. Like Sam, it's often impossible to tell whether Yael really believes everything she says. "I can remember all kinds of things, even back five thousand or so years before I was human. It's all there in my subconscious, yours too. No memories are ever lost."

Adam was certain of one thing. He would remember last night for a long, long time. Sam had worked his way to the back of the boat with Yael. He took the wheel from his father and Yael snuggled beside him. Robin and Keane's ecstasy, both with each other and the bright blue day, drifting with cumulus clouds, was so obvious it assumed an almost palpable reality of its own. Jack, staring across the rippling sea to where it met the horizon, smiled vacantly at Adam. (Was he, too, trying to fit last night into some dimension of his own rather staid New England existence?) Sam held the boat on a broad reach. The light chop slapping against the prancing hull was singing a happy song that entranced all of them. In an hour or so they would be sailing close haul, parallel to the shore; then the boat would buck and heel, and the spray would drive all but the most hardy below deck. Now was the time to relax. If he could relax. What would Angela think when she found out? . . . How would he tell her?

☆ 30 ☆

Angela, I saw your daughter naked. The shape of her pelvis, the contour of her breasts, the angle of her jaw, the shape of her nose, and above all, the dancing sparkle in her eyes . . . is *you.* Angela, your daughter could be my daughter-in-law. My God, what would happen to our Thursdays then?

You absolutely won't believe it. We seem to be involved

126

in some kind of mad "*deus ex machina*." Incredible. Are we characters on a string? . . . Right out of some Victorian novel? Even as I was walking across the front lawn last night, laughing at Yael's joke, deciding that Carswell had made me assume a kind of righteous and Puritanical role with Sam that was completely out of character, I was thinking of you.

In the shadows of my brain you have assumed a reality that makes it possible for me to see my environment, or whatever I may be doing, simultaneously through my eyes as well as yours. Does this happen to you, Angela? I hope so. I can hold tenuous hands with you in my thoughts in a way that I can't with Janice, and I suppose you can't with Jim. Is it a dangerous game to play? The surface answer might simply be a shrug. Is this empathy because we are new to each other? Because we are illicit? Stolen fruits are sweet and all that. Perhaps, but there's something more, I believe. We have a common sense of reality; together we sense what is worthwhile and exciting and what is spurious. It's implicit in your photography. Neither of us can stop exploring life or finding it, a wondrous adventure. Isn't that the unfailing unifying factor between humans?

But for a moment last night I wasn't "adventuring." I was stunned. Not at Barbara Lovell, who opened the front door when she heard us and embraced me in a big erotic bear hug, but at the young girl who was with Keane and helped Sam unload the station wagon. Floating by me, her hair flying behind her, she said, "Hi, Jake . . . Keane said I should call you Jake . . . I'm Robin."

The name didn't ring a bell. Of course, I remembered your daughter's names, Ruth and Robin. I guess we even discussed Keane's fascination with music and Robin's with the ballet. But that Keane should know *your* Robin, that they would have met each other . . . were actually sharing the same apartment in New York . . . never crossed my mind. I knew Keane had a girl. But your daughter? Impossible!

In the light from the lantern on the front lawn, I could see that she was tall, olive-complexioned. Her hair, drawn over her head and behind her ears, framed her heart-shaped face and cheekbones. A madonna right out of a painting by Bellini or Andrea del Sarto. I could tell by looking at her that she had a dancer's suppleness . . . that she could put her palms flat on the floor without bending her knees, and do it without the slightest effort.

In the front hall, as she handed Sam one of his cameras, I saw her face in the full light. Was my shocked surprise apparent? I was looking at you! *You* . . . a younger Angela, in jeans, wearing a floppy blouse, *your* nipples showing through, because *you* had no bra on under it. God alive . . . for a moment I thought I was having a schizophrenic attack of some kind, caused by thinking about you too much.

"Isn't she lovely?" Keane was saying as he introduced her formally. "This is Robin. Robin Thomas. She's going to marry me one of these days when she decides that a woman can be married and still be a dancer."

And then she hugged me with the same kind of unaffected warmth that I once told you was your Italian trademark. "The only reason I'm here," she said, "is that Keane insisted meeting you and Janice would convince me that your son is quite sane. He really would make a good husband, and he has the potential to be a family man and do something besides eat, breathe, and sleep music."

"That's why I need you." Keane was laughing, so proud of his girl I guessed he wanted to dance himself. "Robin, you're music . . . living, breathing music! I can spend a lifetime composing your mystery."

I had to force myself to stop staring at Robin. Fortunately, Janice and Jack appeared from the living room. Jack announced that he had a roaring fire going. He and Barbara had arrived about a half hour before, and were delighted that after knowing us for fifteen years they were going to spend a weekend in the "mad Adams" home.

Everybody was chattering at once, bursting with happy non sequiturs. A four-day holiday for everybody. No. Not quite. Jack had to work Friday morning. Bankers were the last to be rebels. Janice, with her arms around Robin, was asking me how I liked Keane's girl. Wasn't she pretty? Did I know that she was in her last year at Juilliard, that Robin had also studied at Balanchine's school of American Ballet. "Next year," Janice was saying, and I was listening in a daze, "Robin may dance with the Boston Ballet." I could read Janice's mind. Given the chance, she couldn't have picked a more worthy daughter-in-law for her son!

But I was only partially grasping the conversation, because I was wondering if Yael and Sam had made the mental jump with the name Thomas. Thus far they hadn't. About us, Angela, I'm happy-go-lucky careless. Don't say it! I left those pictures you took of me with the Hare Krishna dancers on my desk, and Sam and Yael have both seen them! Believe it or not, they think you might be a photographic genius. My thoughts were doing somersaults. All it would take was Robin to say: "My mother is a photographer. That would bridge the gap. I didn't know then that Robin wasn't too anxious to discuss her parents. She was afraid that you would discover she was in Massachusetts ... practically home ... and she hadn't told you or Jim. I was slowly deciding that if Yael or Sam connected the name, I would pass it off as a charming coincidence, but then I had a scarier thought. Robin was still grinning at me mischievously, as if we had a common secret. Had she recognized me? I could hear your voice saying, "I can't stop taking pictures of you, Adam. I love you. Your pictures are my diary without words. Don't worry. No one will ever see them." You told me that you kept them in a contact print file. No one was ever going to look through more than ten thousand contact prints just to find a few dozen of Adam staring back at them.

I was thinking, Sweet Angela, I'm not the only careless one. While I haven't seen any of those prints, if you kept all the pictures that you've taken in the past weeks, you have some of me with a most marvelous erection, and a few of you and I naked together that you took with a timer. Even though we were both hysterical at our "dirty pictures," and you said that in the contact prints we really looked like innocent babes in the woods ... I'd defy you to convince Janice or Jim ... or Robin ... or any of our kids. In our monogamous years, could we have understood? Interesting thought! Well, anyway, I counted on you. Hopefully, your diary was well protected. But even so, Robin could have seen the pictures of me with the Hare Krishna dancer. Or Sam, who had borrowed them from my desk, and now had them in his attaché case, could suddenly decide to show them to everybody here.

I was beginning to think, what the hell, I can't spend the entire weekend with a guillotine hanging over my head. The simplest thing was to take the bull by the horns. I could ask Robin if she were related to the photographer, Mrs. James Thomas, from Acton. But right then, when the time was ripe, I didn't have the nerve to do it. Thus far, at least, neither Sam nor Yael have said anything or have even mentioned the Hare Krishna pictures. If they do now, my presumed lack of interest in one Angela Thomas isn't going to ring true.

Jan was urging me to hurry and get showered and change into something informal. A pick-up supper of baked beans and brown bread with hot dogs that we could cook over the open fire in the fireplace was waiting. But there was one question I did have to ask Robin. "Do you live in New York?" After all, there was still a possibility there could be *two Robin Thomases in the world.*

Robin grinned, "I hope you and Janice can keep a secret." Her eyes seemed to engulf me. Was she thinking? I know! . . . I know that you're my mother's lover! Actually, she said, "My home is about forty or fifty miles from here, in Acton. If Mother knew that I was so close to home and hadn't told her, she would look and sound so neglected that I'd cry. Which is kind of nutty, but that's the way Mother affects some people when she's sad. On the other hand, Daddy would growl like a wounded lion, and he'd spend hours telling Mother how ungrateful children of this generation are, and how they don't appreciate their parents. I think he would have liked to have brought his children up with more Army discipline . . . and occasionally tanned our behinds, or locked us in our rooms until we repented."

Robin chuckled. "Really, Daddy isn't quite that bad. His theory is that parents without daughters don't have any problems at all. Fortunately, Mother has brainwashed him. He's aware of women's rights!" As she spoke, Robin continued to stare at me with that same kind of innocent, unnerving expression that you occasionally use, Angela, to get your way. Finally, she asked, "Aren't you glad you don't have daughters, Jake?"

I was happy to retreat upstairs to take a shower. With Janice's "Don't be long" ringing in my ears, I thought I'd at least have a moment to reconnoiter. But even before I had closed the shower door, Sam and Yael, completely naked, invaded the bathroom, urging me to hurry and not to use all the hot water. They were smelly, too. When I finally emerged, dripping, Yael handed me a glass of cider. "It's Sam's discovery." She beamed at me, and offered to dry my back. There was nothing to do but let her. It bothers Janice (would you be shocked?) that Yael runs around naked in front of me. But really, she, too, is a product of this house which both outside and inside allows us to dress, or not to dress to suit our moods. She was

130

explaining to me that hard cider is twelve percent alcohol. "It's great with grass. Lighter than wine. Sam is going to freeze some. He read somewhere that is how your forefathers stayed inebriated." Yael chuckled. "Note I said yours, Jake . . . not mine! There were no Pearlmans on those first trips." She told me she laced my hard cider with vodka. "Sam says you're too edgy."

I grinned at her. "If I'm edgy, it's because I'm in the bathroom naked with my daughter-in-law."

Yael shrugged. "So what? . . . Even if Sam wasn't here, so what? It seems quite healthy to me. Besides, I like to see you naked. You don't look so formidable without your clothes."

"The Lovells are quite square people," I told her. "Let's keep it a secret! They think being naked has sexual overtones."

Yael's laughter was tinkling bells, signifying not only her name, but her quality. "Jonathan Adams . . . I'm sure if the idea seized you, you wouldn't have to depend on your daughter-in-law for a roll in the hay." She looked at me quizzically, as if she expected confirmation that I did indeed have a secret life.

While I shaved I listened to Yael and Sam playing together in the shower cabinet. They were giggling and laughing at their nascent sexuality. Again, I was thinking of you, Angela. Why is it that with you I can enjoy the same kind of silly, carefree oneness with life? What happens after years of marriage that a man and woman are afraid to let their hair down and play like children with each other? Would you restrain Jim if he wanted to romp with you like a young puppy? Why do puppies and kittens and human beings grow up and rarely ever snuggle together again? Staring at myself in the mirror, I was wondering if twenty years from now Yael would still have retained her blithe spirit, and the joyous ease that was so contagious and transformed her environment. Watching Yael naked, watching you naked, watching any natural woman naked, I can't believe that any man, with his eyes open, could permit violence or hatred in the world.

When Yael and Sam emerged from the shower, Yael's black hair was soaking wet, molding the shape of her skull. It made her facial features more pronounced, harsher, with a proud peasant beauty. "Sam," I told him as I left the bathroom, "no matter how old she gets, no matter

131

how determined she is to impress the world with the money and genius of Sam Adams, don't let Yael go to a hairdresser." Don't laugh, Angela. I stopped you!

☆ 31 ☆

"Wake up, Jake, a former golfer is sailing the *Wah-kon-tah*!"

Adam grinned and waved at Jack. His reverie with Angela interrupted momentarily, he was vaguely aware that Robin had stepped over his sprawled legs and gone below. Keane and Sam, having convinced Jack to take the wheel, were exhorting him to relax and enjoy the contemplative surrender of sailing. Later, when they changed tacks, he'd find the competition with the sea and wind more exciting than breaking eighty on the golf course.

Yael was listening to their conversation. She grinned at Adam and he wrinkled his nose at her. He followed Robin into the cabin. She was about to pour coffee from one of the Thermos bottles into six styrofoam cups. "The crew asked me to do something useful." She offered him a cup. "Oh, Jake, I feel like hugging you. I'm having so much fun. Keane was right. You and Jan are a joy ... and alive!"

Adam smiled at her. "Your father and mother would probably think we're a little far-out. If you tell them about last night, please don't let them think we spend every evening kissing female behinds, or smoking grass. I think last night, and this weekend, we are all discovering ways of being easy and natural with each other. If any one of us were critical or offended by anyone else's spontaneity, it would cast a pall over all of us. It's a trick of group survival man may have to learn. What does your father do?"

"Daddy's a lawyer," Robin said. "In the middle of things, last night, I was thinking about him. I'm not sure that calmly being whatever kind of person you really are is something you can learn. The times when Daddy seems to have achieved a come-what-may feeling, at least with his children, he reminds me a little of President Nixon. I remember a long time ago when the President tried to

132

convince the kids he was sincerely rapping with them at the Lincoln Memorial at two o'clock in the morning. No one believed him. He *had* to have ulterior motives. Nixon would never be off-the-cuff honest with anybody. Some ways of living honestly *just are* ... you can't work at them. Maybe what makes the difference is inheriting wealth and status. At least, that's the way it seems for most of Daddy's friends. They had to struggle for money and recognition. Daddy worked his way through college and law school. His world is a world of 'survival of the fittest.' "

Leaning against one of the bunks, Adam sipped his coffee. These few minutes of conversation had a strange intimacy. He was experiencing Angela while he was talking with Robin. "It may surprise you," he said, "but the name Adams doesn't automatically insure that one is wealthy or has a certain savoir faire. My father was the owner of a small stationery store. He sold printing as a printing broker. He didn't have a printing plant or very much money."

Robin looked at him with an open-eyed Angela look that was like a body-touch. "But you didn't work your way through Harvard?"

Adam shrugged. "I had to grind for scholarships. But I think the difference is something else. When I was a young man, I was very conscious of transience. I didn't just major in history and government, I lived them, particularly history. Then slowly it dawned on me. Ecclesiastes said it: 'Vanity, vanity . . .' Shelley said it: " 'My name is Ozymandias, king of kings: Look on my works, ye Mighty, and despair!" Nothing beside remains. Round the decay of that colossal wreck, boundless and bare, the lone and level sands stretch far away.' " Adam smiled, enjoying her interest. "Really . . . all man's time should be for discovery and love. Nothing else is important. What's your mother like?"

"I think you'd like Mother . . . Angela is her name." Robin chuckled. "One thing is sure, you'd never get to kiss my mother's behind. But she's sparkly. A self-made iconoclast. Daddy doesn't agree with her most of the time, but she keeps him perking. I think he needs her."

"Does she look like you?" Adam hoped that the bright look in his eyes wasn't independently saying, I need Angela, too!

"She's prettier than me," Robin said. "Cooler. But I guess I look more like her than Ruth or Richy."

"What would she think about your sleeping with Keane? It worries Janice, as if somehow we are sanctioning Keane. I wouldn't want him to hurt you."

"Would you want him to marry me just because we had fun in bed?" Robin shrugged. "I think Keane and I may get married one day. Keane wants to ... so do I really. But I want to be sure I can love him and he can love me—both of us wanting to be each other so much that we can give each other room to grow. That's the most important reason. The first is more practical. I don't want to tangle with Daddy's ideas that young men who contemplate marriage should be able to support their wives."

"Keane may not be earning much, but he certainly can support you."

"I don't want him to have to pay my tuition bills at Juilliard." Robin smiled at him mischievously. "Or ask his Daddy to. Ultimately, I could pay my own way."

Adam wanted to tell her that he would be happy to subsidize her. Instead, restraining his impulse to hug her, he said, "What if you get pregnant?"

"You can ask that again and underline it!" Robin wondered if she were dreaming. Could a girl really talk with a prospective father-in-law so openly? It was charming. "Sometimes, I could bop Keane. He's a lovebug, and I'm too easily convinced. We play Russian roulette with birth control." She handed him two cups of the coffee she had finally poured to bring to the others. "I guess I'm a fatalist. If it happens, it happens. You may be a grandfather sooner than you expect." She kissed his cheek. "We'll name him Jake."

"What about your dancing?"

"Dancers can have babies. If I have too many, I'll have to be a choreographer. It'll probably be no loss. I'm no Margot Fonteyn or Natalia Makarova."

Back on deck, Adam nodded his approval of Jack, who was carefully watching the sails for any telltale flutter. Happy that the air was still blowing steadily, and estimating that it would be about a half hour before they would be sailing close haul, Adam slouched against the railing and resumed his shadowy conversation with Angela. When Thursdays came again, how much would he tell her about last night?

134

Angela . . . Angela . . . I think you would have enjoyed our silly evening together. There were eight of us, but we could have readily embraced your family, too. Ruth and Richy and their friends and Jim . . . even your Gramp and Lena. All any group of people need to function is one premise: that they will consciously work to achieve affection for each other as human beings.

When Yael, Sam, and I joined the others in the living room, I couldn't help noting the contrast between the older females and the younger ones. Yael and Robin were wearing dresses that swirled around their hips and gave the carefree impression that they were naked under them which, in fact, they were. When they sat cross-legged in front of the hearth, opposite Jack and I, who sprawled lazily against one of the sofas, I think we were simultaneously aware that neither Yael nor Robin were wearing panties.

Angela, would you have told your daughter to cover herself? I suppose so. Janice and Barbara would have, but, of course, Robin and Yael weren't their daughters.

It's a subject among millions we haven't discussed. But, of course, I would try to brainwash you. Men enjoy looking at women. Not women who make a flagrant display of their sexuality. But females like Robin and Yael who have a kind of unaffected, joyous ease. Women who are at home with their femininity . . . are happy with their bodies. Neither Robin nor Yael were self-conscious about their dress (should I say undress?). They weren't partially naked as a seductive gesture; simply, they were being their warm, animal selves. I was wondering if it wouldn't be a good idea, if men occasionally wore togas or kilts. Then both sexes, using clothes for their prime purpose of warmth and adornment, could casually enjoy glimpses of their sexual differences. It could add a new dimension to home entertainment.

I suppose it was the combination of the pot, the hard cider, and the music, but ultimately I brought the subject up. But that was a few hours later. At the moment the joy of occasionally seeing a female cleft was diminished by the realization that Keane, without consultation with me or Janice, had introduced Jack Lovell to what Keane referred happily to as "Cohasset green." While I've told you, Angela, that last summer I grew a marihuana garden, I didn't really believe that the president of the Graniteville National Bank, a rock-ribbed Republican, could cope with the idea of escaping his inhibitions with anything except alcohol. But sure enough, while he was smoking his usual pipe, to my astonishment he was inhaling and holding the smoke with an intake of breath that would have made a tobacco smoker fall over in a fit.

Keane and Robin, who were passing a joint between them (yes, Angela, your daughter smokes pot occasionally, even before she visited the Adams home), were watching Jack with unconcealed joy. Janice was cooking hot dogs and Barbara was dishing out plates of beans and brown bread. While I wasn't a hundred percent sure, I guessed that Janice and Barbara were both wearing tight panty girdles. A record was playing through the multiple speakers we have in the living room—a searching kind of music. Keane told me it could best be described as aleatory music. *Alea* means dice in Latin. I have been discovering from Keane this weekend that twentieth-century music (rarely heard on most radio and television stations, but alive and vital nonetheless), along with film and video, is in many instances coming to terms with the scientifically accepted facts of life. There is no teleological purpose in the universe. Within certain boundaries, any of numerous random expectations are possible. A throw of the dice and you and I met. A different throw (but, alas, there is no Known Thrower) and Angel-a and Adam would not be. Obviously, such a concatenation of events, such a perfect gamble, finding embodiment in you and I, should be treated with utmost care and love!

It would have been easy to give in and search with the composer (Keane told me it was called Elliot Carter's *Concerto for Orchestra*), but I was still a little unsure of the company.

Janice was teasing Jack, telling him that he was playing with fire. Smoking marihuana by the pipeful, just because the Adamses had grown about fifteen pounds of it, might turn him on in ways that he never expected . . .

"I can't believe it." She grinned at him. "The president of Graniteville National Bank is going to pot. You'll lose

136

all your depositors, Jack. Or maybe you can work out a deal with Jon. Give all new depositors who open a fifty-dollar account a few ounces as a gift. You'll be overwhelmed. The younger generation will hail you as an Establishment hero."

"It's silly stuff," Jack said gruffly. "I'm only smoking it because Keane says it does wonders for lovemaking." He smiled at Janice. "Makes you very erotic, I understand."

"Don't you believe it." Janice laughed. "I tried it once with Jon and I wasn't there at all."

Both Janice and Barbara were drinking Scotch. I took the last drag from a joint that Sam and Yael were sharing.

"You must have gone mad," Jack said to me. "Why in the name of God would a respectable middle-class citizen grow this crap?"

"Crop not crap." I was determined that Jack wasn't going to aggravate me. If he kept smoking, he'd soon be less aggressive. "Really, it's quite interesting to grow, Jack. Like Jack's beanstalk, you never know if it's going to stop. When the plants were twelve feet high, Jan was trembling. She was certain that people or the police going by in cruising cars could spot them. Jan insisted she'd wash her hands of me if I finally got us arrested. When we harvested it, the next step was separating the leaves. Those near the top, like tea, are the most potent."

"You'll look great behind bars. Prominent Cohasset citizen, J.Q. Adams, arrested on drug charge!" Jack suddenly grinned. *"My God-damned toes are curling!* Jesus Christ. This is a dumb-ass thing to be doing. My feet feel as if they have disappeared."

"Don't smoke it if you're going to loose your feet," I told him.

Jack stood up. "See, I'm walking on my ankles." Sam was doubled over with laughter.

"I didn't say that I didn't like it." Jack was looking vacantly at Barbara, who was shaking her head at him. "I know . . . I know . . ." he chuckled. "Mommy said to stick to Scotch like her and Janice. Trouble with you, Bobby, is you never walked around on your ankles. Jon, old boy, I don't feel this damned stuff at all. All I know is that music has been playing over and over again. Does it go on forever . . . and ever?"

Yael took the pipe from Jack and inhaled it. Speaking in a high nasal, she held the smoke in her lungs. She

137

explained to Jack that probably half the joy of marihuana was the sharing of it. A joint passed from hand to hand gave more of a feeling of intimacy than a solitary smoker puffing on a pipe. "Besides, it's expensive." She grinned. "You'll have to raise your own."

Jack seemed to be listening, but I suspected he was already happily chasing vagrant thoughts through his mind. Suddenly he giggled. "By God, Jon, your wife has a beautiful pear-shaped ass. How expensive is it?" Bewilderment at his uncoordinated thoughts flooded his face. "I mean the grass." Then he roared with laughter. "Maybe I don't."

Janice shrugged at Barbara with an I-told-you-so expression.

"Hang loose." Keane laughed. "By current black market prices, you've already smoked about ten dollars' worth."

"I'm hanging loose." Jack had become a living giggle. "It's beautiful. All these beautiful women. Beautiful Janice. Beautiful Bobby. Beautiful Yael. Beautiful Robin. All with beautiful asses."

"Poor Jack." Janice patted his head. "His needle is stuck in a groove. The world is lucky that you're only president of a bank, and not Secretary of the Treasury."

"Amazing." Barbara grinned at her husband. "We are witnessing the decline and fall of John Raymond Lovell. For the first time in his life, he got down off his high horse. He's acting like one of the hoi polloi. At the rate he's going, he'll soon be an ass-kisser."

Jack ignored any possible sarcasm in Barbara's tone. "That," he said, smiling broadly, "is a great idea. If I were Secretary of the Treasury, I would base the dollar value on the female ass; it's rare as gold, and for most males in just as short supply."

Robin and Keane were in happy hysterics. Listening to the humanization of Jack Lovell, they were sitting at the piano. Keane was softly playing music that he probably never had written down. Dreamy evocations of unending time. Robin, who had first been feeding him a hot dog, was now dancing.

Barbara took a drag on Jack's pipe. "I guess I better try this stuff." She made a valiant stab at dragging the smoke deep into her lungs. "Who knows? Tonight I may even get my ass kissed?"

"Not until you take off your girdle," I told her. "No man wants to kiss a behind that's been turned to corrugated flesh by a rubber girdle."

☆ 33 ☆

Yael and Sam had set up their television monitors and lighting equipment so they faced most of us lounging around the fireplace. As Yael and Sam peered at us through their portable television cameras, we were suddenly aware that even as we were being recorded on tape, we were simultaneously being projected on two screens from different perspectives. Watching ourselves from two different points of view gave all of us an odd sense of being somebody else. *Who am I really?* Sam asked the question and dared us to answer it. Was that "me" on those tubes, full face and profile, watching and being watched, really J.Q. Adams, Jake, Jon, Adam . . . or somebody else? Jack suddenly engaged himself in a dialogue with his television image. He told himself to stop staring at himself. Then he grinned sheepishly at all of us and pointed at himself on the tube. "No matter what he tells you, that ugly-looking character shooting off his mouth, there on that tube, is not me . . . I disown him!"

I think most of us felt the same way. The sharp discovery that sometimes happens when you look in a mirror and tell yourself, It can't be! This surface reflection staring at me is someone else . . . not me! The "me" making the reflection has never really revealed itself. This other me knows that the bland surface of hair, eyes, nose and mouth and chin, staring at me (all carefully arranged for self-protection), doesn't dare to come to terms with the naked, yearning child underneath. The "other me" in all of us, crying to get out and play in the sunshine.

While I was having an internal philosophical discussion with myself on the inability of man and woman to break through the adult barriers they erect against each other, to the delight (at least I thought) of everybody, I also managed to recite the complete "Kubla Khan" and thirty or so lines of "The Ancient Mariner," all accompanied by

Keane (on the piano) and Robin, who were evoking my words in dance and music.

Even as I was blandly raving, I was aware that Janice was holding hands with Jack, and Barbara, her dress hiked over her thighs, was lying on her stomach staring dreamily at the hot orange coals and the yellow, blue, and red flames, dancing hotly on the backlog that Sam had pulled forward on the andirons.

Was I seeing things? Had Barbara removed her girdle? She had! And her stockings too! The lower half of her partially exposed behind was a warm pink from the glow of the fire. Sam grinned at me and aimed his portable camera in her direction. I told Barbara that her ass was becoming immortal . . . a permanent part of the Adams National tape library. She just giggled. "Jonathan, an hour ago, you said that no one would ever kiss a rubber behind. So Janice and I both took off our girdles. We even hinted that we were going to, but neither you nor Jack seemed to care."

"It's kind of mad, the images that we grow up with, isn't it?" Yael said. I noticed that Yael's eyes were glassy and a little red (the effects of the grass she had smoked), but she just grinned into space and picked at the idea Barbara had put into her brain. "Whenever I see a picture of a baby's behind, it makes me feel warm and good. Most of us would think nothing of kissing a baby's rump. It makes me feel soft and mushy inside to see a kid naked with a little behind so fragile and innocent, and needing you. When we grow up, what happens to us? Why can't we see an adult's naked behind with the same warm emotion?"

"It's something to think about," Sam admitted. "We don't even have any warm words for the adult rear end. We call a baby's behind tushy, or po-po. But when you grow up it's just your ass or your buttocks. But even fanny, or just plain behind, don't have loving connotations."

"The reason is a baby doesn't talk back!" Janice's mind, freed by alcohol, was taking a wide leap. "You can pick up a baby and kiss his tushy, and snuggle him all over. And he gurgles because it feels so nice. But how can you kiss an adult behind? It's too big and too ugly. Anyway, even if it was pretty, the average owner of it would probably make some embarrassing comments if you kissed it."

"Jan is right," I said. "If we're going to straighten out

140

the world, we've got to begin with a new image for a human being's behind." Marihuana in your blood often convinces you that there are breathtakingly simple solutions to human problems. "Let's take inventory. There's the word 'ass,' which has crude, sexy, or just earthy images. Ass is not a nice personal-feeling word. There's tushy, which is a description applied largely to babies' behinds, and, of course, there's fanny, which is really a word that is trying to make a silk purse out of a sow's ear."

Barbara decided to join the search. "There's rump, derriére, posterior, backside." She was bubbling with enthusiasm. "Then there's some nasty words. Bum, can, tail, keester, or just plain butt."

"There's heiny. Keane calls mine heiny-butt." Robin blushed. "And there's cooley." She tumbled against Keane, helpless with laughter. "That's Italian, courtesy of the Thomas family."

"Nothing much to go on yet," I said.

"We can try descriptive adjectives," Yael suggested. "But none of them are very nice."

Sam chortled. "It's true. There's all kinds of nasty adjectives that go with ass—like cruddy, smelly, hairy, surly, smart, snotty . . ."

"I know a nice one," Jack interrupted him. "Cuddly . . . cuddly ass!"

"That's a male image," Janice objected. "No female ever thinks of a male's ass as cuddly."

"How about a 'piece of . . .'?" Jack asked. But we all hissed that.

"We can try kinds of asses," I offered. "That might lead us somewhere."

"There's Janice's ass," Jack said. "One of a kind . . . pear."

"I think all the other kinds are nasty," Barbara said. "Fat, scrawny, flabby, tight . . . so we're back where we started with ass-kissing . . . even in Yiddish, *toches-lecker* is not nice."

"There's pygophilemia, which means ass-kissing in Greek," I said. "And that leads us to verbs, which unfortunately have a tendency to orient around the presumed Greek way of sexual intercourse . . . buggery. Which brings to mind 'up yours,' or 'shove it.' In World War II there was the euphemism 'shove it up your barracks

141

bag.' " I shrugged. "But we're still not coming up with a nice word for an adult ass."

"The ass that started all this was Barbara's," Keane said. "For a woman past forty, we must admit from the little we've seen of it, Barbara has a lovely ass. I nominate Barbara Lovell's ass for the Past Forty Ass of the Year, and since the subject has been raised, appreciation should begin with affection; I think someone should volunteer to kiss Barbara's ass." He patted Barbara's rump, over which she had long ago decorously pulled her skirt. I wondered if Barbara was in a state of shock. As Janice pointed out, children in their twenties shouldn't talk about asses or discuss the asses of family friends in their presence, let alone touch them. Of course, the Adams children were precocious. After so many years there wasn't much she could do about it. The Lovells would have to be understanding.

Janice's dissertation brought Jack back to the living. "I think all the females should stand on the hearth." Jack wasn't actually talking, he was burbling. "Lift their skirts, and let all the men kiss their behinds. I remember reading that long ago, in ancient times, public ass-kissing and the display of feminine posteriors was a happy custom . . . much enjoyed by the old men in their eighties, who in this way got their last look and touch of warm, young female flesh."

"My God, Jack," Janice exploded. "These are my children, and my daughter-in-laws." She smiled apologetically at Robin. "At least, I hope you still might be considering joining the Adams clan. I'm afraid we're behaving like idiots in front of you. Smoking grass, drinking, saying any damned thing that comes into our heads. Mothers and fathers aren't supposed to act crazy or sexy in front of their children. When I was your age, I was sure my mother and father had given up sex years before." Janice lost the thread of her thought. "I hope when you tell your mother and father, they will understand. . . ."

Robin told her not to worry. "I think mothers and fathers should talk about behinds and kiss them, and just joyously be with each other."

About an hour later, the females weakened. Sam recorded them on tape. They stood on the hearth facing the fire. Hysterical with laughter at their daring, they lifted their skirts and stuck out their naked behinds in pristine splendor. From left to right, each of us passed down the

142

line behind them and kissed eight female cheeks. No amount of persuasion would convince the males to drop their pants and return the favor.

Later in bed, Jan snuggled naked against me. "My God, what a silly-nice evening," she said. "I hope the Lovells weren't shocked." Janice giggled. "When Sam ran the tape back, you looked so awkward kissing Barbara's and Robin's behinds. I think momentarily you lost your Adams cool."

"It's not something I'm accustomed to doing in public."

"Did it make you feel excited to see all those naked behinds?"

I laughed. "All males feel a twinge of excitement when they see live naked female flesh. It was also an interesting and unusual view of the female bush. To tell you the truth, I had forgotten what a nice behind you have. Rather than feeling orgiastic, I had an overwhelming feeling of how fragile human beings really are."

"You mean with their asses bared?"

"I suppose so. Isn't that how the expression came about? We don't dare bare our asses . . . be honest with each other."

Janice kissed me warmly. "I guess it's something when a wife loves her husband after twenty-three years. I love you, Jon."

"Do you love Jack, too?" I suppose it was a dangerous question, particularly so since Janice was half on top of me and helping me find my way inside her.

She was silent a moment, happily adjusting to the fullness in her vagina. "The other day I was reading a book about changes that the family is experiencing. A sociologist, Andrew Hacker, described marriage as an institution that can't hold two full human beings. It is designed for one and a half. The half being the old-style female who lived her life as a reflection of the male." She glided against me. "I've known Jack a long time. Would you mind if I loved Jack, too?"

In the soft light from the bedside lamp, I could see tears in Janice's eyes. She finally tried to evoke her feelings. "Can one human being love two other human beings?"

She kissed me wildly. "Oh God, Jon, I think so . . . I think so."

Afterwards, Angela, I thought about you. I had made love to Janice, perhaps even while you were making love to Jim. . . . Strangely, I was no less in love with you. "Maybe," I told Janice before I drifted into sleep, "the average human being is flowing with a greater need for love and intimacy than he or she ever gets the opportunity to express."

☆ 34 ☆

About an hour before they arrived in Plymouth, Jon told the entire crew to don bright yellow foul-weather gear. Stationed high on the starboard, they used their weight to keep maximum wind in the sails of the *Wah-kon-tah*. Sam and Keane took turns at the helm. They pointed the boat high on the wind, letting it rear and pound across the increasingly choppy seas. The gusts, occasionally blowing a full thirty knots, created their own certainty. It would be impossible to sail the *Wah-kon-tah* back to Cohasset until the weather quieted.

They were in no danger, but the excitement of the sails tilting under the pressure of the wind to a thirty-degree angle with the water; the spray slapping across the bow and whipping their faces to a tingly, salty red; the turbulent air howling menacingly in the stay wires while the mast creaked and groaned under the strain; the unpredictable lurches as the southwesterly suddenly slacked and the helmsman failed to point up fast enough to prevent the boat from bouncing back in a sickening upward flip; and their yells as the wind smacked them again with increased fury; all these served to weld the crew into a joyous oneness. Perhaps none of them were able to evoke it, but human beings challenging nature together created deep within them much of the erotic joy of a sexual embrace. For a moment they were primitive people wrapped together in an intangible physical ecstasy with each other as they fought to survive against the unyielding sea and relentless wind. Adam wished Angela were aboard to share the ecstasy.

When they were once again in quieter waters with the sails down and the engine chugging impersonally toward the public landing at Plymouth, Sam voiced Adam's feelings from an entirely different perspective.

"A few nights ago Yael and I were discussing the Pilgrims. Isn't it a fact that they were the first American dropouts? Instead of staying in Europe and challenging society—really the business of forcing an accommodation from some of their leaders to their religious and political beliefs—they took the path of least resistance. They set sail for a new land. It's easier to walk away from a sea of troubles than take arms against them. I suggested to Yael that the Palestinian Jews who left Europe long before Zionism and Israel existed—most of them came from Russia and were pure Marxist in their beliefs—went to the Middle East and established the Kibbutzim, based on economic as well as sexual sharing, were also dropouts. If they had stayed in Europe or Russia, and the later creation of Israel, and the exodus of the Jews from Europe and Africa had never occurred, wouldn't they have ultimately forced a reformation of the society that was persecuting them? The point is that man can no longer walk away from those who persecute him. The world is too small. He has to stand pat and fight."

Yael was a little exasperated. "You're talking some sense, but mostly nonsense, Sam. If you weren't a Wasp, you would have held it closer to your mind . . . to your soul. Over the years millions of Jews have been exterminated. But maybe you're right. I was reading that Yeshiva University is now giving courses in karate. To survive in the jungle of New York, against Puerto Ricans and blacks who detest them, Jews are learning to stand pat and fight back."

Sam grinned and hugged Yael. "I'm no longer a Wasp. I'm a Jew by penetration, and osmosis. What I'm saying is this: Wasn't the sacrifice the Jews made in Europe essentially a victory for those who survived? They should have stayed put and made it work for them. After the war Germany was in a mood to expiate. Even if they weren't, the rest of the world was ready to force them to. Many Jews who remained have gained the power formerly denied to them."

"I think that's an untenable idea." Robin joined the argument. "The blacks prove you are wrong. Only by dropping out and creating their own black world have they made any dent in white power. If the Jews hadn't created the focal point of Israel, they wouldn't have the psychological strength to take on their persecutors."

"But nations composed of blacks, or Jews, or Aryans,

145

or Chinese, or Communists, or even tiny enclaves of human beings sow the seeds of their own destruction." Keane had stopped snuggling against Robin's neck. He was obviously happy to have her involved in the discussion. "They inevitably produce leaders who gain power by cultivating group hatred. Fifty years from now, if the blacks have created a separate black culture, or if we force it on them, we all will have lost the battle. The only hope for the world is that we refine our pluralism, blend it in the melting pot. We'll end up with a new kind of stew, but it won't be poisonous like the separate dishes. I agree with Sam: the only way to accomplish that is for each group to stay in and fight . . . capture their share of existing power."

They were still arguing when they tied the boat to the dock. Janice and Barbara greeted them, urging them to hurry. "The town is in uproar." Janice waved toward Plymouth Rock. "Everyone is wondering if there's going to be a riot. The Indians have arrived en masse. All kinds of strange-looking characters have joined them. If the Indians' demonstration is interrupted, there's sure to be trouble. I think we ought to go back to Cohasset."

From the docks they could see hundreds of people walking up Cole's Hill, which overlooks the town and the harbor.

Sam and Yael quickly strapped on their video gear. "You can all leave if you want to, but this is what Yael and I came to see. We'll thumb a ride back to Cohasset."

Outvoted by Robin and Keane, and their husbands, Janice and Barbara, clinging to Jack and Jon, followed them into the middle of groups of smiling, full-blooded Indians, blacks with African hair styles framing their faces, and obviously militant white activists from nearby colleges. Janice was right. The fuse was set. The police, watching various groups from their cruising cars, evidently had been warned not to interfere; to avoid applying the match, if possible. Poker-faced, they watched, Mohawks, Narragansetts, Wampanoags (Indians from tribes who once owned this territory) and Siouxs and Chippewas and Indians from the Far West. The word was being spread . . . to the Indians with "Alcatraz" stenciled on their jackets; to Indians wearing buttons proclaiming "Indian Power" or "Remember Crazy Horse," or "Custer Died For Your Sins"; to Indians with raised fists . . . *there would be no confrontation*. They didn't need the help of white

146

sympathizers. Their closed fists were Indian sign language for "together, unity, God." Yes, the white man could cut off their fingers one by one, but joined together they were still a powerful fist.

Sam and Yael pointed their cameras at an Indian who had climbed up on the weathered bronze statue of Massaçoit. Standing beside the twice life-sized replica of the proud Indian chief who implacably surveyed the harbor and a world he never made, Russell Means, a Sioux, harangued the crowd. Momentarily, he was Massaçoit come to life. A proud, angry Indian. "Look at this statue," he yelled. "He has turned green . . . green with the disease and suffering you have brought him, green with your hatred, racism, and hypocrisy. The white man came to this land to seek religious freedom, but he has denied all freedom to the Indian. Get back on that ship, and take your disease and poverty, your greed and bigotry, your money and your machines and your TV with you.

"For the white man this was a day of Thanksgiving. But for the red man, thank you, for a life expectancy of forty-four years, for a suicide rate among teen-agers ten times the national rate, for the Bureau of Indian Affairs that is the colonial bureau of the government in Washington, which denies us our language and our heritage, and refuses to supply us even with barest necessities of life.

"For years now the U.S. has been locked in Viet Nam, because, as our national leaders insist, the credibility of American commitments had to be preserved. But the U.S. has broken three hundred eighty-nine treaties with the American Indians during the past centuries."

Means jumped down from the statue and led the cheering crowd down to the Plymouth Rock. Ten or twelve Indians scaled the iron fence protecting the "goddamned rock." While they covered the Rock with sand, one of them intoned a sarcastic prayer to the god of the Christians and his religion of hatred. Then they surged aboard the replica of the *Mayflower*, tied up to its own dock in the harbor, a few yards from the Rock. Two of them climbed the rigging of the mainmast, and took down the flag of the English King. "We'll take this to our Indian museum of cultural history, along with your beer cans and condoms."

They hooted at the police, who finally ordered the crowds to disperse. All the Indians participating in the

147

demonstration were invited to Thanksgiving dinner at Plymouth Plantation. Some of the white men wanted to be brothers.

✰ 35 ✰

As the defused crowd wandered toward the town, Jack was trying to fathom what had been accomplished. It all seemed like a tempest in a teapot to him. Jon admitted that he didn't have any answers. Yael, Sam, Robin, and Keane, who had disappeared temporarily with a crowd of Indians, rejoined them. They had a young Indian couple in tow. "This is John—Hawkeye—Whitecloud," Keane introduced them. "And his wife, Susan Whitecloud. We've invited them back to Cohasset to have dinner with us."

Janice grinned her approval at the questioning look in Keane's eyes. "It's kind of a pot-luck Thanksgiving," she told the Whiteclouds. "You're welcome to join us. What about the boat?"

"The Whiteclouds will drive us back to Plymouth," Sam said, "They've got a car. We're all going to sleep on the boat tonight. Tomorrow we'll sail it back to Cohasset."

Keane and Robin drove back to Cohasset with the Whiteclouds. In a quick breakthrough of barriers that escapes people when they get older and self-conscious, Robin and Keane had discovered that the Whiteclouds were doing graduate work in sociology at Boston University, that they were experts in Indian folklore and dance, and that John played a guitar and Susan the piano. Keane and Hawkeye were already discussing an Indian ballet they might create based on an Indian myth that forewarned the coming of the white man.

Back in the living room at Cohasset, once again congregating around the fireplace while Janice and Barbara set up a buffet table laden with a turkey, a ham, sweet potatoes, onions, stuffing, cranberry sauce, and dishes of tomatoes and lettuce, they all sipped champagne and cold duck. And they argued. "Because," as Jon told the Whiteclouds and Robin, "human beings expressing themselves to each other not only may discover themselves, but occasionally they get a glimpse of a common denominator."

He grinned. "They are often surprised to discover that it is love."

Sitting on the floor with his plate filled from the Thanksgiving buffet, Jack apologized for dominating the conversation, but could the younger generation answer the question he had raised in Plymouth. "All I want to know, is what in hell you think was accomplished today?" He explained that as far as he was concerned, eight hundred or so thousand Indians, three hundred and fifty years later—with apologies to the Whiteclouds—were the product of their own stupidity. It was sentimental nonsense to be sorry about savages who had lived in America when the Pilgrims arrived. If the white man hadn't dominated them, eventually one of their own tribes would have created a super-Indian state. In the process millions of Indians would have killed each other.

"That is exactly what happened in the older Indian civilizations in Mexico. Finally a superior force, the Conquistadors, arrived and swallowed them up. In Africa the local black kings happily sold their people to the slavers. The history of the world is the history of the little man pushed to the wall by self-ordained leaders. But the little man rarely rebels spontaneously. Another group of leaders incites him and eventually rallies him around *their* need for power. The little man is conned into a never-ending search for liberty, equality, and fraternity."

Jonathan joined the discussion. "Maybe, Jack, the search is never-ending because it is a condition of power. The need for the leaders will disappear when the little man discovers that liberty, equality, and fraternity will never be realized through conquest or war. The kind of world you and I, all the little men want is at our fingertips, but we can't achieve it by grasping for it."

Jack laughed. "You're too damned idealistic, Jon. Sam was on the right track this morning. Like the Pilgrims and the Jews who migrated to Israel, the Indians were dropouts. The only lasting way to destroy the enemy is to assimilate him. Then, in about a half-century, neither he nor you any longer exist as enemies. You are on *his bandwagon*. Eventually, you have the reins in your hands. At this point, neither he nor you knows how it came about, except possibly historically. A good example is the way the Irish took Boston away from the English, or the Italians and Jews took New York City from the original

Dutchmen. They never knew it was happening to them until it was too late."

Sam shook his head. "Essentially, what you are saying is that if you were an Indian or a black, and you jumped on the white man's bandwagon, if they wouldn't make room for you, you'd fight."

"You can bet your ass on it." Jack chuckled. "But I'd stay alive while I fought. A new kind of passive resistance. Not Ghandi-style. I wouldn't lie down in front of the steamroller. I'd blow it up!"

Sam had Jack out on a limb. Laughing, he sawed it off. "Jack, at the next meeting of the Massachusetts Bankers Association, will you wrap up that idea? Make it a key-note speech. While you're delivering it, think of yourself as one of the self-ordained leaders. The little man is only asking you to move over on your bandwagon. He thinks people like you making a living by charging interest on money for such necessities as home-owning, or buying an automobile, have really found a subtle way of enslaving him . . . and he doesn't like it."

"Then he should pay as he goes, and not get enslaved," Jack said.

Sam smiled. "I'm not an economist. But every time we have a depression, the little guy is blamed because he pays his debts and doesn't spend all the money he makes. If the little man ever decides to pay as he goes, he'll not only dig his own grave, but he'll pull the entire Establishment in with him."

While they were talking, Yael had been video-recording all of them, with closeups of their reactions to the central arguments. Susan Whitecloud asked her what she was going to do with the tapes. Yael grinned. "Ask Sam . . . everything will depend on the editing. I think something interesting has emerged."

Sam explained that their original idea had been to show a New England Thanksgiving in the dimension of the Second Law of Thermodynamics . . . entropic. "But, now I think we are seeing the possibility of Thanksgiving as negentropic. There could be feedback that would revitalize the old ritual . . . thus making it self-enriching and re-generative."

Barbara, holding a plate of turkey and stuffing in her lap, fended off Mike and Ike, Janice's Siamese cats. "I don't know what the hell you are talking about, Sam, but

150

if eating Thanksgiving dinner sitting on the floor has something to do with it . . . I'm for it."

Janice told the others not to look so smug. She'd bet that none of them had the faintest idea what the Second Law of Thermodynamics was. Hawkeye, holding a turkey leg in one hand and a glass of champagne in the other, had a Buddha smile on his face. "You might say, Mrs. Adams, that inviting a couple of Indians to Thanksgiving dinner disproves the Second Law. But first you've got to understand the First Law." With his dutchboy haircut, flashing black eyes, and high cheekbones, Hawkeye spoke with the dignity of one of his ancestral chiefs. "The First Law states that energy is constant. It cannot be created or destroyed. Its form can change, but not its quantity. The Second Law states that the amount of energy tends toward disorder, dissipation, incoherence. All organizations, nations, business organizations, clubs, families, friends—all are entropic; without feedback they lose energy and eventually run down."

Jack looked bewildered. "Quite frankly, I don't think any of you know what you're talking about. You said that the First Law is that energy can't be destroyed."

"True enough," Yael answered for Hawkeye. "But its form changes. It can't chase its tail, or look up its own asshole." She nodded at Sam, who had taken over the video camera. "When we put this tape together and Keane unifies it with music, we'll show you—new . . . adventurous yous."

"I get it." Jack beamed. "Smoking grass and behind-kissing on Thanksgiving eve has made the holiday self-enriching and regenerative."

Ignoring any possible sarcasm, Keane, Sam, Yael, and Robin exchanged an explosion of laughter. "You can bet your ass on it, Jack," Keane said. "Last night and today all of us functioning together may have proved that giving thanks is really to each other. Multiply us about a billion times, and instead of generation gap, you'll have a whole world of joyous, young and old human beings held together by Jake's common denominator.

☆ 36 ☆

Janice's female Siamese cat (Mike), howling her seasonal distress at not having a mate, awoke Jonathan Friday morning. He was sleepily aware that Janice, fully dressed, had bent over him, kissed him, and told him to sleep on. She was going to the hairdresser. That was at least an hour ago. Ever since, he had floated in and out of a strange dream he was having. Angela was a schoolteacher, and between classes he had passed her in the hall. She was wearing a ski suit, and was delighted to see him. But there was nowhere to talk. They dashed into a cloakroom. He pushed up her sweater, unfastened her bra, and was kissing her breasts. Then he slid her ski suit down over her hips to her ankles. They were hilarious over the fact that though he, too, was half naked, intercourse was impossible. The ski pants couldn't slide over her ski boots. Angela couldn't spread her legs around him. Bent over, her behind in the air, her ski pants around her ankles, Angela was untying her boots when the school bell rang. Only it really wasn't the school bell. It was that damned cat, Mike, arching her haunches and wailing her distress for a missing penis that would relieve her agony, and, of course, impregnate her.

Suddenly he was awake enough to realize that Mike couldn't have gotten into the bedroom unless someone had opened the door. Jan, knowing the cat would annoy him, would have closed the door behind her.

Then across the room he saw Barbara. She was standing indecisively near the threshold. "I was wondering if you were ever going to get up." She smiled nervously. "Everyone has gone. It's nearly ten. It's lonesome around here."

"Where is everybody?" Jon knew. The kids had gone back to Plymouth late last night. They were going to sleep on the boat and sail it back today. Jack had gone to the bank. Janice had given him no warning of her early departure. Whether it was premeditated or not, she knew that Barbara and he would be alone in the house. The

152

sexual overtones implicit in Barbara seeking him out in his bedroom were apparent.

"Jack's gone to the bank. He said he'd leave early and be back by one. Janice went to the hairdresser in Graniteville. She said I could make your breakfast."

Adam smiled at her. He wondered momentarily if Barbara and Janice had collaborated. A test to see what he would do. Bobby must be aware that he was naked in bed. "Didn't you have to go to the hairdresser?" he asked. He was aware that Barbara and Janice went to the same hairdresser.

"My appointment isn't until Saturday." Barbara looked like a little girl about to confess a special truth. "Janice usually goes on Saturday, too."

"What you're intimating is that maybe Janice didn't have to go to the hairdresser at all?"

Barbara sighed. She gestured at Mike. "Maybe by the year two thousand, when Women's Liberation is a fact of life, human females will be able to signal their needs as easily as your cat."

"You'll have to admit that you're being a bit devious." Adam chuckled. "Since we're alone, and it's only quarter of ten, you might just as well talk to me under the covers."

Her blue eyes wide and bright with her daring, looking as pristine as a Danish porcelain figurine, Barbara walked slowly across the room. Her face flushed, she stood at the foot of the king-sized bed. "Really, Jon ... I shouldn't ..."

Adam grinned at her. "But you really want to."

Barbara shrugged, "Oh, damn it. All my life my body has said let go ... stop freezing up when a man looks at you. But at heart, I guess I'm an old maid. I keep wondering what Janice would think. She's my best friend."

"For heaven's sakes, Bobby, take off your housecoat and your nightgown. Get in the bed before you freeze to death. I'm not going to eat you."

Barbara laughed. "Gosh, I kind of hoped you were!" Adam had a momentary glimpse of naked breasts, a white body and a prolific nest of pubic hair. Shivering, she burrowed into his arms. "Oh, God! You've got an erection. Do you always sleep naked? What if I'm wrong? What if Janice isn't in Graniteville right now? What if she isn't in my bed making love to Jack?"

Adam burst into laughter. Bobby looked at him, bewildered. He touched her erect nipples lightly with the tips of his fingers. "You mean the reason you're in bed with me is for revenge . . . ye gods! That's silly."

Barbara stared into his eyes, trying to fathom his mind. "You and Janice seem so secure with each other. I have a feeling, if she really is in bed with Jack, you wouldn't even be jealous, or angry with her. I don't know how Jack feels, but I can assure you, I'm not so sophisticated."

"But occasionally you're willing to play games, like what is good for the gander is good for the goose . . . so long as the gander doesn't know about it."

Barbara was enjoying his light tasting of her nipples. "Maybe tit for tat is a better description." She laughed. "Anyway, you don't seem to mind servicing a hungry female. Why aren't I more blasé? After all, I am the mother of two grown children."

Adam leaned on his elbow and smiled at her. "And, in fact, a grandmother . . . three times." He wondered how to calm her tense expectancy. She lay rigid in his arms, like the virgin heroine in an old-time movie. Even though Bobby's hair was dyed a little too brown, and she must be nearly forty-seven (he had never asked her age), she was a pretty woman. He was quite erect. The truth was his unfulfilled dream about Angela had left him with a restless urgency. Damn . . . he wanted Bobby to be Angela. With Angela he could have enjoyed the erotic comfort of her flesh floating against his flesh. Like flotsam and jetsam, they had learned the joy of drifting endlessly. Was intercourse that way an instinctive need, special to both of them, enhanced by their own peculiar interacting chemistry? Adam was certain that it was. Somehow, though he knew that he wanted no future with Bobby, he was determined not to make a surface game-playing contact with her. Would she be willing to be involved, even if only momentarily? Could two strangers ever surrender completely to each other? He guessed that Bobby wouldn't dare to be completely vulnerable. Yet wasn't defenseless surrender the key to complete sexual intimacy and communication?

He tried to explain his thoughts to her, and she listened. Amazingly, instead of being her usual chattering self, she was silent. Tiny tears were in the corners of her eyes. Finally, she kissed his cheek. "Thank you for just talking to me, Jon. I feel so nice and warm and bubbly." She started to get out of bed. "But I think it'll be best if I leave now, before we get in too deep. It's strange, but in all the years Jack and I have been married, this need for another man has happened only once before to me. That was a long time ago, and I wasn't the aggressor." Bobby couldn't hold back her tears. "One thing is certain about affairs . . . they don't last, do they?"

☆ 37 ☆

Adam gently pushed her down on the pillow. "Now you can relax—I'm the aggressor. Bobby, let's not think of duration . . . nor of tomorrow . . . or even time passing. Let's just be. Sometimes, minutes can have as much significance and more joy than hours or days. We're going to make love. Later, when we both think about it, it will be something nice that happened to us. We'll remember it with a warm chuckle . . . and be amazed that we could surrender without possessing."

"Oh God, Jonathan, what's the matter with me?" She kissed him fervently and her hand fluttered over his flesh until she found his penis. Then she slithered down beside his stomach and kissed his penis, too. "Am I a nympho, or being immature? I'm forty-seven years old. My son is a doctor. My daughter has three children. Why do I think about making love all the time?"

"You're not a nympho . . ." Adam kissed her face and lips as she returned to his arms. "You're a very sound, lovely female who is a prisoner in this silly world of ours; a world that renounces love and sex as a natural way of life . . . even for grandmothers."

Barbara nibbled on his shoulder. She clung lightly to his penis as if it might escape her. Although he couldn't see her face, he knew she was smiling. "You do taste good," she murmured. "I even like the taste of your penis. And you feel different than Jack."

"I am different from Jack."

"That's the point, isn't it? That's what makes adultery so intriguing. Oh, my God . . . the reason I'm so madly excited is because the environment is so different. You're different. This bed is different, and you're the husband of

155

my best friend." Barbara sighed. "Once Janice offered you to me, but I think she was kidding. Then last summer when you were giving Bessie Crampton that business about wanting to snuggle on her tits, I was ready to brain you. Whether you knew it or not, Bessie would have been happy to oblige." Barbara suddenly felt secure. Being in bed with Jonathan was fun. What was more, she could suddenly view her marriage in a different perspective. For one thing, unlike Jack, Jonathan didn't seem to mind listening to her. "Maybe the reason I'm feeling so hopped up is that being with you is not predictable." Barbara smiled at him. "I guess that, as men go, Jack really isn't a bad lover. He's just predictable. I told him that a few months ago. The next thing I knew he was reading to me from a book called *The Sensuous Woman* ... telling me about the joys of covering his prick with whipped cream and chocolate sauce and eating it off . . . or vice versa. No kidding! That's what that damned woman advised females to do. Ye Gods, I don't like whipped cream. It's fattening. Besides, whether we were trying to drown each other as we made love in our swimming pool, or Jack was dunking his balls in cold water, or we were playing with each other with a vibrator, or he was tasting me between the legs, when we were in the shower *he was still Jack*. No matter what he was doing, or where we were trying to screw, he was still saying the same predictable things. Christ, I don't know what I mean. I love Jack. I guess I'd be lonesome without his predictability."

Adam laughed. "Maybe he's not so predictable as you think. If he's in bed with Jan right now, instead of sitting behind his mahogany desk at the bank, looking like a reincarnation of Croesus, he deserves an A for effort." Enjoying the warmth of Bobby's breasts, Adam lay silently against her for a moment. The wondrous quality of female flesh might be predictable for the male, but if the male surrendered to it, the predictability had more nuances than he could ever encompass in his lifetime. He leaned on his elbow and looked into her face. Her eyes were closed.

"Did you ever stop to think that after a few weeks or months I would be just as predictable as Jack?"

She smiled at him without opening her eyes. "I guess so. But right now you're not. For one thing, Jack and I don't talk so much."

"That's sad," Adam admitted. "Maybe most human beings don't consciously seek enough input to recharge

156

and catalyze each other." Angela's serene face kept floating in and out of his mind. Angela would understand what he meant. He guessed that Bobby wouldn't. If Angela knew what he was thinking . . . that he had a pleasant little job to do with Barbara . . . she might even have given him her blessing. Or would she? Janice might have. Hadn't Janice occasionally told him that he made love to her as if his mind was half on it? By God, if only to prove to himself that the depth of the enjoyment of sex was the depth of the conscious mental surrender, he was going to try to make this one experience with Barbara something beyond a casual connection of flesh.

"Jonathan?" She kissed his fingers and whispered, "I was going to ask you what you were thinking. But the honest truth is that I'm ready to burst."

He rolled her on top of him. She sighed as she felt him enter her. "Why this way?" she asked.

"Because I can row the boat without falling overboard."

"I'm very excited."

"Bobby . . . Bobby . . . just glide. Feel me rippling under you. Feel my fingers on your behind. Feel my fingers touching your anus . . . feel the erotic warmth of us . . . breathe the odor of our flesh . . ."

"Oh . . . God . . . Adam . . . Adam . . . don't ever stop . . ." Barbara screamed and sobbed her joy and finally lay panting in his arms. Her rapid breathing slowly turned to laughter, and they both laughed hysterically together. "Oh, Adam . . . thank you. Thank you for laughing. That was so nice, I thought I'd never stop coming. Am I heavy? What about you? Oh, aren't we silly? What were we laughing about? Why do I feel so effervescent? Oh, dear . . . I'm being so selfish. What about you?"

"There's time. Just float."

Bobby looked at him dubiously. "I never floated before."

Adam chuckled. "You'll have to explain to Jack that floating is more fun than eating whipped cream."

"This can't be bad . . . can it? Are we bad?"

Adam shrugged. "I'll wager everyone who has ever had extramarital intercourse asks that question a few minutes after they reach a climax. What did you think of Sam and Yael's movie last night?"

"I thought it was very dreamy." Bobby inched up on her elbows and looked in his eyes. "Come to think of it

157

... you've been making love to me the same way. Sam's voice, as the off-screen commentator, was very beguiling. He kept proposing the idea of sex as a reunion with God ..."

"Don't say 'God' with such an awe-inspiring tone ..." Adam kissed her cheek. "Say 'God' like he might be you ... then sexual intercourse could be a voyage into your own mystery. The discovery, as Sam tried to explain in his *Oceanic Love*, of the unity between all the phenomena in the world ... an experiencing of a mystery that defies verbalization, beyond comparison with anything else you might ever experience, a sensing that what has happened to you has opened you to the depths of your being, has given you insights more vivid than any you have ever known ... and then, far beyond whipped cream and vibrators ... a sure sense of cosmic joy; an overwhelming feeling that in the act of love and mutual surrender, you have found the only true value and purpose of being born, and living and dying."

Barbara kissed his neck. "Adam, you sound like a minister. I don't really understand you, but I do like to float with you inside me. You've convinced me! This can't be bad!"

☆ 38 ☆

Adam was lost in his own thoughts. He wondered if man would ever wake up to the truth. It wasn't the merger of an uncommitted penis and vagina that was bad. How could flesh merging with the flesh of another loving person be bad? Was a handshake bad? Was a kiss bad? No. What was bad was the betrayal of the security and reinforcement that had been previously given to another person. Could human relationships be devised that gave those who dared the opportunity to live multiple commitments? Despite the prevalent I-gotta-be-me philosophy, couldn't there be a new kind of people in the making, living right now, who were aware of the greater truth. That each of us were really no more than the sum of those who loved us; that the me I gotta be, is you!

Still inside Barbara, as she lay dreamily across his thigh,

Adam thought of Angela. Making love with Bobby had made him aware of something he instinctively knew all along. The *knowing* of another human being required a time commitment that was self-limiting to promiscuity. For him, at least, unless a female would consciously work with him to embrace the world in their relationship, they could never be fully interfaced. And it was in the interfacing that he and Angela were succeeding where he and Barbara couldn't. And what about Janice? Adam smiled. Time and understanding, over many years, could also create their own interfacing.

Barbara sighed in his arms. "Even without opening my eyes I can feel you smiling. Are you happy? Do you want to come?"

"In a little while. I'm enjoying the erotic feel of your breasts against my chest ... the cool morning air ... the silence of the house."

"Do you know something, Jonathan?" Barbara's voice was a tiny whisper. "I've had sexual fantasies about you many times in the past few years."

Adam grinned at her and kissed her lips. "Most females refuse to admit that they occasionally live a fantasy life."

"I never told anyone else." Bobby snuggled herself enthusiastically against him. "But you do inspire confidence. Did you ever read that novel, *The Collector*? It's about a man who captures a young girl, like a collector would a butterfly, and keeps her imprisoned. He really wants her to love him ... even though she is unconditionally dependent upon him for everything. I used to daydream that situation. I was the woman and you were my captor."

Adam chuckled. "Did I finally give up pleading for your love and rape you?"

"Of course not! Females detest rape. But I pretended that you were forcing me, and ultimately I would capitulate."

"What then?"

"Nothing. I'd start all over."

"No nitty-gritty lovemaking?"

Barbara laughed. "No. I never daydream all the gory details."

"What other daydreams do you have?"

Barbara giggled. "Don't you think we're talking too much? Would you want to see if *I can ... again*?"

"You know you can!"

They reached a climax together.

"It was nice," Adam whispered in her ear. "Thank you, Bobby."

"Can I love you a little, Jonathan?"

Adam shrugged. "You can love me a lot . . . but mostly in fantasy."

Lying in his arms, Barbara told him another fantasy she occasionally indulged in. As he listened, Adam had to admit that this one had more imagination.

She was sitting beside Adam and he was driving an automobile on a remote country back road. A desperado waved them down. At gunpoint, this evil-looking man made Adam drive them high up on a lonely mountain road. Barbara's fantasies didn't include location, so she didn't know where the mountain was. Brandishing his gun, the desperado forced them to enter a lonely mountain lodge which was very cozy, with a fieldstone fireplace, deep rugs, and furniture. Who the lodge belonged to Barbara didn't know. Then he handcuffed them together, Jonathan's left wrist to her right wrist. There was plenty of food in the kitchen, but they couldn't pry open either the doors or the windows. They were prisoners tied together in a comfortable jail. Even though she knew he was Jonathan, in her fantasy they were actually strangers.

"I was wearing a panty girdle," Barbara laughed. "You had to help me get it off so I could go to the bathroom."

"Did I wipe your ass when you were finished?"

"My God . . . no! Anyway I had to pee-pee . . . not the other thing." Barbara grinned at him.

"Well, you had to dry your pussy. Did I help you?"

Barbara smiled. "I asked you to close your eyes."

The telephone on the bed table rang. Barbara jumped away from him, startled. *This was no fantasy.* "My God, it's probably Janice!" Barbara sounded frightened. In a flash, she was out of the bed and into her nightgown and housecoat.

"This isn't a picture phone!" Adam was laughing as he picked up the telephone. "Janice can't see you."

But it wasn't Janice. It was Sam. He sounded both wrathful and intimidated. "I've got bad news for you, Jake. Your loving sons and their women are in the Plymouth police station. We're about to be tossed into the cooler."

"For God's sakes, what for?"

160

"They say we were smoking grass. The police raided us on the *Wah-kon-tah*."

"At eleven o'clock in the morning? Why in hell were you smoking marihuana so early in the morning? I thought you were sailing the boat back."

"Evidently you're still in bed, Jake. If you'll look out your window, you'll find it's blowing about forty knots. We weren't getting high . . . just giving Hawkeye and Susan one more taste of Cohasset green."

"Jesus Christ!"

He heard Sam laugh. "We may need him, too! Robin figured by tomorrow we'll all be in the headlines. She just telephoned her father. When he discovers his baby daughter is in the pokey, he'll take off like a self-propelled rocket! According to Robin, Mr. Thomas doesn't think too highly of the weed."

☆ 39 ☆

Wondering what Adam might be doing the day after the holiday (was he still in bed? had he made love to Janice?), Angela listened to Jim in the kitchen as he dawdled over his second cup of coffee and flipped through the morning newspaper. "Dull day . . . the Friday after a holiday. Everyone I know is taking a long weekend. I've got a brief to prepare on the Jacobi case. But . . ."

Angela knew Jim was waiting for her to tell him he really should take the day off. Jim liked to be told that he had worked hard all his life. It eased his conscience to have her approval for what he had already made up his mind he was going to do. But Angela, watching Lena set up her ironing board, was too irritated at his mother (why couldn't she just relax?) to assuage his guilt feelings.

"Lena . . . please! . . . You don't have to iron today."

"I want to iron." Lena tested the bottom of the iron, which sizzled satisfactorily against her wet finger. "I like to iron. It's the least I can do to help you, Angela. Gramp and I are making a lot of unnecessary work for you." At seventy-five, Lena had become an irresistible force. "Besides, why should you pay to send Jim's shirts out? I'm happy to iron my son's shirts."

Even while Lena was talking, Angela had stopped listening. A flickering picture of naked bodies ... Adam's and Janice's thrusting at each other (or was it herself and Jim?) wove through her mind. She tried to shut the pictures off. It was better not to think of Adam making love to Janice. It not only reminded her of how little she really shared his life (or he hers), but it gave her an uneasy feeling that the intimacy of their Thursdays was an illusion. Really, compared to the six/sevenths of their lives that they didn't share, they were basically strangers. Their involvement was peripheral. Adam's lips kissed another woman's lips. His penis ...(the penis she had kissed) had been inside Janice. Was that nasty? Or immoral? Or evil? Angela smiled. The reverse also applied. If Janice kissed Adam's penis, what would Janice have thought if she knew it had been inside Angela? My God ... these were silly thoughts. Hangovers from a guilt-ridden world. Didn't she really believe what she had told Bettie Kanace? Did a penis or a vagina, or the person who was attached to one or the other, become different because they penetrated or gave entry to more than one penis or vagina? And if not, how many was too many? Freed of many past restrictions, it was obvious that human beings couldn't function without some new guideposts in the bewildering forests of human relationships.

Maybe the real problem was that although she and Adam made love as if there were no other person, for her as well as him, their love was schizophrenic, a self-deception that was almost impossible to cope with. While it was obvious that neither she nor Adam wanted to make comparisons ... wanted to even think comparatively (that would be destructive ... Jim was Jim ... Adam was Adam . . . and she, vis-à-vis either of them, was two different Angelas), still there was the inescapable fact that despite her complete surrender to Adam, and his to her, certain facets of their life experience were beyond discussion with each other. Was there no answer? Was it a condition of life that no two people could dare to be honest and defenseless with each other?

What would Adam think if she told him about last night? Would it sound invidious? A subtle complaint? In truth, wouldn't it be? Even though the upstairs bedrooms were completely occupied (though Ruth was in her own room, Bud was sleeping in Richy's room, and Lena and Gramp were in the guest room), and Jim knew that the walls

162

gave only the illusion of privacy, last night Jim had decided that he was in a romantic mood. There was no dissuading him. So, there was only one thing she could do. Not waste time. That way the bed would creak and groan only for a minute or two. It was a whore's trick. Jim had been able to withstand her passionate responses less than five minutes. Twelve minutes from beginning to end. The late news was still on television when he rolled off her. Was he convinced that she, too, had enjoyed the momentary encounter? The swift transition from passionate lover, enjoying a death-defying orgasm, to comfortable, satiated husband seemed incongruous to her. One moment there was his crying need for her body, followed quickly by what seemed to be only a dim awareness that she was the same person lying quietly beside him. His anger at the nightly news, telling him the inefficient way the country was being run, quickly subsumed his passion for her. But wasn't that fairly normal masculine behavior, particularly after a quarter century of marriage? It wasn't fair to compare Jim with Adam. Time and unfamiliarity was on Adam's side.

"Hey, lover, wake up." Jim was grinning at her, bringing her back to reality. "Was last night too much for you? You haven't heard a word I said." Angela knew that her face was flushed. (Maybe Jim was receiving telepathic messages she was unaware of.) But she had heard what he was saying. Vaguely, anyway. She assured him that she had been listening. He was going to drop into his office for an hour or two and then meet Ed Kanace at the club. There would be time this afternoon to play nine holes before it got dark. Later, around five, she could bring Gramps and Lena to the club for dinner. They could all have a few drinks first in the lounge.

"Nothing heavy." Jim kissed her good-bye. "After yesterday we all need to go on a diet. Maybe tonight we can find a movie that Gramps and Lena would enjoy."

"Gramps likes X movies." Angela smiled at her father-in-law. Looking up from his newspaper, Gramps winked his agreement.

"Well, I don't," Lena said after Jim was gone. "You're a lecherous old fool, Arthur." She shook her head at Gramps. "I never understood men. All that naked stuff makes me crawl. People jumping in and out of bed with each other indiscriminately. It's disgusting. Wonder they're not all diseased." Lena plopped the iron back and forth

163

across Jim's shirt with a heavy hand that indicated her disapproval. "Where's Ruth and that boyfriend of hers?" she demanded. "It's nearly ten-thirty and they haven't had breakfast yet."

Angela answered her with a patient smile. "Let them sleep. Kids that age hate to face life. Ruth can make Bud's breakfast when they come down." It was a good thing, Angela thought, that Jim, Lena, and Gramps didn't really know what was keeping Ruth and Bud. Just an hour ago, when she was sure that Jim and his mother and father were safely downstairs, Angela decided to confirm her suspicion. It was surprising that Jim was so unimaginative. Hadn't they all seen together that movie based on Philip Roth's novel *Goodbye, Columbus*, where the boyfriend sneaked out of his room and joined the daughter in hers? Had the movie paved the way for reality? Ruth and Bud were certainly unflappable. Not even shocked when she quietly opened Ruth's door and peered inside. Thank the Lord they weren't actually making love (Angela guessed it wouldn't have bothered Bud if she had surprised them in the act), but it was obvious from their relaxed dreamy expressions that not too many minutes ago they had been. Ruth was curled on her side, her face snuggled against Bud's neck. Bud was on his back, his eyes closed, evidently enjoying Ruth's fingers cradling his balls. They hadn't shown a scene like that in the movie, though the way movies were going, Angela guessed, it was just a matter of time. Neither Bud nor Ruth were embarrassed. Ruth, her eyes only half opened, snickered a "hi" at her. She didn't even let go of Bud's penis. And Bud just grinned at her and said, "Hi, Mom ... we were just talking about you. Ruth is convinced that she is a love-bug because she inherited her loving nature from you."

Blushing, not knowing what to say, Angela mumbled that Ruth better not let her father catch her in *flagrante delicto*. By keeping Ruth's relationship with Bud a secret, Angela realized that she really was deceiving Jim two ways. Jim certainly would be as shocked at her secrecy as he was at his daughter's "immorality." Maybe the truth was that she was looser morally than Jim. Was Ruth closer to the truth than she knew? Her mother was a love-bug. Years of marriage had only turned the damper on her fires. Maybe her seeming coolness had started on their honeymoon, when she had naïvely and honestly told Jim all the delicious sexual thoughts she had lived with as

164

a young girl. Then she had discovered that Jim was a little shocked that females could be so earthy. He was a husband who enjoyed his women on a pedestal. How could she tell him, for example, that she had recently read a survey made at the University of Louisville that showed young adults in the 18-25 age group thought about sex about once in every ten minutes, and middle-aged people about once in every thirty minutes ... especially when the truth was that at forty-three she was still maintaining the youthful sequence? Could she have told him when she finally returned to the kitchen that she had just seen her daughter's lover's penis ... and for a brief moment a fleeting picture of Jim's penis and *her lover's* penis had flashed across her mind. Or could she tell him about yesterday? Gramps had finally convinced her she should watch at least one pro football game on television. Then she had suddenly realized she wasn't interested in whether the players were called the Packers or the Rams or the Cowboys, or who was winning or losing, but rather that these magnificent men were wearing a new kind of football costume that clearly defined their buttocks, and a proud cod-piece that magnified their genitals. Did females who said they enjoyed professional football ever admit to themselves that they were really watching men? Men bending, flexing, kicking, running, in a lovely male sex ballet? Not that she was interested in any particular male player. Rather the game was a hymn to male sexuality. A virility dance. One day they might even devise mixed male and female athletic games (even football), where each team was composed of both males and females. A new kind of contest that bypassed physical brutality and could become a paean to the essence of maleness and femaleness.

Remembering that she had promised Adam she would send him a collection of her best pictures, Angela told Lena that she was going to work in her darkroom for a while. In the basement, she suddenly had a better idea. She would make a cassette tape for Adam. Would she dare mail it to his office? If she did, would he return a cassette to her ... a rambly one, just talking about nothing and everything? Oh, God! Extramarital communication was such a scary, undiscovered territory. Fortunately, the darkroom was not only lightproof but nearly soundproof. She turned on the outside red warning light and bolted herself inside. If anyone heard her mumbling, she could say she was humming or talking to herself.

☆ 40 ☆

At first her voice on the tape was uncertain, a trembling whisper, but slowly she grew more accustomed to speaking without a listener.

"Oh ... love, I really miss you. It's silly isn't it? How can a human being develop this mad longing for another human being. I've known you a little more than six weeks, and now eight days have gone by and with them the first Thursday we haven't made love. It would be so much easier to curl up in the temporary time capsules we create for each other and blend our words and flesh in a litany of love. Dear Love, I'm speaking into this contraption in my darkroom ... hidden away, feeling sneaky, because I told Lena I was going to print some pictures. I feel so tongue-tied. An ingenue in her first stage appearance. It isn't easy to conjure your face in my mind or speak to you as if you were here. How lovely it would be if I could just hear your voice ... Angel-a, you would say, I love you ... and you would hug me with a warm, laughing look of love on your face. Without you right here beside me, it's so difficult to vocalize my thoughts ... keep them from rambling ... take you inside my scatterbrain. Do I really dare to do that? Darling, I want the fullness of you inside me. Oh God, I better stay away from that kind of fantasy. Suddenly, all of you, your dear body naked beside me is too real ...

"There, I turned this tape recorder off for a second, to clear my mind. It isn't easy, believe me. The laughter you hear in my voice is really a form of whistling in the dark, or singing to make sure I am me, and won't just go up in smoke without you. Did I tell you Monday when I telephoned ... God, that was only three days ago? The days are creeping ... thirty-five more until I see you ... how will I last? Did I tell you that Robin and Richy weren't coming home for Thanksgiving? It's funny about kids. Ruth always calmly tells me what she's doing. If I don't

166

like it, I can lump it. But Robin is a loner. I think she's in love with somebody. But she isn't ready to commit herself. 'Maybe marriage isn't for everybody,' she told us a few Sundays ago when she telephoned. 'Maybe some people are just happier single.' I guess that kind of thinking frightens me. How can a person live by himself all his life? What would Robin think if she knew her mother wasn't satisfied with just one man, but somehow got herself committed to two?

"I guess that would shock Ruth, too. She dared all and asked if Bud could visit with us over this long weekend. Bud's home is in San Francisco ... what there is of it. Both his father and mother are remarried. I don't think he has much rapport with either of his new families. Oh, Adam . . . remember when we were reading Alvin Toffler's *Future Shock* . . . do you remember Toffler's feeling that temporary relationships, rapidly developed in depth, would be the only way of human survival in the transient future? Toffler frightened me. Yet, I suppose, in a sense, we are precursors of that kind of intense relationship. In less than two months I have given myself to you in a depth of communication and sheer trust that equals or even surpasses my years with Jim. But there's something else, too. Something we can't share together, can never have together. Families. Families are important, aren't they? A person needs two-generation or even three-generation roots. Yet, the problem is that one generation rarely learns to accept another on its own terms. How much nicer it would be if I could tell Lena and Gramp that I love *you and Jim* . . . or if I could tell Jim, and we could discuss you and me as a quite natural way of life, without any threat to the intimacy of the life that Jim and I have shared. Or, if you could share me with your family. And since we were lovers, then you could come and visit me here, and not in some impersonal hotel room. (Why should Jim mind on a day he was playing golf?) Or I could visit you in Cohasset while Jim and Janice were visiting their lovers' homes, or, if they preferred not to have the involvement of another love ... they could do whatever they might wish on that day. Couldn't the central core of the family be maintained, and still make room for at least one more involvement?

"Gosh, I'm off the subject. I was talking about Bud. Anyway, I have a feeling that's why Ruth brought him home ... to offer him an alternate family. Hopefully one he could identify with. And along with her home, and her family, she's giving herself and her own warmth. . . . It may not be nice for a mother to say it, but I'm glad that there's lovemaking going on in my house, and that my daughter has brought her friend home. Not to trap him. Simply to let him know that affection and love doesn't have to come with strings attached. . . . Of course, I guess my real fear, when I think about Ruth and Bud, is not what she is doing . . . but rather how I could ever explain what I am doing? I was reading *Time* magazine yesterday and the advertisement of one of the big diamond manufacturers stopped me cold. It was a full page in four colors with a diamond about to be inserted on the female's hand, and this message: 'For the hundreds of ball games you've watched (and I know you hate ball games). For the operas and ballets you haven't seen (because you know I hate them). For all the years of giving, sharing, and caring, Happy Anniversary!'

"Ye Gods, Adam, isn't that advertisement the epitome of our mad world? Diamonds, somehow, become a gift of love that can make up for any kind of day-to-day failures to really be the other person. Is that the kind of ethical and moral guideline I should perpetuate for my kids? On the other hand, if I'm excoriating the kind of stupid lack of monogamous communication this advertisement is exalting, can I tell my children that Mommy has a lover, and at the same time have them believe that all is well in the Thomas household? That somehow, whether they can comprehend it or not, Mommy loves both Daddy and Adam? Oh, honey . . . I'm really grinning and feeling very bubbly. But I think the truth is neither Ruth nor Robin could understand. Not yet. Possibly Ruth might, because she's sleeping with Bud without benefit of wedlock, and she's a little rebellious anyway. I suspect that she couldn't simultaneously at her age love another boy. I remember you saying: 'Love is process.' When they teach that as a way of life, men won't give diamonds for the ballets they refused to attend, and the kind of world that Byron knew when he said, 'Man's love is of a man's life a thing apart; 'Tis woman's whole existence . . .' will be buried in the same grave as Fritz Perls, 'I do my thing . . . you do yours.'

"Oh, dear love, reality has caught up with me. Someone is pounding on the darkroom door."

☆ 41 ☆

It was Ruth. "Mother! Mother! Can you hear me? Robin is on the telephone. She wants to talk with you."

Damn. Jim had often told her she should have had an extension put in the darkroom. Angela snapped off the recorder, tucked it in one of the cabinets, and ran upstairs to the kitchen. She grabbed the phone from Ruth, who was trying, unsuccessfully, to determine where Robin was telephoning from. Ignoring the questioning look on Gramp's and Lena's faces, Angela tried to appear calm. "Robin, how nice of you to call. Where are you? Are you all right?"

"I'm in Plymouth, Mother." Robin's voice sounded a little detached and giddy. As she spoke, it was as if she were perceiving new and interesting relationships between her thoughts, and was enjoying the contemplation of them. "You and Daddy aren't going to be very happy about this." Angela could hear Robin chuckle. "Oh, Mother, it's really quite silly. If I were twenty-one, I wouldn't have to bother you. It's too bad, because sometimes, like now, when I'm talking with you, I know that I'm a hundred and twenty-one, and you and Daddy are really my great-grandchildren."

Angela tried to hide her astonishment. Had Robin been drinking? Robin, for heaven's sake, what's the matter? What are you trying to say? Did you say you were in Plymouth? Do you mean Plymouth, Massachusetts?"

"Yes, Plymouth, Mother, Plymouth where the Pilgrims landed. That was three hundred and fifty years ago. But they're still here. Their great-great-grandchildren have just arrested us. They said we were smoking grass. Sam told them it wasn't grass. It was just oregano. And we're all just pizzas who needed some spice. Mother, the truth is that the descendants of the Pilgrims aren't so great." Robin giggled. "Right now they are acting boorish. I really mean boorish, which is piggish. Mother, do you know what grass is?"

Angela stared into the phone. She was aware that

169

Gramps, Lena, Bud, and Ruth were all listening to her response. "Robin, stop joking with me. I don't like it."

"Mother, *I am not joking!* Right now . . . standing right beside me, is a big fat Pill-grim. He's wearing a uniform and badge, and he's telling me not to take all day. This is a long-distance call. I'm sorry, Mother. But you're going to have to tell Daddy. His darling daughter is going to jail. The Grim-man said so. They're going to take us to the county court house. We'll be arraigned for trial. If you and Daddy won't bail me out, you can visit me in the Children's Detention home. They won't release me except to my parents."

Angela listened increduously. Instead of being in despair or contrite, Robin actually seemed to be quite bubbly and hilarious. She could hear Robin laughing in concert with some voice in the background. "I just told this horrid Pill-grim that I'm old enough to vote, I should be old enough to smoke pot. He told me no one is old enough to smoke marihuana and get away with it."

Angela tried to be calm. "Robin, please come down to earth. Tell me exactly where you're telephoning from."

"I told you, Mother. These Pill-grims arrested all of us. We weren't even bothering them. Just sitting in the cabin of Jake Adams' boat . . . me, Yael, Keane, and Sam, and two very nice Indians named Whitecloud . . . Hawkeye White-cloud and his wife Susan. We're so mad at them, we're all going to declare war on the United States of America. When we win we're going to elect Hawkeye President . . . and he's going to invite me to dance at the White House!"

The name Keane slowly penetrated Angela's shock. My God! It couldn't be: no! . . . not Adam's son! "Robin, did you say Keane Adams?"

"Yes, Mother, Keane Adams." Robin sounded impatient. "I know . . . you thought that I was in Westchester. I'm sorry. There was a change in plans. Actually, the past few days, I've been in Cohasset with Jake and Janice Adams, and their son Keane."

While Angela was trying to control a rising feeling of hysteria, Ruth, who had been listening on the extension, danced back in the kitchen squealing with delight. "My little sister Robin has been arrested for smoking pot! Now, what do you think about that? Jee-iminy wow! Wait till Daddy finds out."

A masculine voice, gruff and cold, replaced Robin's on

170

the phone. 'Madam, are you the mother of Robin Thomas?"

"Yes, I am."

"Your daughter tells us that your husband is a lawyer. Is that true?"

"He is."

"Mrs. Thomas, I'm sorry to have to tell you ... your daughter and five of her friends were picked up by one of our cruising cars about a half hour ago. They had about ten ounces of marihuana in their possession. The fact is they're all still pretty high. You and your husband better get over here as quickly as possible."

"My husband is playing golf." Angela knew that was a silly reply, but she was so bewildered that she simply didn't know what to say. Why was Robin smoking marihuana? Why would anyone want to smoke marihuana?

The policeman sounded crisp and a little irritated. "Madam, if my daughter were in a mess like this, I'd hotfoot it over to that golf course, and trot around all the holes until I found my husband. Your daughter is charged with a felony. She could spend the night behind bars."

Angela put the phone down and stared dumbly at Lena and Gramps. Confused, bewildered beyond any ability to sort out this sudden, unbelievable barrage, Angela burst into tears. "Robin's been arrested for smoking marihuana." She kept repeating the words while the tears streamed down her cheeks. Touched by her mother's misery, Ruth hugged her and tried to assure her that it was no big thing. There weren't enough jails to hold all the kids who had smoked pot.

Lena looked at Ruth amazed but said nothing. Gramps mumbled, kids will be kids, and Bud rubbing his hand through his long hair had an expression on his face that conveyed his hopeless disapproval with the whole mad world.

Even while she was telling Ruth to call the club and try to locate her father, Angela was aware that her careening thoughts and sickening, kicked-in-the-stomach feeling were not wholly due to Robin's smoking marihuana. Momentarily, she didn't dare speculate on the answers, but the questions kept circling in her mind. By what mad coincidence was Robin in Cohasset? How had she got there? Where had she met Adam's son? Why hadn't Adam told her that Robin was coming to his house? She suddenly remembered Adam telling her, last summer he had grown

171

marihuana plants . . . had even smoked grass several times. He was neither impressed nor unimpressed with it. "A mild escape from boredom," he told her. "Making love to you puts me much more in tune with the world." Could Adam have given Robin the marihuana? Worse . . . far worse, did Robin suspect that Jonathan Adams was her mother's lover?

Somehow she finished changing into a prim, brown street dress just as Ruth yelled from downstairs. "Mother, they say Daddy's out on the course somewhere with Ed Kanace. He left the first hole about an hour ago."

"Have someone page him or send someone out to find him." Angela stared in her bathroom mirror and tried to calm her distraught expression. "Tell him it's urgent. Mrs. Thomas will meet her husband in twenty minutes in front of the club."

She refused to argue with Ruth, who had followed her upstairs. No. Ruth and Bud couldn't drive with them to Plymouth. If Ruth wanted to help, she and Bud could stay here and cool Gramps and Lena. "Your father is going to take this pretty hard."

"Really, Mother," Ruth said, "marihuana isn't that bad. All Daddy has to do is try it. Bud has a toke somewhere. We've been tempted to mix some in Gramp's pipe tobacco; then he wouldn't mind Lena yakking at him all the time."

"Ruthie!" Angela tried to keep her voice level. "You and I have had a lot of confidences. We've been friends, but don't push it . . . and don't try anything funny with Gramps and Lena. I mean it!"

In the station wagon all Angela could think of was Adam. Robin smoking marihuana and being arrested was bad enough, but what if Robin knew that she had been unfaithful? Could Adam have let anything slip? Adam smiling at her as he recited poetry flickered through her mind. "Fear not, dear love, that I'll reveal those hours of pleasure we two steal. No eyes shall see, nor yet the sun descry what thou and I have done . . ." Yes, Adam could say that, but he had never been very careful to avoid discovery. When they walked through the streets of Boston, when they registered at hotels, he had made no attempt at concealment. "I love you Angel-a. I'm not ashamed of us." Okay, all right, Angela thought, but you can't say that to my children.

It suddenly occurred to her that when she and Jim got

to Plymouth Adam would be there. Confronted by their spouses, would their guilt be so apparent that anyone could tell? That was silly. But what could she and Janice talk about? And, what about Jim and Janice? Angela knew that her imagination was running away with her. Janice couldn't see inside her brain. Were Jim and Janice faithful to their conjugal vows? Jim was ... of that Angela was sure. He never left Acton. A picture of the big black leather couch in Jim's office flashed through her mind. Of course, Jim could have curled up there on an afternoon with some female client. My God ... at a time like this, how could she have such silly thoughts? Jim was so proper he would never have thought of even making love to his wife on that couch.

What if Robin knew? The question was a dirge in her brain. How had Robin ever met Keane? Was Adam responsible? She remembered Adam telling her that Keane was playing with the New York Philharmonic. Had Adam told him that he should look up Robin Thomas, who was studying ballet at the Juilliard School? It was strange she never thought of it ... Robin and Keane would have a lot in common. Angela couldn't help smiling inwardly at the thought ... not only music, but a father and a mother who were lovers.

☆ 42 ☆

Jim was waiting for her in front of the club. Ed Kanace was with him. Neither had changed from the slacks and sweaters they were wearing on this cool New England day. Perfect golf weather. She didn't blame Jim for the look of disgust on his face. He was thinking, what silly thing was bugging his wife that she would upset the whole damned club? Once he had told her that Alan Shepard had swung a golf club on the moon because he was symbolically staking out the moon as one place women wouldn't follow men to play golf. Men needed liberation, too.

There was no choice but to come to the point. By tomorrow it would be in the papers. Acton girl arrested on marihuana charge. Jim would detest that. "We've got to go to Plymouth, Jim. Robin has been arrested." Angela blurted the words as she stopped the car. "She's in the police station there. She was smoking marihuana."

"Robin?" Jim's shout was incredulous. He looked as if he were about to collapse from some internal implosion. "For Christ's sake, not Robin!"

Ed Kanace patted his shoulder. "Jim, don't let it throw you. All my kids have smoked it. Bettie and I even tried it a few months ago. We never told you and Ange . . ." Jim had made it obvious on more than one occasion that he was not in favor of legalizing marihuana. Ed grinned feebly at him. "After all, Jim, you're the law."

Jim pushed Angela out of the driver's seat. It was one-thirty. She knew that it would take at least an hour and a half to drive to Plymouth. She tried to keep her tension under control, but Jim drove fast . . . angrily, as if his wrath weren't simply over Robin's betrayal, but he was personally at war with every automobile on the road. When she told him that she was frightened enough without having to wonder if they were going to be dead the next minute, and then they certainly wouldn't be much help to Robin, he only grimaced.

"Of all the goddamned unnecessary things to have done." Jim kept repeating the words over and over again. "Smoking marihuana. Good God! I thought Robin would have more sense."

"Some people think marihuana isn't so bad. I think too much fuss is being made." Angela didn't know how far she should go in trying to reorient Jim's beliefs . . . "Anyway, you can be sure that Robin is very much like both of us . . . basically pretty serious . . . she'd never want to lose control of her mind. It was probably just a lark."

"Some lark," Jim said grimly. "These damned kids are going to spoil all their future fun in life. Too much of everything. We give them too much money, and then they get bored and try to find excitement with drugs and sex. What have they got to look forward to? You can't spend your life escaping life."

Angela sighed. Jim could certainly think she and Adam were simply using each other as a form of escape. But actually, wasn't most of everyone's life spent escaping or planning to escape life one way or another? For Adam it seemed to be making love . . . for Jim, golf. "I guess I kind of feel sorry for the kids," she said. "We tell them to straighten up and be righteous citizens but beneath the surface they can see the truth. There's very little real love

174

and affection between humans in this world, and without love what else has any meaning?" Angela tried to reach Jim on a different level. "We were all pretty proud of you when you decided to defend that kid who wore the American flag sewed onto the seat of his pants. Wasn't that the same kind of rebellion? Can you really blame any of the kids? It's a pretty screwed-up world. Who's to say what's good or bad?"

For the first time Jim grinned. "I know, I know . . . I even said that I'd take that backyard nudity case in Cambridge. But the principles are different. Maybe those people were taking drugs, but that wasn't the issue . . . and anyway, I didn't know it. Don't think that I'm completely square. I'd defend Patrick Henry or Eldridge Cleaver. Incidentally, I just read where Cleaver completely rejected Timothy Leary's 'turn on . . . tune in . . . drop out' theories. No drugs, not even marihuana is permitted to Black Panthers. I guess that's what scares me. While America becomes effete and decadent, the tough nuts of the world steel themselves, like old-time Spartans, for the takeover. If the young Americans want to survive with any kind of freedom, they simply can't turn their backs and drop out."

"Oh, Jim," Angela said. "You remind me of that poem. 'Life is real. Life is earnest.' You don't believe it yourself. We drink . . . isn't that dropping out for a few hours?"

"That's what all the kids say. It's no excuse, Angela. A world of alcoholics is just as bad as a world of pot-smokers or LSD trippers. It isn't the drugs . . . no matter what they may be. It's their what-the-hell attitude about life and values that scares me. Right now, all I keep thinking about is that movie . . . *Joe* . . . I can see that big slob with his gross, naked belly groveling with those young girls. They all were smoking pot. The girls slithering naked all over him, two at a time, as if sex had no meaning. Is that the kind of people Robin is mixed up with? Did you say their name was Adams? That sounds pretty improbable to me."

Angela laughed. "I don't know why. The Kennedy children tried marihuana." She guessed that Jim had substituted Robin in his mind for those young girls he had seen in the movie. Robin making love with lecherous old men. Robin . . . his baby daughter, a full-grown, sexual woman. Jim had told the children that in his opinion premarital intercourse was no panacea solution that guaranteed a happy marriage. The divorce cases he had handled proved

175

that. He admitted to them that he and their mother had made love before they were married, but they had been committed, and it had happened only a few weeks before the wedding. The thought of Robin or Ruth calmly entering into long-term sexual relations before they were married was something Jim preferred not to think about. Their mother had been a virgin before they had sex together (at least Jim thought so). Despite all the freedom today, Jim was certain that men preferred women with limited premarital sexual experience.

"I guess there's a boy in it somewhere," Angela said, knowing full well that the boy was Adam's son. It occurred to her, as Jim slowly exhausted every facet of his indignation and finally subsided into bewildered melancholy, that the worst was yet to come. What would she do if Adam so much as hinted that he knew her? What would she say? The inevitable questions of where, when, and how she had met Adam would jump into Jim's legal mind. If she casually admitted to the chance taking of Adam's picture with the Hare Krishna dancers, wouldn't Jim wonder why she had never mentioned meeting Adam? Wouldn't he suspect the obvious? Where there was smoke there was fire. If she had to lie, or tell a half truth, could she make it stick? She knew that she wasn't a good dissembler. She would blush, or act so damned uneasy that a rank amateur could tell she was guilty.

A few minutes before they arrived in Plymouth, Angela was on the verge of confessing the truth. Wouldn't it be better to make a headlong confession than slowly sink into an ugly swamp of deceit? But ... dear God, what could she say? "I love you, Jim, and somehow I love Adam, too." She would have to be that honest. She couldn't say it was just a sex escapade, that she had never really loved Adam, or that now she was sorry, or promise she wouldn't see Adam anymore.

Still, if she were forced to make a choice, what else could she do? Adam had his full life without her. In any event, she wouldn't want his love at Janice's expense. If she told Jim that there would be no more Thursdays, would Jim forgive her? Maybe ... maybe on the surface their life would go on, but deep down wouldn't Jim's security and trust be gone? Wouldn't the knowledge that she had loved Adam gradually erode their marriage? She wondered how she might have reacted if the situation had been reversed. Oh, damn, she might as well face the truth.

If love were jealousy, then she wasn't in love with Jim. Because the truth was that even before Adam she would have hugged Jim ... not to forgive him (why should anyone have to forgive love?) but to tell him she understood.

☆ 43 ☆

When they finally located the police station and Jim informed the sergeant at the desk who they were, a captain appeared and curtly informed them that their daughter was with the Adams family, and their lawyer in the station conference room. His tight smile seemed to say that the Thomases were about what he expected .. indulgent upper-middle-class parents who had never properly disciplined their children. He led them down a corridor and rapped imperiously on a closed glass door. A tall young man with long black hair opened it and greeted them enthusiastically, with no aura of guilt.

"You must be Robin's father and mother. Welcome to Plymouth ... a world we never made. I'm Keane Adams. No matter what you may be thinking, and Robin thinks it's probably pretty horrible, I love your daughter. I'll marry her, even if she is a pot-head!"

Robin hugged Angela and smiled timidly at her father. Jim didn't think Keane's remark was funny. He ignored Keane's proffered hand. Angela guessed that Jim had expected some tears of contrition. The apparent coolness of the guilty ones irritated him. Over Robin's shoulder, she intercepted Adam's cheerful smile and quickly looked away. He stood up from the long oak table they had all been sitting around, and took her hand. His calm expression exuded confidence and reassurance. He almost seemed to be saying, I love you. Don't worry, Angela.

She could feel the blood rising in her face, and she wondered if the other people in the room (one of whom was obviously Sam Adams) were aware of the unspoken interchange. Adam was telling Jim he was sorry that they should meet under such unpleasant circumstances .. not to blame the kids. "It's the law that needs to be changed." But Jim maintained a cool legal distance and refused to thaw under the Adams warmth. Angela felt like a woman reprieved from a hanging. For the moment, at least, her relationship with Adam seemed to be their secret.

Adam introduced Keane and Sam. "These are my boys, and Yael is Sam's wife. Behind them are Susan and John Whitecloud and Barbara Lovell, a friend of the family. My wife wasn't home when the police telephoned, but we haven't let any grass grow under our feet." He chuckled at his unintentional innuendo, and then checked to see if the door was closed. "You wonder, sometimes, if they would bug a room like this." Adam introduced the only person in the room they hadn't met, a tall, tweedy-looking man in his late thirties. "This is Bob Aureen, Jim. May I call you Jim? Bob is our lawyer. I think he has things pretty much under control."

Jim, shaking his head disgustedly, was still being austere. "It seems to me that you're all taking this pretty damned casually. What I would like to know from Robin is where she got the damned stuff and why in hell she was smoking it anyway? Secondly . . ." Jim frowned at Robin who was holding hands with Keane. "What are you doing in Massachusetts? Why did you lie to your mother and me, and tell us that you were going to your girlfriend's house? Quite honestly, Robin, your mother and I can't understand you at all."

"It's my fault," Keane jumped into the fray. From Jim's scowl it was plain to see that neither Keane with his dutch-boy haircut, nor Sam with his beard, nor the Whiteclouds who looked as if they had concealed bows and arrows under their buskins, were the kind of friends he would have picked for Robin. "Robin and I met nearly a year ago in New York," Keane told him. "I'm responsible. I persuaded her to come to Cohasset instead of going to her girlfriend's house. Actually, Robin and I were going to drive over to Acton tomorrow, so that I could ask for her hand in marriage." Robin smirked at Keane and shrugged at the astonishment on Angela's and Jim's faces.

"Keane's trying to pin me down." She smiled at him with an obvious expression of love on her face. "Don't worry. I'm going to finish Juilliard first. It's nothing imminent. As for the grass, it was mine. I brought it from New York."

"That's not true." Adam smiled, particularly at Angela. "I grew the plants last summer. While Robin may have

178

smoked marihuana before, I'm sure that she didn't bring her own supply to Cohasset."

"You mean that you actually grew the stuff in your own yard?" Jim couldn't believe that this proper-looking Bostonian would do anything so foolhardy. "You must be insane."

Bob Aureen laughed. "Let's just say Jonathan dreamed he grew it. Reality is in the eyes of the beholder. In any event, Jonathan, I'm warning you ... keep your mouth shut. The source of the weed is not the issue here. Unless you feel like joining a long list of marihuana martyrs, the path of least resistance will be for the kids to say they bought it in New York."

Adam shrugged. "My boys were smoking in the privacy of their own boat. A statement made by Justice Brandeis that I've never forgotten from my more radical student days goes a little like this. 'When the makers of the Constitution undertook to secure conditions favorable to the pursuit of happiness, they recognized man's spiritual nature, his feelings, his intellect. They knew that only part of the pain, pleasure, and satisfactions of life are to be found in material things. They sought to protect Americans in their beliefs and thoughts. They conferred, as against the government, the *right to be let alone*—the most comprehensive of rights, and the right most valued by civilized man.'" Adam ignored Jim and Bob Aureen's surprise. "Sorry, but my mind is cluttered with things like that. I'm not a lawyer, but the *Wah-kon-tah* where the kids were arrested smoking the stuff is an extension of my home. What's more, when you fellows finally get around to working on the problem of legalization, I suggest you also make it perfectly legal to grow it yourself." Adam grinned at Angela. "Even in dreams it's quite easy to grow ... requires no effort at all. We should make the sale of it illegal ... not the smoking, nor the growing, nor the giving of it. The same principle could be applied to distilled and fermented liquors. Making one's own simple escape mechanisms from this life shouldn't be a source of profit for business, or taxation for government. The Pilgrims and the early Americans made their own liquor ... If we made the sale of alcohol and marihuana illegal, but condoned the home-grown and home-produced product, we'd restore some of the dignity and control to the family where it belongs."

Adam was enjoying his tub-thumping. "If people could

simply grow pot, use it themselves or give it away, we'd prevent one more possible form of personal manipulation by government and business. I have a feeling there are plenty of politicians and industrialists who wouldn't give a damn if the entire so-called New Left and revolutionists "turned on," particularly if they paid taxes to do it Stoned, they would be ineffective politically, while they were simultaneously making the producers rich. The same principle applies to the hard drugs. Treat the user who is hooked, *free*. Let him live in perpetual euphoria, or have the option of *free* treatments at drug addiction centers Dry up the profit and the possible tax windfalls and there would be some hope that the escape mechanisms would assume a more casual perspective in most peoples' lives."

"Mr. Adams!" Jim slammed his hand on the table. "I didn't come here to discuss insane ideas about the legalization of or private growing of marihuana". He stared angrily at Bob Aureen. "Where are we? What are the charges? What have you done?"

Aureen smiled cooly at him. "Leaving aside Jonathan's 'insanity,' as you have so rightly characterized it, and assuming that his diatribe has been for our ears alone, I think we're in pretty good shape. None of these youngsters were smoking the joints in the street. Late last night, evidently feeling the hunger pains that come from smoking pot, they were gaily eating in a local restaurant out of their entire inventory while simultaneously causing quite a commotion. The police were alerted by the owners, but they waited until this morning before they raided the *Wah-kon-tah*. They had no search warrant. Jonathan's privacy bit doesn't apply, of course. But happily, during the three hours we've been here, things are cooling a bit. We're waiting for one more phone call, and that should wrap it up."

While Bob Aureen and Jim were discussing whether they could avoid arraignment for a felony trial, Angela suddenly realized that Samuel Adams was staring at her. Not with words, but by an overfriendliness, Sam and Yael gave Angela the impression that they were all accomplices to some prior understanding that transcended the immediate discussion. Had Adam told Sam about her? God, if she could only talk with him alone for a minute. She had to put together the missing pieces before she tripped on them. And where was Adam's wife, Janice? And why was that woman Barbara Lovell smiling so approvingly at everything Adam said and occasionally holding his arm as if she owned him? Angela's whirling thoughts made her so jittery she finally excused herself and asked where the ladies' room was.

"It's right next to the men's room," Adam twinkled at her. "I'll show you, Mrs. Thomas." Squeezing her hand, he led her quickly down the hall to an appropriately marked door, opened it, and shoved her in. There was only a toilet and sink in the tiny room. He turned the lock.

"Adam . . . for God's sakes, get out of here." Angela stared at him, terrified. "What if Robin or that Barbara friend of yours followed us?"

Adam kissed her mouth closed. "They can't get in. When you leave, I'll lock the door after you, and then, when the coast is clear, I'll leave." He chuckled. "I'll have to admit that I've watched you take a leak under more favorable circumstances. Oh God, Angela . . . I just wanted you to know, I love you, and to tell you not to worry."

"Adam, I beg you. Get out of here. We can't talk now."

He could see that she was close to hysteria. "Angela, this doesn't change anything. Call me Monday . . . somehow . . . you must!"

"No . . . Adam. It's over." Angela's voice was trembly with her fear of discovery. "I don't know why, but I have a feeling that your boys know about us. Sam, particularly. He and his wife give me a feeling they are about to say it right aloud: 'You are my father's mistress. We saw you together!'

Adam had momentarily forgotten the Hare Krishna pictures. Certainly, by now, Sam and Yael would have made the connection. He wondered whether they had questioned Robin already. If Robin had told them her mother was a photographer, Adam was sure that Sam and Yael would have put two and two together, particularly when they saw Angela in the flesh. But beyond the fact that he was obviously more aware of Angela than he might be of some passing housewife who had taken a snapshot of him . . . what could they guess?

These thoughts streamed through his mind in a split second but Angela caught the flicker of uncertainty on his face. "They do know, don't they, Adam? . . . Please, if I don't go, I'll burst." Embarrassed she lifted her skirt, wiggled out of her panties, and sat on the toilet. "Please,

Adam, I beg you ... if you ever loved me, get out of here *now*!"

Adam opened the door a crack and peered up the hall. "Angela ... telephone me Monday morning. You must!" As he closed the door behind him he saw the fright and misery on her face, and he knew she wouldn't.

☆ 44 ☆

A half hour later Jim, Angela and Robin were on their way back to Acton. Monday, the formalities of the law would be preserved. Bob Aureen and Jim would meet in court with the judge and the county attorney ... Robin Thomas, Keane and Samuel Adams, Yael Adams, and the Whiteclouds would be given a warning and released. With a little undercover maneuvering, the charges would be dropped completely.

To Jim's dismay, instead of being thankful that she had escaped so easily, Robin sat in the back seat of the car in tearful silence. She had hugged Keane and kissed him and told him to come visit her tomorrow in Acton, and she generally had made it quite obvious that she would have preferred to spend the remaining days of the weekend with Keane and the Adams family in Cohasset. While Robin hadn't actually said it, Angela was sure that Robin didn't want to be called to account or even questioned for having smoked marihuana. That she and her friends might have gone to trial and been convicted of a felony didn't seem to jar her.

It did nothing to calm Jim, who was spouting on at length about hippie surburbanites and limousine liberals (his description of Jonathan Adams and his sons), when Robin finally told him if she had to go to trial, she wouldn't want her father to defend her. As far as she was concerned, the whole business was absolutely ridiculous and proved how mad the whole society was. If she had to go to jail, it was all right with her. And whether Daddy liked Jake or not Robin was certain of one thing, Jake would never let them down. Jake was a man who would fight for a principle . . . a latter-day Thoreau.

"It isn't that I'm so hopped-up on pot-smoking, either."

Robin cooly expounded her philosophy. "I believe like the Adamses . . . bad laws are meant to be broken. You see, Daddy, Keane's father is a man who asks questions. Questions like, why up until 1956 was there no law at all against marihuana? And then the Marihuana Tax Act came into existence, but it didn't say one way or the other whether grass was good or bad. It just put a federal tax on the sale of it. Why, at this late date, has marihuana suddenly become such a menace? It's been around as long or longer than distilled spirits. I think it's because, just on hearsay, the bluenoses have attributed all kinds of sadistic and heinous crimes to people who were presumably under the influence of pot. The same kind of upright citizens passed the Volstead Act. I remember you telling us that Gramps didn't pay any attention to that silliness. Once he even told all of us that he made gin in his bathroom and sold it by the pint to his friends. You and mother thought it was very funny that he kept it in the bathtub. If the revenue agents came, he would run for the bathroom, lock the door, and let the evidence go down the drain." Robin shrugged. "Your generation finally got fed up and ended Prohibition. Now, if you feel like it, you can go to clubs like the Valley Stream and drink yourself to death. I can tell you, smoking pot has one advantage over alcohol, you don't become so idiotic with grass, or fawn all over each other like your sad-apple friends at the club do.

"One thing you should know, and you don't have to blame Keane or Jake, I smoked grass before I met Keane. The kids I know can smoke it or leave it alone, which is more than you can say about some of your friends and juice."

"Juice? . . . Jake?" Jim exploded. "You sound like all the rest of them. How come you call Mr. Adams by his first name?"

Robin laughed. "That's not his first name. Jake has several names. His kids call him Jake. His wife calls him Jon."

Angela held her breath, wondering if anyone beside herself called him Adam. Had Adam told that friend of his, Barbara Lovell, her name for him? Why had she come to the police station anyway? Where was her husband? God, what difference did it make? Angela had told Adam she wouldn't ever see him again. They had been lucky. They had their "brief encounter" and no one was the wiser. Even if she were sick at heart, there was only one

183

sane thing to do ... "give him up." Weren't those the hopeless words they used to terminate affairs?

For a moment she had tuned Robin and Jim out, but Robin having found her tongue was still rubbing salt in her father's wounds. "The real problem, Daddy, is you don't know what you're talking about. You should smoke a joint or two. If you and Jake would get acquainted, I'm sure he would give you some of his dream seeds. Next summer, you could raise your own.

Jim grunted his disgust. "So, he really did grow that stuff. If this business comes to trial, don't think I won't pursue it. There's something about this arrogant Mr. Jonathan Adams that needs to be punctured. Believe me, I'm just the one to do it."

Angela was silently praying that Robin would drop the subject. The truth was shockingly apparent to her. Adam had not only grown marihuana and given it to his boys *and her daughter*, but for all she knew he had probably encouraged Robin to smoke it with him and her friends. Whatever had been going on in the Adams home since Wednesday night, Angela had suddenly seen Adam with a new insight and clarity. Jonathan Q. Adams had scarcely been as honest with her as she had with him. Why had he never mentioned his sexy-looking friend Barbara Lovell? Was he sleeping with her? Were the Adams and the Lovells wife-swapping? Was Janice sleeping with Jack Lovell? Angela was certain that something strange was going on. Why had the boys and Robin and Yael all been staying overnight on the boat together? It was apparent (though Jim, hot on the marihuana bit, had overlooked it) that Robin must be sleeping with Keane. Angela was sure of one thing. If, somehow, she came through this weekend without Jim discovering that she knew Adam . . . had known him intimately for six weeks ... if the good Lord were watching over her, this must be the end. She must not capitulate. No matter how much she enjoyed those mad Thursdays with Adam, they couldn't continue.

Again as she pursued her own worries, she lost the thread of conversation between Robin and Jim, but Robin had scarcely come up for air. "Daddy, if you ever bring Jake into this ... or even mention that he grew the pot, I'll never speak to you or see you again as long as I live. I told you . . . Jake grew marihuana because he was curious. Curious to try it himself. It would be nice to have parents who were more aware of what's happening." Between sobs, Robin managed to throw some more fuel on the fire. "The trouble with you and Mother . . . particularly you, Daddy, is you don't ever wonder about anything. Mother at least has Thursdays . . ." Angela suppressed her astonished gasp. "And Mother's photographs show that she knows it is a different kind of world than she grew up in. But you're so straight . . . you don't even know that in addition to forward and backward, there's up and down. If you were defending me, before the trial was over, the prosecution would have convinced you that I was guilty."

"You are guilty, Robin," Jim said angrily. "One thing you and your Jake Adams and his hippie sons are going to learn is that we are living in a society. If you defy the laws of your society, don't yell for mercy when it grinds you to bits."

"I'm not defying the law. No one has a right to make a law about what I do with my body. If I go naked . . . make love . . . smoke pot . . . get drunk, have an abortion, or commit suicide, and I don't physically injure anyone else, it's none of society's business."

"Robin, you're a daydreamer." Jim suddenly seemed amused. "No government man has ever devised will give you all those freedoms. Take pot-smoking and drinking . . . suppose they became endemic . . . suppose everyone was turning on or getting drunk. . . . How could we protect ourselves against our enemies? They could simply walk in and take over. Then you can be certain that they, the conquerors, would calmly eliminate marihuana and alcohol from your diet . . . the only high you'd be allowed would be cheering for the state. In case you don't know it, a few years ago when the Russians began to backslide and drink too much, the government simply increased the price of vodka so that finally only the wealthy could afford to get drunk."

Robin was cut from the same cloth as her father. She liked to argue, particularly when the heat was off her. "If you stop to think about it, Daddy, revolutions start with people just below the top. . . The rest of us are peasants. Those at the top better not try to cut off the vodka supply for the second in command. If they do, they might find themselves in the middle of the second Russian revolution."

Angela didn't intervene in the argument, and miraculously Jim didn't ask her to sustain his convictions. The truth was that if someone had passed her a marihuana cigarette (what did they call them? . Joints?) she guessed she would have smoked it. A few months ago when they were discussing marihuana at the club she had said as much. Jim had wanted to know, if someone told her to inject heroin, if she would have tried that, too. Jim made his point. Most human beings were pretty gullible . . or as Ed Kanace (finishing his fourth bourbon and soda) had said, "We'd all eat shit, if some scientist said it was good for us."

☆ 45 ☆

When they finally got home, while Lena and Gramps were trying to grasp the fact that their granddaughter had escaped a marihuana trial by the skin of her teeth, and Ruth and Bud were joyously trying to extract all the details from Robin (a heroine to them at least), the telephone rang. Angela answered it and was greeted by a cool female voice with a quiet but precise New England accent.

"Hi, is this Mrs. Thomas?" Even before she introduced herself, Angela guessed that it was Janice Adams. Her estimation of Janice suddenly went up a few points. If the situation had been reversed, she would have called Janice. Or would she have? *Oh God*, this was Adam's wife. She had made love with Janice's husband. "This is . . . Janice, Janice Adams. I'm so sorry I wasn't home when the boys telephoned from Plymouth. Jon couldn't wait, of course. When I got home from the hairdresser and read his note, I was in the same state of shock that I'm sure you were in when Robin telephoned you. Really, this is such a terrible way to meet . . . sight unseen" (not quite, Angela thought, I know what you look like) "but Keane tells me you're just as attractive as Robin." Janice chuckled. "That's saying something. Robin is lovely. Keane is absolutely crazy about her. Angela . . . may I call you Angela? Both Jon and I feel very badly . . . especially because the boys were smoking marihuana that we grew. It's as if we condoned marihuana smoking. Jon may, but I don't. Of course it was Jon who grew the plants. But when you know Jon, you'll discover there is no stopping him when he gets an idea in his head . . ." (Angela couldn't help grinning. She was quite aware of Adam's persistence.) "Even so, the boys would never have had the stuff in Plymouth, if Jon had listened to me. Personally, it turns me off." Janice rambled on, evidently gaining confidence as Angela told her that she and Jim were taking it in stride. Jim's only fear was that by Monday the judge or the prosecutor might have changed their minds and decided to make a big deal over it.

"They won't," Janice reassured her. "We've got all of Cohasset and Plymouth working on it. Jack Lovell (you met Barbara Lovell, I believe) knows the judge. He has children himself. Bob Aureen has talked with the attorney for the county. He's assured Jon that they can squash it. Your husband must realize that no one wants to make a big deal out of marihuana anymore. No one knows how to handle the problem. If it's legalized, half the country will turn on. I think those at the top are hoping it's a bad dream that'll go away if they ignore it." Janice laughed. "I told Jonathan, if the police had walked into our attic a few weeks ago and discovered the whole place hung with stalks of it, he'd be really having a bad dream . . . behind bars. I'm trying to convince him to dump it all in Cohasset Harbor. Maybe you and your husband would come and help us . . . *the Adams' Good-bye Grass Party.*" Before she hung up, Janice told Angela that she really hoped Jim and she would come to dinner soon in Cohasset. "After all, the way things are between Robin and Keane . . . who knows, we may be relatives?"

As she listened to Janice, Angela kept thinking, she's really rather pleasant. A nice person . . . *and I'm not!* I've been making love with her husband as if this woman didn't exist. A feeling of despair enveloped Angela. She had been vacillating back and forth. Should she telephone Adam Monday? How could she not ever see him again? Now, Janice's call reinforced her basic convictions. Somehow, she would have to forget Jonathan Adams. She believed what she had told Bettie Kanace. If Jim had been involved with Janice, for example, or any other woman, and she knew it, and Jim would say (as she was sure Adam would), "Our marriage is not threatened," Angela was certain she could accept his extended involvement, or at least try to understand his needs for a different kind of female. Or was she reasoning post facto . . . rationalizing because she wanted Jim's approval of Adam and her?

187

Really, there was no choice. Two lone individuals couldn't make new rules for themselves. Thursdays were based on lies and deceit. Even if she were quite certain that the few Thursday hours weren't depriving Janice or Jim of anything essential . . . now, a new throw of the dice had involved Robin and Keane. Unbelievable . . . but one day Keane might be her son-in-law. What would Keane think if he knew that his mother-in-law was sleeping with his father? Oh God . . . it sounded like one of those horror stories out of *True Confessions* magazine.

Angela's mental buffeting was only beginning. Back in the living room where Bud, Ruth, Gramps and Lena were gathered . . . even before she could explain that the phone call was from Janice Adams . . . she realized that Jim, Robin and Ruth were playing a blunt game of showdown.

Jim had evidently been probing into Robin's relationship with Keane and was asking her why she couldn't have been honest and told them she was going to be in Cohasset with her boyfriend.

"Because if I told you the truth, you and Mother would have wanted me to come home."

"Is that so bad?" Jim demanded.

"Could I have told you that Keane was going to sleep in my room with me? Or would he have to pussyfoot around like Ruth and Bud do?"

Lena gasped. Bud and Gramp both looked startled. Ruth softly clapped her hands in approval of Robin's challenge.

Angela had heard enough to know that Robin wasn't about to be intimidated by her father. "Jim, why don't you just drop it?" she asked nervously. It didn't seem like a subject three generations should thrash out together.

"The hell, I will," Jim said angrily. "So, *you have been* sleeping with Keane Adams?"

"I've not only been sleeping with him," Robin said calmly, "I've been living with him in his apartment for the past two months." Jim was startled, but he held his temper. "So, it's obvious that the Adamses would have no objections if you slept together in Cohasset?"

"Is Robin on the witness stand?" Ruth demanded. "This is quite silly, Daddy. Who Robin goes to bed with is her own business."

"I suppose it is." Jim suddenly looked a little bewildered. "Let's say I'm a little confused with the new rules of the game. What happens if you get pregnant?"

"Oh, Daddy . . . where have you been the past ten years?" Robin looked as if she wanted to hug her father and protect his innocence. "There are no rules. I love Keane . . . Keane loves me. So, we have intercourse and gradually find out about each other . . . not just sex, but what kind of people we really are. And then, one day, if we think each of us is the best reinforcement that we can possibly find for each other, and we decide that we can actually make it together for the long haul, then we get married."

"Okay." Jim shrugged, and they all listened in amazement at his sudden turnabout. "I'm not going to fight city hall. If it's all right with your mother, and I suspect it is, then you can telephone Keane, and tell him that he can sleep with you in your bedroom in your own family's house."

"Why do you 'suspect' it's all right with me?" Angela demanded, a little shocked.

"Ange . . . you must think I'm completely stupid." Jim stared at her. "I'm against it. I don't believe it's right. I don't approve of it, but I know damn well that Bud hasn't spent the entire last two nights in Richy's room. The way things are, you better tell Richy to bring a girl home for Christmas holidays and we can have a family love-in . . . And maybe someday, someone will answer the question I'd like to place on the table. Once you girls do find that one person you are sure is the one you can live with in perfect harmony, what happens next. . . ? What makes you so sure it will last a lifetime?"

Jim grinned at Angela. "I have a feeling that when they finally do get married, neither of them will know how to handle a man as well as their mother."

☆ 46 ☆

During the December weeks, Jim's sudden acceptance of the sexual reality of Ruth and Robin slowly transformed their environment. Finding a breach in their father's and mother's role of admonishing and critical parents, Ruth and Robin rushed in to widen it. Friday night Bud went to bed in Ruth's room, and while both Jim and

Angela felt strangely embarrassed, the arrival of Keane, Saturday morning, gradually dispelled their awkwardness.

It seemed to Jim that Robin and Ruth had cast Keane and Bud in the roles of husbands and were "playing house." He told Angela he had played games like that with little girls, long, long ago. Then, the little boys tried to look under the little girls dresses while they were cooking mud pies, but that was as far as they dared to go. That, of course, was the first sexual awakening. In those years the little boys "couldn't get it up." If they could have, the little girls wouldn't have known what to do with it anyway.

As she thought about it, Angela wondered if letting Robin and Ruth bring their boyfriends home to sleep with them (and Richy his girlfriend, when he finally discovered the new state of affairs in the Thomas household), giving them the security of their parental home, wasn't simply an advanced stage of the male-female learning process. If little girls played with dolls, older girls should be able to play with living boys, and together discover the joy possible in the union of their genitals, and ultimately whether they would want to make the "doll commitment."

Angela couldn't quite believe that her daughters were suddenly calmly discussing the Pill and contraceptives with her (Ruth didn't like the Pill. She used a diaphragm. Robin thought a diaphragm was too premeditated and messy). When they asked her what she used, Angela laughingly told them, at forty-three, she was a little careless . . . a combination of diaphragm, condoms, and Russian Roulette! As she said it, she had a vision of both Adam and Jim erect and wanting her, and she blushed.

But even beyond the exchanges of female confidences with Robin and Ruth, was the joy of the whole family, including Gramps and Lena, and Bud and Keane defenselessly discussing love and marriage, and Lena, two generations removed coming to the conclusion that her granddaughters were much more aware and sensitive than she had been in her twenties . . . Lena had suddenly hugged Gramps and thanked him for putting up with her. Or, Saturday night when all four of them—Bud, Keane, Robin, and Ruth—were cavorting in the bathtub and shower stall together, while Jim controlled his temper and wondered when arms or legs would come through the ceiling, and then the sudden quiet upstairs, followed by a screaming chorus: "Get ready for the *treatment*." Devised

190

by Robin and Keane (learned from Sam and Yael), the *treatment* was a naked march through the house with the hi-fi blasting, and Jim shrugging and admitting that as the zoo-keeper who unlocked the cages, it was all his fault, and Lena looking a little horrified, and Gramp grinning from ear to ear ... charmed to see his granddaughters (whose diapers he had occasionally changed years ago when he and Lena had minded the kids) were now prettier naked than any of "those floosies" in the X movies.

Scarcely had they gotten used to Keane and absorbed him a little into the family (they were in the living room finally all dressed, listening to him play the piano) when Sam, Yael, and the Whiteclouds arrived.

Angela couldn't escape Sam, who embraced her. "We were supposed to sail the *Wah-kon-tah* back to Cohasset, but Keane finked out, so we decided to visit the Thomases." Sam grinned at Jim. He finally released Angela's hand. "Don't worry, we didn't bring any grass. Jake and Janice send their best wishes. I'm supposed to give Robin a hug for Jan and tell Keane to drive back to New York with caution. He will have Robin, precious cargo, a future Adams. . . . But that isn't the real reason we have descended on you."

Angela wondered if Sam or Yael were going to blurt out something that would reveal the truth about her and Adam. She couldn't help it. Sam was charming, but his intensity made her feel absolutely jittery.

"Robin told us about your interest in photography." Sam stared coolly at her. His face revealed nothing. "We brought our Sony video rigs. If you'll let us hook up your TV, we'll show you an entirely new kind of moving world in living color. Adams Video is looking for new talent, Mrs. Thomas. The video camera is no better than the brain looking through the lens."

It was Yael who innocently (Angela still couldn't believe that it was entirely innocent) convinced Angela that she was walking a tightrope. While Sam was hooking up his Sony video playback equipment to their television set so that he could show them his unedited *Negentropic Thanksgiving*, Yael inveigled Angela downstairs to see her darkroom and Angela's basement exhibit of photographs.

Yael was excited and entranced. "Wait until Sam sees these. You have a poetic touch with the camera. You could exhibit with any of the pros." Angela noticed that Yael was carefully examining all of the framed photographs as if she were in search for a missing one. Yael finally dropped her bombshell. "Sam and I saw the Hare Krishna shots you did of Jake. They're great. That's why Sam is so anxious to talk with you."

Angela hoped she looked cool, that her shock wasn't showing. She already suspected that Sam had seen those pictures, but why hadn't Adam told her? How much did Yael know? Should she plead for Yael's confidence? She knew that she was practically stuttering. She tried to pass the pictures off as a strange coincidence. It was a small world. In September when she took the pictures, Jonathan Adams was just an interesting stranger. Who would have guessed that Robin actually knew Jonathan Adams' son, or that they would be arrested smoking marihuana? Angela was afraid that she wasn't sounding casual enough.

"Yael . . . have you told Robin about those pictures?" Angela's eyes were bright with her tears.

Yael shook her head and quickly touched Angela's arm. "From the way Jake reacted when Sam told him that he had borrowed them, Sam and I realized they were private." Yael quickly changed the subject, leaving Angela certain that she and Sam either knew or suspected much more. "Honestly, Angela, Sam and I are both certain that you are completely unaware of your talent. Sam will be convinced when he sees what you have done."

During the remainder of the evening, Angela made it a point not to get in a private conversation with Sam, but it was impossible to keep him out of the darkroom. Robin and Ruth escorted him downstairs, with Angela finally reluctantly bringing up the rear. At least she could make sure they weren't exploring the many cabinets in the darkroom. Once Sam had seen the pictures he found his theme for the evening: Angela Thomas should work, at least part-time, for Adams National. Once she had mastered the basic video techniques she could produce her own tapes. Sam was high pressure. He visualized a series of tapes called *Angela's World*. "How's that for a title?" he demanded. "You'd be on your own . . . you could interpret any aspect of life you wished, from the ghetto to suburbia in Acton. . . . If you can probe beneath the flesh with the video camera the way you do with a still camera, you'll be sensational."

She couldn't dampen Sam's bright enthusiasm. "You're unique," he kept telling her. "You have a way of letting the inner person shine through." Sam put it up to Jim.

"We could teach your wife the business one or two days a week ... then she'd be on her own. You wouldn't mind if she worked, would you?"

"Angela can please herself," Jim told him. "Making videotapes should be right up her alley." Whatever Angela wanted to do was all right with him.

But Angela wouldn't commit herself. She tried to brush Sam off lightly with maybes. "I'm not looking for a career. I'm happy doing the simple little things I'm doing." But she didn't dare look into Sam's face when she said it. Damn him, anyway. She suddenly wondered if Adam had put this idea in Sam's head. But that would be insane. If she worked for Adams Video, Thursdays would be out of their control. Even Adam wouldn't be able to regulate the kind of work or plans that Sam might dream up for her. Crazy thought ... Thursday was already out of control. A thing of the past. The joyous invasion of the Adamses was slowly turning the fun house into a nightmare.

Sam and Yael were playing their videotape *Oceanic Love* on the television set before Angela (suspecting the worst) could convince Gramps and Lena they should go to bed. To top it all, while it was playing, Sam and Yael were aiming their portable video cameras at all of them, catching the change of expressions of shock and surprise on the faces of Jim and Gramps and Lena (and probably on her own face, though she was sure that now she was beyond shock) as they watched the tape. And after that came the pièce de résistance. At Robin's insistence they decided to show the complete tapes they had made of the Adams family Thanksgiving. ... Just two nights ago in the Adams' living room. To Angela's complete surprise she was watching Adam and Janice (strikingly sophisticated) on her television screen and their friends the Lovells (Janice seemed unusually affectionate with Jack Lovell). All of them were talking excitedly (obviously they were all high on marihuana or alcohol). Amazed, Angela watched Adam reciting "Kubla Khan," and then all the women, including Robin, were standing on the hearth with their behinds in the air ... and Adam (as well as the other males) thoroughly enjoying himself as he kissed all the naked females asses, including Robin's ... their own daughter!

Alone, without Gramps and Lena (Angela wasn't too sure of Jim, though he had had a few drinks and seemed

193

in good spirits), she might have thought it was kind of hilarious. But maybe not. She felt a strange tinge of jealousy when Adam kissed Barbara's behind. (Janice's behind was actually prettier, but after all, Janice was Adam's wife.) But Angela couldn't really concentrate on the video exposé of Adam's home life. It was difficult enough to try to empathize with an Adam she scarcely knew, but the agonizing suspense of what Sam might inadvertently reveal, coupled with Gramps and Lena . . . right in the middle of the confusion, watching, tight-lipped . . . turned Angela frigid and shivery with cold perspiration oozing out of her skin.

Well, actually Gramps was laughing and he seemed to be enjoying the younger generations to the hilt, but Lena's smile was still pretty grim. She reminded Angela of the woman in Grant Wood's painting "American Gothic." . . . Even the two vodkas and cranberry juice she had drunk seemed to have had little softening effect on her. Tomorrow Angela was sure that Lena would explode as she recalled the immorality and absolute shame of what she had witnessed in the past twenty-four hours.

The pressure didn't finally relax until Sam and Yael and the Whiteclouds were at the front door, with Sam prolonging his leavetaking endlessly as he thanked everybody for a marvelous conclusion to his Thanksgiving tapes, which had culminated (at his urging) in a practically nude ballet scene improvised by the Whiteclouds and Keane to Jacque Brel's music *Les Timids*, which Keane played over and over on the piano, while Robin, dancing, in love with Timid Frieda, insisted she knew just how Frieda felt (a poor little prostitute) with "her valises clutched so tightly in her hand."

Probing Jim after they had gone (it was nearly two A.M., Angela tried to encourage him to reveal his feelings about this mad Saturday evening and "the crazy Adams boys." He shrugged. "I felt like a visitor from another planet whose spacecraft stopped working and he couldn't leave." Undressing, at first he was little uncommunicative. Was he shocked?

He turned the question on her. "Were you?"

Angela wasn't sure. "I guess so. Bewildered, a little. The Adamses seem to live in an "anything goes" environment. The boys are very open with their parents. I guess what bothered me most was your reaction, and what Gramps and Lena were thinking."

Jim laughed. "Lena probably will never admit it, but she had the time of her life. All of the kids, even those Indians, were so affectionate with her, they took her off-base. How can you be critical of someone who loves you, someone who is so happy that you're alive and happy that they snuggle their face against yours? I saw Robin and Ruth doing that with Lena. Later, Susan Whitecloud and Yael had Lena in a long dissertation, while she reminisced about love and sex in her youth.

Naked, Jim looked at himself in the mirror. "I still don't have too much belly." He grinned at his reflection. Angela, in bed watching him, agreed. Jim was in fine shape. "It's a different ball game, Ange," he said. "Yesterday, I suddenly was aware that I was fighting a lost cause. I had an unpleasant vision of myself, the patriarchal father completely out of touch with the world, spouting the inflexible codes I had lived by. Basically, I suppose I was trying to stop the world because it's moving so fast I was getting dizzy." Jim flopped on the bed and snuggled against her uncovered breast. He smiled at her. "For an old lady, you have marvelous tits. ... Believe me, I'm still bewildered and worried about Robin and Ruth. I can't help wondering where they'll be twenty years from now. But suddenly I realize I can't legislate their moral life. It's funny, even though I cringe a little and can't believe that right now they are in bed, *in our house,* sleeping with their boyfriends, and though I'm scared to death that they'll get hurt and one day Keane or Bud won't seem so wonderful ... for the first time in a long time, Ruth and Robin have been openly loving with me. Tonight they hugged me, and I swung them around the way I used to when they were babies ... and I realized that if I can take it ... and not pass judgment before I understand the facts, that we have something deeper than paternal power emerging between us ... like maybe trust and concern, which is a sounder basis for love than duty."

Leaning on his elbow, Jim pulled the sheet off her. "Tonight, for the first time in years I saw my daughters naked ... but their mother is still prettier. A mature female body has a comforting softness. God, God, Ange, all this happy sexual glow is catching. Even though I'm pooped, you better stop staring at me with that little-girl, big-eyed look ... I might even think you like me."

"Honey, honey." Angela couldn't control her sobs, or
195

the tears that blurred her eyes. "I've never stopped liking you." My cup runneth over, she thought. Two men like me and I love two men.

☆ 47 ☆

To Angela's amazement, as the days between Thanksgiving and Christmas crept by, Lena would happily recall something Robin or Ruth or Bud or those Adams boys had said. While Lena confessed she had been shocked, particularly by Jim's sudden decision to give the girls carte blanche to sleep in his house with their boyfriends ("For heavens sakes, Angela, take my advice and don't tell your friends!"), Lena couldn't help missing all the youngsters and their noisy confusion.

"Kids liven up the place," Gramps admitted. "Give you something to think about." In the morning, after breakfast, he set up the cribbage board for a continuation of his and Lena's endless game, during which they both managed to watch television and generally ruminate on the state of the world. "Here, Lena." Gramps pushed his pipe at her. "Before she left, Robin gave me some of that marihuana . . . take a puff. It'll make you dreamy."

Angela stared at her father-in-law unbelievingly. Did he actually have marihuana in his pipe? She was glad Jim had gone to work. Blessedly, the charges had been dropped against the children, but while Jim had become amazingly permissive about his daughters' relations with their boyfriends, he had made it quite clear to all of them that he still was against letting one's mind be dominated by any drug, except perhaps an occasional drink of liquor.

Lena refused the pipe with a few shrieks and dire warnings that Arthur would go to jail. She couldn't understand why anyone would want to inhale tobacco, let alone that nasty stuff, in their lungs. What was more, while Bud and Keane were nice young men, she certainly hoped they would announce their engagements to her granddaughters right away. It was difficult to understand why the younger generation all wanted to go to bed with each other so early in life, but if that's the way a girl had to get a man nowadays, she supposed it wasn't too much different from her youth. Running around naked, like they did ... now, that might make some sense. Maybe it was better to be natural about being naked. It certainly would save on laundry. Bud and Keane slept naked and they only wore those little jockey things for underwear. All his life Arthur had put on his long underwear, summer and winter. Three sets of woolen underwear a week she had to wash for nearly fifty years. At night when Arthur finally went to bed, he wore pajamas. Neither of them went into the bathroom when the other was in it ... so they rarely had seen each other naked.

"I swear," she said, "I've lived seventy-six years and I never saw anything in my life like those two boys, or your girls, floating around the upstairs, naked as jaybirds. I'd yell to them that I was coming through, and they'd just giggle and yell back: 'Close your eyes, Gram ... don't look if it bothers you.' Well, I never ..." Lena harumphed, but she couldn't suppress a tiny grin. "Angela, they're so young. Really, so innocent. They think they're very mature with breasts and hair on their bellies, and the boys with floppy jiggers, but they're really babies. The way the world is, I don't blame them for trying to be happy."

Lena wasn't too sure about the older Adams. . . . It was a shameful thing to have a man with a name like Jonathan Quincy Adams and go around kissing naked female behinds ... and that other man, was he really president of a bank? She wouldn't put her money in a bank run by a man like that. He looked like an old lecher. She took it in stride that it was possible to take color television movies right in one's living room and show them back immediately. But she was dubious about the awful kind of pictures people would inevitably make ... that sex picture Sam Adams had shown them with his own wife stark naked proved what the world was coming to.

The Monday after Thanksgiving, Angela might have convinced herself that she couldn't telephone Adam (after all, Robin and Keane had stayed over an extra day for the hearing at the Plymouth court), but Tuesday she no longer had any excuse. All she had to do was escape Gramps and Lena and telephone from a pay station at the shopping plaza. If she wanted, she could have mailed the cassette and a collection of thirty 16 x 20 enlargements she had made for him of her best pictures. But even though she was plagued with a dull, gnawing sense of loss, she steeled herself. Their affair was over. God must have been watching over her. She had survived the aberration safely. Adam and Angela were a temporary dream. They might have gone on for a few more months—even a year—but ultimately the dream would have ended. It was better this way. She read Morton Hunt's book *The Affair* and wanted to share it with Adam, but what was the use? Hunt proved what she already knew. The average affair lasted about four months and rarely ended happily. Maybe the kind of dream Adam envisioned would be possible if people could wall off a tiny portion of their lives from the world of families, friends, and children. But what kind of world could two people create alone against the normal tide of monogamy? The small security they had of living in separate towns, miles from each other, no longer existed. Robin and Keane had enmeshed them, and now Sam and Yael were trying to tighten the net. Thankfully, she could avoid Sam's offer. If Robin and Keane did get married (and she prayed they would), at least she and Adam lived far enough away from each other so that she could keep the inevitable family meetings (which she knew she would dread, because she knew she would never stop caring for and loving Adam) on a formal basis. As she thought about the two families spending an evening together she couldn't help smiling. How would the Adamses and the Thomases behave as in-laws? Would they end up kissing each other's behinds, too?

Day after day she wracked her mind with torturous questions, and she was certain that there were no solutions except tragic ones. Despite the new premarital freedom, not even the swingers and wife-swappers had any viable post-marital solutions. The marriage counselors and family planners claimed monogamy would survive, but in new forms. Maybe serial monogamy . . . one marriage after another, with the children from several fathers raised by their mother in day-care centers. A rootless kind of non-caring world. Of course, her children and Adam's children were adults now. But in their early years, they had grown up with the security of their families.

What was the purpose of a big home in the suburbs when the nest was empty? Really, for her and Adam it was no longer children that held either of their marriages together. At this point in life, wasn't it true that she and Jim and Adam and Janice were so interdependent that divorce was kind of ridiculous? Better than divorce would be a merger . . . or at the very least Thursdays . . . for adventure.

As the days dragged toward Christmas, Angela knew that the "cure" wasn't going to be easy. In two weeks the holidays would be over. Gramps and Lena would be on their way to Florida. January, February, March would be a long expanse of empty time and lonely days. Without Adam there would be no more Thursdays. She wondered how she could have once walked the streets of Boston alone. Adam had infiltrated her tiny escape world and made it apparent that her Thursday picture-taking had been an incomplete way of fending off her basic loneliness. Boston without Adam would only magnify her sense of loss.

Thursday before Christmas—a few days before Robin and Ruth and Richy would return for the holidays—feeling miserable and dragged-out for no accountable reason, Angela made breakfast for Jim and Gramps and Lena and then, after Jim had left for his office, she crawled back into bed and watched the gray winter sky, remote and cold through the bare, interlaced branches of the silver maples that edged the half-acre of the Thomas home.

Adam, I need you. God, I need you!

Thinking. Tears in her eyes . . . wondering why he hadn't telephoned her (even if she hadn't had the nerve to call him), she drifted into a mixed-up dream. She was in bed and she was ill, and Adam had come to visit her in the hospital, only he kept insisting that she shouldn't worry. It was all right if he took off his pants and climbed into the hospital bed with her. He was already in the bed when the call bell started ringing, and a nurse who looked suspiciously like Janice poked her head in the door and, ignoring Adam, asked if she were all right. Embarrassed, frightened, she told her she was, and quickly pulled the covers over Adam's head so that the nurse (was it Janice?) couldn't see him. But damn . . . the nurse's bell kept ringing and it wouldn't stop. Suddenly Angela was awake. The ringing bell wasn't in her dream! It was her own front doorbell! Why hadn't Lena or Gramps answered it?

As she flung her housecoat over her nightgown, she could hear Lena talking with someone in the front hall. Who could it be this time of morning? The newspaper boys collected on Saturdays. It was too early for the postman. She checked her bedroom clock. It was nine-thirty. As she hurried down the front stairs, she shivered.

199

She had heard the voice in the front hall before. *It couldn't be*! *Adam*! For a moment she was convinced that she was still back in her bed dreaming. Adam couldn't be in her home, calmly talking to her mother-in-law! He wouldn't dare!

She gasped as he smiled brightly at her. "Good morning, Mrs. Thomas!" Adam returned her astonished look with a big grin. "I hope I haven't awakened you too early." Angela tightened her grip on the banister. Surely, now she would wake up in a cold sweat. Adam would disappear. He had to! What ever could have possessed him to come right into her house in Acton?

Adam was in complete cool control of the situation. "Jim's mother just gave me permission to call her by her first name. Lena . . ." He smiled at Lena, who was lapping him up. "Once Helena, I presume. I was apologizing to your mother-in-law for those videotapes that Sam brought over here. Sam's a bad one, Lena, he never has learned where privacy begins and leaves off. I just told Lena that the reason for my visit was, that if the mountain doesn't come to Muhammad . . ." Seeing Angela's consternation, as she clung to the stair railing, Adam momentarily lost his aplomb. "Well, you know the cliché Mrs. Thomas."

Lena, entranced by a middle-aged stranger who looked the way a President of the United States should look, evidently forgiving him mentally for kissing all those behinds, filled in the conversational lull.

"Mr. Adams said that you promised to send him some of your pictures." Lena seemed slightly indignant that Angela should be so forgetful. "I do remember your son Sam asking if he could bring them to you . . ." Happy for a change of pace from morning cribbage and television, Lena had already taken Adam's overcoat. She invited him into the kitchen for a cup of coffee.

Torn between delight at seeing Adam and panic that he was actually unbelievably in her home, Angela felt like a youngster on a carousel, screaming, her mouth open, with no sound coming out. She wasn't sure whether she felt ecstasy or cold fear. Summoning every ounce of strength, freezing her face, hoping she would shatter Adam with her icy expression, she said, "Really, Lena, I told Mr. Adams' son Samuel several weeks ago, I'm not interested in having exhibits, or going to work. Jim may say he doesn't mind. But I'm quite certain Jim wouldn't want me too involved with photography. Mr. Adams, you and Samuel are being very nice, but you are overestimating my abilities."

Adam was ignoring her. As if he had come to visit Lena instead of her, he followed the old lady into the kitchen, shook hands with Gramps, and in a few minutes, while Angela listened dumbfounded, he was in an extended discussion with him about the pros and cons of a senior-citizen center near Daytona, Florida, where Gramps and Lena had put their savings into a retirement apartment, which was now ready and waiting for them. Finally, refusing a second cup of coffee and a piece of her own homemade fruitcake that Lena offered him, he told Gramps, "Your daughter-in-law is selling herself short. She has a great deal of talent. Just on the basis of a few pictures we have and those he saw here a few weeks ago, Sam has arranged an exhibit of her photos in a gallery on Newbury Street. All Angela has to do is say yes." He smiled at her. "I don't think Lena and Arthur would mind if you let me see your photographs. I understand that you have a complete darkroom in the basement. I'd like to see that, too."

Trembling, wondering whether Lena was encouraging her because she really liked Mr. Adams, or whether she suspected the truth and was setting the stage so that Angela could incriminate herself, Angela led Adam down the basement stairs. At the bottom, chuckling, Adam grabbed her and kissed her wildly. "Mrs. Thomas . . . you're a bad woman!" he whispered. "Two weeks have gone by and you haven't telephoned me. You didn't even send me a cassette, or your photographs."

"Adam, for God's sake, not here." Angela was so frightened she was actually panting. She looked up the basement stairs, fully expecting to see Lena staring at them from the landing. But there was no one there.

Angela snapped on the red light in the darkroom and pushed him inside. She closed the door behind her. "Adam, you've gone mad!" Sobbing, she clung to him. "Oh, God . . . God . . . over and over again, I've promised myself I'd never see you again." She couldn't stop kissing him as she said it. "Adam, we can only stay down here a minute or two. Oh, what am I going to do?"

Adam held her hard against him. She could feel her housecoat, nightgown and all, sliding up over her calves. "Adam . . . No! . . . No!" she gasped as she felt his hands caressing and holding her naked buttocks in a tight grip.

His penis, through his trousers, was hard and erect against her. "Oh, Adam . . . you're so excited!"

His face was a shadowy red grin reflected in the darkroom lamp. "I like your darkroom. It's a warm little womb. A nice place to make love."

Helpless in her need for him, yet thoroughly frightened that Gramps or Lena, treading on the kitchen floor above them, would follow them to the basement, Angela couldn't resist when he sat on a straightback chair, and pulled her down astride him. To her amazement, she realized he must have dropped his pants. She could feel his naked penis rubbing against her vulva. She kissed him frantically. "Did you watch the astronauts?" he asked her softly. She looked at him through puzzled tears. He chuckled. "You're the command module, sweetie. Lift up a little and help the lunar module steer its way to safety."

Choking with laughter, she told him that he was a loony module. "Oh, Adam . . . Adam . . . I wanted to telephone you . . . I wanted to. But I just couldn't."

"It's Thursday." He snuggled against her neck, and his hands under her nightgown, tracing her back and the curve of her breasts, were question marks. "If I were inside you, we would be in the favorite position of the Tantrics. They stay joined together for hours . . . seeking Nirvana."

"Adam, no! Not here! With Gramps and Lena upstairs? No! We can't!" Even while she was protesting and telling herself this was completely insane (how could she have intercourse with her lover while her in-laws were upstairs, guarding the sanctuary?), even while she was exhorting him to leave, telling him they were acting like children, this madness couldn't continue, she was helping him find his way into her, and then suddenly she was pinioned to him, and he felt so full and warm and deep inside her that she could no longer control her excitement. Tears of joy in her eyes, she rode him with a passion that carried them both to a violent climax in seconds. Breathing her noisy, gasping ecstasy in his shoulder and neck, she could feel the broad grin on his face against her breasts.

"My God, Adam." She was breathless with her passion and controlled laughter. "You have satyriasis and I'm a nymphomaniac. Why are we so starved?"

"Don't worry. It's not generalized. It's a very particular hunger for each other."

She tried to separate from him but he wouldn't let her

go. "A few weeks ago," Adam whispered in her ear, I dreamed this . . . only you were wearing a ski suit. You got all tangled up in it. And then before anything happened I woke up."

"Adam, you have to go." Gingerly she separated from him, found a towel, and quickly patted herself and him dry. "I beg you. While I'm temporarily sane. *Please get out of here*." She listened apprehensively for a moment. There was no sound on the floor above. "Oh my God, what if they heard us? Adam . . . please, I'm pleading with you. It's obvious that I have no morals or brains. You're going to have to protect me from myself. What will I ever do? What will I tell Jim?"

Adam kissed her bewildered tear-stained face. "Have you any photographs you can give me?"

Angela turned on the full lights in the darkroom. She handed him a thick portfolio. "All the time I was printing them, I told myself I would never give them to you, or ever see you again." She sighed. "Obviously, I don't listen to my own good counsel. You might as well have the cassette, too. It's in the package."

Adam kissed the tears in her eyes. "Tonight, tell Jim that Jonathan Adams was on his way to Concord, and he dropped by the house. Be casual. Mr. Adams wanted your photographs. Sam wants you to at least look in and see Adams Video."

Angela shook her head. "If you were thinking clearly, you'd know its too complicated. One day we're going to be found out. Then what will I do? Janice will probably forgive you. Women forgive men their sins . . . but not vice versa."

Adam hugged her. "You and I are not a sin. The seventh commandment should have defined adultery. By loving each other we have neither corrupted ourselves nor our spouses. He watched her as she tried to repair her face in the darkroom mirror. "Shakespeare just popped into my mind. 'Let me not to the marriage of true minds admit impediments. . . . If this be error, and upon me prov'd, I never writ, nor no man ever lov'd.' " Chuckling, Adam fished in his coat pocket. He handed Angela a tiny box. "Actually, though it doesn't look that way, I had something else in mind beside making love to you." He watched her surprise as she opened the box and found a tiny microphone and a house key. "That's a fractional part

203

of your Christmas present. The rest is too big—I couldn't bring it with me."

"What on earth is it?"

"It's a Dictacall." He handed her a card with a phone number written on it. "This afternoon or tomorrow, dial this magic number . . . 617 471 8583 . . . and you'll find what the beeper is for, and all about the rest of your present." He kissed the surprise on her face with a hundred little kisses. "Angel-a, Angel-a, I wish I had a picture of you right now. Your expression has all the wonder and curiosity and mystification of a two-year-old on Christmas morning."

Despite her pleas he refused to tell her any more. "I love you. Come on, we'll go upstairs and allay any suspicions Gramps or Lena might have. If you won't let me tell them that you're a magnificent photographer, I'll have to tell them you are a post rider without equal!"

☆ 48 ☆

Late that afternoon, Angela, certain that she was twenty years old (mentally at least)—bubbly, effervescent, in love with Adam, in love with Jim, in love with love—dialed Adam's magic number . . . 617 471 8583 . . . and listened, astonished.

"Angela-love, it's me. I'm talking to you on a tape. When I've finished, if your money hasn't run out" (Angela could hear him chuckle) "use the gadget I gave you . . . the Dictacall. Just hold it up to the phone. The signal will activate the tape and run it back. Then, with one more signal you can start the tape forward and listen to me say 'I love you' all over again. You are connected to a machine called an Ansaphone. I'm telephoning to it from my office. That's where I am now . . . talking to you, and imagining the puzzlement and surprise on your lovely face when you finally dialed the magic number, and here I am.

"Are you listening? Are you suddenly super-conscious? Aware? Blissful? Are you smiling? Look outside that telephone booth I know you are standing in. Look at the people in the shopping plaza, the signs, the cars huddled in the parking lot, the sky, the winter ruts of snow in the road—are they all suddenly glowing with some lovely music and inner light that only you can hear and see?

"Angela ... this morning in your darkroom, I *was* you. And now, for days I'll relive those short moments, and remembering, I'll smile, and feel good and buoyant and alive to the very depth of me. The warmth of your flesh, the joy on your face, your early-morning fragrance. (Were you wearing sweet pea, or was it your own natural odors?) Even now, I can smell you on me, and the elusive quality of you being near and yet not near is both erotic and maddeningly lonesome. Were you sleeping when I arrived? I forgot to ask you. Were Gramps and Lena happy with the new, blooming you? Even, now, Angela, I'm still holding hands with you across this distance ... tenuous but unforgettable.

"Good Lord, before I rattle on to the end of this tape, let me tell you more about it. It's a one-hour cassette ... not just ordinary plastic and magnetized tape on a reel, but really our Thursday lifeline, and during the week when we are apart, a means of communicating, if the need or mood seizes us. . . . A bridge across the six-sevenths of life we can't share. And after the holidays ... the first Thursday when you leave Acton ... all you have to do is dial the magic number, and you'll hear me saying, 'Honey, we've done it. We've lived to live another Thursday.' Or, if I should be late or get tied up (God forbid), you will know it and not have to be nervous or fearful. And Thursdays just before you leave home, you can dial this phone and say, 'Hi, Adam ... I'm on my way ... I love you.' And when you arrive, I'll be there, waiting for you.

"Where is 'there'? Let me tease you a little. First I want to tell you more about the useful gadget you are holding in your hands (I have a similar one). It signals the machine, using it you can rewind the tape, listen to it again on the phone you are calling from, and then record your own message. The tape will record for an hour. We'll have to devise a system for during-the-week calls (in case either you or I should get too rambly). An agreement that we will record over previous messages only when we're sure that we're erasing what we've already heard.

"So, this is one part of your Christmas present ... really the smaller part. Where the Ansaphone is located ... where this impersonal tape is now very personally talking to you, is the big surprise. Hold your breath! A week ago I leased this lovely three-room apartment for one year. Fifty-two Thursdays! A little more expensive, perhaps, than Thursdays in hotel rooms, but a lot more joyous and less constrained. If you are feeling economical you can make our lunches. This is our Thursday home on Beacon Hill. Somewhere nearby Louisa May Alcott lived and wrote *Little Women*" (Adam was laughing) "—maybe she even lived in this very house. Perhaps her spirit will listen to us making love. and she would decide, if she were living now, that she would write a new book, *Brave New Women*.

"So, now you know what the key is for. The number of the house on Pinckney Street is engraved on it. The first Thursday morning after the New Year begins, when you arrive in Boston, drive up Charles Street from Boylston . . . park your car in the garage under Boston Common . . . walk across Beacon along Charles to Pinckney. Then, walk up the hill. When you find the doorway—there's a gas lantern on the sidewalk in front of the ancient brick building—open the lovely old mahogany door with brass fittings and walk up to the second-floor landing. Open the only door, and I'll be waiting for you. Oh, loved one, I'm beginning the long wait now . . . impatiently. Visualizing a million times in advance the laughter and the hysterical joy when you flop down with me and we float together on the only furniture in our new home . . . a king-sized water bed! Good-bye sweet . . . for the moment."

Angela continued to listen, but there was nothing more, only the hum of the tape on the phone, and the thump of her heart beating so frantically she thought it would jump out of her chest. . . . Oh, Adam . . . Adam . . . you are completely joyously mad . . . sparkling crazy . . . blithely insane. What am I going to do with you?

Outside the telephone booth, she suddenly couldn't stop laughing. She went back inside, dialed the magic number again, and listened to Adam, on tape, once more. Then she talked.

☆ 49 ☆

Long before Spring, her Thursday-home, the Adam-Angela environment they slowly created together, and the occasional Tuesdays and Wednesdays she had worked with Sam and Yael at Adams Video, discovering the fascinating world she could create with the video camera and tape (without pay, and only occasionally saying hello to Adam on those days) were subtly changing Angela from a passive suburban "dying matron" (her description of herself to Adam) to a "come-alive-female." The first buds of the new blossoms, erupting in her brain before Thanksgiving, now, in the next-to-last week in February, were in full bloom. Twelve Thursdays altogether ... that was the total of the time she had been with Adam since the beginning, less than a hundred hours, and yet the metamorphosis was complete. Where she was going was impossible to guess. All that she was certain of was that it would be equally impossible to retrace her steps.

Jim's happy reaction was that Angela seemed sparkly as a new bride. Amazingly, though she was almost self-conscious about it, Angela knew she actually looked more vibrant. She walked younger, with her head high. For the first time in years she looked forward to tomorrow. Not that she was a youth-worshipper, nor was the effect consciously achieved. She still wore only a touch of perfume (sweet pea on Thursdays) and little or no makeup. The new burgeoning life, the renaissance of Angela, was in the new twinkle in her eye, a new sense of wonder and humor, a new appreciation of herself as a sexual female, and a new confidence, and no embarrassment in letting her female sensuous responses shine through.

Was it the excitement of stolen sweets? A momentary escape from boredom? Not simply from marriage but from the whole senseless way of the world? A cloud-nine patina that one day would wear off? Angela was sure that it wasn't. For one thing, the depth of her relationship with Jim had actually improved. She was much more objective about herself than she had ever been in the past ... able to laugh at her own moods, and fears. And as if in response, for the first time in their marriage, Jim was taking his own sexuality less seriously. Not only the act of love, but their day-to-say encounters were tinged with a new humor. The joy that she had discovered with Adam was really the joy of being able to give herself defenselessly. Unconsciously, she shared the secret with Jim and together they were slowly changing the locus of their subjectivity from themselves to each other.

At first, when Adam had been delighted and amused with her obvious enjoyment of "lovemaking," she had been embarrassed. Now, she wondered if the real change going on inside her wasn't really biological. Maybe there was a crucial underlying relationship between aging and the generative drive involved in the act of lovemaking. Men and women didn't give up sex because they grew old; they grew old because they gave up sex. But with Adam, since they had the apartment, joining their bodies had become much more than a pursuit of an orgasm. Rather, it was a Tantric kind of communication as they drifted, momentarily detached from their own consciousness, being each other for hours at a time so that even their spoken words had a composite character.

But guilt was not easy to jettison. Almost as if she were driven by some fearful compulsion, she suddenly seemed to be wallowing in books and movies about adultery, as if the whole world was trying to find answers on how to coexist monogamously. Without exception, these were ugly, and the affairs they described were dehumanizing. During Christmas she had seen a movie with Gramps and Lena and Jim about doctors' wives. Everybody was mixed up with everyone else, and finally one wife was discovered by her husband who was a doctor ... in bed with his friend who was a doctor. Of course, a murder was committed. All the movie added up to was that doctors didn't know any more about sex and love than anyone else.

Then there was the Late Show she watched uneasily with Jim ... featuring an older Ingrid Bergman as the wife of a colorless, boring history professor. In the picture, Ingrid was presumably in her middle forties. She had a daughter and a grandson two or three years old. At first it was easy to identify with Ingrid and respond to the earthiness of Anthony Quinn. Ingrid was nearly ready to capitulate. But then, inadvertently, she was responsible for the murder of Quinn's son by Quinn himself. The moralists were assuaged. Ingrid was saved from a fate worse than death . . . surrendering to Anthony in the hayloft. (Even Jim thought that movie was implausible.) In another movie, a young housewife, presumably mad, but really saner than her contemporaries, had a hateful lover, and a rather hateful husband. Jim thought the wife and husband both got what they deserved . . . each other. On the other hand, he couldn't empathize with a wealthy young doctor, in another movie, who began to play around because his wife had become so boringly domesticated. It was obvious to Jim the man was an ass not to appreciate a good mother and homemaker. He did, by gosh. What's more, from now on, he'd pick the movies. He was fed-up with movies about adultery.

And then there were the books distributed by the book clubs (fortunately Jim didn't read these). One based on a woman discovering from her husband's notebooks that he has been making love to her best friend. Her husband is in the hospital dying when the story starts. So that solved that problem. Another about a loving wife whose husband is uninterested in her career as a social worker (and of course she really isn't interested in his life as an advertising executive), so she falls in love with her boss. They obviously should have many more interests in common. But sadly her boss doesn't ever plan to leave his wife and share their interests together. The truth is that he only enjoys her as a sexpot and not as a fellow-worker.

It got to a point where Angela was afraid to read a book or watch a drama with adultery as a theme. There never was any lasting happiness in the stories that man told to man about his inability to be faithful. On the contrary, it seemed as if adultery, as a deviation from the presumed norm, was one more way for human beings to express their hatred and aggression toward each other.

Were she and Adam on a collision course? Were they pursuing some kind of death wish? Were they simply sexual orgiasts? Those were the conclusions of most of the writers who wrote about affairs and tried to prove one way or another that man must suffer and pay for his sins.

Adam told her there was only one immorality . . . lack of love. Of course, he enjoyed her sexually, but more important, he liked her. She was both a sexpot and a friend. Before she ever saw the apartment on Pinckney Street, their intimacy and involvement had multiplied a thousandfold in a fascinating duologue (Adam said it couldn't really be a dialogue since they couldn't immediately talk back to each other) via the Ansaphone. Recording their thoughts and feelings on a tape they knew the other waited avidly for was a little like holding hands across the distance. They learned about each other in depth by the simple process of listening.

In the morning Adam would dial the magic number, listen back on the tape to recapture Angela's afternoon conversation of the day before, and then he would ramble and ruminate for five or ten minutes, answering her questions, posing hundreds more himself ... challenging her to break through the cobwebs of middle-class thinking and reexamine every aspect of life and living.

And the certainty and confidence this tape lifeline gave her was never more apparent than on Thursdays. Now she didn't leave Acton fearful, wondering whether after a long week, Adam would be able to see her; she didn't have the uneasy feeling that someday he might be waiting somewhere for her and she would be unable to come. Now, all she had to do was dial the apartment, and Adam would say, "Hi, love, it's Thursday! February 17th," or whatever date it was, and then he might say, "Hurry, but drive carefully. I need you." Only once so far had he said, "I'll be late ... but I'll be there. Have patience." And once she had to tearfully tell the impassive tape, "Oh, Adam, I can't come. I'm so miserably feverish and sick ... and crying because I can't ..." But at the worst (and the two times since New Year's that the chain of Thursdays had been broken had given them both a hopeless feeling of futility) ... at worst they still had a communications center.

This Thursday, as she walked from the garage under Boston Common up Charles Street to Pinckney, almost dancing to some internal Thursday music that filled her body from head to toe, the "second beginning," as she called the first Thursday after New Year's, was still vivid in her mind. After those long weeks of insecurity, fear, terror of discovery, all mixed together with an overwhelming loneliness (their quick mating in her darkroom had been hilariously funny but was nowhere commensurate to her needs), she was going to be with Adam again.

It was a bitterly cold day. Her stomach was doing frightening somersaults. The reality was irrevocable ... once again she was meeting her lover, and this time in an apartment that he had rented for just one purpose ... so that they could make love. She had told him on the Ansaphone that it seemed like pretty expensive sex to her. If the apartment cost two hundred a month, and they could only use it on Thursdays (and it was unlikely they would be together every Thursday), she was at the very least a fifty-dollar-a-day call girl. She told him, via tape, that she guessed he was rich enough to afford such a luxury, and he had answered, "Sweetie, at fifty dollars a day you're inexpensive. A call girl of your character could command a hundred." He knew that would make her a little peeved, so ultimately he had countered with: "I'll prove to you that you're wrong. It's not your body I crave. Next Thursday, though I'll be rigid with desire, I'll command this uncontrollable creature at my middle to lie down, and Angela and Adam will spend the afternoon like brother and sister."

That first day, the key to the apartment she had never seen, clutched tightly in her gloved hand, Angela Campolieto Thomas from the North End, with a Boston Brahmin for a lover, walked right out of the twentieth century onto Beacon Hill. As she climbed the steep incline of Pinckney Street, past Louisburg Square, she looked back for a moment. The Charles River, a shimmering curve of cold winter water and ice, sparkled below her. Was it because she was in love, or did the narrow street meandering between eighteenth-century buildings, mostly three to four stories high, with leaded panes, and window casements, and winding stairways with no elevators, have a kind of built-in warmth and friendliness that modern man seemed unable to recapture in the cement, stone, and glass towers that were turning other parts of Boston into one more American lookalike city? Modern man evidently enjoyed walking through caverns to his new downtown caves with windows that looked out on the other animals in their glass caves.

Even before she located the number of the building and entered the mahogany-paneled hallway and tried to stop herself from running up the carpeted stairway to the doorway that her key should fit, Angela knew that she was enthralled by this tiny world of gaslighted streets. It was an illusion, of course, a hideaway for those Bostonians rich enough to pretend they were living in a more benign and less hurried world. Still, though Henry Longfellow or Nathaniel Hawthorne or Ralph Emerson might not walk by and tip their hats at her, it was nice to know that across the centuries they shared these buildings in common.

☆ 50 ☆

On the second-floor landing she hesitated. There was one massive mahogany door. She read the tiny card inserted in the doorplate. *Angela Adams.* My God, Jonathan Adams really was dangerous! Even before she unlocked the door she pulled the card out of the bracket. And inside . . . there he was, lying on the king-sized Aqua bed, reading a book, stark naked! A huge grin on his face, he greeted her, and she knew that he thoroughly enjoyed her consternation.

Closing the door behind her, aware that music was softly playing, any remaining fears vanished. She burst into laughter and tumbled into his arms without even taking off her coat. "Oh, Adam, Adam . . . I'm so glad you're here. You're an absolute nut . . . you're bad! Angela Adams! . . . God . . . do we have to advertise us?"

With tears of joy in his eyes even while he was kidding her, he slid the zipper on the back of her dress, and slowly eased her out of her coat. As hungry for him as he was for her, she made no attempt to create order in her undressing. Her arms were out of her dress, the shoulder straps on her bra quickly unfastened, and he was gently kissing her breasts.

"Adam, Adam, I've missed you," she murmured, feeling his hands under her dress, inside her pantyhose. "Oh, love, I've missed you." She giggled, remembering the door card. "Angela Adams! Adam . . . be sensible, please . . . I'm not your wife."

"Of course you are!" A mischievous kid, he was enjoying the erotic effect he had created. Angela's pantyhose were around her knees, her dress was high around her waist, and her bra dangled over her breasts. He kissed her mons, tasting her clitoris for a second as she tried to wriggle out of his embrace. "You're Angela Adams on Thursdays. Angela Thomas the rest of the week. You've landed yourself a second husband. What's more, half undressed, you prove at a glance that a woman over forty can be a wildly sexual creature, if she knows how to personify two words."

"What are they?"

"Happy abandon!"

Angela eased herself off the bed. The words had turned her cold. She wanted to be the female that Adam expected her to be. She wanted to run blithely naked around the apartment and explore it in detail and tell him how delighted she was. (And she was delighted!) But his impression of her, an abandoned, sexually charged female, struck the chord of her guilt. It was as if the reality of the apartment, and her need for Adam, suddenly magnified the uneasy fears that were always trailing at the back of her mind. She wanted, somehow, to keep them from seeping into the moment, corrupting their love, and somehow making it sordid. Had her Catholic upbringing been so brainwashed into her psyche as a child that it had become inescapable? ... An echo across the years of the mortal sin she was well embarked on? An old-time preacher had once said of the female adulteress, "and her bowels will burst."

Adam immediately sensed her mood. "I said the wrong words, didn't I? I should have stayed dressed. I should have greeted you more formally, showed you the apartment, and then told you it was yours to decorate. But, Angela, after all, beyond the happy-go-lucky lovemaking in your darkroom, it's been six weeks. Angela I want you ... Don't get the wrong impression, not for fucking ... for immersion, for blending." He shrugged. "You have to understand, you're my flower-girl come to life. Every male has one and most likely never finds her again. But whatever that girl was for me at that moment in my life, she's branded into my brain tissue. For me you're that girl. Every word you say, every gesture you make, the style, the odor, the chemistry of you is predisposed in my psyche. Did I love you in another world? Is this you, you reincarnated?"

Angela couldn't help smiling. "You're working on a pretty dangerous assumption. In reality I may not be that kind of person at all. Maybe you're seeing me through rose-colored glasses."

Adam watched her slowly undress. "I've thought about that. If I were trying to remold you to fit some inner vision of mine, it might have some validity. I might be making you up. But I've had no need to do that. The human being you are ... you being you ... daring to take me into the inner recesses of your thoughts and feelings, daring to dress with a simplicity that escapes most older females, daring to wear no jewelry except that plain wedding band, daring to wear little or no underclothes, daring to simply brush your hair and tell the hairdresser to go to hell ... being you. Not playing games. But I guess those are just facts of your life and have nothing to do with daring."

Listening to him, Angela was only partially aware that she was finally as naked as he was. She was suddenly conscious of the room ... that the bed was in what should have been the living room (why not? they obviously would have no friends to entertain), that the ceilings were at least fifteen feet from the parquet floor. Once the entire building, instead of being apartments, had been some Boston Brahmin's home. The ceramic tiled fireplace, now burning cannel coals, and warming one side of her, had probably been the only winter heating on this floor of the house.

"Adam." She snuggled into his shoulder. "You're delightfully unaware of the subtleties of the female. I have makeup on. I'm dunked in sweet pea. I took off my engagement ring. It seemed ostentatious and made me aware of Jim. The wedding band I can't get off. And if you haven't noticed, I do have earrings on ... and the day before yesterday, I went to the hairdresser. Oh, God ... I love you. But I can't help it. Sometimes when I tell you I love you, I wonder if Jim might be hiding in the woodwork, listening. This morning I told Jim I loved him. Sometimes I get the uneasy feeling that one day either you or Jim will tell me to make up my mind. That's what my mother told me a long time ago when I thought I loved another boy. It was a month or so after Jim came along." Angela leaned on her elbow, enjoying Adam's face and mouth as he nuzzled the fullness of her breasts. "What's more, Adam . . . you're changing me! It's scary.

"I listen to you, and absorb your mad ideas like a stagestruck schoolgirl. And if I know you, before long this place will be full of books. Already there's music. What's that playing? It's very unworldly music."

Adam grinned at her. While she was talking she had been playing with his penis and examining it in a loving, detached way. "It's called *As Quiet As*, by Michael Colgrass, a young composer," he told her. "As quiet as a leaf turning colors, as quiet as an uninhabited creek, as quiet as an ant walking . . . children sleeping . . . time passing . . . a soft rainfall . . . the final star coming out." Adam curved his body so that his face lay against her stomach. "Listening to Keane tell me that my musical ear was still in the nineteenth century, it occurred to me that you and I, scarcely exerting ourselves, on Thursdays could become experts on twentieth-century music. The radio stations play pop music, rock, or Mozart and Beethoven. Most people don't know what is happening in the world of music that parallels art and sculpture. I bought us a dozen or so records. We can listen from the new beginnings at the turn of the century to Schoenberg, Alban Berg, Erik Satie, Webern to Igor Stravinsky, and contemporary composers like John Cage with his prepared piano, Edgar Varese, Virgil Thomson, Elliot Carter, Luciano Berio, Stanley Silverman and hundreds of others."

Suddenly, he kissed her wildly. "I need to be inside you. I can't help it." He laughed. "Talking and seeing you listen so seriously . . . as you unhesitatingly let me be your guru . . . makes me very excited. You look like that song, 'Through the black of night, I want to go where you go.' "

She chuckled. "I'm glad you're aware that I need two kinds of input."

"Me too," he murmured. "If you're ever down a well, ring my bell."

An hour or so later, happy that it still wasn't noon, and that most of the afternoon lay before them, they talked about their children. Angela told him about Jim's sudden reversal with the girls and with Richy, who was positively dumbfounded. Richy's only problem was he didn't know any girls who would be so nonchalant as to sleep in his family's house with him. And while she hadn't discussed it with Adam, she hoped he realized how deeply Robin and Keane were involved. She presumed that if they slept together in her house (as they had at least three nights during the Christmas holidays), that they did the same in his house. Adam admitted Robin bunked in Keane's room. Janice had encountered Keane on the subject when they were alone. She had told Keane that she and Jon liked Robin very, very much and they certainly didn't want her to get hurt by Keane. His answer had been, "Jan, how am I hurting her? I don't have an iron penis, so her vagina can't be hurt. If she doesn't want to marry me, or if I shouldn't want to marry her—unlikely since I ask her about twice a week—then one of us may have a tear in the eye and a longing memory, but we won't be hurt, and I presume we'll survive."

Angela shook her head. "Sometimes I can't believe it's happening. My daughter has had some of your flesh inside her, too. Sometimes, I feel incestuous." She looked at him sadly. "You know, Adam, if they get married that's the end for us. I simply couldn't see you, knowing that Robin might discover that you and I were lovers."

"What you really mean is that you would have given your daughters a pretty bad example. You want them to be what you couldn't be, strictly faithful."

Angela had tears in her eyes. "Don't tease me. I still don't know where my head is at. I suppose you're right. As it is, I'm positive that Sam and Yael suspect something."

Adam shrugged. "You should take up Sam's offer to learn video. He'd never believe that you'd walk into the lion's den, especially if you were actually sleeping with the head lion."

☆ 51 ☆

And then, because she convinced herself working for Adams Video might be good red herring, she telephoned Sam. She was interested. Not to work for pay . . . at least not for the moment . . . but to have the option, one or even two days a week, to learn video techniques. The last Wednesday in January, when she drove to Adams National for the first time, she was feeling a little lightheaded. Now she really had screwed herself up. She didn't dare tell Adam her worry. In fact, other than a kind of breathless "hi" to Adam as Sam took her through the plant and finally into the Adams Video area, she made certain on that day, and the following days when she was in the factory, that she confined herself strictly to the video department and stayed far away from Adam's office. She even refused to let him know the exact days when she was so near and yet so unavailable. The problem was that somehow Jim had assumed that now she was working at

Adams Video on Thursdays as well as Wednesdays. Instead of fully enjoying the learning contact with Sam and the intricacies of videotaping, or rising to Sam's enthusiasm that one day she could be one of the most creative video artists around, now, on Thursdays, she lived in the uneasy fear that if Jim wanted to contact her for some reason, he might call Adams Video, and of course, Sam or one of the employees would have to report that Mrs. Thomas never, ever came to work on Thursdays.

When she finally confessed her fears to Adam, she inadvertently plunged headlong into a sad discussion of the ultimate futility of their love, and her separate relationship with him, and his with Janice. If the strain of lies and deceit didn't finally erode their love, they would be found out. Of the latter Angela was sure. Even though they had the apartment and would have been happy to hide out in it, Adam insisted that love needed a sharing of experience.

"You and I are going to be involved with each other for the rest of our lives," he told her as they were walking around the Prudential Center on Thursday in broad daylight, as casually as husband and wife. "If we don't build a life together of common experiences, beyond our sexual need, we'll miss the joy of remembering together."

"The common experience that we're going to have one day," Angela couldn't help laughing, "is explaining to Janice or Jim, or your children or mine, why you and I are necessary in the first place. Note ... I didn't say anything about your friends. But the way some of your executives at Adams National look at me ... like Harry Carswell, for example, who you say is out for your scalp ... I have a feeling they've seen us together somewhere on Thursdays already ... mooning at each other as if the rest of the world didn't exist." She squeezed his arm. "Youngsters can do that, Adam, but when people our age act completely whacked-out toward each other, the whole world watches in dismay. It's against the rules to be starry-eyed when you're forty."

"Some rules need to be broken," he told her, as he calmly took her to lunch at Pier Four. "I know some Adams National people might be in here. But not Thursday. Friday is the big expense-account day." He ordered them a drink. "This is the first time I've taken you out to eat since New Year's. I love you. I'm proud of you. I take Janice out to dinner."

"I know," she laughed. "It's Thursday. On Thursday, I'm Mrs. Adams."

"In a sane world you could tell Jim, and I could tell Janice. This is no passing fancy. I need you. I need Janice."

"Oh God, Adam. You're such a daydreamer. Janice would hate me. Jim would hate you." There was no answer. He was her Don Quixote, dreaming impossible dreams ... and she had grown up believing in "knights of old."

Back in their apartment, naked, they basked in the vast lostness of each other and watched the late afternoon shadows creep over them. Adam had found a book, *Infidelity* by Brian Boylan, and was skip-reading it to her. "Listen to this." He held the book on the pillow over her head, and she was only partially aware that he had managed to find his way inside her. "It's pertinent to us. 'Most married persons define infidelity as adultery ... but infidelity as it is actually practiced ... is much more extensive and involved than simple adultery ... there is emotional infidelity ... psychological infidelity, plus many lesser forms. ... A more accurate definition of infidelity is that it takes place whenever a married person repeatedly has to look outside marriage for a need not fulfilled by the person's spouse ... It is the rare couple who can be all things to each other ... the thought that infidelity is the offspring of need is enough to make the moralists and marital "experts" gag. ... Judging from the contents ... of the women's magazines, infidelity is the hottest issue today, more debated than the Pill or marihuana ...

" 'The phenomenon is not too difficult to understand, because infidelity represents traditional morality's last stand. ... Premarital sex has been liberated ... now the sacred institution of marriage is threatened by the increasing public and personal tolerance of extramarital sex. ... American traditionalists regard sexual fidelity in marriage (monogamy) with the same reverence in which they hold the American flag and belief in God. ... To question any of these publicly is reprehensible and will bring down upon the questioner the wrath of society.' "

Angela grinned at him. "You're trying to indoctrinate me again. I agree with the writer, especially the last about the 'wrath of society' ... but something that is even more difficult to cope with is that I have discovered Janice through your eyes. A mistress should hate the man's wife, if only for her own protection, but I like Janice. In many ways we are alike. Maybe the 'need' I satisfy for you is a kind of nonquestioning carte blanche for the Adam side of your personality. The Adam-you makes Janice feel insecure." While Angela nibbled on his shoulder she twisted the hair on his pubis into little points. "Maybe if I lived with you day-in day-out, I'd be afraid of Adam, too, and be searching for Jon . . . or J.Q."

Adam chuckled. "Which would simply be rediscovering Jim in me. Janice doesn't want J.Q. For her, Jon, who actually is only a fringe me, is the competent, respected businessman . . . not so gone in the industrial world that he wouldn't put his family and friends before money and career . . . liberal but not radical . . . careful, having achieved the kind of success that hasn't dirtied him in the marketplace . . . not a trend-setter . . . but aware of trends . . . occasionally carefree but never abandoned."

Out of the corner of her eye, Angela could see the time. It was three-thirty. In an hour she would have to leave . . . and Thursday would be seven days away again. Angela wondered if she and Janice were typical of most middle-class women. When they finally dared to live a little dangerously, be abandoned, care about things beyond the tiny walls of their nest, it was impossible to decondition their spouses. The average female defused her man early in life . . . made him conform, and in the process created her own straitjacket.

"Maybe," she told Adam, as he followed her to the apartment's old European-style bathtub (big enough to stretch out in, and the pride and joy of their Thursday home). "Maybe it's really quite simple. I suspect that Jim's attraction to me and Janice's to you, though they might never admit it, is our basic unpredictability. Something which in their early childhood conditioning was denied to them as a way of life, or as Jim says, 'He grew up.' Their seeming smugness covers their insecurity. Maybe that's why encounter groups are so popular . . . they're filled with Janices and Jims who wouldn't dare to make love in a bathtub full of water, unless they read it in some book that said it was all right . . . and in any event, if they did it once they'd say, 'Why suffer?' "

They watched the water fill the huge tub. Dangling their feet in it, they soaped each other with castile soap. Angela told him about trying to seduce Jim in their own back yard, the first summer they owned their house. She wanted to make love with him, rolling in the soft brown earth she had spaded for a vegetable garden. Roll together in it naked, sweaty from their labors ... wildly erotic. "Not that you consciously plan something like that." Angela slid her behind down into the tub and Adam splashed in beside her. "If I told Jim, let's run out in the back yard naked and screw in the snow, he'd make a production of it, or be convinced that no sex was worth pneumonia." At the water level, Adam kissed Angela's floating nipples. They slid down into the tub ... mouth to mouth ... floating against each other's flesh, a symphony of two bodies slowly building to a triumphant climax, followed by the comparable joy of the second movement ... a lovely water dance of wonder and giggling joy at the sheer impossibility that they had survived such ecstasy.

Brushing the water from his face and whispering that he had nearly drowned her (but it was a nice way to go), Angela picked up the thread of their conversation. "But what if there were no Janice or no Jim. . . . If we were married to each other, would we have passed beyond this nuttiness? Would we have burned each other out? Would I be home in Cohasset, and Janice here?"

Adam grinned as she showered him with cold water from a "telephone" shower connected to the tap. "In Cohasset I have a shower cabinet, but I've sacrificed intimacy for luxury. I'll hire you for a lifetime to give me tub baths." Drying her back, enjoying her squeals as he tickled her anus and her determined, giggly no as he took tiny bites out of her pink behind, Adam asked, "If you knew that Janice was in love with Jack Lovell, would that make you feel better?"

"Is she?"

Adam smiled. "I never asked her. I hope she is. Not because of you and me. But because like you, with someone else, a new mirror, she might discover a new reflection of herself. After hunger and keeping warm, the third most important thing in man's life is loving and being loved. The tragedy of our times is that we have let the moralists and the preachers interject so many spurious needs and values. Love ... the Third Force that gives meaning and purpose and provides the axis for all the rest ... why are we so fearful of it? Why can't we cope with it?"

As the weeks went by, Angela stopped probing her guilt. There were no answers for her generation. Maybe another generation, another world, could embrace the marital and comarital into a secure relationship. Maybe one day there would be a new kind of woman (because this new world would be female-oriented, not male) who could proudly tell two men she loved them, and accept with equanimity that other women loved her two men.

Of one thing she was certain, there was no false note between them. If they were adventure for each other, a more joyous form of escape than most, it was a committed adventure. Adam never made her feel insecure . . . nor she him. Even when she had managed to uncover the total extent of his sex life . . . three girls before marriage to Janice . . . one, a few years after Janice and he were married, and Barbara Lovell (which shocked her momentarily), she realized that Adam's basic Puritanism made it impossible for him to enjoy promiscuity.

"Bobby's really a nice human being," he told Angela, kissing the tears of doubt from her eyes. "I should have resisted, I suppose . . . but if a woman really signals a man that she needs him, it's damned difficult for a male to resist."

"I suppose that's how you feel about me," Angela sighed. "It's too bad you didn't get involved with her first; then all four of you could have wife-swapped."

"That's the pat way that novelists write it in books," Adam said. "Unfortunately, life is more complicated. It would be pure luck if two couples discovered each other in later life and found they were perfectly compatible mentally and sexually."

"Maybe they could work at it. I read a book like that once." Angela found herself smiling, despite her temporary indignation at Barbara Lovell. "I guess it's not plausible; people are so hung on the inviolability of their own egos, they would never make the concessions necessary to love each other."

Adam laughed. "Or maybe the real problem is that

221

Barbara never can be my flower-girl, nor probably can any other man be your Don Quixote. Of course, what you call my Puritanism is a basic human drive. You have it too. A need for commitment ... pivot points for one's life. Otherwise the centrifugal forces would whirl us in bits and pieces to the outer edges of space."

But the overriding emotion for Angela ... and she guessed that it was the same for Adam ... was the ever-present fear that what little continuity their Thursdays gave them was subject to the winds of chance. Business problems at Adams National, sickness of their own, or in either family, even the weather could snap the fragile thread. And something else that Thursdays could never provide ... as simple a married thing as waking up together and smiling their love and good mornings into each others faces ... or making early-morning love, determined in their joy that the day would never begin.

Then, without too much maneuvering, the last week in February, from Tuesday morning through Saturday night, fell into their laps. Four days and nights together. A gift from the gods. Adam was aware of it first. The annual play-offs for the Massachusetts Golf Club Championships were being held at the Mid-Ocean Club in Bermuda. Jack Lovell was a leading contender in the pay-offs. Barbara Lovell had planned to go, but her mother who lived in Florida was ailing ... and she had been promising for more than a year to visit her. Janice's suggestion to Jon—that it was only four days, Bermuda was so close, and anyway they hadn't taken a winter vacation for several years—failed to intrigue him. Suddenly, a better idea occurred to him. He tried to keep it at the J.Q. level, and at least give it the dignity of a chess game. Why couldn't Janice go to Bermuda with some of the other ladies from the club who were contenders in the women's play-offs? After all, it was going to be a charter flight of golf enthusiasts. When he first dropped the idea, Janice pooh-poohed it ... but he noticed a sparkle of interest. Could she guess that he was consciously offering her an adventure with Jack? He tried not to make it obvious. It wasn't that he was exactly uninterested, he told her, but Harry Carswell was stirring in muddy waters. The stockholders meeting scheduled for February 15th had been postponed until March 5th. He wanted to be sure that the factions warring over Adams Video were brought into line. What's more, he would take the opportunity while Janice was away to run up to Montreal and visit their Canadian plant. He hadn't popped in on Jean Martineau since last July, when he and Janice had driven up to Quebec.

Sipping a before-dinner Scotch with Janice in the living room, he said, "Jack called me today . . . something about our building mortgage. I told him you might join the charter flight to Bermuda and root for him. You can play a little golf yourself in between the tournaments and have some fun. Would Barbara mind?"

Janice shrugged. "Not everybody is so easygoing as you are, Jon. I don't know about Barbara. If you'd fly to Los Angeles with her, I'm sure she'd give Bermuda her blessing. But coming down to earth, people would talk. Jack in Bermuda without Barbara. Me there without you." Janice looked at him with raised eyebrows.

As she got up to put dinner on the table (they ate alone in the kitchen when there were no guests), Adam pulled her down in his lap and kissed her. "Your problem is Barbara!"

She snuggled against his face, and then looked at him clear-eyed and calmly sophisticated. He was aware that Janice was a cool, self-possessed, attractive female. "Janice, we're beating around the bush," he said. "First, I love you. I enjoy you. But I read somewhere that women in their forties, having belatedly discovered their dammed-up sexuality, and finally daring to explore the joys of love, can quite easily handle two men. Whatever your feelings may be toward Jack Lovell, I want you to know I like Jack . . . and you've never made me feel like a second-rate citizen."

Tears in her eyes, Janice hugged him. "Okay, if you'll still love me, I'd like to go. But I want you to know that I'd be just as happy if you came, too." She sighed. "Damn it! . . . Jonathan . . . sometime we should have a real encounter with each other. Why don't you like Bobby?"

"I do." Jon shrugged. "I think Bobby, unlike you, is a typical middle-class hausfrau with no basic interests whatsoever . . . and no talents she has ever developed." Playing with Janice's fingers as he said it, thinking about her abilities with oil painting, sculpture, and pottery, he wondered why she would ever think that he would be attracted to such a shallow woman as Barbara Lovell. He mentally crossed his fingers as he suddenly remembered the morning after Thanksgiving. Had Barbara told Janice about it? Evidently, from the way Janice was reacting, she hadn't. "I just have a feeling, if I made love to Barbara, I wouldn't like myself, because by morning, I'd be trying to escape her." As he said it, he was suddenly Adam, and he remembered Barbara's fantasy of being handcuffed to him. He laughed. "God, if Bobby and I were ever imprisoned together, I'd die of sheer boredom. She really hasn't two ideas to knock together in her brain."

Janice asked him why, after so many years, he hadn't found her boring. Jon hugged her. "Let's say, in the words of that song, I've grown accustomed to your face! You're Janice. If sometimes you're dull, it's a familiar dullness more often than not that matches mine."

The following Thursday, lying on their water bed, Adam reported the conversation to Angela. "Janice would be delighted with some kind of two-couple arrangement . . ."

"What a lovely daydream." Angela was snapping pictures of him as he rode an imaginary bicycle, his legs high in the air. "Maybe someday Jim will discover Janice. They'll both sink a birdie on the eighteenth hole, and it will be love at first sight!"

"We could all meet together," Adam told her. "Janice has suggested several times that she's been thinking of inviting you and Jim to dinner. She feels negligent. After all, the Adamses were responsible for the infamous marihuana affair . . . and Robin and Keane are in love . . ."

"No thanks." Angela shuddered. "How could I spend an evening in your home indulging in superficial pleasantries when Janice was right there, and Jim . . . all I would be thinking about is you and I making love."

Monday, when Adam checked the Ansaphone, Angela was on it . . . vastly excited. "Adam . . . Adam . . . the impossible has happened. Jim is going to Bermuda on the same charter with Ed Kanace. Ed is representing the Valley Stream Country Club, and Jim is one of the runner-ups. Bettie still isn't reconciled with Ed, so when I suggested that Jim go with him, and together they could have men fun . . . that I had seen Bermuda and it was not such a big deal . . . Jim was really elated." Adam couldn't help chuckling at Angela's bubbling enthusiasm on the tape. "Jim is really acting like a big kid. He can't believe that I won't mind being left alone for a few days. Sunday, he was trying to assure me that he would be in bed early every night. If Ed wanted to chase females, okay . . . but he was there to play golf, and after eighteen holes every day, by eight or nine he'd be in the sack. Of course, I had the mad temptation to tell him that Janice Adams would be there, but other than using Sam as the excuse as to how I knew, that didn't seem too logical. Well, who knows, maybe they'll meet. They do know each other . . . at least by hearsay . . . and Janice could be his daughter's mother-in-law someday. Damn, if that friend of yours Jack Lovell wasn't going, Janice might be at sixes and sevens and run into Jim in the cocktail lounge. Jim might be lonely. Janice might not like an empty bed. For the tournament they could be each other's 'in-beds.' Ha! How's that for a new kind of relationship? 'In-beds' would find it much easier to relate to each other than in-laws, for example. Oh, Adam, can't you convince Jack to go to Florida with his wife . . . or maybe something good would happen and Jack would get the flu. We really need to give this a chance. But of course, it has to happen independently of us. We must have nothing to do with it. Imagine . . . Jim returns from Bermuda and he talks about golf, but there's a faraway look in his eye. He's remembering Janice. He's in love with her. First thing you know, he's taking Thursdays off. Instead of playing golf he's discovering romance. Then, one day when we are really old and it doesn't matter what people think, we discover for years that we've all been in love, and, of course, we're all in our seventies anyway and ready for the senior-citizen centers, and we're determined that won't happen, so we move in your house in Cohasset, or into this house if we all prefer . . . or if houses are too much and we did all end up in the old folks' home, we could scandalize everybody, because the Adamses and the Thomases were wife-swapping.

"Oh, God . . . Adam, I'm so elated, I'm two feet off the ground. Now . . . at least once in our lives, we can have four days and nights together. I'm going to telephone Sam today and tell him next week I won't be in. Oh dear—maybe you'll have to go to work normally; otherwise Sam will be sure to put two and two together . . . especially on Wednesday. He'll be certain that we're somewhere together making love!"

Adam didn't tell Angela, but his theory was to explain nothing to Sam or anyone else. Adam had never told Angela that Sam's opinion was that next to Yael, Angela was the best discovery of his life. In fact, if he weren't married, even though she was old enough to be his mother, he would have talked his way into bed with her. The way Sam said it was too boyishly good-humored to suggest any insinuation or testing of his father, but he could imagine Angela's shock, if she had heard Sam state quite calmly, "Frankly, if I were you, Jake, even though she's obviously pretty straight, I'd have asked. All she could do is say no."

☆ 53 ☆

Tuesday morning between eight-thirty and nine-fifteen, the Adamses and the Thomases would all meet each other for the first time at Logan Airport. It was Adam's idea. On the Ansaphone, Angela had listened to the tape. Joyous, Adam blew a bubbly fantasy for her. "It will be just what you hoped for. Jim will meet Janice, and they'll fall in love at first sight. But more to the point, the minute the plane takes off for Bermuda with our golf-loving spouses, our honeymoon will begin."

How could you argue with a happy madman? It might be simple for Adam to suggest to Janice that he would drive her and Jack Lovell to the airport (Barbara Lovell had left the day before for Florida). Presumably Adam had to go to work in Boston anyway. But Jim had other ideas. Why should Ange have to get up so early and drive thirty miles or so in heavy traffic? Ed Kanace had plenty of automobiles at his agency. Ed would drive . . . they could leave Ed's car at the airport garage until Sunday. Tuesday morning he would kiss Ange good-bye, and she could sleep on, undisturbed.

It wasn't easy, but Angela finally convinced him she wouldn't be happy unless she could wish him a bon voyage at the airport, and meet him when he returned. After all, why shouldn't a wife be happy that her husband was going to have a little fun and enjoyment? That turned out to be the wrong tack. Jim quickly pointed out she was more than welcome to come with him. In fact, he wanted her to come with him. Flustered but determined, Angela finally convinced him, for the second time, that he'd be much happier knowing he could play golf to his heart's content and not have to worry about her. Of course, she couldn't reveal her true reasons for wanting to drive him to the airport.

The idea of not wasting a precious minute of Adam-time was one reason, but it also was the perfect opportunity to meet Janice Adams in the flesh, without getting too involved. Angela shrugged away the truth ... simple curiosity. What was her lover's wife like? And, another thing, while Adam might think she was daydreaming, it would be a perfect way for them to introduce Jim and Janice to each other. While she had never met Jack Lovell, she would bet anything that Jim was much more handsome and interesting. If she were Janice, she would have liked Jim and wanted to know him better.

Of course, she knew it was wishful thinking. The chances of Jim liking Janice, or even vice versa, were incredibly remote. Worse, she knew the whole daydream was something she had cooked up to assuage her own guilt—proved by the fact that she was counting on a spontaneous happenstance meeting and hadn't dared to tell Jim she knew that Janice Adams was going to Bermuda without her husband.

Tuesday morning, finally at the wheel of the station wagon, listening to Jim and Ed discuss the pecularities of certain holes they would be playing on the Bermuda golf courses, Angela reflected that all she had finally achieved was her own inconvenience. She had really wanted to pack a small suitcase, but at the last minute she realized she would have had to put it in the back of the station wagon. She could have told Jim that her sisters Kathy and Alma had invited her to visit them in the North End for a few days, but that might have made Jim a little more curious about the how, why, and where of the days he'd be gone. She decided that Adam's theory about simple lies was the best. By being purposely vague as to what she might be doing, she avoided embarrassing dead ends, and could invent simple escape hatches if and when the need arose.

So, here she was, on the threshold of a lovely adventure, with just the clothes on her back. A few weeks ago she had brought an extra dress into the Pink (Angela grinned as she recalled Adam's code name for the apartment), as well as a few pairs of pantyhose which she really didn't need, because Adam was slowly convincing her that pantyhose were simply a twentieth-century version of the chastity belt. In the eighteenth century, women made themselves much more accessible; if the female were willing, a man could simply lift her skirts and there she'd be, naked and delectable. Wriggling out of pantyhose on the spur of the moment (as Adam, rambling on the Ansaphone tape, had pointed out), in a telephone booth, for example, should the need arise, could be time-consuming and damned near impossible.

Chuckling inwardly that at forty-three, she, Angela Thomas (Adams?) could have such silly sexy ideas, Angela felt as if she were really ten or eleven, a laughing youngster, skipping rope or playing jacks. Her hair flying in the wind, she wanted to fling herself into Adam's arms, laughing and saying, "I love you." If she needed more clothes, she could drive back to Acton. But that was silly. They had made no particular plans. Hadn't Adam told her that this really was their honeymoon? They should act quite normal and spend most of their time in bed. What would she need clothes for?

Carrying their clubs and suitcases into the Eastern Airlines Terminal, waving enthusiastically to friends and challengers from other golf clubs, Jim and Ed, with Angela tagging after them, were quickly swallowed up in the confusion. Thirty minutes before departure, more than two hundred golf enthusiasts, waiting for the announcement that the Massachusetts Golfers' Charter Flight to Bermuda was ready to board, were milling around in happy confusion, exhorting each other to bring home the victory cups and enjoy the days ahead. While the bar wouldn't be open until the plane was winging over the Atlantic, most of them were already high at the thought of playing hookey from the dull world of work, and the deadly process of commuting back and forth to it.

Standing on tiptoe, scanning the crowd in all directions, desperate as the minutes fled by, Angela finally spotted Adam and tried to wave casually at him. "It's the Adamses," she told Jim. "I forgot about it. Sam told me last week that Janice might be flying to Bermuda for the tournament. J. Q. is bringing her over to meet us."

With Janice in tow, grinning and looking so beamish as he squeezed through the crowd that Angela had a momentary fear he might flip and actually embrace her, Adam shook hands with Jim and introduced them to Janice and Jack Lovell, who had followed them. Angela, completely off balance, returned Janice's friendly cheek-to-cheek hug. "Now, I know where Robin gets her beauty." Janice

228

grinned at Jim. "Not that the male Thomas isn't quite handsome. Are you coming to Bermuda with us, Angela?"

Angela shook her head, praying that her careening thoughts made some kind of sense. "Jim wanted me to, but golf really isn't my cup of tea. Instead of enjoying himself, he'd be worrying that I was bored." As she spoke, she could almost see the connection forming in Janice's mind. But maybe it was her imagination.

Janice smiled. "That's a shame . . . Jonathan isn't coming either. If he had known, you could have both come and entertained each other. Jon and you could have sailed together. Do you like sailing?"

Angela wondered if she were blushing, but Janice didn't seem to notice. "For a moment," Janice said, "I was hoping that we would finally get to know each other. Anyway, I promise you, the week after next I'll telephone you. Keane says that Robin has a Spring vacation. If Keane can get off, it would be a nice time to have a family get-together."

Janice didn't sound insincere, but Angela suspected that, at the moment, a gathering of the Thomas and Adams clans was the farthest thing from her mind. Even as they exchanged pleasantries, Angela couldn't help staring at her. Janice was wearing a beige suit. Tall, model-thin, a cool Nordic face with high cheekbones and hair (dyed?) natural blonde, she laughed easily as she told Angela about her embarrassment when Sam confessed that he had shown those silly videotapes of Thanksgiving to the Thomases. Angela was aware that she and Janice were strikingly contrasting females. Janice could have walked out of the pages of *Vogue*. Angela guessed that she didn't weigh too much more than Janice, but by comparison her breasts and behind were much more lush. Angela couldn't help grinning at her thoughts. Jonathan Quincy Adams' wife and mistress were Isolde and Iseult. She prayed that Adam was a better manager than Tristan.

It was impossible to maintain any connected conversation; the noise and churning excitement of those about to leave had already created a separation from those who would stay behind. Janice's farewell plunged Angela into further confusion. She squeezed Angela's hand. "I really mean it. We'll get together soon. It's a shame that Jon is flying up to Montreal for the week. Otherwise I'd insist that he take you to dinner."

The frightened question on Angela's face . . . what's this

229

about Montreal? ... must have been apparent to Adam, but he only grinned at her. As the call to board the plane sounded through the terminal, they all became strangers again, physically separated not only by other travelers and their families ... but by an invisible wall of privacy that husbands and wives and even friends are able to quickly erect in the middle of a crowd. Angela was a little disappointed. It had been impossible to determine Jim's reaction to Janice. At the moment he seemed far more interested in the discovery that Jack Lovell and Ed Kanace might be matched against each other in the play-offs—jousting knights determined to bring the trophies home to their particular club.

She assured Jim for the hundredth time that she was happy that he was going. No, she wasn't disappointed, nor had she suddenly changed her mind. She had a thousand things that she wanted to do. This afternoon, she might even drop into Adams Video ...

Jim interrupted her rambling, nervous cover-up. "I suppose you'll be having lunch with Adams." Jim's courtroom expression revealed nothing of his thoughts. "Don't look so guilty. I give you permission."

Trying to control her jittery feelings, Angela hoped she sounded casual. "You heard Janice. Jonathan is flying to Canada. Adams National has a Canadian plant."

Adam better not be flying to Canada, she thought grimly. Not after this. "Really, Jim, J.Q. never takes employees to lunch ... and my status is lower than an employee. I'm just an unpaid apprentice. His son thinks I have potential, but I may never produce anything."

Out of the corner of her eye, Angela saw Adam give Janice a fond farewell kiss, and then a quick handshake for Jack Lovell. Jim hugged her and pecked her lips. Distraught and overwhelmed, suddenly, with the sure knowledge that she loved him, she kissed him back. She tried to hold back the tears in her eyes. With a cheery smile and the usual "take care of *you*, I love you," he followed Ed Kanace into the tunnel that connected the jet plane to the terminal. Just before Janice disappeared onto the plane, she waved at Adam and puckered her lips in an airborne kiss. Was the grin on her face covering her loneliness? It seemed so to Angela.

Adam edged through the crowd back to where she was standing. "Okay, Angela Thomas. I know what you're

230

thinking ... that you're a bad girl." He took her arm. "Come on ... we haven't much time."

Jittery and fearful that some of the passengers who still hadn't boarded the plane might recognize them, Angela quickly pulled away from him. "Adam, please ... act as if we're just friends, will you?" Her voice was trembly. "Oh God, I feel so guilty, I could sit right down here and cry my eyes out. You must be made of iron. Did you see Janice? She wanted you to come with her. She loves you. She's really very lovely. What do you ever see in me? Why do you need me? Janice is a fine-looking woman." Angela couldn't hold back the tears flooding her eyes. "Before, Janice didn't seem real to me. Or when she did, I simply wouldn't let myself think about her. ... But now ... oh, Adam ... maybe the world is right. One wife ... one husband should be enough."

Adam squeezed her hand. "Angela, I love you. I love Janice. Maybe once long ago when I was a young man, I might have thought that loving two women was very bad or immoral. Today, in this screwed-up world, I think just the other way around. Loving is the only path to a new kind of world sanity. The real problem, which makes me feel badly at the moment, is that I can't tell Janice and you can't tell Jim." Adam smiled at her. "Really, Angel-a, I'm not impervious. When Janice blurted out that bit about taking you to dinner, my stomach did a flip-flop."

They were at the entrance to the terminal. Angela assumed that they would go to the airport garage and leave, either in his car or hers, but Adam had captured her arm in a firm grip. He pulled her in the opposite direction. "What I couldn't tell Janice and haven't been able to tell you up until now is that Angela and Adam are both flying to Montreal." Adam burst into laughter at her shocked surprise. "We haven't time for discussion. Come on, Air Canada is quite a way down the line from here. We're booked for the ten-thirty flight. ... That gives us about a half hour."

He ignored her astonished protests. and she was almost running to keep abreast of him. "Jonathan Adams ... you really must have flipped. I have no clothes with me ... no suitcase ... nothing. I thought you were using the Canada trip as an excuse ... Adam." She wailed, "You're not listening to me. Why do we have to go to Montreal? I'm happy right here, I want to spend our four days together in the Pink. Why do I have to chase all over the world with nothing to wear?"

"I'll buy you a dress in Montreal. Stop fretting. All I have is this overnight case. I promise you we'll be back in Boston by noon tomorrow."

Angela immediately felt better. After all, it was just Tuesday. They had until Sunday, and she had assumed that Adam might have to work. At least he was taking her with him. At the reservations desk, as he checked their seating arrangements, Angela said, "It would be interesting to see your Canadian plant, but I suppose that's impossible. You could never explain me . . . or why I was with you."

Adam hurried her toward the departure gate. "This is not a business trip. I'm not going near the plant, but if I were, I'd just say to Jean Martineau, 'This is Angela Thomas. She works in our Boston video department, and she loves me.' "

Walking into the plane, almost afraid to look into the faces of passengers already seated, praying that there was no one aboard who would recognize them, Angela fastened her seat belt and scrunched down in her window seat. She watched Adam, sitting beside her, open his overnight case.

"How's your French?" he asked her. Fumbling underneath a shirt and underwear, he produced a paperback book.

"Where I left it in college," Angela said. "Never mind my linguistic ability. I see that you brought a change of underclothes for yourself. Don't you think I need to be clean, too? Please . . . Adam, you told Janice you were visiting your Canadian plant. If that's not true, then why are we going to Montreal?"

Adam was grinning like a kid who had held a surprise so long that he was about to burst. "To get married!"

"Married! Have you gone crazy? We are married!"

"Not to each other."

"Oh, Adam . . ." Angela stared at him with tears in her eyes.

Chuckling, he handed her the book. "We won't be in Montreal for at least an hour. After you've read Father Lereve's book, you won't feel so hopeless."

Between laughter and tears, Angela read the title aloud. "*Le Synergamie* par Jesonge Lereve . . ." She flicked the pages. "A long time ago I could read French pretty well

232

and understand it, but not words like *synergamie*. What does it mean?"

Adam was adamant. "The author explains it. The book isn't very long. You can read it in an hour."

Angela grinned at him. "Maybe you can, but in French, under the best of circumstances, it would take me somewhat longer." She touched his hand. "What's this book got to do with the madness you've dreamed up about getting married? My God ... you've got me nearly crazy as you are ... we can't get married."

"Yes we can. Father Lereve has arranged the licenses. I telephoned to him yesterday." Adam smiled indulgently at her bewilderment. "All right, let's start from the beginning. A few weeks ago, Jean Martineau, who *really is* the manager of our Canadian plant, sent me a copy of Father Lereve's book. He didn't send it with any forethought. You see, in addition to financial printing in Canada, we print what is known in the trade as quality paperbacks. So that I'm aware of what we're producing in the Canadian plant, copies of all printed material completed the previous week are sent to my attention." Adam grinned. "Hence, the copy of Father Lereve's book, which is being published by a small Canadian publisher. Since you already know my reading compulsions, I was very soon engrossed in the book, reading it in almost complete disbelief. While many obvious changes have taken place in the Church ... almost a complete radicalization in some areas, I couldn't believe that a Catholic priest would dare to propose an idea like this, even speculatively. When I telephoned Father Lereve, he assured me that *synergamie* was only one facet of a bright new Catholicism he was exploring. I told him that the reason for my call was that I was interested in synergamy (to anglicize the word) because a very lovely female and I were involved in just the type of relationship he describes in his book."

Adam touched the tips of Angela's fingers. He wanted to kiss the wonder and suppressed laughter in her eyes. She looked like a child listening to a fairy tale she didn't really believe but hoped might, somehow, be true. "From our conversation, Father Lereve convinced me that if you approved, he could marry us. Now, don't you think you should read the book?"

The pilot, who had been waiting for the signal from the tower, revved the engines and the plane roared down the runway. Adam looked at his watch. "It's eleven o'clock.

We have reservations at Le Chateau Champlain. We'll register first, and then buy you a dress and panties or whatever you need. Father Lereve plans to meet us in the rectory of L'Église de Sainte Marie de la Vie at three o'clock. Before five we'll be married." Adam couldn't repress his enthusiasm; grinning at her, he kissed her cheek. "We'll spend the first night of our honeymoon in Montreal."

☆ 54 ☆

Angela unfastened her seat belt and stared at him, wide-eyed. "If I didn't know you better, I'd think you had flipped. I'll just assume you're in one of your testing-teasing moods to see if you can jar me." She touched his brow lightly with her hand. "At least you haven't got a temperature." She interlaced her fingers with his. Adam knew that if there hadn't been an armrest between them, she would have snuggled against his shoulder. "Okay." Angela tried her most beguiling voice: "What is synergamy?"

Adam sighed. "Angela ... you are unquestionably female. If you had started reading when I first asked you to, you'd know by now. You're obviously indulging in one aspect of marriage already ... contrariness." He picked the book out of her lap. "I'll read you bits and pieces and translate as I go."

With his reading glasses on, looking like the headmaster of a New England boys' school, Adam read softly while Angela listened and tried to concentrate. But her brain waves were playing "ring around the rosy." Oh Lord, she thought, whether this man reads to me or just looks at me without even touching me, he makes me so sexually aroused I can scarcely follow what he is saying. At least (and she grinned), not until I'm undressed and in snuggly contact with all of him.

"They should have curtains around these seats," she murmured. "You read better naked, inside me."

"You're not listening."

"I am, but I can't believe my ears. Synergy isn't easy to understand. Read it again."

"Webster defines synergy as 'the cooperative action of discrete agencies such that the total effect is greater than the sum of the two effects taken independently.' In his book *Operating Manual for Spaceship Earth*, Buckminister Fuller has defined synergy as 'the behavior of whole systems unpredicted by separately observed behavior of any of the system's separate parts or any sub-assembly of the system's parts.'" Adam smiled. "In his book, Father Lereve is offering synergamy (a word he created) as an alternate form of marriage. He visualizes synergamy as an earlier commitment that might or might not precede corporate or group marriages, depending on the growing ability of many human beings to handle more sophisticated types of interpersonal relationships. Whether synergamy actually was resolved in a structured group relationship is not the entire key. His theory is that synergamous marriages can coexist with monogamous marriages without disrupting the prior marriage commitment . . ."

"Adam," Angela interrupted, "I'm bewildered. In simple words, for my befuddled brain, what is synergamy?"

Adam laughed. "You and I . . . our relationship. The sum of you and I (two effects) have created a total effect that embraces our separate relationships to Jim and Janice and creates a new gestalt that enlarges our capacities. In Father Lereve's proposal, synergamy is viewed as expanding previous monogamous ties without destroying them. Obviously, this is not the usual effect of an extramarital relationship, which would tend to be anti-synergetic. By contrast Father Lereve is proposing that what we now refer to as adultery could be structured (for those who wished to undertake it) in a second commitment, which would be truly comarital. The key would be a growing understanding of interpersonal human responsibility. The synergamous marriage brings the second relationship out into the open and gives the participants an opportunity to produce an overriding commitment that embraces both marriages. Here's Father Lereve's own words." Adam read: "'Synergamy is a form of committed relationship which can be embraced not so much as a legal form of marriage, but as an emotional commitment (preferably in the form of a church ceremony), in which ordinarily adulterous or extramarital relationships are given a status approximately equal to the first marriage commitment. In a perfectly operating synergamous marriage, the spouses making the second commitment would be responsible for

235

any children emerging from the second marriage; though in most cases synergamous marriages probably would be childless, as a matter of preference as well as population control. Financial responsibility for the second family which would be embraced in the synergamous marriage would be optional. Thus the original husband and wife would be able to relate to a second wife and husband without destroying the original monogamous marriage, but in a sense enlarging it. The contemplated relationship in a synergamous marriage, unlike a group marriage, would be two separate dyads . . . two males relating to two separate females and vice versa, but with no necessity for a complete relationship (as would occur in a group marriage) between the two males or the two females. It would be assumed in a synergamous marriage that the spouses would change households, or basic home environments, a portion of each week: one, two, or three days, and enjoy complete involvement in the second relationship with the children of the second spouse equivalent to the love and involvement of the blood children. Synergamous marriages might lead to group or corporate marriages of two couples, but not necessarily. Synergamous marriages are predicated on the fact that most individuals can discover a second member of the opposite sex with whom he or she could relate fully, but it is considerably more difficult for a monogamous couple, a dyad, to effect a mutual relationship with another monogamous couple not only in the areas of sexual exchange, but in the simultaneous, multilateral, interpersonal encounters of a quartet or sextet.' "

As Adam was translating, Angela shook her head. Father Lereve was obviously a dreamer. "Adam, I love you . . ." she said finally, "but how do you think Jim or Janice would react. Really, it's quite silly. Father Lereve is assuming that two of the spouses in the original marriage would give the other two permission to marry. Maybe they would, if like wife-swappers they were in the mood to do the same thing. But supposing, for example, Jim didn't want a second commitment . . . that he was perfectly satisfied with one wife . . . Angela. Do you think he'd be happy if I married you?" Angela couldn't help laughing. "He'd tell me, 'If you want Adam . . . take him and say good-bye to me.' The missing words that all monogamous marriages are hung up with are 'instead of' . . . Try it on Janice. Tell her you want Angela in addition to her. She'll ask you if you think you're the king of Siam."

Laughing, Adam disagreed. "Father Lereve is a futurist. He thinks that the male or female of the future will react quite differently. Synergamy, of course, isn't for everybody. But there's no question that there are many males and females, like you and me, who really enjoy the opposite sex and one way or another somewhere in their lifetimes will actively seek the second involvement. Maybe that drive is sexually rooted, but it has numerous other facets, too. Of course, if Jim or Janice didn't like that kind of adventure for themselves—and who knows, if the opportunity existed, as a socially approved relationship, it might change their attitude—they might be very happy to give you and me an opportunity to try our wings."

Angela shrugged. "Only a Frenchman could have dreamed up synergamy. Years ago, wealthy Frenchmen had mistresses, and their wives had lovers, without destroying their basic marriage. Of course, in most of those marriages the original marriage was economic . . . not romantic, like American marriages . . ." She laughed. "Anyway, if I'm crazy enough to marry you today it will really be bigamy, not synergamy. This Father Lereve of yours must be quite mad." Angela shivered. "Ye gods, even though I haven't been to church in years, my early conditioning shouts that the whole idea is impossible. Marriage is a sacrament. You're saying that the Church, or rather Father Lereve, who most certainly will be excommunicated, can perform a marriage that would in effect condone adultery."

Adam was obviously enjoying the discussion. "Why not? Ultimately if the old religions are to survive, they will embrace concepts that could solidify marriage and the family. There are many new approaches to Catholic doctrine. Religious organizations are no different from any other life-forms. The dinosaurs couldn't adapt to the changing environment and they perished." He smiled. "The lowly cockroach has lasted for millenia."

Angela still wasn't convinced. "Why in the world would anyone want to legalize an affair?" She sighed. "Except silly utopians like you and me. Basically, wouldn't we be asking our present spouses to assume the role of mother and father and give their blessing on the follies of the children they married . . . you and me?"

Adam took her hand and nibbled the tips of her fingers. "All husbands and wives should occasionally play the mother and father role for their spouses . . . that's love.

Didn't e. e. cummings say? . . . "Unless you love someone, nothing else makes much sense." But cummings said *someone*. Man is slowly discovering the many dimensions of human love. Because you and I care for each other, we pray for continuity to our involvement. If we didn't have that deeper need, we would have dismissed that first day in bed as a temporary lust and then fled from each other. A few weeks ago you were feeling sad at the sheer fragility of our Thursday love affair . . ." Adam handed the book to her. "You really should read it. If synergamy ever becomes an accepted relationship, the guilt aspects of you and I would disappear."

Angela smiled at him through tears that turned her eyes into amber pools. "Of course, I'll read the book, and I'll marry you. It really doesn't matter whether it's sane or not. The insanity is caring so much for you in the first place."

"Monogamy and pure fidelity wouldn't have seemed sane to many people who have lived on this earth. A few days ago, you were daydreaming that Jim and Janice might discover each other and maybe fall in love. What if that had happened?"

Angela chuckled. "I knew it was a pipe dream . . . but I went even further; all four of us could move in together. I read a book like that a few years ago . . . it was very idealistic."

"Maybe it might happen, eventually," Adam said. "Our house in Cohasset is big enough, but there's the more likely possibility that the four of us wouldn't immediately like each other, or even if we did, we might not be emotionally balanced enough to function as a foursome."

"I still don't see why synergamy is better."

Adam grinned. "To paraphrase Father Lereve: 'synergamy simply rationalizes a human need. It recognizes that monogamous love based, as it has been, on strict fidelity, is, for many individuals, self-limiting. For some people it strangles human growth. You and I have discovered that we can love two adult human beings of the opposite sex . . . with an innate sense of responsibility both to each other as well as to Janice and Jim. Responsibility is the key."

Later, even Adam would admit that their day in Montreal and their marriage in L'Eglise de Sainte Marie de la Vie had a dreamlike quality to it. After the houseboy, who brought them to their quarter-circle room near the top of Le Chateau Champlain had gone, Angela stared unbelievingly out of the floor-to-ceiling curved glass window. A light snow lazed its way down over the city below them, blending the buildings and the streets and Mount Royal into a moonscape monotone. The gray haze of winter softened the reality of the man-world, and from this vantage point afforded them the momentary detachment of human gods watching a world that existed solely for them.

Angela pulled back the covers on one of the double beds and chortled with joy at the surprise luxury of orange sheets and pillowcases. She hugged Adam. "I just decided, I don't need a dress. I'll rinse out my underclothes tonight." He flopped on the bed beside her, and she looked at his watch. "It's one-thirty . . . do we have time?" She pointed out the window, which gave the illusion they were floating in the sky. "I've always had a secret wish . . . to make love, naked, with the snowflakes falling on me, melting like tiny caresses on my body." She shivered. "Sometimes, I think I'm too honest with you. You might not like such a sensuous woman."

Adam's gentle kiss assured her that he did. The room was a womb with a view, and they revelled in their need to be reborn in each other. Angela would have been content to dream away the afternoon and night, but Adam was a man with a mission.

The taxi driver who picked them up in front of the hotel had heard rumors about Sainte Marie. "It's in the University area," he told them. "Nothing is sacred anymore . . . not even the Church. From what I've heard, that parish is overrun with radicals trying to make a new Church without Jesus."

Turning into a narrow twisting street, he stopped in front of a small Gothic cathedral that long ago had been encroached on from both sides by taller, secular buildings. As they got out of the cab, a priest opened the door in a granite-faced building across the street from the church and waved at them. He introduced himself. *"Oui, je suis le Frère Lereve."* A tall man with a trimmed black beard covering an emaciated face, he had the appearance of a latter-day saint. *"Bonne chance, vous arrivez à temps. Venez, nous pouvons parler ici dans ma chambre."* Then he switched to heavily accented English. "You must be Monsieur Adams and is this Madame Thomas? Delightful. You honor me to have come so far. Alas, I see you are alone." He smiled forlornly. "In many marriages *de la synergamie*, the other spouses come and they give their blessing to the new union."

He ushered them into a tiny book-lined office. A small tile-faced fireplace glowed with hot coals in an iron basket. "You are fortunate. In a few minutes there will be a rehearsal of the Ballet de l'Annunciation. Afterwards, the dancers will be delighted to witness your marriage. I presume that you have read *Le Synergamie*. New types of marriage commitments, to preserve family structures, is only one of the many ideas we are experimenting with."

Sitting on a leather couch beside Angela, Adam said, "Angela and I have discussed your book pretty carefully. Angela thinks you must have written it tongue-in-cheek. She still can't believe that it is more than an exercise in fantasy."

Staring at them from his chair, behind a Queen Anne desk, Father Lereve seemed almost insubstantial . . . lost in some nonexistent dream world. There was something about Father Lereve that made Angela want to comfort him . . . to tell him that Adam was wrong, she really did believe . . . or wanted to. Finally, just as he seemed about to vanish forever into his own thoughts, he recovered himself and smiled absentmindedly at them.

"Forgive me, I was thinking about one of your American religionists, Harvey Cox. When you said fantasy, Madame Thomas, it reminded me of his delightful book *The Feast of Fools*. To understand what directions we are taking here I suggest you read it. In Cox's words: 'Ritual is embodied fantasy. The word body is important. It indicates that the ritual fantasy is not merely mental!' Cox also asks, 'Which of the great traditional rituals shall we choose as our environment for fantasy?' and he says, 'Fantasy is essential to human life. Perhaps one day if our petrified, churchly rituals are cracked open and their buried dimensions exhumed ... maybe that will be the day, as Berdyaev says, the whole world "will dissolve in creative ecstasy." ' "

While he was speaking, Father Lereve watched Angela and Adam with an intense expression that gave the impression he might be peering through their skulls into their brains. It seemed vital to him that they understand the roots of his thinking. He picked a book off his desk. "Here," he said, "let me read to you directly from Cox. 'Political fantasy goes beyond the mere political imagination. ... It envisions new forms of social existence, and it operates without first asking if they are "possible." Utopian thinking is to the *polis*, the corporative human community, what fantasy is to the individual person. It provides the images by which existing societies can be cracked open and recreated. ... It can be dangerous if it tempts people from dealing with the real issues. There are societies which have gone mad in this sense. But a society without the capacity for social fantasy faces equally serious dangers. It will die of sclerosis instead of schizophrenia, a very much less interesting way to go.' "

Angela was captivated by him. "It's not that I'm against fantasy, Father Lereve." She gestured at the camera she was carrying. "I'm a photographer. Every time I take a picture I try to go beyond the surface reality to reach the child-person, the dreamer behind the facade." She smiled. "But really, synergamy is something else again. I think it will be a long time before Canadians or Americans will really want responsibility in an extramarital relationship. Monogamy is binding enough."

"Perhaps, because of synergamy, monogamy wouldn't be so binding." Father Lereve smiled. "Properly understood, this kind of commitment could loosen the bonds of monogamy. *For those who dare* ... because interpersonal reaching out requires daring and risk-taking. Why isn't it possible to create a new kind of shared duality, with many elements of play and fantasy that could become a bridge between the first marriage and the second?

"Thus far I have brought into being eighteen synergamous marriages, and they are all working well. No one of these second marriages is exactly like another, except in the one basic commitment, a caring responsibility that removes the insecurity and guilt that can't be escaped in most comarital relationships. Each adaptation is what

241

makes these marriages continuously fascinating. Even the amount of time and the character of the involvement in these synergamous marriages varies with the needs and the moods of the families and the people who have made the commitment."

Father Lereve's eyes were dancing with his enthusiasm. "I hope that you don't mind my dominating the conversation. While I'm happy for your interest in synergamy, it is one blossom on a much larger plant. In a few minutes we will go into the Church, and you will witness, in the form of a ballet, an entirely new approach to the mysteries and the sacraments of the Church. To give you some perspective, let me tell you how it began. A few years ago with some of the students who live in this parish, I raised the question of the divine birth of Jesus to the Virgin Mary. I suggested that the early fathers who wrote of the event, a hundred and fifty to two hundred years later, simply diverted the river of an idea which in those days was well accepted by most people ... the possibility of divine birth and personal intercession of God in the affairs of man. By putting Mary on an equal plane with Isis and Astarte and Krishna's mother, Jasuda (all of whom gave birth to divinities, through various forms of divine impregnation, by the gods of Egypt and India), it was possible to substitute the worship of one for the other. In a sense, these ancient fathers of the Church were on the right track. But they were living in a male-dominated society. At the crossroads, they chose the easiest path. Instead of creating a yes-to-life religion, a religion of affirmation ... and sacraments that could have quite calmly exalted the ultimate mysteries ... the impregnation, the gestation, the birth, as a joyous part of everlasting mystery of life, the early fathers got hung up on the credo of Justin Martyr, who had written: 'Eve paying heed to the words of the serpent conceived disobedience and death; Mary paying heed to words of the angel conceived him through whom God defeats the serpent and rescues from death those who do penance for their own sins.' "

Father Lereve shrugged. "Presumably in this extended historical view Eve wrought our downfall and Mary our redemption. Christ stands in the same relationship to Adam. These beliefs, inculcated through the centuries, are the soil that gave root to much of our present-day neuroses. There are some of us in the Church who believe that the time has come to start over. We hope to create a

Marianity that will embody and transform Christianity. In our world, where all the old religions are failing man, where all the old absolutes of behavior and conduct that one could guide his life by have become existential and situational, we are proposing a religion that will restore the Catholic Church to its early promise of leading man, not following him." Father Lereve chuckled at the astonishment on Angela's face. "You ran see that I'm preparing you for the worst."

"Why me?" Angela asked.

"I assume from your Mediterranean beauty that you or your family must have once had roots in Catholic doctrine."

Angela smiled. "I was brought up Catholic ... so was my husband. We drifted away."

Father Lereve nodded. "Hopefully, new approaches will recapture you. What we are proposing is a very gradual abandonment of the nay-saying aspects of ancient Catholic theology. Ultimately, we hope to create a new mystique of humanity that will have vibrant meanings for the kind of world in which we are living today and the coming future. Thus we exalt the living sexual body of each man and woman, glorify the ultimate mysteries of human living and dying, and in a symbolic sense show that *the birth of Christ is continuous* ... reflected every second in each human birth. This yes-to-life hosanna will embrace the unceasing life aspects of the Vedantic religions as well as modern physics, and ultimately subsume the negative after-after-life aspects of Christianity into a world of no-death, but of continuous changing life forms of which we are all a part and which are equally valid as human life. Some of our approaches to human sexuality and life and death existed in early paganism. It should have been the chosen path. But unfortunately, perhaps necessarily at the stage in human evolution, the early Christian fathers, certain that man could only be controlled by divine fear, denied the flesh and proclaimed the joys of the after-life.

"In that period of the life of man, early fertility religions, coupled with demon worship, promulgating terror and fear, were a far cry from the message of love that was offered by Christ. But the needs of early man are not our needs. If man is to survive on this earth we must have a religion that offers visions and new hopes that coincide with life as we now experience it. We believe that the basic Catholic approach, with its roots in the ultimate

243

mystery and the ineffable aspects of life, is ideally suited
to provide the nonverbal meanings ... the sacramental
relationship of human beings *to all life*. We believe the
time has come to offer readaptations of old beliefs that
man can receive with joy and wonder and pride at his
being human."

Father Lereve stood up. "Come, we will go into the
church to witness a new interpretation, a gradual recreation of the sacrament of marriage in one of many
ballets that we are creating. Perhaps, what we are offering
may be a fantasy, Angela Thomas ... but before the
century closes, the Calvary aspects of Easter and the
tortured Christ on the cross will have disappeared forever.
The impregnation ... the Annunciation ... on March
25th will be recognized for what it is ... a never-ending
hymn to renewal ... a continuous Resurrection. At least
in the Northern Hemisphere. In the Southern Hemisphere,
we may have to change the meaning of December 25th
from the Birth to Annunciation." Father Lereve chuckled.
"One of your famous American bishops said: 'No one can
understand the sacraments unless he has a divine sense of
humor.' The Lord Incarnate never ceases walking the
earth. The difference now is that we are just beginning to
be aware that He is really We."

☆ 56 ☆

Father Lereve led them from the rectory to the cathedral. He opened the doors, and they walked into the nave.
The soaring Gothic interior, the soft gray of twilight
through the rose window and the stained-glass windows,
the candles flickering on the altar, and the ephemeral
music of the organ, seemed to blend Angela's body with
Adam's in an immaterial way. She tried to whisper the
thought to Adam, and he nodded his agreement ... "Man
expressing his need to wonder in stone," he said, and he
kissed her cheek. "The wonder is flesh too, and the tear in
your eye."

As they followed Father Lereve through the south tran-
sept of the church, the volume of music grew louder. The
choir section, which had been elevated as a stage, was

244

bathed in a pale blue light, creating a dreamy, floating world of its own. Young people on the stage, and standing nearby, obviously dancers, greeted Father Lereve. One of them, a young man, spoke rapidly in French to him.

"Le Ballet de L'Annunciation will begin in a few minutes." Father Lereve was bubbling with enthusiasm. "The dancers are delighted to have you share their rehearsal. This is our third company. We have no lack of young people who believe that the dance and music and the festival will become the basic bridge between man and man, and man and God communicating the inexpressible. The living encounter with the basic mystery of life is nonverbal. The New Church will slowly discover for man the path beyond words. While we are waiting, I will show you the altar."

Angela knew that Adam was entranced. She guessed that he was thinking the same thing she was. The kids ... Robin, Keane, Sam, Yael, Ruth, Richy ... even Jim and Janice should be here. She had a momentary vision of Robin in a leotard gliding across the stage, but then becoming aware of the statuary behind the altar, she couldn't contain her sudden shocked surprise. "I must be dreaming," she gasped.

In the position usually occupied by the crucifix was a four-figure grouping at least three times life size. Cast in a compound that resembled ivory, with the soft patina of age, the foreground figures of a female, male, and a young boy were all naked. The female was of a young woman sixteen to eighteen years. With long hair to her waist, she leaned slightly against the young man, who stood a head taller than she. She was a timeless female, lithe, small-breasted, ethereal. Her head, like that of the male figure, was tilted forward. Their expressions were companions in delight, as they looked down on the young boy, about three years old, whose arms were interlaced behind her left knee and the man's right knee. Pulling them forward, as if to see the vision of pure wonder and joy that lighted his face, he gave the group a sense of arrested motion.

Father Lereve was amused by their obvious surprise. "Madame Thomas was expecting to see Christ on the cross. . . . While you're assimilating this new aspect of Mary and Jesus, let me tell you about the music you are now hearing. It's an organ adaptation of Maurice Ravel's *Daphnis and Chloe* ballet music. Ravel uses a chorus throughout this ballet singing wordless syllables. The human voice, as you will hear, moves a step beyond the orchestral instruments or the organ and enhances the emotional human quality of the ballet. I think Ravel's music works rather well, but you must understand that each of our ballet companies is privileged to create its own interpretation of the Christian myths, as well as develop their own choreography. Of course, we believe that ultimately we will have modern composers who will work directly with the choreographers. Using churches and temples throughout the world for a new kind of religious drama, the choreographers could create a new blending of music and the dance that will reach the masses. Our second company is using Igor Stravinsky's *Agon* ballet music for their interpretation of the Annunciation. Along with it they have added the human voice. The first company tried Paul Hindemith's *Noblissima Visione* music, which is a ballet designed to interpret St. Francis' embracement of poverty. This hasn't worked so well. They're now experimenting with Virgil Thomson's *Variations on Sunday School Tunes* which were originally composed for the organ and have a subtle warm humor which many of us have enjoyed.

"All the ballets cohere to a basic approach that exalts the human being as creator. Man, who is simultaneously joyously mystified and wondrous at his power of creation, as well as his unlimited potential to express the ineffable awe that is the mystery of impregnation, birth, and death." Father Lereve smiled. "You might say that we are practical Utopianists. Using the old forms, we are searching for a new blend; a life-exalting religion that reinforces man not because it denies evil, but because it convinces man that his own potential for loving goodness can overcome any man-made, self-induced evil. Isn't this really the essence of most evil in the world? Man as the enemy of man. We will express this by recreating the old mysteries and myths with new interpersonal value structures. Man learns best by metaphor and simile and symbol. We will provide a correlation that really interprets and defines the needs and dilemma of man."

As the organ prelude to the ballet tiptoed around the shadows of the cathedral, Angela and Adam continued to stare at the statuary over the altar. All of the foreground figures were idealized, their genitalia natural and uncovered, almost alive with their ecstasy. Behind the three figures was a fourth figure of a man in his late fifties. His hand was holding a staff, and from what could be seen of his shoulders and chest he was wearing a simple peasant costume. His face was warm with the benign expression of a grandfather. He, too, was obviously captivated by the child's tugging enthusiasm.

Angela heard Adam whisper, " 'Heard melodies are sweet, but the unheard are sweeter; therefore, ye soft pipes, play on; not to the sensual ear, but, more endear'd, pipe to the spirit ditties of no tone.' "

Father Lereve was delighted. "Ah, you do understand."

"It's Mary and the Child and the old shepherd must be Joseph." As she spoke Angela could feel the sense of awe in her words. "It's lovely. It gives me goose pimples. But Mary naked? And who is the naked man beside Mary? The Good Lord better protect you, Father Lereve."

Father Lereve shrugged, but his eyes were dancing. "I'm happy you sympathize with this grouping. Some Catholics who have seen it have come close to apoplexy."

"Who is the man?" Adam was fascinated. "Obviously, you are moving away from a virgin birth."

"The man is the father of Jesus. Who ... which man is not important."

"The Holy Spirit?" Angela asked.

"In a sense. You will note while Mary's face is clearly delineated, the man's face is a face in process. Like one of Michelangelo's later sculptures, he is all men rather than a particular man. If we succeed in our new interpretation, March 25th, the day of Impregnation, will also be the beginning of Resurrection culminating in Birth. The Easter aspects of fertility are, of course, preserved in the act of impregnation.

"In the future at Easter we will deemphasize Christ rising from the grave, and focus on conception and birth. Christ's birth will be continuous. The joy and appreciation of the Impregnation, and the Birth will coincide with the world need to limit human procreation. Ultimately this will have the effect of making the act of creation a unique privilege." Father Lereve had a dreamy look on his face. "As Mary reassumes the ancient earth mother concept, the time of conception and birth will become a holiday of human love, a hymn to the wonder and mystery and loveliness of sexual communication. The crucifixion will be left to scholars to debate. Christ not rising from the dead but instead being reborn in each human birth. Actually, if you are familiar with the Eastern philosophers, and the

247

myths that preceded Christianity, you may be aware that we are pursuing a lovely fantasy. Assume that time has stood still, and it is nineteen hundred years ago. We writing a gospel for the kind of world that we *now know* will come into being two thousand years later ... with this prescience we can do a better job."

Adam couldn't help smiling at the magnitude of Father Lereve's dream. "By the time the Middle Ages arrive, you may be burned at the stake."

Father Lereve shrugged. "I think not. Even the Church these days seems to be aware that it lives because of man, and not because the supernatural gives it life.

☆ 57 ☆

The music, which had been pianissimo, slowly increased in volume. The lighting on the stage in the choir section dimmed slowly diminishing from pale blue-green until the stage was black and then gradually returning to life in floating vernal colors. Spring yellow and green, it drifted cloudlike around the bodies of five female dancers, who danced in a circle around a scarcely visible sixth female dancer. They were barefoot and naked under pale orange diaphanous skirts which flared over their hips and hung scarcely an inch below the lower curve of their buttocks. As they danced away from the center of the stage, the sixth dancer, whom they had surrounded (dressed in the same style skirt except that the color was a mixture of purple and scarlet), danced free into the center of the stage.

"Mary ..." Angela whispered both shocked and intrigued. "It can't be Mary ..."

Father Lereve nodded, apparently unconcerned that the dresses of the Virgins fully revealed their youthful pristine bodies. As they danced—laughter and childish abandon on their faces—their skirts swirling exposing the soft curve of their buttocks and the fragile dainty hair of their deltas— they were life, and living, and God, and Love incarnate.

Standing beside Angela, watching the ballet, Father Lereve asked her if she remembered the Virgin's names. But of course, she didn't. They were lost in the memories of her First Communion. "They are Rebekah, the plump one," he told her. "And Sephora, the bookish; Susanna, the Joyous; Abigea, the Restful; and Calah, the Faithful. You'll remember when Mary leaves the temple, they go with her to Joseph's home." He chuckled. "You will note that the dancers are epitomizing the particular qualities attributed to each of the virgins, including Mary, who already has some inclination of her purpose in life. As for their nakedness, which I presume you find a little sacrilegious, let me assure you that it is premeditated. In all the "Mary ballets" we go to great lengths to glorify the living male and female body ..." Father Lereve grinned at her. "We left shame in the Garden ... we're 'not leaving it to the snake' any longer."

The dancers, who were dancing playfully around Mary ... encouraging her to be carefree with them ... crowned her with a garland of flowers, and then drew back to study their handiwork. Their friend ... she was Queen of the Virgins. Smiling warmly at them, she walked around the stage, enjoying her new image, and then tiptoed to the music and slowly glided into a lovely dance. It needed no explanation. Every gesture was the awakening sexuality of a young female.

"Mary at this moment is an orphan," Father Lereve told them. They had moved back and were sitting in the shadows, all of them entranced by the lovely figure of the dancer who was interpreting Mary. A dark-haired French girl, about seventeen or eighteen, she portrayed in a tender, delicate dance a young Jewish Mary of fourteen or fifteen. "Her father Joachim is dead," Father Lereve said. "And Anna her Mother has married first Cleophas, and then Shalom, and has had two other daughters whom she has called Mary. At the moment preceding the opening of the ballet, Zacharias, whose reed floated on the stream, has been appointed Mary's guardian. You understand, of course, that the Mary myths are many and various. Beyond brief references in Luke and Matthew, little or no biography of Mary has come down to us that everyone agrees on. The Apocryphal Books ... *The Pseudo Gospel of Matthew*, and *The Protevangelion*, which was presumably written by Mary's stepson, James the Less, gives us the folklore, which, if you pursue it into the Syrian and Mussulman sources have further details, some of which are quite startling. "Ah, here come Zacharias and Abiathar."

Two male dancers in leotards leaped onto the stage and

danced around Mary, examining her with obvious interest.

"Abiathar is asking for Mary's hand for his son." Father Lereve chuckled. "This puts Zacharias on the spot. It is obvious that Mary has passed into her puberty. Along with the other virgins, she can no longer remain in the Temple. What Zacharias doesn't know is that Abiathar's son has already met Mary, and Mary is both frightened and charmed by him. She has already told the astonished Zacharias that it can never be. She will never take a husband." Father Lereve grinned at Angela's quizzical expression. "Of course, the joy of being human is the realization of the many conflicting "yous" inhabiting one's brain. See . . . words and actions are often at variance!"

As Father Lereve was speaking, Zacharias and Abiathar disappeared from the stage, and a young man, visibly naked, in transparent leotards, but as obviously virginal and wondrous as Mary, approached her bashfully, dancing awkward boyish dances to attract her attention. Finally Mary, laughing, delighted with him, took his hand and they danced a pas de deux in a wondrous innocent dance of childhood.

As they danced, the lights on the stage softened to a hazy purple. Mary's dress slipped to the floor, and naked and sublime, still with a lovely innocence, she reached to Abiathar's son, and as the dance continued, he swirled with Mary's arms around his neck. As they sank to the stage in a delicate kiss of young love, the stage slowly darkened.

The stage remained black for a few seconds and then the voice of the chorus singing wordlessly but with tender feeling echoed throughout the cathedral.

"Are they telling us that Abiathar's son is the father of Jesus?" Adam asked.

"Perhaps." Father Lereve smiled. "Perhaps they are simply exalting human love. Of course, if Abiathar's son had actually impregnated Mary, it would explain the next episode as being carefully preplanned and staged by Zacharias, and probably aided by the Pharisees, who would have quite obviously had a problem on their hands. The dove lighting on the rod that belonged to Moses, and the rod blossoming with almond blossoms, and Joseph bringing Mary to his house along with the other virgins, and Joseph, a gentle old man, aware perhaps that Abiathar's son had met Mary on one of her visits to the fountains at Nazareth . . . Joseph, covering for her, but immediately leaving for Capernanum so as to be guiltless in his own wife's eyes (was he really married? did he have two sons?) . . . all this is the timeless human plot that happens over and over again in much young love. It's not evil. Many, many marriages begin at pregnancy. Yes, Abiathar's son could be the father of Jesus . . . but as you will see this is not important. We prefer to keep the element of mystery alive."

Charmed by the living presence of the dancers in a church, drawn deeply in an empathetic recreation of the Mary myth, Angela and Adam were momentarily involved in an eternal love story. As she watched the dancers portraying Mary arriving at Joseph's home with her friends, and Mary, already a mother in spirit, playing tenderly with Joseph's baby son, James . . . Angela couldn't stop the tears flowing from her eyes.

The scene shifted and Mary . . . full of grace . . . not divine (but as Father Lereve said, pronouncing the Greek word of Luke, *kercharitomene* . . . "beautiful, comely") danced around the fountain at Nazareth symbolically filling her pitcher. She suddenly looked up into the eyes of a young man, and as she did, the stage lighting diffused and the stage emptied of the throngs of other dancers, leaving Mary and Gabriel dancing together. And Mary was tearful . . . frightened, but Gabriel was understanding, tender.

As the spotlight gradually focused on the dance of Mary and Gabriel, the chorus sang a poem in English by Emil Deutsch.

> Nothing is as holy, nothing as lovely,
> nothing can touch our heart to its depth
> as a woman, heavy with child,
> reminder of sweetness, tenderness,
> promise of new life, of renewal—
> the greatest, most enchanting mystery.
>
> Not before man as species
> learns to look at every living thing,
> learns to look at every other man
> as a mother looks at her children,
> concerned, caring, and loving,
> has he any chance to turn
> the hell he prepared for himself
> by hubris, greed, by fear, and hate

into the heaven he wanted to make
of life on earth.

The salvation lies not in the stars,
the moon, the thousand discoveries;
lies not in power over things
which turn into his masters for his
    destruction.
Only love can combine the details
by its wisdom, into true knowledge
of connections, interdependence,
and mutual caring.
Love alone can lead to God.

As the song concluded, the lights slowly abandoned the dancer's bodies and concentrated on their faces for a few seconds. Finally the stage was black, and the music stopped.

"Is Gabriel telling her that she will be divinely impregnated?" Father Lereve asked. "Or is he telling her that she is already pregnant and the birth of any human is divine? Does it matter? He is an angel ... a messenger from the source of life. Mary's child will be wondrous, because man loving man is wondrous. Come, the dancers are looking forward to your commitment."

Father Lereve led Angela and Adam to the altar and stood one step above them. Behind them the dancers, now huddling together with overcoats over their costumes, because the cathedral was cold, watched with warm sympathy on their faces.

"In a synergamous marriage," Father Lereve said, "I believe it is important to emphasize aspects of synergy by reading briefly from the writings of men and women who have thought deeply about the interrelated nature of human love and sex. The first reading is from Abraham Maslow, an essay titled "Toward a Humanistic Biology." The second from a pamphlet titled "Toward a Quaker View of Sex" by a group of Friends, and the last from a book by Michael Valente titled *Sex, Radical View of a Catholic Theologian*. The interest in these paraphrases, to me, is that from entirely different backgrounds and disciplines we can discover a common perspective that one day may provide a cohering center for all men.

"And Abraham Maslow says: 'But "love is knowledge,"

252

if I may call it that, has other advantages as well. Love for a person permits him to unfold, to open up, to drop his defenses, to let himself be naked not only physically, but psychologically and spiritually as well. ... In ordinary interpersonal relationships, we are to some extent inscrutable to each other. In the love relationship we become scrutable. But finally, and perhaps most of all, if we love or are fascinated or profoundly interested, we are less tempted to interfere, to control, to change, to improve. My finding is that if you love, you are prepared to leave alone. In the extreme instance of romantic love and of grandparental love, the beloved person may even be seen as perfect, so that any kind of change, let alone improvement, is regarded as impossible or even impious.'

"And from the essay by the Friends: 'Nothing that has come to light in the course of our studies has altered the conviction that came to us when we began to examine the actual experiences of people—the conviction that love cannot be confined to a pattern. The waywardness of love is a part of its nature, and this is both its glory and its tragedy. If love did not leap every barrier, if it could be tamed, it would not be the tremendous creative power that we know it to be and want it to be ... we recognize that while most examples of "the eternal triangle" are produced by boredom and primitive misconduct, others may arise from the fact that the very experience of loving one person with depth and perception may sensitize a man or woman to the lovable qualities in others. We think it is our duty not to stand on the peak of perfectionism but to recognize in compassion the complications and bewilderment that love creates and to ask how we can discover a constructive way in the immense variety of particular experiences. It is not by checking the impulse to love that we keep love sweet. The man who swallows the words "I love you" when he meets another woman may in that moment, and for that reason, begin to resent his wife's existence; but it is also true that love may be creative, if honestly acknowledged though not openly confessed. We need to know much more about ourselves, and what we do to our inner life when we follow codes or ideals that do not come from the heart!'

"And the last from Michael Valente: 'Sexuality can no longer be approached in terms of what the individual cannot do. It must instead be approached in the context of an individual's attempt to build a life that is productive

253

and used as one of the means by which the individual is oriented towards growth in self-awareness and openness to self-development. In other words, sexuality is to be used as in any other area of potential in one's life: for developing greater self-consciousness. Properly used in accordance with its intensity and importance, it should serve as the integrating factor in the mature individual's life. Creative development is only possible in the context of interpersonal relationship. No one can mature in an impersonal vacuum, apart from feedback and response from another. Thus sexuality functions as an important facet of the person's self-development and becomes a means whereby the individual reaches out to others, a means whereby his life is given direction, energy and vitality. . . . In the notion that there is nothing intrinsically evil in any sexual act, there is a certain openness which makes possible a better life-style. Instead of repressing, fearing, and trying to turn away from a part of his personality, one can integrate it into the mainstream of his whole life. . . . The determination of moral responsibility was in a sense much easier for the individual when sexual acts had a negative moral valuation placed upon them. Now he bears the burden of freedom and the responsibility of deciding for himself whether certain acts are moral or immoral. But it is only in the assumption of the burden of freedom in this, as in all human life, that anyone can ever hope to grow to be something better, something more than he is now.'

"Angela and Jonathan . . . as lovers you have come to this humble church to consecrate your love in a form of marriage which has no sanction in the law of the State, nor of the Church. Yet the truth is that the marriage or commitment of two human beings to care for each other has neither strength nor stability because of any divine origin nor sacramental quality, nor pronouncements of man, but rather because the individuals dare to transcend their own ego and in the process be each other. Such a commitment is something one gives out of his own desire. Duty, obligation, responsibility may be contained in the word commitment, but these states of being tend to be outer-induced . . . pressured into existence by society. Such feelings tend to define love in terms that are self-destructive. A marriage of the kind you are entering into, ideally, should be witnessed and approved by your present spouses, and in view of the prior giving of oneself the limitations of the new commitment informally agreed

254

upon. One day we may be able to offer this open strengthening of the family by a responsible process of accretion and blending of existing family units."

Father Lereve smiled as he noted that Angela and Adam were holding hands. "There is no ring in this ceremony. The words I ask you to repeat after me are only as strong as your joy and love for each other as interacting human beings. Repeat after me this syngeramous bond, you willingly assume. 'I, Angela ... I, Jonathan ... with no less love for my present spouse and my family, do accept the commitment to love and to cherish. ... You, Jonathan ... you ... Angela. I am aware that my love for you does not modify my prior commitment to my husband ... to my wife. While our relationship to each other is supportive, it should also grow and gain strength because it reinforces and strengthens and adds perspective to the nature of our love both for each other and for our first spouses and children.'

"I pronounce you man and wife. May God love you!"

☆ 58 ☆

Suddenly, they were living in a new dimension of time. Incredibly, less than eighteen hours ago they were in Montreal being "married." Angela could only think the word married in quotes. Could it really have happened?

Either Montreal was a dream, or this was. Now, they were racing along the Mid-Cape Highway below Hyannis, heading for the deserted winter beaches on the outer Cape Cod at Truro. But it was February and it was snowing. Utterly impossible! Who in their right mind vacationed or, God forbid, "honeymooned" (Adam's words) on the Cape in the middle of winter? But, of course, Jonathan Quincy Adams would ... her Adam ... The "third Adam"? Maybe? Why not? If Jesus had been the second Adam, why not a third? And what would this Adam's mission on earth be?

Smiling at her disconnected thoughts, she realized that lately she was even beginning to think like Adam—lovely, irrelevant non sequiturs that often led one into strange byways. Adam called it creative thinking. Free-floating ideas merged and became something new. She leaned against the door of the car and watched him through her eyelashes—a flickering, unsubstantial Adam, humming a little song as he drove. No, she wasn't watching him. *She was sensing him*, absorbing the strange encapsulation of the moment into her body processes. She was vibrantly aware of the soft hum of the tires and the engine, and the flip-flop of the windshield wipers. Janice's car . . . an El Dorado Cadillac which Adam had driven to the airport garage. Lord, was that just yesterday? Madness. And now a man with the mistress he had married, in his wife's automobile, driving sixty miles an hour on a deserted, snow-covered highway, late in February . . . toward Provincetown, the end of the earth. Who were they? Angela's thoughts were detached giggles. Not tourists, certainly. Not Cape Codders. Angela and Adam from another planet making a world and time to their own measure.

Smiling at her, Adam touched her fingers stretched toward his. From the beginning they had discovered a depth of agreement and empathy that defied words. Deliciously exhausted, Angela drifted in and out of sleep. Was it only Wednesday afternoon? Oh God . . . yes! Tonight, and Thursday and Friday and Saturday were still ahead. And *she had told him*: "We don't have to keep moving. We have the Pink."

"I know, I know," he said. "But I want a life with you in retrospect as well as in the future. Synergamious marriages gain sustenance from memories, too."

They had left Father Lereve with Adam's assurance that their marriage would link them to L'Eglise de Sainte Marie de la Vie for their lifetimes. After a candlelight dinner at Cafe Martin, they taxied back to the Chateau, tumbled into bed, delirious with laughter, as they simultaneously admitted that having drunk sherry, Bordeaux, and madeira, accompanied by courses of frog's legs, and roast beef, they were so delightfully full, detached, and logy, that even though it was their "honeymoon," to make love would be impossible. Well, not impossible. But certainly carrying coals to Newcastle.

But they weren't too tired to fall asleep in each other's arms, flesh pressed against flesh, until they awoke with stiff arms and prickly with "pins and needles," and they grinned sheepishly to discover that already the sky was growing lighter on the horizon.

"Hi, Madame Adams-Thomas."

"Hi, Monsieur Thomas-Adams."

"Wasn't it a lovely, silly marriage?"

And they recalled bits and pieces of their discussion with Father Lereve after the ceremony, partly in English, partly in French. Happy talk ... as the youthful dancers, all of whom had hugged them and congratulated them on their marriage, sat on the stage with them and involved them in a dialogue about man's religious beginnings and primitive people's awe of nature. Early tribes of the Near East ... Sumerians, and others who wrote their understanding of God and Life on stone tablets. Pictographs that told how the gentle rain from heaven was God's Word ... His semen pouring softly from the sky out of His penis, or being ejaculated in the fierce ecstasy of a thunderstorm onto the warm, throbbing labia of Mother Earth, God's semen producing the life that man lived by and with. And the sun, red-hot in the early morning, was the red glans of God's penis, erect and glowing after the long night ready to penetrate the body of Earth.

A mystery, a sacrament, revealing in a lovely, indefinable way that all birth was virgin birth. And as they remembered, Angela and Adam, lost in each other's flesh, acted out the unceasing cosmic life drama. Slowly awakening to each other's touch, and responding to the amazing, panting wonder of being each other, they made love with a joyous laughing surrender that would dance in their heads for hours. And then lying in his arms, because their love had no before or afterwards but was continuous, Angela was partially aware that her charm for Adam was her own subconscious necessity to sway on the wind-seeds of his ideas, not losing her own roots as a person, but coming alive and blossoming for him and herself because neither of them alone could provide the cross-fertilization.

"Would you be a little crazy with me?" He had whispered the question in her ear. "Would you walk the loneliness of a winter beach with me? . . . Feel the cold, salt wind biting against your face? Play Thoreau on Cape Cod? We could explore the miles of frozen sand, and the winter debris of once-live-things and a blue-gray Artic world of beauty that belongs only to us because the gregarious, the outdoor people are in the North country ... probably not enjoying that either, but standing in long lines to be towed up a mountain so they can have the thrill of skiing down it a hundred miles an hour."

His words captured her imagination. Her only demurral

had been feminine and practical. "What do I wear? This dress?" She kissed his neck, and breathed his sleepy morning warmth. "Okay, Admiral Byrd, but we'll have to drive to Acton first. If you'd really prefer to go skiing, I do have a beautiful ski outfit. I'm not the best, but I can stand on skis."

But Adam wasn't interested in skiing. "It's too much like golf. The paraphernalia become more important than the simple purpose of breathing clean and feeling the sun and the sky and the air on your face. I leave skiing to those who can't relax, or who are afraid of being lonely, or being alone together. There's only one kind of skiing that makes sense to me, that's cross-country skiing, just taking off and enjoying the snow-covered land, not standing in line with thousands of other people, impatiently waiting to get to the top of a mountain. Why does man have to make a business out of his leisure? I believe that if humans will survive and live joyously, they need to fight unceasingly against being massed together. Even crowds having fun have no humanity, only implacability. As a radical-liberal, hiding out in the bloodstream of the capitalist system, I will fight unceasingly the profit that man makes on man by purposely massing his leisure."

Adam bounced out of bed. "Good God, I'm raving again." He jigged naked around the room, and grabbed her. "Come on, the plane leaves for Boston in an hour."

They showered together, washing each other's genitals and thanking them for the nice enjoyment they had provided each other, and while they dried each other, Adam remembered a poem for her. "Calm Soul of all things! make it mine to feel amidst the city's jar, that there abides a peace of thine, man did not make and can not mar. The will to neither strive nor cry. The power to feel with others give! Calm, calm me more. Nor let me die before I have begun to live."

Smiling, he told her the poet was Matthew Arnold, and she wondered if Matthew might once have recited it to his mistress with an erection as big as Adam's. Adam was sure that he had. "Some of the calming Matthew was pleading for is only available merged with someone you love."

Before they landed in Boston, Adam finally convinced her they shouldn't lose time by driving to Acton. They could stop at the Pink for the Ampex portable video camera. Though they could never show them to anyone, it would be fun to take tapes of the winter world. And when they stopped in Cohasset (which was on the way) for his winter clothes, he was certain they could find plenty of stuff to keep her warm. They were hurrying across the covered bridge to the airport garage (Angela proclaiming a little loudly that no matter what mad idea Adam might be entertaining, she wasn't borrowing any of Janice's clothes), when Angela noticed a man crossing the bridge from the garage. Adam recognized him at the same time. It was Harry Carswell! There was nowhere to turn off the bridge. They couldn't pass him and ignore him. There wasn't even time to confer on what to say and what not to say. Angela had met Carswell only once. Six weeks ago when Sam had taken her on a tour of Adams National, he introduced her to various executives as a free-lance employee of Adams Video. Even then Carswell had examined her suspiciously. "We don't have many employees at Adams National with your style, Mrs. Thomas." She knew that Carswell was Executive Vice-President, the man next in command of the company, and he was, in Adam's words, "pretty straight," and he wasn't at all sure that Adams Video was a good venture.

While Carswell greeted her smoothly, remembering her name, "Good morning, Mrs. Thomas" . . . his inflection revealed his thinking, So this is the boss' little playmate. "Surprised to see you back from Montreal so soon, J.Q. I thought that since Janice was in Bermuda, you were going to stay the week."

Angela was trembling. She didn't dare to look at Adam's face, but she admired his fast and cool answer. "As a matter of fact, I didn't go to Canada, Harry. I flew over to New York. Angela was kind enough to meet me at the airport."

Carswell wasn't surprised. "I gathered you hadn't flown up. I was talking with Jean Martineau yesterday. He said you weren't even expected."

Angela was aware that Adam had momentarily vanished. In his place, J.Q. was fencing with Carswell. "Obviously, if I had I would have preferred to surprise Jean and avoid the big brass treatment. Where are you bound, Harry? I was talking with Charlie McMasters, Monday . . . he thought you might be popping in on him again." J. Q. shook his head. "You want to be careful, Harry. Sam didn't ask me, but he has asked McMasters if his group would like to put up some venture capital and spin off Adams Video."

From Carswell's expression, it was obvious that he was momentarily on the defensive. "I thought I'd call on a few accounts in New York. I'll be back tomorrow." Carswell looked at his watch.

"Is Saul Meers out of town?"

"No. Why? Should he be?"

J. Q. chuckled. "I was just wondering why one of our New York salesmen couldn't handle any of the accounts in the city. Calling on accounts is a little out of your province, Harry."

"These aren't sales problems ... they're credit problems." Carswell shrugged. "I've got to run. I'm on the ten o'clock shuttle. Charlie McMasters called me yesterday. I thought I'd kill two birds with one stone and have lunch with him." He grinned at J.Q., but his eyes searched Angela's face. "Have a nice day, you two."

Driving to the apartment to pick up the video camera, Adam tried to calm Angela. "Stop worrying. Harry was just as uncomfortable at being discovered as we were. The truth is, he's on his way to New York to try to persuade McMasters to head up some dissident stockholders for a takeover of Adams National." Adam shrugged. "He thinks that J.Q. Adams has become too radical, that the company is losing its conservative image."

"Maybe he's right." Angela felt jittery. "Maybe he knows I'm taking your mind off business. Supposing he tells Sam that he met us. . . . What if he mentions meeting us to Janice? Oh, Adam . . . I hope you know what we're doing, because I don't. I'm lost."

"I suppose I should fire him, but he's damned good in his way." Adam hugged her. "Don't worry, Harry's a gentleman of the old school. I happen to know he once had a 'back street' arrangement. Harry would never tackle a man on the basis of his sexual peccadilloes."

"Am I your sexual peccadillo?" There were tears in Angela's eyes.

Adam laughed. "You're my wife. Remember? We're married. You have the certificate from Father Lereve that proves it. I really should have told Harry. That would have blown his mind."

"You just better not tell anyone," Angela warned him. "If Jim ever knew what I've been doing while he's innocently playing golf, he'd call the men in the white coats

260

and have me put under observation . . . and you, too, for leading me astray!"

An hour later in Cohasset, standing in his bedroom while he unearthed a sheep-lined lumberjacket for her, and insisted that she take off her dress and try on a pair of his ski pants (she could have belted them just under her arms), he was still discounting her worries.

"I can't help it," she sighed. "I have moments when I forget, and I think we really aren't hurting anyone, and I feel like a youngster alive and carefree, and then the mood shifts and I see myself for real, sitting here in a bra and panties on Janice's bed. This is the bedroom you share together, and I shouldn't be in it."

Holding her on the bed and kissing her breasts, Adam had completely undressed her and would have made love to her right there and then, but she refused. "No, Adam, God, no! Not here. Janice is alive in this room. I can feel her presence almost as if she might walk through that door and stare at us in complete shocked dismay."

Finally, once again in the car, the back seat piled high with Thermos jugs filled with coffee she had made, and cans of clam chowder that he had warmed up, and peanut butter and bread, and cans of salmon and tunafish and cookies that he had found in one of the cabinets (he was certain there would be no restaurants open on the Cape this time of year), relieved that she was finally out of the house and Janice's bedroom and kitchen, he told her that she really hadn't been listening to Father Lereve.

"In synergamous marriage, it would be expected that you would make love in the other spouse's bed." Adam, grinning, was feeling very bubbly. He slowed the car down while he bussed her cheek. "If synergamy is to succeed, we would share each other's home. We would extend our involvement and not get hung up on the ethics or morality of who enjoyed which bed."

They argued all the way to Hyannis.

☆ 59 ☆

She told him that he was a dreamer. She was sorry that she couldn't make love to him on Janice's bed, but he was

261

really worse than Father Lereve. He had swallowed the impossible, hook, line, and sinker. Did he really believe that Janice would accept another woman sleeping with her husband? If she did, it would be under duress, and not because she approved. She would simply be like many women who discovered that their husbands were involved with another female. If you really loved the man, it was better to be permissive than go down the lonely road of divorce. Whoever would marry or live with a past-forty female?

"Is that the way you would feel, if you were Janice?" Adam asked her. Angela wasn't sure. "Maybe. I think I'd be a little jealous, too, because I'd be sure that Janice, as your lover, would be getting something from you that I wasn't."

"Are you jealous of Jim?"

"How do I know?" Angela smiled. "I know he's human. He likes women but he has never, to my knowledge, ever pursued any of them ... not beyond a typical evening of surburban sexual play. You know, dancing in the playroom ... squeezing or hugging a little in a dark corner ... telling dirty stories—shockers—in a mixed group ... even occasionally showing stag movies to determine, indirectly, whether other wives enjoyed cunnilingus, or would 'go down' on their husbands." Angela shrugged. "To be honest, Adam, if Jim found somebody he liked ... Janice or your Barbara," Angela wrinkled her nose at the thought of Barbara, "well, what could I say?"

Adam's eyebrows were raised, mocking her. "You could say: 'Jim, I really understand. You can bring Janice or Barbara home. She can sleep with you in my bed.' "

"And where will I be?"

"If it were Janice, in Janice's bed, with me. If Jim brought Barbara home, you could spend the night at Pinckney Street."

"Where would you be?"

"If we were at all coordinated, with you."

"Good heavens. Wife-swapping, or swinging, or whatever they call it sounds less messy and involved."

"Of course it is. Wife-swappers don't want to be involved. Synergamy is something else entirely. It's an agreement to adventure intimately together with one other human being. Wife-swapping isn't an adventure, just a roller-coaster thrill." Adam chuckled "Anyway, look at how most families live. Whether they are in their own suburban home or an apartment, the same enclosed space seen year after year through the same eyes finally fails to stimulate the people who live in it. Imagine how it would break up the week to know that I was coming to *your home* for dinner, and that I would sleep with you in *your bed*. All the old rooms that have become dull and familiar to you would look entirely different, because you were seeing them through my eyes.

"You know the old saying. 'If you want to appreciate your own city or home town, take a stranger sightseeing.' What is more ... me ... in the bedroom where you have made love with Jim ... will ultimately dispossess you. You won't own it and it won't own you anymore."

They were still arguing when Adam stopped in front of a store in Hyannis that obviously catered to fishermen. Inside, Adam patiently explained to the owner, a grinning beer-barreled Portuguese, that his wife wasn't interested in style ... just warmth. Did he have pants and boots that would fit a female? His wife and he were going to walk the beaches below Truro. "John Silva feet anybody," the old man told them. Peeling Angela out of Adam's mackinaw, he encircled her hips with a measuring tape, surreptitiously feeling her behind at the same time, with an approving glance at Adam. While Silva was rummaging through heavy woolen pants to find a size for her, Adam spied a double sleeping bag. "Maybe we can sleep on the beach."

Angela advised him emphatically she wasn't sleeping on any beaches in the middle of winter. "My God ... You really do need two wives ... one an Amazon." Adam bought the sleeping bag anyway, plus woolen face masks and a white turtleneck sweater for her. The purchases came to ninety-six dollars.

Back in the car Angela sarcastically observed that for synergamy to work, one obviously had to be rich. "What is more, Jonathan Adams, I'm not sleeping in any sleeping bag with you. I'm not twenty ... and you're not that Hemingway character. What was his name?"

Adam laughed. "Robert Jordan ... his complaisant girl friend was Maria. But to contest your pique, if this were synergamy, we would have planned a little better. .. At the very least, you could have borrowed Janice's ski clothes."

Angela gasped. "You are mad!"

"Not really. I didn't suggest it. But since you raised the

263

question, if you stop to think about it, synergamy doesn't require a lot of money. Caring, involvement costs nothing. The whole idea of changing homes or apartments, having a lover to dinner and spending the night ... would be a lot more stimulating than watching television or going to the movies. If there were young children, they would look forward to it ... one or two nights a week they'd have a new mother and father to relate to. Think it over. If someone had told you a year ago that you might be sleeping on the beach in the middle of winter with your lover, you'd have said he was insane. Yet the truth is, if you will admit, it's more exciting and costs less than any adventure you can conceive."

Angela couldn't help smiling. "But you have to be a little daft."

Adam grinned. "Maybe. But now that we're married, if you don't let yourself get hidebound, and you're willing to jump out of your skin with me ... I guarantee you'll go through menopause and scarcely be aware of it." Angela stared at him astonished. "Don't look so surprised," he said. "I have a theory that menopause as experienced by Western females is the product of sexual boredom and glands atrophied from disuse."

Angela choked with laughter. "Adam, sometimes I have the feeling that Janice and I should call in Women's Lib ... we're both one big experiment with you."

"You don't have to worry. The experiment will take a lifetime. In the process, the experimentees are in full command of the experimenter."

Adam seemed entirely unconcerned with the wind and snow whipping the car as they traveled further out on the winter-deserted Cape. Finally, with his headlights on, he turned off the highway onto an unplowed secondary road. The snow splattered fiercely against the windshield. The late afternoon sky was menacingly dark. And now the snow was falling so heavily that it was impossible to see the road more than a few yards ahead. It occurred to Angela that had Jim been driving, she would have been tense, even disagreeable with him. Now she was simply shrugging, maybe even enjoying the fact that the shape of things to come was out of her control. If Adam got Janice's car stuck in the snow, eventually someone would find them. Like it or not they did have the sleeping bag and enough clothing to sleep outdoors in Antarctica. Maybe the essential difference between Adam and Jim was that Jim would never have exposed himself to such a silly adventure ... and if by chance he did, his own insecurity at his inability to change fate would have been communicated to her, and she would have responded like a tuning fork vibrating his fears back on him. For what? Was it so impossible for her simply to trust? With Adam there was no other way. I'm learning, she thought ... at forty-three I may not know the answers, but I'm daring to ask myself the questions.

Adam skillfully guiding the car in and out of skids, and ignoring the foul weather, was singing, "Sleigh bells ring, are you listening? In the lane, snow is glistening ..." He seemed completely confident, but he was tuned to her "I know ... you're feeling pretty grim. We're alone in a place as desolate as the North Pole. You're wondering how we'll sleep, if the car skids off the road?" Adam laughed. "What bugs me is how could we ever make love sitting in these damned bucketseats?" That thought sent Adam pursuing a wilder one. "Really, when you think about it, Angela, the way they build automobiles is quite insane. If automobiles were sold for transportation, nice six-passenger jobs with front seats that folded down and merged with the back seat, every family would have their own bed on wheels. If they would make the automobiles like those old Checker taxis to last for ten years instead of having to make ten million of them a year, the manufacturers would only need to make a million. Great for ecology. Of course all those people who wouldn't have to work so hard would have to be taught how to enjoy making love on Thursdays and other days. Angela, I love you. How come you haven't demanded to know where I think I'm going?"

"I don't dare." Angela leaned over and kissed his cheek. "If I were first Mrs. Adams instead of Mrs. Adams-Thomas, by now I'd have probably been fighting with you, telling you to turn around." She shrugged. "Sitting here, watching you fight the wheel, seeing you peer through the windshield at a road that isn't here, I feel as if I'm on the Russian steppes with Dr. Zhivago. I can even hear the music playing. Only instead of 'Somewhere My Love,' it's 'Che Serà, Serà.'"

Ahead of them, Adam pointed to the long black outline of a building that looked like a motel. It seemed deserted. They passed an unlighted neon sign that read *The Dunes*. Adam slurred the Cadillac to a skidding halt in front of the building. A room marked "Office" behind drawn curtains seemed to be dimly lighted. Someone peered out of the window at them.

"This is our home for the night." Adam grinned at her. "I telephoned them a week ago and made reservations for us. The owner and his wife live here in the winter. It's one of the few places this far down the Cape that is open this time of year."

Angela wondered if he had been here before ... with Barbara Lovell, perhaps? She asked him, and he hugged her.

"*You*, lovely one, are my first and last affair. Don't you remember I married you! A real-estate man I know in Eastham located this place for me." Adam was effervescent. "To tell you the truth, you are partially responsible. At least twice you've told me you always wanted to make love bare-ass in the snow. ... Now you're going to put up or shut up."

The owner, a man in his late sixties, led them along a shoveled path to one of the rooms. On her left Angela could hear the surf pounding the beach, but the black, blizzardy night completely obscured the water. She was certain from the way the man looked at Adam when he signed the registration card that he guessed they were lovers.

"My wife wouldn't let me turn the heat on until I knew you were coming ..." he told them. "But don't worry, the system's connected to the main house. The room'll warm up real quick. All of these room's got window walls, may be a little drafty in the winter. But there's a nice view of the ocean. The Atlantic's down there about twenty feet below you. Do you live around here?"

Adam told him their home was in Cohasset. "My wife and I enjoy the beach in the winter."

"Best damned time." From the tone of his voice Angela knew that Adams had found a companion spirit. "No confounded tourists messing up the Cape this time of year. You've got the place to yourself. This storm is gonna blow out to sea. By midnight, if you're lucky, we'll have a full moon. Wife and I watched it over the water last night. Kind of beautiful, but it makes you feel pretty insignificant."

When he closed the door behind him, Adam grabbed Angela in his arms and swirled her around. "Only one thing we can do. Undress, get dressed again for winter in

266

bed." While Adam poked in the cartons of clothes and food he had lugged in and produced a bottle of Scotch, Angela stripped naked. She put on the woolen pants and the white turtleneck sweater he had bought in Hyannis. Shivering, she took the drink Adam handed her. "How do you like my nightgown?" She modeled the sweater which hung to her waist and the trousers that seemed to walk without her.

The walls of the building shuddered under the impact of the wind and snow slashing against them. They could still hear the thud of the waves as they crashed on the shore. Bending over, Angela unrolled the sleeping bag on the floor. "Maybe we should put this on the bed and sleep in it . . . I'm beginning to see . . ." She was about to say "why you bought it" when Adam pulled down her floppy fisherman pants and kissed her bare behind.

"I couldn't help it," he chuckled, as she fell to the floor, squealing, with Adam on top still kissing her. "You were bent over like a lovely Italian *paisan*, with your ass in the air, tempting me. You know that you wanted it to be kissed." He pulled her on to the bed and she realized that under his sheepskin mackinaw he was naked too. "The sleeping bag's not for tonight. We'll need it tomorrow when we make love and snuggle together on the beach."

"In the daytime?"

"Why not? There'll be no voyeurs."

Angela recaptured her drink from the night table. The Scotch was making her suddenly warm and glowy. "Are you really going to make love to me in the snow tonight?"

Still in his sheepskin, Adam pushed up her sweater and burrowed in her breasts. "I'm game if you are."

"When?"

Adam burst into laughter. "My God, you're fantastic. A few drinks from now. It's only seven o'clock. Aren't you hungry? We have clam chowder and peanut butter sandwiches. When our bellies are full, and we're half crocked, I'll grab you and we'll run out naked in the twenty-below wind and do it."

"I'm getting cold feet." She shivered. "Where?"

"We'll search around and find a snowdrift. Then we'll tumble in it together."

Lying in bed, they ate the clam chowder; Angela fed Adam while he read from an inevitable book that he had brought along from Cohasset. Adam thought the author, Paul Ehrlich, and his book *How to be a Survivor, A Plan to Save Space Ship Earth*, was too Utopian. Angela discovered she was entranced with Ehrlich's vision of a new world. "I think down deep, Adam, your conflict with the author is that you're really a materialist."

Adam disagreed. "Even though you think I am, I'm not a dreamer. Ehrlich believes the only way to change the world is one fell swoop. It just isn't going to happen that way. His solutions, even if they are partially achieved, presuppose either a dictatorial government—hopefully beneficent—or a highly educated majority who recognize the social and ecological problems that the world is facing, and would be agreeable to sacrifice now for a world they will never live to see. The people who run this country, the business leaders ... the fellows like Harry Carswell, and the hard-working middle class, the "hard-hats" who control the vote, are all emotionally conditioned to a philosophy of more and more. They are fully brainwashed that heaven is achievable by simultaneously increasing the gross national product and their own consumption."

Angela put the Thermos jug of clam chowder on the floor beside the bed. She burrowed into the sheepskin collar of the mackinaw and held Adam's penis, sleepily listening to Adam rave on.

"The only way the average man will give up his Horatio Alger dreams is to educate him to enjoy the alternatives." Adam was aware of her fingers lightly probing his flesh. "Like synergamy, for example ... instead of consuming more and more man-made junk, depleting and exhausting the world's resources so that a few million of the billions alive can live high off the hog, I propose a world where the greatest joy is man and woman simultaneously loving and wondering and searching together. . . ."

Adam slid down beside her, south to her north. The book still in one hand, he inched down her pants, kissed her belly, and tasted her clitoris.

"Adam . . ." Angela murmured her appreciation.

"Yes. . . ?"

"Going to bed with you is like going to bed with a sexy schoolteacher. You should patent the approach . . . 'Sex reinforced learning' by Jonathan Q. Adams, the father of his country."

"All right. You asked for it."

Adam pulled her to her feet and stripped off her pants.

"You can keep your sweater on, but it's time to screw in the snow."

Laughing hysterically, shushing each other not to wake the owner of the motel and his wife, Angela in her sweater, Adam in his mackinaw, their only other clothing the boots they had slipped into, they opened the door of their room and slid down the snow-covered dunes on their naked behinds. At the bottom of the cliff, in five feet of snow that had drifted between two large dunes, panting, her eyes sparkling, Angela flung herself against Adam. Yelling he disappeared in the drift and she flopped on top of him. She felt his penis wet and cold between her legs and she quickly contained him. Thrashing gleefully, together, still inside her, he flipped her over. The icy wet snow squeezed up between her legs and the cheeks of her behind.

"Oh, my God ... I love you." She moaned and rocked beneath him sinking deeper in the drift. She was aware that above her the sky had cleared and was pinpointed with stars. Two thirds of a moon hung over the black, white-crested ocean. "Oh ... Adam ... Adam my behind is numb ... but I'm too excited to care! ..."

☆ 60 ☆

Adam awoke before Angela. Turned toward him in the bed, her face was youthful and vulnerable in her relaxed sleep. She still wore her white turtleneck sweater. Her black hair interspersed haphazardly with gray streaks, was askew on the pillow. A mature woman, she dared to be a trusting child. Adam kissed her nose, and she opened her eyes and smiled at him. A brown-eyed fragile smile. Sighing happily, she closed them again, interlaced her fingers with his, and with an utter relaxed contentment continued to sleep on.

Adam was in love with being in love. Watching the tiny smile on Angela's face (was she dreaming of the young girl she momentarily seemed to be?), he remembered his father, one evening, long years ago, expounding on the nature of love. "Women tend to fall in love with love, son."

The way the senior Adams said it, this was obviously acceptable feminine behavior, but not a philosophy on which men should pursue the founding father's dream of happiness. Whatever his mother's thoughts might have been, she hadn't contested her husband. Had it been agreement, or simply passive acquiescence toward a superior power? It was sad that the words parents spoke with their children were mostly a thick veil drawn over their real emotions. Whatever . . . Adam was sure that Lucy Adams would never have dared to tell her husband that perhaps being in love was the axis on which all else turned. Then and now such thoughts were maudlin. Love was the dessert of life, not the main course. But what was the main meal? If you loved and discovered the warmth of love, the giving of love, the amazing surrender of love . . . if being in love became a way of life for you, weren't your priorities in the only possible sequence that could give life and living some kind of meaning and purpose? If you were in love with love, you couldn't escape being in love with human beings.

Angela snuggled her face against his chest and was dimly conscious of his chest hairs tickling her ear. Her calf crossed his, so that she was gently spreadeagled over his middle. Her eyes closed, she continued to doze, delighting in the erotic feeling of his fingers tracing her buttocks. Easing her slightly to his side, he pushed up her sweater, cradled her breast for a moment, and kissed her sleepy nipple. While his fingers were exploring the individual hairs on her labia, and he felt the almost imperceptible moisture of her readiness for him, he thought of Janice.

He knew that he loved Janice differently from Angela. But really, should one worry about the kind of quality of love that human beings could share with each other? To do that would reduce love to equations and comparisons. Because Janice (often bewildered by the unpredictable man she had married) had never learned how to fully surrender or merge herself with him as easily as Angela was silently doing right now, didn't make Janice's "I love you, Jonathan" less a gift than Angela's "I love you, Adam."

He wondered if Janice might discover how to release her essential self with Jack Lovell. What would happen between them in Bermuda? With every night to themselves, would they dare to make love and let the world of golf be well lost? Probably not. Neither Jack nor Janice

270

ever questioned the basic mores and traditions. Traditions that in most cultures discounted the possibility of a completely interwoven relationship between a male and a female. That was a dream of the poets that vanished in the cold light of living.

Angela breathed in his ear. "Hi, sweetie ... you're making me feel like a pond lily. I'm drifting idly on a long, long stem that reaches down, down to the bottom of the lake. ... But I can't escape ... don't want to escape." She was silent, and then after infinite floating minutes, she asked him what he was thinking about.

Adam kissed her still closed eyes. "That you need me inside you. Are you awake?"

"Not really. I'm dreaming. This has to be a dream." She glided fully on top of him. Hard but indolent, his penis pressed the lips of her labia ... light, unhurried, slowly, a fraction of an inch at a time, it became an erotic questioning touch, probing, now to her inner lips, poised ... hesitant, giving her an excruciating feeling of sheer loveliness, followed by their simultaneous gasping wonder and amazement as the flower opened and her vagina slowly drew him into the warm liquid depths of her.

"Oh, my God ... my God, Adam ..." she whispered, and her words were his words. And then: "How can this be? How can I be wanting and needing you so much and be worrying about Jim?" She couldn't hold back the tears in her eyes. "Gosh, I guess you must think I'm pretty god-awful. I'm making love to you and talking about my husband." She stared down at him and Adam was immersed in the planes and curves of her face, and the warm feel of her body against his.

"You have two husbands now, remember?" He chuckled. "So long as it's nice talk, does it matter?"

"You mean it's all right that I love two men?"

"I don't think we'd survive any other way. Anyway, if you really love, you can't forsake all other loving."

Angela was silent for a moment. "Do you think we might be lucky ... that Janice and Jim would find each other in Bermuda?"

Adam shrugged. "I don't need their loving each other as an excuse for loving you. Anyway, I wouldn't count on it. Right now Janice is feeling guilty enough for daring to go to Bermuda without involving herself with a third man."

"Do you think that Janice might be making love with Jack Lovell right now?" It didn't seem in character, but

Angela occasionally wondered if Adam was playing around because his wife did.

Adam kissed her nose. "Sweetie, the next thing you're going to be thinking is that I'm here with you in retaliation for Janice's behavior. But the truth is, it's entirely conceivable that Janice has never made love with Jack Lovell nor any other man since we've been married."

"Oh God . . . I hope she has."

"I do, too . . . especially, if she could experience this kind of merger." Adam held her face with two hands and savored her lips.

"If it can't be with Jim, I hope Janice is with Jack and they're making love right now."

Adam's eyes twinkled at the impossibility. "It's only six in the morning in Bermuda. Janice wouldn't make love with Casanova himself at six in the morning."

"What time is it here?"

"It's seven."

"We're making love."

"You and I would make love in a howling snowstorm in Siberia."

"Or a typhoon in Malaya?"

"Even a hurricane in Key West while the roof was blowing off our heads!"

"Why?"

"Because we like each other."

"Jim and Janice might really like each other. Jim only likes to make love in the early evening." Angela chuckled. "Maybe they have other things in common."

"Do you feel guilty because you make love with two men and Jim presumably only makes love with you?"

Angela was silent. Adam had a way of crystallizing her worries. Finally, she arched herself on her elbow and looked in his eyes. "Do you want me to feel guilty?"

"No!" Adam kissed the question on her face into a grin.

"Oh, Adam . . . Adam whether it's moral or not, I do enjoy us. With Jim I'm much less involved."

"Which is really his choice."

Angela was puzzled. "Why do you say that?"

"Because Angela Campolieto Adams-Thomas is a love-bug. Your entire approach to life . . . even your photography . . . is an expression of your loving, affectionate nature. The immoral thing would be to turn your love off or on, depending on the man you were with."

"But the highs are higher with you." Angela giggled.

"Maybe it's because you talk me into an orgasm. Right now, you'd never guess what just popped into my mind. A week or so ago I was reading a book called *The Couple*. It's about two people who paid Masters and Johnson twenty-five hundred dollars so that the man could learn how to be sexually adequate. The poor soul would lose his erection right in the middle of things. Nothing his wife could do would bring him to life ... Adam ... why is it that you don't have that trouble?"

"Because I don't try!" Adam laughed. "I'd hate to think that having an orgasm was a life or death matter. All his wife had to do was hug him, be glad he was alive and with her, and not make his erection or lack of it an issue one way or the other. It's really a screwed-up world. Most married people haven't even learned to like each other. Maybe if we could create a society where young men and women were educated to enjoy each other as fallible, silly people, and make love naturally from their teens, in later life they wouldn't end up such a mass of inhibitions and frustrations."

"Are you offering yourself as a case in point?" Angela was kneeling over him. Her eyes closed, joined to him, a smile of a wonder and mystery on her face, she swayed lightly side to side. Adam could feel the curve of her stomach caressing his stomach. "God, no! When it comes to love I'm a Johnny-come-lately." He swung her off the bed. "With that treatment I wouldn't last another ten seconds. Come on ... we're going to get dressed and save this orgasm."

While Adam peeled oranges for them and poured coffee that was still warm from the Thermos jug, Angela unearthed the Instavision video camera and took pictures of him. Then while she was sitting cross-legged on the bed, munching graham crackers, Adam told her he'd continue the sex documentary of Angela and Adam. He aimed the camera at her exposed vulva. "I like the way it looks at me." He leaned over and tasted her. "It's kind of soft and downy ... independent of its owner ... smiling. If it had a tongue right now it would say "Hello, Adam, I love you."

Angela closed her legs.

"Why did you do that?"

"The middle of me is blushing." She grinned mischievously at him. "I just remembered Sam ... he told me about the tape that he and Yael had made of them

273

making love." Angela shook her head. "I don't think I could do that."

Adam admired the mid-length of her body. Angela, with only her sweater on, stretched indolently naked on the bed as she sipped her coffee. "Sam was testing you. I warned you. He and Yael are exhibitionists. They enjoy each other so much they want the whole world to participate. Sam offered to show the tapes to Janice and me, but he got no takers."

Angela was fascinated. The world was changing. If the son would dare to show his father videotapes of himself and his wife making love, would the father and mother return the favor? "I wouldn't mind seeing their tapes." Angela grinned at him. "Just a minute ago, I preserved your most marvelous erection for posterity. I like your penis. It's very much a Jonathan Q. Adams penis with a character and personality all its own." Angela felt bubbly. "Should a female talk about her lover's penis? Do you think I'm too erotic?"

Adam shook his head. "It just occurred to me that we might produce a better movie than Sam's. Maybe, tomorrow in the apartment, we should make our own tape. I'd rather watch us making love than anyone else."

Laughing, Angela hopped off the bed and slid into her panties. "No thanks, sweetie, I really couldn't do it! I'm too self-conscious." She pulled on the woolen trousers that Adam had bought for her in Hyannis. Grimacing, she eased the woolen face mask over her head and surveyed herself in the mirror. "On the other hand, I suppose if we could work out a little scenario, it might be fun. I can see it now. The camera exploring the lonely empty Pink, and then you and I bustle through the door, dressed in mackinaws and trousers and face masks. We slowly undress. But we are so busy admiring each other, so anxious to make love, we can't wait, and we jump into bed naked except for these silly masks." Angela's eyes behind her mask were a dancing question mark, but Adam seemed unimpressed. "Well, it might be funny," she said. "What's your plot?"

They finally emerged from the motel room. Two overstuffed visitors from interplanetary space, hilarious as they surveyed each other and the cold world around them. The owner of the motel, evidently an early riser, was repairing a snow fence at the front of the motel. He waved and watched them as they cautiously retraced their last night

274

tracks down to the first snow-covered dunes and past them to the snowless frozen beach.

Her finger nearly frozen to the camera release, Angela panned the shoreline, and then closed in on Adam cavorting on the wet, hard-packed sand. Dancing and shouting his enthusiasm, his yells were dissipated by the biting cold wind, and the shuush and thud of the surf crashing on the shore. He hugged her, and their eyes staring at each other from behind their masks were overflowing with love.

"Maybe we should leave the camera," he bellowed. "It's too heavy, and it's pretty damned cold. With this wind it must be ten below."

Angela shook her head and pointed at seagulls far up the beach, lazily circling over the dunes. "Even if I freeze ... I want them on tape."

She was already leading the way along the deserted beach.

"Thataway is Race Point and Provincetown. I hope you feel athletic."

Angela was beaming. Athletic wasn't the word. She was fine-tuned to the deep throbbing beat of the turning earth. The sky was almost painfully blue, the atmosphere wiped clean by the brisk wind. But the surging winter ocean, unlike the same Atlantic a few thousand miles south, was not a placid-mirror-green reflection of the white sand beneath it. Here it was angry. Steel blue and gray, it was furrowed to the horizon with spray-whipped rolling whitecaps. The storm had passed, but the gods of the sea, roiled beyond endurance, wouldn't regain their equilibrium for days.

The tide was going out and the beach, previously watercovered, was a firm wet roadbed, leading to a nowhere infinity where sky and sea formed a misty blend. As they leaned against the wind, unable to hear each other over the crashing surf, Angela knew that she and Adam were twin-alive, vibrant. The clean cold salt air was recharging their blood, washing them clean of civilization. Here the junk and accumulation that man lived by was no more important than the disappearing imprint of their boots on the wet sand.

As they walked past miles of primary and secondary dunes on their left, and the infinite ocean on their right, they merged with a timeless rhythm that was beyond human life. But not quite beyond their subconscious comprehension. Somewhere in the primitive recesses of their brains strange stirrings, inchoate memories, welled to the surface of their consciousnesses, and they were simultaneously Angela and Adam and the gulls and terns watching them overhead, and they sensed the unheard music of billions of miniscule life-forms brimming through the ocean water.

As their strength to brave the cold wind diminished, they headed toward the warm deep sand cradles between the dunes that faced the ocean and secondary dunes, covered with dune grass, that held this shifting world together and protected the heather and the backwoods of scrub pine from an invasion of sand and rolling ocean. Treading lightly on the dune grass, they found a hollow protected from the wind. The sun nearing the meridian was trapped in sandy saucers. Near the bottom of the dune it was like stepping out of winter into early spring.

Adam unrolled the sleeping bag. "We've found our gull-watching station," he told her, and to Angela's amazement, he stripped completely naked and ran in circles around the curvature of the dune. Shaking with laughter, she tried to steady herself sufficiently to tape him, and then, enjoying the sheer insanity of taking off her clothes in broad daylight in the middle of winter, she ran after him, tumbling on the cold dune sand near the top and yelling her joy as he videotaped her.

"Oh, my God ... we're absolutely nuts," she gasped. Adam was lying on his back aiming the camera at her crotch. "Fathers and mothers from Cohasset and Acton don't do this! If anyone can see us they'll call the nearest asylum and bring straightjackets."

Adam inclined the sleeping bag against the windward side of the dune. Shivering, suddenly aware of the cold air whipping across their bodies, they crawled into the sleeping bag and kissed each other's bubbling laughter. And while their coursing blood quieted and they warmed each other, the gulls banked in flight above them occasionally glided in a few feet above their heads, eyeing suspiciously the wild disorder of the clothing they had flung haphazardly over the dune.

Adam's face was nuzzled in her neck. "In my next life I'm planning to return as a herring gull, but only if I can arrange it for you, too. There are at least twenty-five varieties of Atlantic gulls. The herring gull has a pure white body, a blue-gray mantle, flesh-colored legs, and a little orange spot on its yellow beak."

276

They lay on their backs, legs intertwined in the sleeping bag. Holding hands, they watched the birds. "See those smaller brown mottled birds . . . they're only a year or two old."

The gulls swooping lower and lower over them, curious, kyooing at them, were evidently irritated that their feeding ground was invaded. "In the Spring," Adam was tracing her delta as he whispered in her ear, "when the females are nesting, they're very ferocious. They'll peck at your head and face if you come too close. Some people think they're very nasty rapacious birds. Maybe they will even eat their own eggs if they're hungry, but they clean up man's debris, too. Watch the sheer grace and ease of their flight. I'd like to do that with you. Climb a few hundred feet in the air and then glide and float together on the wind currents." Adam told her that a few summers past, Janice had found a baby gull on one of the outer islands. They had brought it home and tried to raise it. "Gulls don't fly for at least three months after they're born. They have a long life, too . . . thirty or forty years."

The gulls were swooping over a long inner estuary of water left behind by the retreating tide. As Angela and Adam became silently engrossed bird-watchers, studying the personalities of particular birds, the gulls finally ignored them and returned to their never-ending business of eating. Angela retrieved her Ampex camera. Wiggling partially out of the bag, her head and shoulders and breasts bare, half sitting, half leaning against Adam, who occasionally kissed her nearest dangling breast, she followed the flights of individual birds with her close-up lens and captured the continuous life-and-death transaction of gulls swallowing their uncomplaining prey.

"What happened to your baby gull?" Angela asked.

"Every day for months we flapped our arms at him, and he stared at us with beady eyes and flapped his wings back, but he was too overweight to take off." Adam kissed her and pulled her back down into the sleeping bag. "Brewster was his name . . . a very cocky fellow. At three months we were sure that he was in control of his own destiny. He ate everything in sight. He even brazenly yakked at Janice's cats. Presumably, he could repel any attackers. But we forgot that Ike is very short-tempered with birds. One night Ike pounced on Brewster from the rear. Very proud of his conquest, he deposited him half-eaten on the doorstep."

Angela shivered. "I read something by Alan Watts once that I never could get out of my mind. Alan was watching a gull that had picked up a crab from a tidepool. The gull was pecking through the shell to the crab's flesh. He imagined the gull saying, 'Let me in! I love you so much, I could eat you to the very core, especially the soft juicy parts, the vitals most tender and alive. Surrender to this agony and you will be transformed into Me. Dying to yourself you will become alive as Me. We shall all be changed in a moment, in a twinkling of an eye when the last trumpet sounds. For behold! I am He who stands at the door and knocks.'"

There were tears in Angela's eyes. She hugged Adam and burrowed with him deep into the sleeping bag.

"Who are we, Adam? Will we live again? Is it wrong for us to be here, naked making love? Would you eat me if I were a fish and you were a gull? . . . Oh God, dear love . . . in the act of love with you I die to myself and momentarily am transformed into you."

"And I into you . . . and I into you . . ."

☆ 61 ☆

Saturday morning it was snowing again. Lying on the water bed, half on her stomach, one arm across Adam's chest, Angela could see the snowflakes flick and melt as they touched the leaded glass window in the front of the room. Sleepily, she reminded herself that today she must water the geraniums and sanseveria she had bought for the window garden and she felt melancholy at the thought. Tonight their honeymoon was over. Tonight was the last night. Had the past four days actually existed? Next week back in Acton, waiting for Thursday, would she still be able to bifurcate her two realities? How long could she maintain two separate worlds; hold onto separate compartments without mixing the clutter and memories of one with the daydreams of the other?

In the four days she had become so immersed in her Adam responses that the Angela Thomas who lived in Acton, Massachusetts, the mother of three children,

278

seemed like a person in her dreams, and this Angela, the Boston-Adam-Angela was momentarily the only reality.

Saturday . . . oh God, where had Friday gone? The days had almost lost their identity . . . a flowing, delightful blending of time and love that at the first seemed limitless, and then unbelievably the last grains of sand in the hourglass had gathered a faster momentum. Time that had trickled slowly and confidently at the beginning suddenly swished through the tiny aperture, and the top of the glass was empty.

Two days ago at this time they were at the bottom of the sand dune, a blissful, naked huddle in the sleeping bag that had careened down the hill, as they had suddenly erupted in their thrashing ecstasy and joy in each other. At the bottom of the dune, they had wiggled out into the trapped warm air, waving hilariously at the curious, staring gulls who were sailing above them again, cackling their annoyance at these interlopers who made such noisy love.

"Oh, thank you, Adam . . . thank you for loving me so warmly, so crazily." And as they dressed, she suddenly realized that tomorrow was Thursday. "Adam could we hurry home? Back to Boston? To the Pink? This may be the only Thursday I can ever wake up in your arms."

Four hours later, they parked the Cadillac under Boston Common, hysterical with laughter at their exhaustion (too much lovemaking?). They plodded through Louisburg Square in their mackinaws and face masks, enjoying the bewildered expressions on the faces of passersby (didn't mothers and fathers know enough to grow up?), and finally flopped gratefully on their water bed . . . too tired to eat . . . too tired to undress, but not too tired to recall their days together, and chuckle at their silliness (were they really in their forties? why was it against the rules for fathers and mothers to be joyous lovers?). And they remembered two days ago. Were they really married in Montreal? "My God, Adam, don't tell a soul!" And her fingers stealing into his trousers finding him erect again. And they had squirmed out of their clothes, and temporarily joined but unable to proceed further, fell asleep in the middle of their "I-love-you's."

Friday . . . was that yesterday? My God, yes! Yesterday afternoon she and Adam had been discovered again! This time by her sisters. For the past sixteen hours she knew she had been consciously trying to forget that it had ever happened. Their honeymoon was nearly over. In the lonely days ahead she'd have plenty of time to worry about what her sisters might be thinking.

"First it was Harry Carswell," she moaned to Adam. "And now Kathy and Alma. One by one, every one we have ever known will accidentally run into us."

Adam had only grinned. "And Janice and Jim, the wronged spouses, will be the last to know."

"What will we ever say when they find out about us?"

"I'll take the responsibility," Adam told her. "We'll have a big conclave at your home or my home. . . . 'Jim,' I'll say, 'I love your wife . . . so I married her. Not to take her away from you, just to enjoy her, one or maybe two-sevenths of her life.'" Adam smiled at Angela's unbelieving expression. "You, of course, will have to assure Janice that in a very real sense you are taking the strain off her. Or, if you prefer, we can simply blame it on the middle-aged syndrome; we were afraid we were losing our sex appeal so we needed each other as reinforcement."

Angela couldn't shake his laughing equanimity. As he pointed out to her, while he had been delighted to meet Alma (an older and plumper version of Angela), and he was sure that her sister Kathy loved him, too . . . they would never have met at all if she hadn't dreamed up the idea of shopping in the open-air market on Blackstone Street.

It really had been madly risky. "I want you to know my Boston," she had told him yesterday. "If I can't convince you that you should go to work this morning, and you're not afraid what your friend Harry Carswell may be up to, or what ideas Sam might be entertaining about his vanished father, then you can go shopping with me. I'll show you the North End, where your *paisan* "wop" girlfriend spent her childhood while the rich Adamses were basking on the North or South Shore."

But it was much more than that. What she had really wanted to do was pretend. Pretend one more day that they were really married, and the Pink really was their home. Tonight she would cook for him. His first Angela dinner. Real Italian food for her Boston blueblood. Insane! How could you go to a bustling open-air market and buy enough food for two people and one meal? But she was so intent on her daydreams that she hadn't given a thought to the fact that she was playing at love in her sisters' backyard.

Adam caught her fervor and was suddenly ecstatic. He hadn't been in Haymarket Square or wandered through European-style streets like Hanover and Salem Streets for years and years. Here, he was suddenly reminded, instead of cold, human robots adding up the endless streams of purchases, shoved in front of them on a moving belt in regimented supermarkets ... here lingered the warmth of old-time grocery stores and old-time butchers hawking their meats and vegetables and fruits and bakery products to the passersby ... carrying on a warm, personal, almost loving interchange between the buyer and seller that existed nowhere else in the impersonal city. Here you were more important than the money you were spending. Here human beings were mutually involved both in the joyous bounty of the food they sold and the food their customers would eat.

The butcher on Salem Street discussed the quality of his veal cutlets in detail with Angela, assuring her that the slices he was personally cutting for her would make the finest meal they had ever eaten. The liquor merchant, Martignetti, opened a bottle of Bordeaux Chateau Tremblant from Saint Emilion, vintage 1966, for Adam and tasted it appreciatively in paper cups with them. Of course it wasn't Chateau Lafite Rothschild 1900, but ... the price! Before she could stop him, Adam bought a mixed case of Bordeaux and Beaujolais. How to get them back to the apartment?

But why worry? They had only begun to buy. It simply was impossible not to. If they filled the apartment with food and liquor, when would they ever use it? Adam wasn't listening, and she was caught in the sheer whirling joy of the late-afternoon crowds of workers and their wives, all temporarily rich and squanderous with their Friday paychecks, slowly turning into a week's supply of food. Like kids in a candy store, they squirmed and shoved through a noisy quarter mile of pushcarts and peddlers, haranguing their dickering customers, suspicious over bargains that sometimes weren't really bargains.

"Hey, two dozen Chiquitas ... twenty-five cents a dozen ... not too soft. Just freeze em ... need some onions? Hey, tomatoes ... hey, mister, where'd you ever see such tomatoes in February ... hey, grapes from California ... never mind the boycott. Feel these melons—delightful as a cool tit. Hey, looka these peppers, oranges from California, navels from Israel. Looka here, lettuce four heads for

281

a dollar! Brussels sprouts? Twenty-five cents a box. Wanta case, Mister? A dollar-fifty for twelve boxes."

"No, Adam . . . they won't keep," Angela wailed. "Not a case. We only need a box."

"It's such a bargain and I love brussels sprouts."

"Everything's a bargain. Look at you . . . I told you one pound of tomatoes and you bought six pounds. You have enough lettuce to make salads every day for a month."

Adam was hilarious. "This is great! Next week I'm going to open up here myself, with my own pushcart."

"You want a job, Mister?" A stubble-faced big-bellied man with a knit cap over his head and ears, his breath condensing in a cloud around his face, standing next to a pile of discarded crates and boxes left from the broccoli he was selling, stopped yelling his bargains for a moment. But he forgot his job offer when he suddenly saw Angela.

"Hey, I know you! . . . It's gotta be! You're one of the Campolieto kids . . . I used to work for your old lady, Maria." He grinned at Angela's embarrassment. "You're the youngest one—*Angela!*" he yelled, happy he had remembered her name. A circle of shoppers stopped in their tracks, enjoying Angela's blushing confusion as the big man hugged her and kissed her cheeks. "I'm little Frankie! Frankie Veneto . . ." Angela remembered, but all she wanted to do was to crouch down and vanish—crawl away on her hands and knees in the crowds. But even before she could escape Frankie's enthusiastic appraisal of her good firm shape, before she could actually confirm that she was indeed the former Angela Campolieto, Frankie's shout of "Angela" was returned by a two soprano echoes.

"Angela! . . . Angela!" Two women shoved their way past the shoppers and embraced her. Even now she wasn't certain how she had fended her sisters' torrent of questions. She was certain that her blushing, tongue-tied bewilderment revealed the truth. Adam was her lover. If only Adam had less effrontery . . . if he had just disappeared in the crowds, it would have solved everything. It might have been difficult to explain what she was doing in the North End shopping, without having visited her family, but it would have been far simpler in the long run. But Adam didn't go away. He stood calmly beside her, too close, possessive, grinning as he listened to Alma and Kathy complain that they hadn't seen Angela for months. Where was she keeping herself? (They inventoried Adam with raised eyebrows.) And how was Jim? And what were her children doing? Adam, feeling left out, right in the middle of their gossipy exchange introduced himself as Jon Adams . . . Angela's boss at Adams National. This immediately required further explanations. Yes, she was working part-time. No, Jim didn't mind. Jim was in Bermuda playing golf (more astonishment, why wasn't she with him?). Yes, she was "doing photography" with Adams National. Today, she was helping Mr. Adams buy some fresh vegetables. (Angela could hear them now. Since when does a married woman go shopping with her employer? *And her husband away?* Ho. Ho. A likely story) No, really, she finally told them, as much as they would like, Mr. Adams and she wouldn't be able to visit with them this afternoon. Some other day . . . Adam coolly assured them. Hiding her astonishment at Adam's words, Angela finally told them she would telephone them next week.

Back in the apartment, after the taxi driver had helped them carry the bags and cardboxes full of food and wine up to the Pink, Angela exploded. "Good Lord, I was horrified enough when I saw them descending on me, I even thought I was handling them pretty well until you took over, put your two cents' worth in." She was peeved with him, but it was impossible not to hug him. "Did you have to be so pleasant? Did you have to tell them that the Campolieto girls must have been the most beautiful girls in the North End? Did you have to act as if you'd really want to go back to their homes, as if you were getting ready to join the family? . . . And the pièce de résistance, telling Alma she had the style of Sophia Loren! You've made an indelible impression on their feeble minds."

Adam only smiled. "Alma and Kathy and Angela are joyfully unrefined . . . warm, earthy-looking women."

Angela wasn't sure that was a compliment . . . but later, wearing nothing except a cotton dress, barefoot, making dinner for him while they listened to two new records he had bought—*Pli Selon Pli* by Pierre Boulez and *Geod* by Lukas Foss . . . the music strange, other-worldly, evanescent, searching . . . Adam in slacks and a sweatshirt read to her from a conversation with Lukas Foss, "With *Geod*, Foss says: " 'You don't have the sense of a masterwork unfolding in front of you . . . you feel there are sounds which you are getting on the other side of . . . like sitting in a tree and feeling that you finally have become a part of the tree ... the growth ... the juices go through you ... you become very quiet inside and you feel something. *You listen in on nature* and become a part of nature, rather than contemplating a masterwork." Adam chuckled. "That's what I mean by earthy."

While she was scooping a cup of butter into the scalding milk, telling him that the noodles were ready and the swiss and parmesan cheeses shredded, he was about to eat a fettucine that would bring tears to the eyes of all the Alfredo's in Rome. Adam was unzipping the back of her dress. Over her protests he pulled her free of the sleeves and caught the top of the dress around her waist. He watched her, delighted. "Earthy is not knowing whether my roots buried in you, are the effect or the cause. Do we hold each other together, do we give each other sustenance and strength?" He kissed her breasts. "Earthy is watching you, half naked, by candlelight, the music playing, your breasts in natural rhythm as you whip together butter, cheese, milk and noodles, and your eyes are overflowing with love."

Lying dreamily beside him, Angela recalled each time they had made love in the past four days. "Do you know something?" Tuned that he was finally awake, she murmured in his ear, "Last night you made love very nicely, after my big Italian dinner."

He grinned at her sleepily. "It's Saturday. Already, I'm feeling lonesome for you."

"Me too. Even now, I'm living in the memories. I just figured it out, twenty-five percent of the time that we've been together, we've been making love."

"I'm going to give you Carswell's job. You should have been an accountant." She felt his hand on her behind. "But your facts are confused. I may have been inside you twenty-five percent of the time, but I've been making love to you one hundred percent of the time." He reached for his wristwatch on the table beside the bed. "We need a digital clock. Then, on gray mornings, like this, I would only have to open one eye to see what time it is."

She snuggled against him and trickled her fingers through the hair on his belly. She knew she was on the verge of tears. "I hate clocks. Nasty timekeepers, measuring out the moments. This is our last full day. Why do we need a clock? There may never be other mornings ... gray or otherwise."

"Of course, there will be."

"How? This has been a little miracle. There may be times when Jim is away or Janice, but they'll never coincide like this."

He kissed her cheek. "I know . . . you're feeling melancholy. So am I a little. We've made a discovery. We need more continuity than Thursdays between ten and four."

Angela nodded. "We need a few Thursdays that let us wake up together Friday morning." She kissed his cheek. "Okay, I refuse to be sad. After all, you are married to me! You can never escape me now. What do we do together this snowy day? I've got an idea!" She bounced out of bed. "I've suddenly found a reason for making a videotape of us making love."

☆ 62 ☆

While Adam lay on the bed, contentedly enjoying the New England stormy weather that had turned the Pink into a warm protective cave (for a few more hours he had effectively disappeared and, in a sense, they, and they alone, were the *only* reality to each other, a daring kind of enjoyment for even intelligent human beings to attempt), Angela bustled around the room, naked, putting the Ampex camera on a tripod, aiming their only floodlight toward the bed, and checking the lighting and footage from various locations.

"Whatever changed your mind about making a videotape of us making love?" Adam was enjoying her preoccupation with her preparations.

"To blackmail you, silly." She moved the camera extension cord nearer to his side of the bed. "Oh, Adam . . . not to blackmail you . . . I want this tape to bring home, and those days when it isn't Thursday, and I'm alone and feeling at sixes and sevens, I can run it off and grin a little between my tears."

She lay down beside him. "That's not the reason, either. It just occurred to me that one day when our Thursdays are over, I could look at the tapes and be both sad and glad that it happened to me."

"Honey . . . you are in a mood."

She smiled at him through her tears. "Let's say I'm blue

285

... and this is our *Blue Movie* ... it will be better than Andy Warhol's. Are you ready?" Angela reached for the cord switch she had placed near the bed. "This will turn the camera and lights on, all at the same time."

"Okay. Now, I want to say something on the tape."

Adam lay with his head against the headboard and took her in his arms. They both stared self-consciously into the eye of the camera. "I'm not an actor playing a part," Adam said. "I am Adam, or Jonathan, or Jake, and I married Angela Thomas in Montreal and I love her and our Thursdays will be over when I can no longer breathe. And with one of my last breaths I will say, 'Angela, I love you.' "

The tape whirled placidly through the camera. The lone impersonal eye stared at them. "Oh, Adam ... Adam ..." she sobbed. "That was very nice."

But before the first half hour of the videotape had run through, laughter had replaced tears. It was so hilariously insanely impossible to make love with someone watching you ... even if the someone was the inanimate eye of a video camera. But it was intriguing to anticipate how they would look on tape making love; especially so because Angela, recapturing her good spirits, had discovered a new reason for making the tape. "If Thursday would last, even ten years, and our sexual drives diminish ..."

"What makes you think they will?" Adam was certain. He would be just as intrigued with making love with Angela at fifty-seven or sixty-seven.

"Well, just in case," Angela was bubbling with laughter as she held his erect penis, kissed it, and displayed it to the camera. "In ten or twenty years, if all we're able to do is keep each other warm, it will be interesting to remind ourselves of our lost capabilities."

"Since this tape is both visual and vocal ... I give you my guarantee." Adam was choking with laughter. "I'll be as good or better than you need me to be."

Forgetting the camera for a moment, Adam assured her that whether he was fifty-six or sixty-six, all Angela would have to do is to look at him like she was doing now. A little lost, a little wondrous, beseechingly (ah, that was a nice word!) ... or simply pat him (like that flower-girl embedded in his brain), and he would quickly become as rampant as he was now. However, he wouldn't guarantee himself at seventy-six. Although he suddenly remembered that his mother had complained about his father. Just a year ago, before he died at seventy-eight, according to her, the senior Adams "still had sex on the brain."

When they ran the tape through the playback and watched themselves on the tube, they tumbled together, gasping and choking with laughter. They were both absolute hams. The tape was terrible. A turkey! Instead of being lovely and erotic, the tape was self-conscious, corny, and as contrived as a stag film.

"We look like country cousins just arrived from Mexico." Adam was hiccoughing from laughing so hard.

"Middle-aged wrecks!" Angela sat cross-legged on the bed, tears of laughter running down her cheeks. "Frustrated old sexpots!"

But Angela was suddenly intrigued to try again. The video camera in the fixed position was the basic problem. It created wooden characters. Even though she had placed the camera on a forty-five degree angle to the bed, they were much too elongated. The single perspective was boring to watch.

"We were too eager to make love," Adam said. "Somehow, we've got to stop in the middle. Change focus. We really need several cameras, switching from one to the other . . . and we need to be less self-conscious. Be ourselves. Warhol's *Blue Movie* proves that. The picture was a bore. When Grove Press finally published it in a book, it turned out that the dialogue was more interesting than the hours of belly-bumping."

Angela agreed. "In the movie, Andy Warhol lost the mental interplay almost entirely. Most people weren't aware of how delightfully silly the conversation between lovers can be."

While they ate breakfast of coffee, oranges, and anise bread, discussing the problems of videotaping themselves, like old professionals, Angela decided to try a different approach. They would shoot tapes of each other from every conceivable angle, alone and together, and later she would edit them into a changing perspective. "We've got to create the aura of lovemaking without words, and then we can intersperse these, later, with dialogue shots."

Adam wondered if that approach wasn't too mechanical. But it was a delightfully mad way to spend a snowy Saturday morning. Insisting that if he reached a climax he would be an uninteresting male actor (most pornographic movies had impossibly flaccid males whom the females couldn't arouse no matter what they did), Adam somehow

287

managed to delay his orgasm until Angela finally, after three climaxes, threw in the towel. "I'm hollering uncle . . . temporarily."

Adam had never heard the expression.

"Weren't you ever a kid? The boys in grammar school used to spend all their spare time wrestling with each other. When the underdog hollered 'uncle,' it was an admission of defeat." Angela grinned. "The little boys I knew wrestled the girls, too! Some of us were very belligerent and refused to holler uncle, no matter what was happening to us . . . even if we were losing our knickers."

Lying on the water bed, they reviewed their latest tapes and watched with amazement exposures of their anatomy they had never seen.

"My God, Adam, that's my anus! Ooooh, that's awful!"

"Look at my balls . . . do they really dangle like that from the rear?"

"Oh Adam, you have such a tight firm behind."

"I like your crotch, it's smiling at me."

"The only thing we can do with this tape is to erase it." Angela hugged him. "Poor you, you must be exhausted from so much lovemaking."

Adam grinned at her. "I wouldn't call it lovemaking. But as a form of exercise . . . well it beats golf all to hell! But I'm sad. During that last reel I have no erection." Adam rolled on top of her. "But, even though I, and the camera, were practically exploring your womb, this time we were more professional."

And then late in the afternoon they had the maddest idea of all. Was it Adam's brainstorm or hers? Angela would never be sure, but it ended up like a plunge from heaven into the screaming terrors of hell.

Both of them knew that the basic problem with the tapes they had made was the limitation of the equipment. With a portable television camera and inadequate lighting, they could scarcely expect the professional quality of a studio. Angela remembered that Sam had told her he and Yael had used the Adams National studio to make their tapes.

"You must be an expert on that equipment by now." Adam lay on his side and watched her, talking dreamily at the ceiling.

"Not quite . . . but I know how to run the cameras. Sam has a rig that permits you to control all three at once."

Even though Angela was dubious, she could see the gleam spring into Adam's eye. "No! . . . no . . . we can't! So what if it is Saturday? Sam and Yael could be there. How would we ever explain ourselves? Why are we together on a Saturday afternoon while Janice and Jim are in Bermuda?"

"To have them help us make tapes of ourselves making love," Adam said, without knowing he was being prophetic.

Even while she was protesting that it was too risky, Angela was intrigued. With the Adams Video equipment, she could control a complete closed circuit television system. It would be possible from just one location to switch from camera to camera every twenty seconds, and in addition she could produce corner inserts, switches, position reversals, fades, superimpositions, and horizontal and vertical splits. With that kind of equipment they could produce a fantastic "love tape."

Adam knew he should have telephoned Sam and Yael to determine what they might be doing on this bleak Saturday afternoon, but as he listened to Angela explain what was possible working with studio equipment, and reinforced with several Scotches to wash down the tomato and lettuce sandwiches Angela made for lunch, they both let themselves be convinced that they would be perfectly safe. After all, Adam had the keys. They could lock themselves in the studio.

Giggling . . . bubbling with their daring . . . telling themselves they were too old to be acting like children, they took a taxi to Adams National. The long, low building and the parking lot beside it was Saturday-deserted. In this part of Boston on the weekends there was practically no automobile traffic. The driver left them at the front door, reassured by Adam that he was the owner of the plant. He and his secretary had some overtime work to do. They all laughed conspiratorially. The taxi driver drove off after telling them he wished he had someone to knock off some overtime with.

Adam turned off the alarm system with a special key. Inside the building, feeling like thieves, they tiptoed through empty press and composing rooms, past rows and rows of stored paper, to a door marked *Adams Video*. Adam unlocked it, located the power control panels for the studio, and flipped them on.

Thirty minutes later, locked in the studio, with the hot kleig lights warming them, they lay naked together on a

289

studio bed that Angela had improvised. The command control wiring lay on the floor beside the bed. Fascinated with the complications of arranging the equipment, they were completely impervious to any thoughts of discovery. Angela showed him how she could direct the cameras that were now watching them from three different locations and elevations.

And then, almost forgetting why they had come, feeling languorous and blissful, they were whispering to each other, and actually, amazingly, unbelievably they were making love again. "Oh Adam . . . to hell with the tapes . . . we don't need them. I just love you because you're zany enough to come here." And their whispered words and their touching of each other had no sequential importance, but all that had any meaning was the wonder of themselves and their own delightful awareness of each other as one.

Adam was on top of her . . . a warm smile on his face, slowly entering her body, saying softly: "Love . . . love . . . once I remember Henry Miller describing how he and his wife made love in a mud puddle . . ."

He was about to say, "We are obviously just as nutty . . . " when a voice bounced off the cement block walls of the room. "Good God . . . it's Jake and Angela . . . naked as jaybirds! . . . screwing!" Followed by embarrassed laughter in the darkness.

"My God! It's Sam!"

Screaming, Angela leaped off the bed.

The dream of love had turned into a nightmare. They were naked on a blazing, lighted stage. Caught in the split-second horror of the earth and their lives disappearing beneath their feet. They tried to force the cones in their eyes to adapt to the blackness of the studio around them. To see who was out there . . . beyond the stage . . . in the shadows.

Frantic, almost frozen with fear . . . afraid that she was going to faint, Angela ripped the sheet of the mattress they had been lying on and tried to wrap it around them.

"Oh dear God! . . . dear God! . . . It's our kids, Adam! Oh, God, don't let it be!" Angela's whispered words became sobs of despair.

Sam and Yael, followed by Robin and Keane, all of them looking decidedly flustered, emerged from the dark shadows of the room. Only Sam managed a cool grin. For a moment their mutual embarrassment was beyond words.

Angela, crouching against Adam, only half covered by the sheet, sick to the depth of her bowels, kept thinking, Robin. *Not Robin.* It couldn't be! What was Robin doing in Boston? Tears streaming down her cheeks, all Angela could say, over and over again, was: "Oh, Robin . . . Robin. I'm so sorry!"

What explanation was there for her daughter, or for any of them? The truth? What was the truth? She and Adam were two oversexed, middle-aged adulterers.

Yael was apologetic. "Honest, Jake, we're sorry. We weren't spying on you. We didn't even know anyone was here until Sam unlocked the door."

Adam shrugged. He gave the sheet to Angela. Calmly naked, he retrieved his boxer shorts and put them on. He grinned at them. "I often wondered. Now, I know what it's like to be caught *in flagrante delicto*." He kneeled beside Angela. "Angela Adams-Thomas . . . stop crying! It's only our children. They shouldn't be shocked by love."

☆ 63 ☆

June . . . thirteen Saturdays later (and thirteen Thursdays), sitting with Gramps and Lena on the bride's side of the First Church of Acton, Angela listened to the choir singing the chorus from Carl Orff's *Catulli Carmina* in Latin:

> Eise aiona! Tui Sum.
> O mea vita!
> Tu mihi cara, mi cara amicula corculum es!
> Corcule, dic mi, te amare
> O tui oculi, ocelli lucidi, fulgurant
> efferunt me velut specula. . . .

In eternity I am yours. Oh my life! Dear friend, you are my little heart. Little heart, tell me do you love me?

With tears in her eyes Angela followed the translation of Catullus on the program. *The Wedding of Robin Maria Thomas and Keane Bradford Adams.* Jim, father of the bride, was in the vestry with Robin. Not to give his daughter away, but to walk down the aisle and give her the freedom to love that she had already taken. Ruth, maid of honor, Yael a bridesmaid, Sam, best man, and

Richard, a handsome beaming usher . . . the Adams and the Thomas families were being joined by their children. (Across the aisle, sitting next to Janice, Adam smiled at her . . . and Janice was grinning happily at her, too.) Would she be so happy if she knew that Father Lereve, who would marry her son to the Thomas girl, had already married her husband to Robin's mother?

Robin and Keane, with Father Lereve's help, had written their own marriage ceremony. Reverend Duncan had graciously offered his church, and to the amazement of friends and relatives of both the Thomases and the Adamses . . . two dancers in classical ballet costumes danced an exotic love Pas de deux to the *Carmina Catulli* chorus, while the congregation waited for a Catholic priest from Montreal to perform the wedding ceremony in a Protestant church.

There was no escape from her memories. Video technicians from Adams National were taping the ceremonies, prearranged by Sam, who cornered her for her specific permission ("Angela . . . Angela . . . it's no tragedy . . . we all love you").

Listening to the lovely music while the church filled to capacity, overflowing with an uneasy mixture of joy and apprehension, Angela wondered if her destiny was completely out of her control. She, the spider, whose happy Thursday web had been knocked down, was dangling. Three lonely months later and there was no new corner where she dared spin another. Adam's certainty that the kids would keep their love duet a secret overlooked the obvious. Without any choice, Sam, Yael, Robin, and Keane had become a party to their guilt. There was no alternative. Even though the when and where of their lovemaking (beyond that terrible Saturday) had remained their secret, there could be no more Thursdays . . . no more hours in the Pink. Their guilt couldn't be compounded.

Had Robin told Ruth or Richy? Probably not Richy, but Robin and Ruth were very close. Was it her imagination, or had she noticed Ruth staring at her . . . lost in some disbelieving wonder? Was this really her mother? Could a woman with three children be such a blatantly sexual creature? . . . taking pornographic movies of herself screwing with a stranger? But, maybe her queasy thoughts were simply projections of her guilt. In the few weeks that Ruth and Robin had been home from school, gay bright weeks filled with wedding preparations, they had overwhelmed her with their affection. Without bringing the subject up herself, all Angela could assume was that Robin's feelings were summed up in the words she had whispered to her this morning. "I love you, Mother . . . both of you, Angela Thomas and Angela Adams."

The choir, which had slowly faded to a whisper, joined the organ in a chanting version of a poem with music that Keane had written announcing the arrival of the bride and groom. "Look on us and smile . . . share our joy. We are in love with each other and with you . . ."

Father Lereve appeared in the sanctuary. His smile not only embraced Robin wearing a pale sea-green satin dress and Keane in a white evening suit, but seemed to Angela to have a special message for her. As Robin and Keane approached the altar, the choir hushed and then sang, "This is a day that the Lord hath made . . . let us rejoice and be glad in it."

> This is indeed a day which the Lord hath made
> Let us rejoice in it and be very glad and
> let us count our many blessings; particularly,
> of course, on such a very joyous occasion.
> We are here tonight not just to observe
> but to participate with one's heart . . .
> in an event that has interwoven meanings
> for two families and Keane and Robin who
> have brought them together. . . .

Whose children found us naked in the act of love. While Angela listened, part of her was Angela-past, crying her heart out, a sheet wrapped around her naked body.

"Mother, Mother . . . don't cry." Ignoring her advice, Robin was sobbing with her. "I love Jake, too. We weren't spying on you. Keane and I came home this weekend to tell you we decided to get married in June when I finish Juilliard. We don't know if we want a wedding. But we guessed you and Janice might."

Yael with tears in her eyes too. And Sam . . . Sam, the Rock . . . imperturbable, checking the cameras, winding the tapes back. "I knew you were a genius, Angela," he marveled. "Even Yael and I, when we made our screwing tapes, never could have figured out this ingenious hookup."

Adam (J.Q.?) taking command. "Okay, get the hell out of here. Wait for us in my office while we get dressed. Make us a drink. We all need one."

293

And the children had left and Angela, now really sobbing . . . close to hysterical panic . . . the sheet, unheeded, draped on the floor at her feet. Clutching him, naked. "Adam . . . Adam . . . what will we do? I can't face them. I'm not sophisticated about anything. Certainly, not about us. Oh, God . . . how did I ever let it happen?"

And Adam, amazingly calm. "They don't have to know about the Pink. Whatever way the wind blows, don't lean against it. I love you. Maybe the time has come to tell Janice and Jim . . . Let's first see if the children can bear the sins of their fathers."

And Robin and Keane are the Way (Tao). They live, in their lives, the successive movement of *yin* and *yang*. What issues from this is good, and that which brings it to completion is the individual nature. The man of humanity recognizes it and calls it humanity, the wise man recognizes it and calls it wisdom. But no human life has any meaning whatsoever unless it is related to other human lives. And no people living together in a loving relationship can have any meaning from themselves apart from the group, and the friends and people with whom they relate. Keane and Robin know this. And so they have invited us to share their wedding vows because essentially they cannot live together as man and wife and as two people who care for each other unless they have a community of people who care for them . . .

Because essentially they cannot live together. Adam waiting while she dressed. Combing her hair, still trembling. Oh God . . . what was going through Robin's mind? What kind of lifetime trauma would be hers? A young girl discovering her mother, naked, copulating. An adultress? And what words of love had Robin heard her mother saying to her lover? While they were waiting for them in Adam's office, what were the four of them saying to each other? Had they come to an agreement? To be sophisticated. "Parents swinging was where it's at!" Could they create a cover to hide the reverse side of the same doubts and guilt that plagued her?

Keane slumping in a leather chair. Sam behind Adam's desk, his feet in a drawer. Yael and Robin sitting on the leather couch. Festive. Drinks already poured. A libation to their errant parents?

Adam jaunty before they walked in his office. "Angela,

I love you. I'm not ashamed of us." And then, injecting a light note as he greeted the kids, "John Quincy Adams, when he was defeated for president (much to the embarrassment of his son Charles, because it was unseemly for an ex-President to reenter the political fray on a lower level) ran for Congress and was elected to the House of Representatives." Adam laughing. "He had a very good reason. He was broke and needed the eight dollars a day a Congressman got. His wife Louise hated politics, but was probably happy as hell to get rid of the old codger. At eighty-one years, on the floor of the House, John Q. slumped to the floor. His last words were, 'This is the end of the earth, but I am composed.' "

Adam, delighting in the kids' surprise and joining their whoop of laughter. Adam saying: "While I'm Jonathan and not John . . . some people might consider that Angela and I being caught with our bottoms bare, bumping bellies and enjoying the warmth of each other's flesh, was the end of the earth . . . but not Jake . . . I am composed." Adam tenderly with his arm around her. "Robin, I love your mother. If you care for us at all, we all have to compose Angela . . . and convince her it's really not the end of the earth."

The event that they unite themselves in tonight as husband and wife is probably the single most deep relationship two people can enter into. It has tremendous significance; more than I am going to even indicate here tonight. Robin and Keane know that this relationship is no guarantee of growth and understanding. It is no guarantee of creative quality, no guarantee of happiness and well-being. You have to be very obtuse to think that marriage automatically produces those beautiful life-sustaining qualities, but Keane and Robin are not obtuse. They are sensitive, aware, informed, curious, and eager.

They were sensitive, aware, informed, curious and eager. Where to go? Saturday, their last night . . . snatched out of their hands. Would she ever wake up in Adam's arms again? No. Even now . . . how to say to her daughter, "I hope you may always be exclusively in love with one man." Could a monogamous love have been possible with Adam and her? That was an unknown, beyond any hope of knowing in this lifetime. How to convince her daughter that her mother basically believed in monogamy . . . and

yet to be honest. "Robin, it could happen to you. Not now
... but someday." How to evoke the completely impossible? "Robin, loving Adam . . . Jake . . . doesn't lessen my
love for your father." As mad an idea as telling your baby
daughter that someday a man's penis would penetrate the
tiny, unopened, hairless little notch between her legs. Incredible. But ultimately understood and embraced and
joyously wanted. How to tell your grown daughter that
maybe because you have been loving, you are vulnerable
to being loving.

Adam amazingly in control, unembarrassed . . . not hiding his love for her. "Let's all go to Cohasset. We'll have
Saturday night supper together and talk."

Piled together in Sam's car ... heading toward the
underground garage to get Janice's car. Screaming silently
inside, wanting to say "You can let us off here at Beacon
Street. We can walk to the Pink." Wanting to disappear
and never to face the world again, to escape the self-
consciousness of the six of them. The old structures
gone forever. No one knowing exactly how to relate to
each other. The king is dead. But, no reiterating "long live
the king" would reconstitute this microcosm exactly as it
had been.

Desperately not wanting to go to Janice's house. She,
the mistress . . . in the wife's home. But where to go? To
Acton alone? To Acton with Robin and Keane while
Adam returned to Cohasset? Angela Adams-Thomas? Really insane.

They know that marriage because of its potential for
importance may lead into depths of degradation and
despair and misery that no one can adequately plumb.
They also know as you and I must know, and their
parents must know that the same relationships can
lead into experiences so sublime that that which we
call heaven becomes part of our day, so that the two
lives which are separate may seem to be one. And in
the wisdom of Lao-tzu in the *Tao Teh Ching*: we learn
to:

> "Welcome disgrace as a pleasant surprise.
> Prize calamities as your own body!
> Why should we welcome "disgrace as a
> pleasant surprise?"

Because a lowly state is a boon.

Getting it is a pleasant surprise
And so is losing it!
That is why we should "welcome disgrace
as a pleasant surprise."
Why should we "prize calamities as
our own body?"
Because our body is the very source of
our calamities.
If we have no bodies, what calamities can
we have?
Hence only he who is willing to give his
body
For the sake of the world is fit to be
entrusted with the world.
Only he who can do it with love is worthy
of being steward of the world.

And Robin and Keane are confident that their love and devotion will be sufficient to their needs and that it will enable them to continue to grow in wisdom and stature and depth of their creating, loving relationship. And I am sure that you must share, with me, this very deep and basic confidence.

☆ 64 ☆

Alone, finally, in Janice's Cadillac. Fifty minutes to Cohasset. Then what? "Adam, how can I face all of them for a whole evening? What can we say to each other? Where do you and I sleep tonight?"

Adam was holding her hand. "Honey, it's too late to be dishonest. You're going to sleep with me."

"Tomorrow ... you and I are over." Her tears a fountain. Would it never run dry? "Adam and Angela was a fairy tale."

Adam smiling. "In fairy tales that I read, when the gallant knight slayed the dragons, he always won the fair princess."

"Oh God, Adam, this dragon is unslayable. Tomorrow, when Jim and Janice come home, we'll have to tell them. If I take the initiative and tell Jim, maybe he'll think our brief affair was confined to these few days. I'll tell him that I must have just got carried away." Angela sobbing, "I'll tell him that it wasn't love, just a mad passion. I'll tell him that there will be no more days at Adams Video."

And Adam saying softly, "And no more Thursdays? Angela, that can't be. I'm married to you!"

Adam . . . the dreamer. But there was no bright light at the end of the tunnel . . . only impenetrable blackness. If Jim knew the truth, what could he say, except, "Do you expect to have your cake and eat it?"

Keane, living in the faith which your love for Robin and her love for you creates, and being concerned for the goodness and love and understanding which can alone give your life and marriage the richness and significance and meaning and worthfulness which you desire, do you dedicate yourself to the growth of this love with Robin as your wife?

I do.

Eating hot dogs and beans and brown bread in Janice's kitchen in Cohasset. Drinking champagne. Avoiding the obvious. Adam telling the children stories about the early Adamses. "Quite human beings, really. George Washington Adams committed suicide because he got a girl pregnant out of wedlock . . . John Q.'s son was a drunk. Wise Abigail (who was a Smith) writing on marriage. 'Years subdue the ardor of passion, but in lieu thereof a friendship, deep-rooted, subsists which defies the ravages of time . . .' Adam, taking Angela's hand. "It may be incredible to you but we love your mothers and fathers."

Robin, living in the faith which your love for Keane and his love for you inspires, and being concerned for the goodness and love and understanding which alone can give your life and your marriage the richness and significance and meaning and worthfulness which you desire, do you dedicate yourself to the growth of this love with Keane as your husband.

I do.

All six of them sitting together in the Adams living room. Still drinking champagne. Five bottles gone so far. Would Adam tell Janice they had a wedding party?

Keane saying: "We think you and Jake should know. We're sorry that we walked in on you. But we're not shook that you love each other."

Sam laughing. "Really beautiful. Janice and Angela . . . Jake, you have both sides of the same coin."

Yael being pensive. "If Sam ever goes exploring and finds an Angela, I won't complain."

And Keane chuckling. "Two mothers. I hope you get to know each other."

And Robin with a trembly smile. "Oh Mother, I do understand. I'm in love with Jake, too."

All of them trying to bring a smile to her tear-stained face.

And Yael, practical. "So far as Sam and I are concerned, your love is your secret."

And Adam finally rushing in where Angel-a's would never tread. "Angela and I were married last Tuesday in Montreal. It isn't easy to explain. We love each other . . . I love Jan, and Angela loves Jim. The marriage in Montreal is our commitment *not* to forsake all others. We each have two hands to join firmly with those we do love. Maybe it will sound silly, but this is how it was. . . ."

Who gives Robin to be married to Keane?

Because of her ability to make decisions and her freedom, she gives herself, but she does so with the blessing, the approval, and the best wishes of her mother and I, and all of us who hold high these ideals.

Robin and Keane repeat after me: "I pledge ourselves to the growth of our love. I will be patient, considerate, understanding, devoted, honest, open. I will respect your freedom. I will respect your integrity. I will respect your privacy. I will respect your judgment. I will respect your uniqueness. I will keep our love open and unfinished that it may be an inspiration for everything we cherish, and for all that is vital and good in our lives.

For all that is vital and good in our lives. Adam telling their love story from the beginning and finally saying, "Love is process, kids, a phenomenon which is characterized by change and discovery."

Robin and Keane being brightly enthusiastic. "We want to meet Father Lereve."

Sam and Yael seconding. "The four of us could drive up to Montreal before Spring."

Angela suddenly saying, "Somehow, I must tell Jim."

Robin unbelieving. "But what can you tell him?"

Angela shaking her head. "Oh God, honey ... I don't know ... I don't know."

Robin hugging her. "I don't think Daddy could take it." A mind-holding evening. Children caring ... loving.

Robin and Yael snuggling their faces for a second against hers and Jake's as they said good night. Sam and Keane encircling them with a big hug.

The big room. The fireplace a red glow. Their final moments alone with Janice hovering in the shadows.

Adam saying, "Let's go to bed."

Angela being adamant. "No, Adam. Not in Janice's bed. We'll sleep here on the couch."

There is a symbol in this church that Reverend Duncan tells me has been of deep significance to a great many of the young people here. It is a symbol that has intense and deep significance for me, and I am sure that there are many adults in this congregation that have come to treasure and respect it. . . . It is the symbol you see in front of me, the yin and the yang. This perhaps is the most ancient of all symbols. I do not believe that you could possibly exhaust its meaning. It is the division of life that makes up its unity. The polarities that are so deeply important to all of us whether we know them by name or not. The opposites. There was a time when people in our society considered life to be a very simple thing. It is intensely complicated. Keane and Robin enter their marriage knowing something, intellectually and emotionally, of these complications, these polarities, these opposites. They know, as I have said, that the marriage relationship may lead to terrible evil or may lead to transcendent good. The Chinese symbol of the *tao* is a circle with a separating line which divides it like a winding serpent. The line itself is equal to a half circumference. If one draws instead of the separating line a line composed of four half circumferences with diameters half again as large, these will be equal to one half circumference of the main circle. Furthermore it will always be the same, if the operation is continued, and the winding line will be approaching and tending to coalesce with two. Three into one. In all things the *yang* and *yin* are present. The ancient

300

Chinese say the yang and yin yield the ten thousand things of creation. They are not to be separated; nor can they be judged morally as either good or evil.

Robin alone with Angela, for a moment that Sunday morning. "I guess I always would have to be faithful to Keane."

Angela wondering about the thoughts behind the words. "Honey, I hope you always will be."

Robin sighing . . . youthfully honest. "You see, Mother, how could I make love with Keane one day and another man the next?"

Angela supplying the missing words. "But your mother could."

"Oh, Mother . . . I didn't mean you."

Angela, tears running down her cheeks. "Robin . . . Robin, the act of love isn't dirty. Human beings wash their hands and their faces and their genitals. I love your father . . . the love I have given him has something of Jake . . . Not his gisum, but his mind. Beyond the sum total of all the people and things you have experienced, who are you? What is your love? Aren't you a myriad, many-faceted gestalt named Robin? Can you know yourself forever?"

So, not only for Robin and Keane, but for their mothers and fathers, and every one sharing this marriage, the only transcendent evil would be for the eternal balance not to persist. Men are involved in all women and all women are involved in all men. In the loving and caring and deep body and sense commitment of men and women for each other, the perpetual flowing together, and life itself begins and ends . . . with no man ever knowing what is beginning and what is ending.

While the choir sang a song composed by Keane to excerpts from Walt Whitman's *Leaves of Grass*, Angela noticed Jim smiling, a smile that embraced Robin and Ruth and then her and Janice.

I have heard the talkers were talking. The talk of the beginning and the end. But I do talk of the beginning or the end.

There never was any more inception than there is now. Nor any more youth or age than there is now. And there will never be any more perfection than there is now. Nor any more heaven or hell than there is now.

301

I say no man has ever been half devout enough. Nor has ever yet adored or worshipped half enough. Nor has begun to think how divine he himself is, and how certain the future is.

Printed in the program, Keane had dedicated the song *"To my three women . . . Robin, Janice, and Angela."*

Oh, Jim . . . how certain is our future? Could you understand? There never is any more inception than there is now!

The vow which Keane and Robin have made to each other and the new relationship which is theirs will be signified symbolically by the giving and receiving of a ring. It is very important that this ring be understood as unitary, encompassing the significance and meaning of the perfect circle, but also the meaning of the yin and the yang must be included. As the prophet Gibran has said, "Let there be spaces in your togetherness. Drink and give each other to drink, but drink not from the same cup. Do not stand in each other's shadow. And do not give your heart and life into each other's keeping for only the hand of life can contain your hearts and the oak and the cypress do not grow in each other's shade."

So the two are one, but they are separate and distinct persons and the oneness is the creativity of diversities and so Keane will give a ring to Robin with this understanding.

Robin, let this ring be a symbol of our love which binds our separate lives into one.

Keane, let this ring be a symbol of our love which binds our separate lives into one.

Was Janice smiling as she was? Adam and Jim wore no wedding rings.

Jim said all rings made him nervous. Adam said he preferred bells on his toes.

Let us all pray. Let it be our prayer that Keane and Robin will have sufficient wisdom and understanding to be able to meet and transcend any and all difficulties which may be theirs. That they may find the diversity

302

of their personalities and of their eternal persons in and through each other and that the unity which binds them will be enriched and deepened by their individual personalities and that they will find that their relationship is that which creates a good and a beauty and a wonder which neither one would have been able to find in and of himself or herself.

Let it be our prayer that they will find such a loving community that in any hour of distress or in those hours of defeat which come to all of us that they will find the encouragement, the support, which gives them the strength to be able to do what they need to do. Let it be our prayer that through the growth of their love and of ours and of their spirits and of ours the kingdom will be in our hearts and one day come to be in our world.

For as much as you Keane and Robin have pledged yourselves to each other here in the sight of this company and in the presence of God whom we know as love indicating a mutual desire to seek the goodness of God together, I do now pronounce that you are husband and wife and may God add His blessing to this act.

The tears running down Janice's and Angela's cheeks as Robin and Keane passed between them beaming, merged in their own happy embrace. Their kids were man and wife.

At the Valley Stream Country Club, the Thomases and the Adamses stood at the beginning of the reception line. Jim was beside Angela beside Adam beside Janice. Adam's eyes said, I love you, Angela, but she turned away, trying to hold back her tears. Later they toasted each other and their children and their friends.

"To the Adamses," Jim said merrily. "The Thomases are happy to join the first family."

"To the Thomases," Adams responded. "There is no first or second family. Just the four of us."

After she had danced with Jim and Keane, Adam could finally ask her to dance. . . . "Hello, Angela Adams-Thomas. I've missed you terribly and I love you."

"Adam . . . Adam . . . please! We're being watched. Oh God, Adam, my will power is running out. What will I ever do?"

"Do you love me?"

"Do you have to ask?" She stared at him, her eyes a liquid kiss.

"Please. It's been too long. The Pink is crying. Come home."

Angela was silent for a moment. "I talked with Father Lereve. He thinks Janice is aware of us. I told him that I had given you up."

"What did he say?"

"That all of the puzzles created by man could be solved by man." Angela couldn't help smiling. "Like you, he quoted poetry at me, Lao-tzu. He believes that much of Jesus' teachings was a new blend of Chinese and Indian philosophy filtered through and transformed by an activist mind. I wish I could remember poetry like you."

Adam held her close, enjoying the feel of her body against his. "You don't have to . . . you've got me. Father Lereve is concerned that we haven't admitted to our marriage. Is this what he quoted to you? 'Bend and you will be whole. Curl and you will be straight. Keep empty and you will be filled. Grow old and you will be renewed. Only simple and quiet words will ripen of themselves. For a whirlwind does not last a whole morning. Nor does a sudden shower last a whole day. Who is their author? Heaven and earth! Even heaven and earth cannot make such violent things last long. How much truer it is of the rash endeavors of men?' " Adam was almost hugging her. Angela was happy the dance floor was crowded with wedding guests. It made it more difficult to observe them.

"Angela . . . Sam needs you at Adams Video. We're spinning it off. Carswell didn't win the whole battle. J.Q. is still in command at Adams National." He brushed her hand quickly across his middle. "Don't rush away; I'll be conspicuous with an erection."

"Adam . . . for heaven's sakes . . . behave yourself!" Angela couldn't help laughing. "You look like a bad, deprived kid."

"I am. In need to be with you. You've done your duty. The kids are married and unconcerned about us. It's only four days to Thursday. Do you want me to ask Janice's and Jim's permission? Don't think I won't!"

Angela grinned at him through her tears. "Oh, God . . . yes! Adam . . . yes . . . yes . . . at least, we should have Thursdays, my love!"

Afterword

When I was very young, I was an aficionado of "fairy stories." In those days there was no television. For me, Jack Armstrong, the All-American boy, on radio, could scarcely compete with the Brothers Grimm, Hans Christian Andersen, The Arabian Knights (with lovely Scherherazade to tell you tales for one thousand and one nights and make love to you at the same time), or King Arthur and his Knights of the Round Table.

Ah, the remembered delights of trudging several miles on a cold wintery Saturday morning to the public library, carrying home as many books as the librarian would let me and my friends take for a week (ten in one week, impossible!). And finally back home again, after sneaking in a Tom Mix movie, late Saturday afternoon (half frozen in long woolen stockings and knickers), warming my feet to life before the open door of a coal stove while I ate peanut butter, (globs of it, on saltines—not homogenized) and plunged into the lovely world of beautiful princesses and fearful dragons, and knights on white horses wearing their lady's scarves.

And as I grew older, I kept wondering about the reality of people in fairy tales versus the presumed reality of you and me, and then I discovered Shakespeare and "we are such stuff as dreams are made on," and later Descartes and George Berkeley and David Hume (long-forgotten seventeenth-century philosophers in pursuit of the nature of reality) and Schopenhauer's the World as Will and Idea; and Vedantic philosophy, and the Hindu world of "maya," or illusion, and it occurred to me that Launcelot and Guinevere, and Tristram and Iseult, and Paul and Virginia, and Daphnis and Chloe, and Romeo and Juliet, and Mary and Joseph, were not just stories at all, but quite real. Certainly, more real than my great-grandmother or great-grandfather, who may have lived but were never a part of my reality. And in some respects were more real than even my father and mother, of whom I knew a very little except in their role of parents. Certainly, I didn't know my mother, or later the women I have loved, as well as I knew some of the females in stories I had read. And I began to wonder, if perhaps the reason for this wasn't that we are victims of religious traditions that basically have demanded a marriage to God and not to each other. Why should we pray to God and not to each other? Is it because we are conditioned by a society that is so pragmatic that it doesn't dare to teach its children to wonder . . . to live by metaphor and simile?

Whatever the reasons may be . . . before you ask me, I'll tell you. Yes, of course Angela and Adam are real! Do you really believe that I could have created them out of the whole cloth? The truth of Adam and Angela is alive, if you want it to be, in their Thursday home just above Louisburg Square. One of those few places still existing in America that is both a reality and a state of mind . . . as are of course, Angela and Adam.

If, like me, you have discovered two worlds of reality, and can never be sure which is the illusion, you might even walk up Beacon Hill and find the mahogany door with brass fittings in the ancient brick building on Pinckney Street. And, of course, you won't be able to resist looking at the mailbox in the entry . . . and perhaps discover a lovely sense of mystery as you read "Adams-Thomas" printed on it. And you might dare to venture further into the duality of appearances, and walk up the single flight of carpeted stairs, wondering whether you were dreaming of a new kind of *Berkeley Square*, a plunge into the future. Certainly not a return to the past.

And if you knock on the door, as I did (holding my breath—it was late afternoon), and a woman opened it, and behind her another woman was smiling at you, and almost simultaneously they said, "Welcome, Bob" (or John or Kathy or Bill or Joan) ". . . you really did find us! Adam said you might . . . Jim wasn't sure . . . I'm Angela . . . and I'm Janice."

Well, you'd be astonished.

Maybe, if like me you are male and really enjoy females who make you aware that you're male . . . like me, you'd want to ask them a thousand questions. But they

306

were leaving (I didn't dare ask where they were going or when they'd be back), and it wasn't really the time to probe. Angela offered me a Scotch, aware that I was staring at at least a thousand books that lined one wall of the apartment. She told me to make myself at home. "Browse, if you like." And guessing my interest, she said, "They represent quite a few Thursdays ... input, as Adam would say."

Both her laughter and Janice's was joyous and fun-filled. "It looks as if you have found another reading friend, Angela." Janice smiled at me, and from the expression on her face, you could tell she liked Angela.

At the door Angela squeezed Janice's arm affectionately. "Reading isn't everything. There's loving, too." Her eyes twinkled at me, and then they were both gone.

Suddenly I realized that it was Monday, and that was something I would need to think about too. So, for whatever reality they may add to your life, here are a few of the many books that I found in the Adams-Thomas apartment on Pinckney Street. The comments are mine. Not Angela's or Adam's. As you can see their choice was eclectic and catholic, which, like the love you give in monogamy or synergamy, is the only way.

Bibliography

Adams, John F. *An Essay on Brewing, Vintage and Distillation . . . or How to Make Booze,* Dolphin, Doubleday, N.Y., 1970. While John F. and Jonathan Q. are unacquainted, they have much in common, as this delightful book will attest.

Allegro, John M. *The Sacred Mushroom and the Cross,* Bantam, N.Y.,1970. The author of *The Dead Sea Scrolls,* in a fascinating scholarly, but easily readable book, traces "the son of God" from the psychedelic mushroom (God's penis), which ultimately becomes Jesus Christ as a cover-up.

Allen, Gina, and Martin, Clement, M.D. *Intimacy, Sensitivity Sex and the Art of Love,* Henry Regnery Company, Chicago, Illinois, 1971. Gina and Clement explore the human need for deep interpersonal involvement as the key to joyous sexual surrender. A "come-alive" book that at long last puts the horse before the cart.

Atcheson, Richard. *The Bearded Lady,* John Day, N.Y., 1971. As a travel editor of *Holiday* Magazine, Atcheson sets out to explore alternate life-styles objectively, but slowly becomes subjectively involved. The concluding chapter about friends of his who are involved in a carefully thought-out group marriage finally convinces him that there may be other joyous ways to live one's life. The title refers to the author's belief that we are all basically bisexual.

Bartell, Gilbert D. *Group Sex. A Scientist's Eye-Witness Report On The American Way of Swinging,* Peter Wyden, N.Y., 1971. Don't confuse swinging and synergamy. Many swingers are escapists, as Bartell's book proves.

Bischof, Werner, Capa, Robert. *The Concerned Photographer,* Grossman Publishers, N.Y., 1968. Photographs of six photographers whose concern is man. Inscription in the book "For Angela, Love, Sam."

Blitsten, Dorothy. *The World of The Family, A Comparative Study of Family Organizations in Their Social & Cultural Setting.* Good reading to discover that the nuclear, monogamous family is one alternative among many.

Boylan, Richard Brian. *Infidelity, The Way We Live Today,* Prentice Hall, N.J., 1971. An interesting survey of extramarital relations; where we are currently, and where we may be going.

Brook, John. *Along the River Run,* Scrimshaw Press, San Francisco, 1970. A book of photographs by a master who would appreciate Angela. The book is unfortunately too expensive. Brooks deserves wider exposure for the depth of his photography.

Bull, Richard E. *Summerhill, USA,* Penguin Education Special, N.Y., 1970. If you like Neill, you'll enjoy this book.

Christofel, Tom; Finkelhor, David, and Gilbarg, Dan. *The American Myth,* Holt Paperback, N.Y., 1971. A radical critique of corporate capitalism based on the controversial Harvard College Course Social Relations 148-149. A book that would delight Adam, and make J. Q. wonder!

Clanton, Gordon. *The Contemporary Experience of Adultery.* A fascinating article that covers every aspect of adultery and explores the contemporary co-marital experience in the arts by examining *Bob, Carol, Ted and Alice,* Updike's *Couples,* and Rimmer's *Proposition 31.* The article is unpublished at this writing, but for a copy contact Gordon Clanton, Douglas College, Rutgers University, New Brunswick, N.J. 08903. Or, wait for a book titled *Co-Marital Sex* by James and Lynn Smith. See below.

Cox, Harvey. *The Feast of Fools,* Harper Colophon, N.Y., 1969. If you are interested in the road religion could take in the future (and you should be), you should read this delightful book.

Cox, Harvey. *On Not Leaving It To The Snake,* Macmillan Company, 1964. In this book and *The Secular City,* Cox is rethinking the religious experience, at least for the *twenty-first* century.

Craveri, Marcello. *The Life of Jesus*, Grove Press, N.Y., 1967. This translation from the Italian is a must-reading life of Jesus which explores without denigrating.

Crane, Frank. *The Lost Books of the Bible*, World Publishing, Cleveland, 1926. This illustrated book contains *The Gospel of Mary, The Protevangelion*, and *The Forgotten Books of Eden.* Despite many Bibles that include Old Testament Apocrypha, very few of them have these writings. Some paperback publisher should reissue it.

Duyckaerts, Francois. *The Sexual Bond*, Delacorte Press, N.Y., 1970. This book and its joining of sexuality with aggression irritated Angela and Adam so much that their copy is littered with nays and ughs!

English, O. Spurgeon, and Heller, Melvin S. *Is Marital Infidelity Justified?* Two M.D.'s carry on a spirited pro and con debate in the first issue of *Sexual Behavior,* a new magazine published by Interpersonal Publications, Inc., 299 Park Avenue, N.Y. 10017. A subscription to this magazine is $7.50. The first few issues are well done.

Ehrlich, Paul R. *How To Be A Survivor,* Ballantine, N.Y., 1971. United States needs Ehrlich and Nader as beneficent dictators.

Every, George. *Christian Mythology*, Hamlyn Publishing Group Ltd., 1970 Every's study, with pictures of Christian origins, is quite interesting. Watch for this book at bargain prices on overstock counters. It's worth owning.

Fabre, J. Henri. *Life of The Spider,* Blue Ribbon Books, N.Y., 1912. Can you make love discussing spiders? Angela and Adam are convinced the "loving talk" approach is the most joyous way to orgasm. This book is out of print and should be reissued.

Fairchild, Richard. *Communes, U.S.A.,* published by Alternatives Foundation, P.O. Drawer A, Diamond Heights, San Francisco, California. Price $3.95. This comprehensive survey, with hundreds of pictures and text by the author, will be published by Penguin Books in an expanded format. If you are interested in Alternate life-styles, you should make contact with Dick Fairchild. Alternatives Foundation is his brainchild.

Feinberg, Gerald. *The Prometheus Project,* Anchor, N.Y., 1969. Read this fascinating paperback and join Feinberg in the search for new goals! He tells you how, and what's more his idealism will appeal to you. Summed up by William Faulkner's "I believe that man will not only endure, he will prevail."

Firestone, Shulamith. *The Dialectics of Sex,* Bantam, N.Y., 1971. I like Shulamith, and I'm sure Angela and Adam wonder if synergamy would be accepted in the Alternatives she offers in the last chapter of her book. Alternatives, which, incidentally (shades of *Harrad* and *Proposition 31*), are legally structured!

Fleming, Dave. *The Complete Guide to Growing Marihuana,* available from Sundance Press, P.O. Box 99393, San Francisco, California, 94109. $1.25. If marihuana is ever legalized, it is doubtful if Adam's approach (of making it legal to grow it, smoke it, and give it away, *but illegal to sell it*) will ever become the modus vivendi. If you dare to join the ranks of those who use marihuana occasionally, but don't let it use you, then this book is a wealth of information on how to cultivate your own.

Fuller, Buckminster. *Operating Manual For Spaceship Earth,* Pocket Books, N.Y., 1970. Absolutely must reading. If you have never read Bucky or believe that a man (or woman) need grow old mentally . . . this book by a seventy-year-old child of wonder will excite you and set you straight.

Gaer, Joseph. *The Lore of The New Testament,* Grosset & Dunlap, N.Y., 1952. A very good source book for creating ballets for the new Church. Keane Adams obviously supplied it to Adam and Angela.

Goble, Frank. *The Third Force. The Psychology of Abraham Maslow,* Grossman Publishers, N. Y., 1970. Abe's foreword to Goble's book is testimony enough to the value of this book.

Goldman, George, Millman, Donald. *Modern Woman, Her Psychology and Sexuality.* Charles C. Thomas, Springfield, Illinois, 1969. An interesting collection of writings that range from the widespread fear of loving to the role anatomy plays in a woman's perception of herself.

Goldstein, Martin, Haberete, E. Z., and McBride, Will. *The Sex Book,* Herder and Herder, N.Y., 1971. This dictionary of sex, published by a Catholic-oriented publisher, has been put down by the intellectuals who find it superficial. But it is the first pictorial sex book that has found its way into regular bookstores. While there are many detailed photographic sex manuals around, most of them don't have the

311

joy and warmth and human qualities of this book. Good reading for youngsters, and a lot better than *Everything You Always Wanted to Know.* . . .

Greer, Germaine. *The Female Eunuch,* McGraw-Hill, N.Y., 1971. Germaine might not approve of synergamy, but I have a feeling she'd like Angela.

Grey, Alan L. *Man, Woman, and Marriage,* Atherton Press, N.Y., 1970. Various essays which overall reveal group interaction in the family. Good reading.

Grinspoon, Lester, M.D. *Marihuana Reconsidered,* Harvard University Press, 1971. This book wraps it up. After you've read it, like Adam, you'll want to grow your own. You still may return to juice, but no one should say you can't compare.

Harnold, Karen, and Sven. *Adult Love,* Det Frie Forlag. Kronprinessgade 54, 1306 Copenhagen, K. Denmark. While this picture book of sexual love may never be sold in the United States, it probably can be ordered from the publisher. The amusing thing about it is that the four-color photographs by Peter Fleming are far superior to the extended printed dialogue that presumably accompanies the lovemaking. Touching and nonverbal communication needs to be supplemented by an extended vocabulary of love, so that the depths of feelings and needs can be expressed vocally, too.

Haughton, Rosemary. *Love,* Penguin Books, Baltimore, 1970. A wide-ranging study of permissive and repressive love as the basis of social control. Rosemary says little about female liberation . . . but she doesn't have to. Even in print she comes through as a joyous 45-year-old . . . a new breed of thinking, widely educated women. Men like Adam would find her kind of female an inspiration in bed and out. Good conversation and sex! Angela's notes in this book indicate that she relates to Rosemary a little more than Germaine.

Heron, Alastair, editor. *Toward A Quaker View of Sex,* Friends House Service Committee, Friends House, Euston Road, London, N.W. 1, England. I don't know whether this pamphlet is available through the Friends General Conference. Some Quakers were a little shocked by it. I read it with tears of joy in my eyes. It should be expanded into a book. Absolutely must reading for any Christian!

Houriet, Robert. *Getting Back Together,* Coward, McCann &

Geoghagan, N.Y., 1971. The best book on communes around. Why? Because Bob Houriet is not only an observer but a sympathetic participant. His chapter on the failure of the Harrad West group marriage in San Francisco, and the study of Twin Oaks, the Walden II Community, are only two of the many fascinating sections of this book.

Hunt, Morton. *The Future of the Family*, *Playboy* Magazine, August, 1971. A good overall view of the alternatives and where we may be going, but Morton needs to have more intimate contact with communes. His wonder (and fear) about group marriage as the possibly great revolutionary development is chuckly.

Ishihara, Akira, and Levy, Howard. *The Tao of Sex*, Harrow Editions, N.Y., 1970. This translation and descriptions from the ancient Chinese manuscript *Ishimpo* will not only improve your sexual vocabulary with charming metaphors, but since it is predicated on acts of love of long duration (for a long life, numerous women in one evening are prescribed), it prescribes methods of "avoiding leakage." Read it joined! It will give you a warm chuckle.

K, Mr. and Mrs. *The Couple*, Coward, McCann & Geoghagan, N.Y., 1971. This anonymous book will make you feel sad. Would synergamy have solved Mr. K's problems of sexual inadequacy?

Karlen, Arno. *Sexuality and Homosexuality, A New View*, W. W. Norton, N.Y., 1971. Karlen's encyclopedic approach gains justification from his own words. "Our knowledge would be immensely greater if fifty years ago, and even now, scholars felt there was as much to learn from man's sexuality as from the forms of his economy."

Kateb, George. *Utopia*. Atherton Press, N.Y., 1970. If synergamy seems Utopian, then read this book to get significant insights into the process of Utopian thinking.

Keen, Sam. *To a Dancing God*, Harper & Row, N.Y., 1970. The Dancing God lives in you. An interesting essay in this book is called "Education for Serendipity."

Kirkendall, Lester A. *The New Sexual Revolution*, Donald Brown, Inc. A very good collection including Rustum and Della Roy's *Is Monogamy Outdated?* Order it from Prometheus Books, 923 Kensington Avenue, Buffalo, N.Y. They'll tell you how to tie it into a subscription to *The American Humanist*.

Kirstein, Lincoln. *Movement and Metaphor, Four Centuries of Ballet,* Praeger, N.Y., 1971. If the ballet is as much a part of your life as it is the Thomases' and the Adamses', then you'll want to own this expensive but definitive and beautiful book by one of the pillars of American Ballet. If you can't afford it, persuade your library to buy it.

Koble, Wendall, and Warren, Richard. *Sex in Marriage,* Academy Press, San Diego, California, 1970. There are at least five volumes so far of this too expensive, illustrated how-to-do-it sex manual. Unfortunately, only "dirty bookstores" handle it (which is a commentary in itself on the sad condition of our sex attitudes). The text is comme ci, comme ça, the photographs in Volume One are of the most beautiful male and female you have ever seen (copulating and enjoying oral genital sex in detail), but they fail in one respect . . . they are joyless! I guess you can order these books direct from Academy Press. Adam and Angela can afford them because they have a friend, John Raffo, who owns an adult bookstore, the Boylston Book Store on Boylston Street in Boston. Adam and Angela collect the titles of pornographic fiction, which show more creativity than most of the contents!

Lang, Theo. *The Difference Between Man and Woman,* John Day, N.Y., 1971. Even if you are self-assured and certain that you know all the differences, you'll find this book by a wide-ranging scholar a delight and an eye-opener.

Lereve, Jesonge, S.J. *Le Synergamie,* Provocation Press, Montreal, 1971. Father Lereve's book has never been translated, and unfortunately has limited circulation. Like any alternative marriage form, synergamy should be experimented with and thus amplified in practice. This book simply opens the door.

Lewis, Barbara. *The Sexual Power of Marihuana,* Ace Books, N.Y., 1970. Don't let Barbara kid you. If you need either pot or alcohol to help you surrender your little ego, you've only begun the sex trip!

Linder, Staffan. *The Harried Leisure Class,* Columbia University Press, N.Y., 1970. If you believe Linder, we're all too busy pursuing materialistic pleasures to dare to enjoy each other as male and female.

Maeterlinck, Maurice. *Life of the Ant,* John Day, N.Y., 1930. Think of the worlds we completely ignore. The ants blithely spin along without us. When they are sexually

314

joined, humans could find the ants worth meditating about. At least Adam thinks so!

Malcolm, Henry. *Generation of Narcisscus*, Little Brown, Boston, 1971. Malcolm uses the Prometheus and Narcissus legends to isolate the same phenomenon as Reich did with Consciousness III, but Malcolm's approach is more convincing. A good searchlight, if you are in the dark.

Margolis, Herbert, and Rubenstein, Paul. *The Group Sex Tapes*, David McKay, N.Y., 1971. These taped interviews with spouse-swappers in many cases reveal the kind of people who might eventually seek the deeper commitment of synergamy or *Proposition 31* type marriages.

Marshall, Donald S., and Suggs, Robert C. *Human Sexual Behaviour*, Basic Books, Inc., 1971. Subtitled the range and diversity of sexual experience throughout the world as seen in six representative countries. The Chapter *Romantic Love Among the Turu* introduces the fascinating concept of *mbuya* a structured and permissive form of co-marital relationship, and the key to the sexual relationship of a Bantu tribe of 175,000 people.

Mazur, Ron and Joyce. *Open Ended Marriage: Creative Intimacy for Adults*, Beacon Press, 1972. Ron and Joyce celebrate a form of marital relationship which values the freedom to enjoy sexual intimacy with others. They explore the issues of living alternative life-styles and offer guidelines for creating an open-ended marriage in contemporary society. As an indication of the changing world, Ron, a graduate of Harvard Divinity School and a minister, obviously has a common ground with Father Lereve!

————. *Commonsense Sex*, Beacon Press, 1968. In the Chapter "Parents and Lovers," unmarried adults and parents are challenged to question the human relationship and the limitations of traditional monogamy.

Montagu, Ashley. *Touching*, Columbia University Press, N.Y., 1971. Absolutely must reading! The *why* of touching, not the encounter group how. It may make you think that we should learn how to lick each other . . . with our tongues!

Muldorf, Bernard. *L'Adultère*, Casterman Poche, Paris, 1970. To my knowledge this book has not yet been translated. Instructive reading for those who believe the French with their mistresses and lovers have solved the problems of monogamy. They haven't! If such a permissive structure actually ever existed, it was confined to the upper-class

315

families around the turn of the century. Frenchmen have the same problems, as do most other Western people, about marriage and the family, and where it is heading.

Neubeck, Gerald. *Extramarital Relations,* Prentice Hall, N.J., 1969. In case you've forgotten, Jerry gained national fame for his classes at University of Minnesota, for his open and defenseless approach to interpersonal relations including casual use of dirty words. This book is an interesting collection of writings with no solutions.

O'Neill, Nena and George. *Open Marriage, A New Life Style for Couples,* M. Evans and Company, N.Y., 1972. A joyous concept of monogamy that squarely faces the fact that no two people can be everything to each other. In the open marriage, liking is loving, and trust is better than fidelity. The Mazurs, O'Neills, and Skolnicks project the monogamy of the future. Via their books they are good friends to know.

Otto, Herbert. *The Family in Search of a Future,* Appleton Century, N.Y., 1970. Many interesting essays on alternate family and marriage styles.

Peterson, Joyce, and Mercer, Marilyn. *Adultery for Adults,* Bantam, N.Y., 1970. Read it and while you're laughing you'll weep, too! Almost, but not as bad (from a total social concept) as the *Boys and Girls Book about Divorce* by Richard A. Gardner, M.D. But I suppose both books might make you reconsider synergamy as an alternative.

Poor, Riva. *4 Days 40 Hours,* Bursk and Poor, Cambridge, Mass., 1970. A survey of the kind of work week rapidly emerging in some areas of industry. While we are only on the threshold of the four-day week, a later proposal of a three-day week with one half of the working population working three 12 hour days (Monday, Tuesday, Wednesday) and the other half working (Thursday, Friday, Saturday) the remainder of the week, would not only use the productive equipment to capacity, but would give men and women two hundred days a year of leisure, and plenty of time both for synergamy and monogamy.

Prabhupada, Swami, A. C. Bhativedanta. *On Chanting the Hare Krsna Mantra* Available from Iskcon Press, 38 North Beacon Street, Boston, Mass. 62134, for 50¢. If you want to know more, order the pamphlet *Krsna, The Reservoir of Pleasure,* which is also 50¢. You may even end up subscribing to their magazine *Godhead.* But don't drop out! We all need each other . . . active!

Rasberry and Greenway. *The Rasberry Exercises.* Buy this

book from the Freestone Publishing Company, 440 Bohemian Highway, Freestone, California 95472. Dedicated to the millions of children still in prison in U.S. and the handful of adults trying to help them. A delightful book. The fact that it is in "the Pink," is a comment on Angela and Adam's interest. Even though they don't yet have grandchildren, they care about education.

Rollin, Betty. *The American Way of Marriage: Remarriage*, *Look* Magazine, September 21, 1971. A good look at the style of marriage in the seventies that underlines the need for a structured premarriage system (similar to Harrad?) and postmarital styles that offer open-end commitments, Proposition 31's, and synergamy.

Saint Exupery, Antoine de, *The Little Prince*, HarBrace Paperbound Library, 1970. In the frontispiece of this delightful fairy tale originally published in 1943, in Angela's handwriting are these words: "On Thursday, February 24, Adam and Angela read this book together. Naked and mostly joined, they decided never to be 'grown-ups.' "

Salzman, Eric. *Twentieth-Century Music, An Introduction*. Prentice Hall, N.J., 1967. This book should be in the paperbacks. Adam and Angela found it the perfect guidebook. The Pink has at least a hundred records of key composers spanning the years of the revolution in music during which the amazing Igor Stravinsky lived and created, from the beginnings, until his death in 1971.

Sheen, Fulton J. *These are the Sacraments*, Doubleday, N.Y., Image, 1964. If you want to understand the mystery element of Catholicism, this book is a delightful introduction.

Shupe, Deena. *The High Art of Cooking . . . New Grass Cookbook*. Published by Synergisms, 601 Minnesota Street, San Francisco, California. This attractive book is filled with tested recipes. Deena not only tells you (based on how much you eat of these culinary improvements) approximately when to expect results. If you don't enjoy smoking, this could be a new approach. The problem is that most of the recipes require grass in quantities and would suggest self-cultivation is the only economical approach. Available from the publisher for $2.95.

Skinner, B. F. *Beyond Freedom and Dignity,* Alfred Knopf, N.Y., 1971. Skinner might not have terrified his critics so much if he had simply said that man can be reinforced to know how to love simply by creating the social environment for love. With love the joys of a *pluralistic* Utopia become possible, and would require no beneficent Skinnerian dictators.

Skolnick, Arlene and Jerome H. *The Family in Transition, Rethinking Marriage, Sexuality and Child Rearing,* Little Brown, Boston, 1971. A comprehensive collection of writings covering practically every new view of the family. If, like Angela and Adam, you are long past your days of formal education, read this quality paperback from cover to cover and catch up with the future!

Smith, David E. *The New Social Drug, Cultural and Legal and Medical Perspectives on Marihuana,* Prentice Hall, N.J., 1970. There are almost as many books on pot as there are on women's lib. This is a good one.

Smith, James R. & Lynn. *Co-marital Sex.* The manuscript of this as yet unpublished book is in the Pink. It's many contributors and viewpoints will make it must reading when it finally finds a publisher.

Snyder, Wendy. *Haymarket,* M.I.T. Press, Cambridge, Mass., 1971. A book of photographs of the Boston open-air market. Wendy's photographic approach and Angela's have much in common.

Thompson, Jay. *I Am Also You, A Book of Thoughts with Photographs,* 1971. Delightful. Filled with Angela-style photographs by a man who loves his fellowman. Well worth its $1.95 price.

Thorp, Roderick, and Blake, Robert. *Wives, An Investigation,* M. E. Evans Company, N.Y., 1970. Tape recordings with forty American wives who not only reveal *all,* but perhaps indicate that synergamy or *Proposition 31* might expand the horizons of many monogamous couples.

Turner, James. *Thy Neighbor's Wife, Twelve Original Variations on the Theme of Adultery,* Stein and Day, N.Y., 1968. Angela's and Adam's library has many stories and novels on adultery. Most of them, like the stories in this book, have a sad ending.

Valente, Michael F. *Sex, The Radical View of a Catholic Theologian,* Bruce Publishing Company, N.Y., 1970. Whether you are Protestant, Jew, or Catholic, read this remarkable book and cheer!

Warhol, Andy. *Blue Movie,* Grove Press, Inc., N.Y., 1970. The complete dialogue and 100 photos of Viva and Louis making love. A little crude . . . but here and there fun. Angela and Adam finally did much better, but it's unlikely their tapes will ever be publicly available!

Watts, Alan. *The Alan Watts Journal*, published by the Society for Comparative Philosophy, Inc. S. S. Vallejo, P.O. Box 857, Sausalito, California 94965. A monthly newsletter. Annual subscription which is tax deductible $20.00. Enjoyable. Makes you both think and emote.

Weston, Edward. *The Flame of Recognition,* Grossman Publishers, N.Y., 1971. Another Aperture Monograph on a photographer (with comments from his diary) who was one of the first to create photographic art.

White, Minor. *Be-ing Without Clothes,* Aperture Inc., 276 Park Avenue So., New York, 1971. Price $3.50. A collection of photographs from eleven hundred submitted to the Creative Photography Laboratory at Massachusetts Institute of Technology to develop special approaches to photographing naked human beings. The text in this book and the photographs reveal over and over again, the sheer, fragile, beauty of naked man, woman, and man and woman in human family situations. Humans *be-ing* even more human while *be-ing* naked! If you are as interested in photography as Angela then you should investigate membership in Aperture.

Wyden, Peter and Barbara. *Inside the Sex Clinic,* World Publishing, N.Y., 1970. Interesting how many husband and wife teams are writing books! This one is a story of one more couple going through the Master and Johnson treatment (not the Wydens). It's interesting to note that most Americans still believe so thoroughly in mechanical solutions to their problems that the metaphysical approach of two people simultaneously abandoning their own petty little egos and *being* the other never occurs to them. It could be a better cure for impotence or frigidity than stroking each others eyelashes.

Youngblood, Gene. *Expanded Cinema,* E. P. Dutton, N.Y., 1970. If you want to know where it's at, in the world of film, videotape, and intermedia, read this book. If you are a futurist read this book . . . it's a clue to the exciting worlds of tomorrow's art. Read this book anyway, it's great!

SOME OTHER THINGS

Radical Software 22 East 22nd Street, New York, N.Y. 10010. A fascinating quarterly newspaper bringing all the burgeoning elements of videotape and cable television (the coming revolution!) together in one complete package. Subscription $5.00 annually. Volumes I, II and III are already published, and a gold mine of information.

Videorecord World, Box A-Z, Irvine, California. Annual subscription $24.00. This is the first magazine that reports in depth everything that is occurring in the infant video industry. By 1975 when home video is a billion-dollar industry, Bill Periera, the publisher, along with Adams Video, will be known as the prophetic ones!

Forum, The International Journal of Human Relations, 1650 Broadway, New York, N.Y. 10036. Yearly subscription $12.00. One of the best magazines focusing on sexual relations published anywhere. The letters and answers from the editors and consulting experts, represent the kind of exchange that is not available in any other U.S. publication.

Big Sur Recordings, Box 4050—Dept. R, San Rafael, California 94903. A repository of tapes and cassettes of practically everyone interested in interpersonal relationships. Write them for a complete catalogue and prices. Angela and Adam, among others (in the Pink) had these exciting people to listen to on tape:

Paul Bindrim: *On the Nude Marathon*
Harvey Cox: *21st Century Religion*
Ronald Laing: *The Politics of Experience*
John Holt & George Dennison: *Alternatives in Edution*
Paul Krassner: *Summer 1970 Report on The Inner Space Revolution*
Robert H. Rimmer: *"A Day with Rimmer at the University of Missouri"*

and a fascinating LP phonograph record, *Music of Tibet, The Tantric Rituals*, based on multi-toned chanting of the lamas.

Elysium, Incorporated, 5436 Fernwood Avenue, Los Angeles, California 90027. In addition to publishing books, Elysium runs a delightful sensitivity colony in Topanga Canyon, California, where being naked is a way of life. *The Wonderful World of the Webbers* and *Eros in Art*, both available from Elysium at $10.00 each, are in Angela's and Adams' Library, a gift from Sam.

Jesus Christ, Superstar. A Rock Opera by Andrew Webber and Tom Rice. While operas of this type (including *Godspell*) cannot by their nature explore the mystery element of religion, Father Lereve considers them a step in the direction he is taking. Independent of the stage, the record version of *Jesus Christ, Superstar* is an interesting listening experience.